A Shilling on Good Friday

A SHILLING ON GOOD FRIDAY

VOLUME TWO

A Dream Fulfilled

Adrian John Hoare

Man of Kent Publishing

British Library Cataloguing in Publication Data
A catalogue record for this book is available from the British Library

ISBN 978-0-9933369-1-1

Typeset by Amolibros, Milverton, Somerset
www.amolibros.com
This book production has been managed by Amolibros
Printed and bound by Lightning Source

Hark! 'tis the voice of angels,
Borne in a song to me,
Over the fields of glory,
Over the jasper sea.

From the hymn by F. J. Crosby (1820-1915)

Photograph of Mina Reynolds by Trasks of Philadelphia: sent by William Reynolds to his mother in the autumn of 1865.

DEDICATION

To my wife, Theresa Eily Hoare.

In appreciation of her considerable forbearance on those occasions, since 1970, when I may have appeared unduly pre-occupied as I ventured in the footsteps – both at home and abroad – of my collateral ancestor, William Reynolds.

Foreword

The history of the United States is tightly stitched to that of England. After all, the American "Tree of Liberty" was grown from English seed. And so, it is not unusual to find a young English boy begin his career in Queen Victoria's Royal Navy, only to wind up a soldier in Abraham Lincoln's army. Of the two million-plus soldiers that made up the Union army nearly half were of British ancestry and, of those, over 50,000 were British subjects (Canada added another 10,000 men in the Union ranks). Such is the story of William Reynolds as told through the engaging writing of Adrian Hoare.

I first met William Reynolds, the English seaman and Union soldier who found himself an unsuspecting player in the hunt for Abraham Lincoln's murderers, in the summer of 1993. At the time I had spent well over two decades researching and writing on the events surrounding John Wilkes Booth and his murderous act. That summer, I received a phone call from a good friend and fellow historian, Charles Jacobs. While my interests centered mostly on Lincoln, Charles was interested in the exploits of a local Marylander named Elijah White who served as a colonel in the Confederate army. We often shared our research and knowledge, swapping stories about the Civil War and its interesting people.

Charles told me he had been contacted by an Englishman who had a relative who served in the Union army. The soldier had kept up a regular correspondence with his mother back in England, apprising her of his exploits in America. The letters survived, eventually winding up in the hands of a descendant. As so often happens with historical documents, the letters took on a life of their own and soon consumed the interests of his descendant. He was, of course, the author of this remarkable narrative, Adrian Hoare.

Reynolds' letters detailed his unusual story as a fifteen-year-old boy who enlisted in the Royal Navy in 1857. After five years in Her Majesty's service and, aggrieved with his treatment, he jumped ship during a layover in Halifax, Nova Scotia. Making his way to Baltimore, Reynolds enlisted in the Union army where he saw service in Louisiana during the Red River Campaign under General Nathaniel Preston Banks. Wounded during the battle of Pleasant Hill, he was invalided out of the army and found work as a coal miner in Pennsylvania. However, when he became restless with life in the mines, Reynolds re-enlisted in the 213th Pennsylvania Volunteers in 1865. Assigned to protect the Baltimore and Ohio Railroad near Relay, west of Baltimore, he was chosen to lead a small unit of soldiers in search of the assassin of President Lincoln and any conspirators attempting to escape north.

It was while leading his patrol one miserable, cold, wet night in April 1865, that Reynolds stumbled into history. Roaming the Maryland countryside in search of George Atzerodt – one of Wilkes Booth's fellow conspirators – he ran into another patrol charged with the same duty. Invited to join forces, Reynolds agreed and soon found himself at a farmhouse near Germantown, where Atzerodt was hiding in the belief that he was safe from arrest.

Reynolds' letter home to his mother, describing his rendezvous with history, took hold of Adrian's imagination and wouldn't let go. Delving into every aspect of his remarkable life as a seaman and soldier, Adrian developed a strong desire to visit the site where Reynolds became a part of American history.

The phone call from my friend, Charles Jacobs, was in the form of a request. He told me Adrian was planning a trip to the United States and a visit to Germantown and the site of Atzerodt's capture. Charles knew I had researched Atzerodt's capture and written on the subject. Would I be willing, Charles asked, to take Adrian under my wing and show him around the area and tell him what I knew about the story? Of course, my answer was yes, both out of friendship to Charles and because I had my own motive in meeting Adrian.

In the course of our conversation Charles mentioned that Adrian lived in the village of Hildenborough, in Kent, England. It was from Grafty Green, a small village in Kent, not far from Hildenborough, that my great-great-great grandfather had gathered up his wife and four children and emigrated to America in 1835. Two of his children, along with a son-in-law, enlisted in the Union army, serving in the same theater of operations as William Reynolds. It was exciting to think that the four men may have crossed paths at some point in their historic venture. I had spent a great deal of time researching my family genealogy and wanted to know more about the place where my ancestor had lived. Perhaps, I thought, Adrian might just be able to help me with my research while I helped him with his. We proved to be a perfect match.

It was a fresh morning following a night of rain, much like that which occurred when George Atzerodt awoke on April 20 1865 to find a Colt revolver thrust in his face, when I met up with Adrian and his family. With Adrian and myself in the front seat of a rented car and Theresa, his wife, and sons, Richard and Philip, we began our day tracing the footsteps of Atzerodt as he fled Washington and the scene of Lincoln's murder. We began in Germantown in the District of Columbia, close on the heels of Atzerodt as he made his way through the military pickets surrounding the city to the small village of Germantown in Montgomery County, Maryland.

Atzerodt, assigned by Booth to assassinate Vice President Andrew Johnson, lost courage at the last minute and fled from the hotel where Johnson was staying. After a few hours of fitful sleep, he decided to leave the city for rural Maryland. His destination was his father's old homestead, now owned by his cousin, Hartman Richter. The dull Atzerodt had visited his cousin on several occasions during the war and had found solace away from the bustling city overrun with Union soldiers. Confused and frightened at first by Booth's act, Atzerodt felt sure that Germantown was well beyond the military's reach. He was mistaken; a mistake that cost him his life. Captured by a military posse, Atzerodt was taken to Washington where he was soon tried as an accessory in Lincoln's murder, found guilty, and hanged along with Mary Surratt, Lewis Powell and David Herold.

While official records make no mention of William Reynolds or his part in Atzerodt's capture, there is little doubt that he participated, as he claimed in his letters. Like so many soldiers who found themselves caught up in America's great Civil War, Reynolds was a prolific letter writer. Far from home and loved ones, he kept in touch with his family through his mother, writing her about his great adventure in America. Although he was not well educated by his own country's standards, Reynolds had a keen eye for the smaller as well as the larger events of his own life and those around him. And, like so many of his peers, he was capable of writing lucid and interesting letters to loved ones back home; and, as with the letters of many of those peers, these important documents were cherished and carefully preserved, being passed from generation to generation for us today. Because of William Reynolds and his letters, we have the good fortune to travel by his side through some of the more exciting times in history; to witness, through his eyes, everyday events, both small and large, that still interest us today.

William Reynolds' letters are, of course, only one part of our good fortune today. Without Adrian Hoare's dedication and beautiful prose the letters might well remain carefully stored away in a family trunk unknown to history. Adrian's research is impeccable and his skill in translating Reynolds' story into an interesting narrative enriches our history. Like Lazarus of old, William Reynolds rises from the dead to live once more through the pages of this novel.

Perhaps this is the true meaning of immortality.

Edward Steers Jr.
Berkeley Springs, WV.

Dr Edward Steers Jr. is a retired microbiologist and former Deputy Director of the National Institutes of Health in Bethesda, Maryland. He lives in the mountains of West Virginia, near Berkeley Springs, with his wife, Pat and is the acclaimed author of Blood on the Moon (*The University Press of Kentucky 2001) and* The Lincoln Assassination Encyclopaedia (*Harper Perennial 2010). In addition, he has written a wealth of other books relating to Lincoln and the conspiracy against him. In his New York Times bestseller,* Manhunt: the 12-Day Chase for Lincoln's Killer, *James L Swanson describes Ed Steers as the premier contemporary historian of the assassination.*

INTRODUCTION

At the end of Volume One, in the late autumn of 1862, William Reynolds was newly arrived in the city of Baltimore, Maryland, having worked his passage aboard the *Snowgoose* from Nova Scotia. Here he could realise his long held ambition to become a soldier. The Union Army beckoned…

Some sixty miles to the south, in Port Tobacco, Maryland, George Atzerodt had recently been approached by postmaster and tavern keeper, John Surratt. For the German carriage painter and underground ferryman it was an encounter which would ultimately lead to fateful consequences…

One

Baltimore And Beyond
Late November / Early December 1862

William Reynolds' first night in Baltimore was something of a milestone. It was spent comfortably upon a well-sprung mattress and in pristine bed linen that smelt of powdered sassafras. Yet more momentous was his finding, for the first time since closing the door on the family home in Portsea and joining the *Excellent*, that he was not tied to anyone… not beholden to a soul. First it had been the Royal Navy, not least the wretched *Cygnet*; then the penitentiary…fleetingly, again, the gunvessel, then the kindly Tom and his cousin, Henry. And finally, Captain Jacob Burns…bless him. Bless him, because that very afternoon, after William said his farewells aboard the *Snowgoose*, amid the noise of one hundred and fifty bullocks being herded onto the quayside, the skipper had sent him on his way clutching a few greenbacks and the inner warmth from a parting tot of his chart-room blackstrap. The old man's reckoning was that William – although having agreed to work his passage – had shown greater alacrity than most in going about his work and hence was worthy of some reward. And so the Englishman disembarked with a few dollars to amply pay for a night's lodging and advice to seek out a boarding house on nearby Hanover Street with which the old man was apparently familiar and could warmly recommend After all, he said, Missus Jane Rutherford, the proprietrix, was a staunch Unionist. Were he to seek her counsel upon army enlistment in the neighbourhood, this she would willingly provide. Yet, he should above all be discrete and certainly not raise the subject in the presence of other guests.

A few hours earlier, as the *Snowgoose* had reduced sail, got steam up and made her way out of the Bay and into Baltimore's inner harbour, William had felt a glow of expectancy. It was time to turn over a new leaf.

"Well, I wish you good fortune, young Reynolds," exclaimed the rheumy-eyed Skelly, as once again, William had happened upon the company of the old sailor on the upper deck.

"We've just got to dismantle the animal pens and clean and scrub up, once the bullocks have been taken off...then I'll be on my way," had proclaimed the younger man, excitedly. "The other temporary hands will be staying with you and returning to Boston. They've proved a hardworking and likeable bunch of fellows. I hope the master keeps them on."

"Seeing as you're looking to join the army, there's a reminder of past conflict," the old Canadian had observed as the steamship passed Fort McHenry on its port side. "But not for the British. I believe the fort is now a prison, in the hands of the military, but the best part of fifty years ago its guns repulsed a British bombardment and saved the city."

Then, in a short while, having rounded Locust Point, and gently steamed into the upper reaches of the harbour, there emerged sobering evidence of the present struggle The lofty heights of the fortified Federal Hill appeared, their impressive eminence and heavy armament of cannon and mortars a constant reminder to all Baltimoreans...a reminder that Southern sympathies and talk of secession would be firmly checked were they to spill into insurgency. For such feelings were endemic. After all, Maryland was a Southern slave-owning state. And here, in Baltimore, raw hurt continued to fester in the wake of the previous year's Pratt Street riot when a violent secessionist mob attacked Massachusetts troops and caused the war's first bloodshed.

"I think we're heading for one of the piers along the Light Street Wharf... straight ahead," Skelly had murmured as, in awe, William was struck by the multitude of vessels which packed the inner harbour, the density of masts resembling a forest, the yards and rigging having a likeness to intermingling lianas.

"Now, to enlist, my lad, you'll need to seek out a recruiting station. Ask a soldier as to their whereabouts. If not, just make your way east on Pratt Street and you'll come upon Patterson Park. I know a lot of the regiments are tented there in preparation for whatever the war will deal them."

And so, having bidden his farewells, and taken hold of his drawstring bag, William had made his way down into a Light Street that throbbed with all manner of noise and activity, not least the ring of horse-drawn traffic across its cobbles. Having jostled his way through the crowds, he had sat himself down and rested a while on the steps of the Methodist Church. Tomorrow he might be a soldier, something to which he had constantly aspired. With that thought he had risen to his feet and made his way towards the boarding house recommended by Captain Burns.

The house on Hanover Street lay two blocks to the west of Light Street. On its approach, William found himself shuffling through large, brittle leaves, newly shed from paulownia. The shade trees added elegance to the street and, during the summer months, must have been a welcome screen from a sometimes brutal Baltimore sun. Missus Rutherford's boarding house was a tall, narrow property, ably presided over by the proprietrix, a widow in her mid-forties. She was a lady of neat and prim appearance. In her manner she was fastidious, yet her attention to detail did not prejudice a natural affability. She drew competent assistance from three house servants – free blacks – in running her establishment. These comprised two women – a cook and general housemaid – and a butler named Gideon who doubled as gardener and stable hand and would sometimes be called upon to convey guests in the widow's buggy to destinations within the city limits. The parlour, for the general use of guests, was well appointed and comfortably upholstered with its haircloth armchairs and sofa. Yet, of an evening – excepting perhaps in the summer – it was invariably dingy. This was because Missus Rutherford made a habit of regular inspection and, where she deemed it necessary for the sake of economy, would have little qualm about lowering the gas intake by adjusting the wall sconces. It was an example of her fastidiousness and, according to Jacob Burns, far from conducive to the guest wishing to while away an evening reading or writing letters. However, in his experience this mattered little, for Missus Rutherford's table was fit for a trencherman and one of her suppers could frequently send a guest into prolonged post-prandial slumber, to the exclusion of conscious pursuits. Indeed, Missus Rutherford would jokingly refer to the guests' parlour as the snoring room.

The afternoon light was beginning to fade as William paused at the threshold of Missus Rutherford's establishment. It had been a bright day but, being late in November, the days were short. Gideon, the negro butler, responded to William's knock. He was resplendent in his appearance, dressed in a tight-fitting, green velveteen waistcoat and corduroys. Below the knee, leather leggings terminated in brown buckled shoes. In the gloom of the spacious entrance hall his billowy-white shirt sleeves emitted a brilliance only exceeded by the whites of his eyes.

"Can I help you, sir?" enquired the butler in a rich and refined timbre, his diction a cut above anything William had heard from a negro's lips.

"I'm looking for a night's lodging and a good supper, if that can be arranged," said the visitor. "I come here on the recommendation of Captain Jacob Burns."

"A moment, sir," and with that Gideon turned and retreated into the house. A few minutes passed before a faint rustle of skirting announced the approach of authority in the form of Missus Rutherford.

"So Captain Burns sent you?" said the proprietrix in search of elaboration, her eyes simultaneously scrutinising the figure that stood before her. For his part, William felt mildly awkward, for while he had made some cursory effort to tidy himself, he still bore the signs and smells from his day's work. "And what of Captain Burns, himself? Does he require a room?"

"No ma'am," said William. "We've just arrived today from Boston with a cargo of fresh beef on the hoof…for the army. The *Snowgoose* is to return north tomorrow and the Captain has matters with which to attend. He's remaining on board overnight."

"Then what of you young man? What prompts the Captain to afford you the luxury of spending the night ashore?"

"I've left the ship, ma'am, having worked my passage from Nova Scotia." William was loath to disclose too much of his circumstances, but, heeding what the Captain had said, and seeing that nobody else appeared to be in earshot, he took the opportunity to make passing reference to his immediate intention. "Tomorrow I'm hoping to enlist in the Union Army."

Missus Rutherford gave the hint of a smile. "You'd better come in, young man," she said, ushering William into the hallway. "Yes, I do have spare rooms…and I take it you have the money to pay your way? You'd better take a look at our schedule of fees before committing yourself," she continued, without pausing to enable the visitor to respond. She beckoned to a list of her tariffs that lay upon the hall table…lodging, 50 cents…breakfast and dinner, each 65 cents…supper 75 cents. William nodded in affirmation.

"I'll only be needing supper, a room for one night and breakfast, ma'am."

"Fine. Now sign the guest book, will you, and I'll get Clara, my maid, to show you to your room. Supper is at six thirty." And with that and a swish of her stiff skirts against the wainscotting, the lady disappeared.

Clara, the housemaid, shortly emerged, clutching a pitcher of hot water.

"Follow me, sir. I'z jes' take ye t'yer room," she murmured, meekly. The girl immediately began ascending the stairs, politely rejecting the new guest's offer to carry the heavy receptacle. "In here, sir," she continued, once they had reached the second floor landing, her voice laden with breathlessness from the exertion.

The room was clean, newly decorated by the smell of it and well furnished. William took note of the bed...plump and cosy-looking, topped with a richly patterned marseille bedspread, its appearance exuding the kind of comfort he had never experienced. While he pondered it, he listened to the noise of swirling water as Clara emptied the steaming contents of the pitcher into the ironstone basin that occupied a nearby washstand.

"Missis says she specks you'z wanna wash and smarten y'self up 'fore supper."

Indeed, I do, thought William to himself, realising that Missus Rutherford's remark to her servant had been a contrivance, the intent that it be repeated in all innocence by the girl. Understandably Missus Rutherford did not want a malodorous and rather dishevelled cattle tender at her table.

The proprietrix was in the habit of taking meals with her guests and, in doing so, was always quick to snuff out any discussion about the fighting. For although she had strong convictions of her own, Missus Rutherford considered that talk of the war was potentially divisive, especially in a place like Baltimore. Pontificating upon the rights and wrongs of either side or upon the conflict's progress was in consequence taboo around the dining table in Hanover Street. As to Missus Rutherford's feeding of her guests, Jacob Burns was right. She was not frugal when it came to food and her cook was clearly accomplished in her work. Supper on this particular evening at the close of November was no exception, enjoyed by the lady of the house and a total of four guests, William included. The others were two quite elderly ladies travelling together, who had chosen to break their journey in Baltimore for two nights to visit old friends. Lastly there was a gentleman of middle years, who William gathered was a commercial traveller from some obscure place in Vermont. He had already stayed several nights under Missus Rutherford's roof while going about his business in the city.

The conversation over supper was of little substance or significance: the weather... the price of certain goods...railroad travel...subjects upon which William had scant, if any, knowledge and could therefore contribute little. In any event, he preferred to remain on the periphery of the conversation, being keen not to draw particular attention to himself. One thing he did not relish was others wishing to elicit information upon his background. Not that he was unprepared but it meant lying in front of Missus Rutherford who William had considered sufficiently astute to have already drawn her own conclusions upon his background. Indeed, he sensed that the good lady was careful not to involve him in too much conversation for the very same reason. Yet that was not difficult, since, apart from the occasional brief remark from the commercial traveller – a naturally taciturn man by nature – the elderly ladies from Frederick appeared more than eager to monopolise the conversation. It emerged that these not unpleasant – yet ebullient and garrulous companions – had journeyed from their home town upon the railroad. It had been a largely uneventful trip excepting that there had been a delay at a place called Relay where troops had searched the cars. Yet their only cause for complaint was the lumpy seating "which sorely lacked the degree of comfort to which we are normally accustomed." William was amused by the lady's inadvertent choice of the word 'sorely.' Its inevitable relevance required him to stifle a snigger. Well, eventually the train had proceeded to nearby Camden Station, the Baltimore terminus of the B & O, and "fortuitously, Missus Rutherford, some kind gentleman recommended us to your fine establishment."

"Tomorrow morning you will have nothing to worry about," came the response. "After breakfast I will ensure Gideon makes ready the horse and buggy to get you and your luggage to President Street Station for your onward journey. I think you said the Philadelphia train leaves at eleven o'clock, so you will have ample time. However, being a small conveyance at our disposal, Gideon will need to take you both separately but it's no distance."

"Well, thank you kindly, Missus Rutherford," said the two ladies in unison. The fact that they both uttered the very same words was, in itself, quite remarkable, causing William and the commercial traveller to glance at each other in disbelief.

"Think nothing of it," said Missus Rutherford, smiling sweetly.

"We have enjoyed our short stay and your hospitality, ma'am. Your boarding house is most commodious," chortled one of the ladies, as the other nodded cheerily in agreement. "We must remember to insert some apt and kindly commentary upon our stay in the guest book," said one lady to the other.

"We must," came the retort.

"Well, thank you," exclaimed Missus Rutherford, "and perhaps you will grace us with your presence if once again, ladies, you find yourself in Baltimore."

"Most certainly."

"This peach pie is grand...most delectable and the best I've tasted," exclaimed the commercial traveller, as much bent upon interrupting the ladies' chitchat as in making the observation.

"I'm pleased to hear it, Mister Meredith. It's one of Martha, the cook's, specialities. The fruit's not fresh, of course, on account of September-time being the height of the peach season but it's preserved in a good French brandy. I'll convey your compliment to Martha. She'll be pleased, having turned up her nose at the fruit this year."

"Why would that be ma'am? I agree with this gentleman...Mister Meredith. The pie was superb." For William it was a rare foray into the conversation as he cleared his plate.

"Well, I've always been happy with the peaches we get in. I purchase them from an old gentleman who, for years, has kept a fine orchard up on Stuart's Hill. The trouble is that this summer a succession of regiments has been bivouacked on neighbouring ground. It seems that some soldiers constantly infiltrated the peach orchard to supplement their army rations and regrettably the best of the fruit disappeared. Yet, if you gentlemen are impressed with Martha's pie she has clearly done well with what she was given. Now, if, as it appears, you are all about to finish your supper, you may care to retire to the front parlour and I will instruct Gideon to bring you coffee."

"I think I will go straight to my room, if you don't mind, ma'am," said William apologetically, as he set down his napkin and rose to his feet.

"Tired are you? I'm not surprised after the day you've had. Breakfast will be at eight. Now, if you'd like coffee I will get Gideon to bring it to your room shortly."

"Thank you, ma'am. Goodnight."

"Goodnight, Mister Reynolds." Missus Rutherford smiled warmly as she spoke her guest's name. "Sleep soundly. You'll not need a candle, by the way. Clara should have lighted a lamp in your room."

"She has already, ma'am. Before I came down to supper."

"Of course, she did. Whatever am I thinking...after all, it's the end of November, not high summer," chuckled the proprietrix.

And with that William bade goodnight to the other guests as they made to depart the dining table. His early retirement was in part due to fatigue but, principally, because he wished to be spared entrapment in a room where, deprived of the tempering presence of Missus Rutherford, he could well find himself interrogated by the elderly ladies from Frederick. Unknown to William, as he ascended the stairs, was that his departure proved a grave disappointment to the gentleman from Vermont. The thought of settling down with those same two ladies and their wearing tittle-tattle, without the countervailing influence of any male company, proved too much for the commercial traveller. Instead he took himself off to the backyard. There, despite the evening chill, he enjoyed a cigar before likewise slipping away to the privacy of his room.

William was not long out of bed. He had picked up a copy of the *Baltimore Daily Gazette* that lay amid a selection of newspapers in the front entrance hall. Once in his room it was to discover that, during supper, young Clara had set and kindled a fire in the grate. As a consequence, any nip had been dispelled and the room's occupant drew forth an easy chair before the fire which he took time to stoke and tend, finally adding a few more coals. Gideon arrived with his hot beverage. Once the butler had departed, William took a sip or two, then nestled into the fireside chair with his newspaper. It did not take long before the combined effect of a hearty supper, the room's warmth and tired eyes wrestling with newsprint, combined to soporific effect. Within minutes William was asleep. When he woke, forty minutes later, it was to find the cheery flames had fallen to flickering embers, his paper strewn upon the hearth rug, his coffee cold. It was only nine o'clock, yet time enough to transport himself into bed. Bleary-eyed, he stumbled to his feet, turned back the counterpane and undressed. Then, extinguishing the light, he felt his way into bed assisted by the faint light from the grate's faltering embers. He slept well until a rapping on the door signalled Clara's arrival with hot water and, somewhere beyond, a distant chiming struck the hour. It was seven o'clock.

William was dressed and downstairs soon after seven thirty. He had made himself as presentable as he could, being only too aware that he needed a fresh stock of clothes. Yet, his intention of joining the army would presumably reduce the urgency of such, for he would be issued with whatever constituted a Union soldier's wardrobe. He peered into the front parlour. A welcoming fire spat and crackled. The maid, Clara, busied herself dusting the walnut casing of a stout-looking parlour organ.

"Do go in and sit yourself down, young man," came a voice at William's shoulder. It belonged to Missus Rutherford.

"Good morning, ma'am," said William, immediately complying with his hostess's invitation.

"Clara, my dear, leave that now and go into the kitchen to help Martha with the breakfast preparations," said her employer as she followed William into the parlour. "Oh, and I notice the table is presently lacking napkins and the spooner is bereft of spoons. Attend to it please."

"It is fortuitous that I might steal a quiet word with you young man," began Missus Rutherford, as soon as her maid was out of earshot...before the other guests appear. No problem, I'm sure, where Mister Meredith is concerned, but the two ladies are Marylanders and I've no idea where their loyalties lie. I can't afford to upset my guests you'll appreciate." A short hesitation ensued before she continued. "So...you told me yesterday you had intentions of enlisting in the Army today. Have you given thought to how you propose going about it?"

"I was told by a shipmate that I should go to Patterson Park."

"I think not. You see, regiments are just encamped there, going about their drills and such like...waiting to be sent to wherever they're required. There's been a lot of activity this fall, what with regiments leaving Camp Washburn...Patterson Park, that is...and other camping grounds in the city. This month we've heard the strains of many a military band escorting its regiment down to the docks. The soldiers have been embarking on transports and taken down the Bay...bound for somewhere in Virginia I imagine. Wherever they're going, bless them, they're needed. The Union has fared very badly this year. We could have made far greater advances in Virginia but we dithered and weren't up to it...not the soldiers, you understand...oh, no, far from it...brave fighting men if ever there were. No, they say it's down to the men at the top...nobody of the ability of General Lee I'm afraid." For a moment Missus Rutherford appeared to lose a little of her composure as she allowed recent events to raise her hackles. "Still," she continued, "the President has just appointed a new commander...General Burnside. Let's hope he can turn the tide." William wondered when she might revert to the gist of their little chat, knowing, at any minute, the other guests might appear, leaving him no wiser as to his best course of action. Fortunately, Missus Rutherford realised her mistake. "Sorry, Mister Reynolds, I'm rambling on...wavering...a bit like that poor General McClellan. I was about to say that you need to present yourself at one of the recruiting offices. There are now several in the city since the Government is keen to attract new recruits. The young men aren't as enthusiastic to join up as they once were, what with the bad year we've had. But don't let that deter you. I know that one of the offices is in West Baltimore Street. Now, you won't know how to get there, but don't worry. Gideon is taking those two ladies to the railroad station to catch the Philadelphia train. Once he's finished that you can join him in the buggy and he'll take you to the recruiting office. Just remember to give him a few cents if you would…for his trouble. He'll be much appreciative."

"Thank you, ma'am. That's wonderful," said a grateful William.

"Oh…and a little motherly word of warning. If, once a soldier, you find yourself with a pass to leave camp, remember there's safety in numbers. Above all remain sober. Don't be inveigled into the evils of strong liquor. I say this because there are a good many ruffians about the city who have a pernicious dislike of Union soldiers. They roam around with the sole purpose of setting upon those the worse for drink. Plug uglies is, I believe, the vulgarism by which they are referred. I'm sure…"

At that moment the sound of subdued voices on the stairs caused Jane Rutherford to cease talking. She rose to her feet, then resumed, but now in a whisper.

"Excuse me Mister Reynolds. That sounds like the ladies from Frederick coming down for breakfast. Now, if we don't have the opportunity to speak again, confidentially, I wish you well in the Army. May God bless you and keep you safe." Missus Rutherford made for the door, then checked her progress, turned and pensively whispered a final comment. "You know, young man, you should look most dignified in your smart blue uniform. It'll suit you." Her words were touching and there was a twinkle in her eye.

"Good morning ladies. Did you sleep well?" uttered the kindly proprietrix as she breezed into the hallway, closing the parlour door in her wake.

"Tolerably well. But it's never quite the same without one's own mattress," came the reply.

In the parlour William sat alone for a while with his thoughts. "…your smart blue uniform. It'll suit you." He stared into the grate's shimmering flames. Somewhere, down in the recesses of his mind, something flickered. It was something long lost to recollection, buried deep in his memory, layered beneath the mind's record of subsequent experience. Out of that sediment of stored information it now percolated to the forefront of his mind. He was back on Southsea Common…an autumn day…a breezy afternoon, salt spray being whipped off the sea and driven into the furze. William had found his way to the gypsy encampment and Ned's wizened old grandmother was reading his fortune. The old hag spoke of him joining the army…she had seen a row of soldier's buttons but not upon a scarlet tunic, so William had dismissed her pronouncements as nonsense and relegated them to the back of his mind. Now her words came to him in the front parlour in Hanover Street…*I see the colour blue.* She had been right, after all…the old woman had been right, damn it. William continued to sit upon the haircloth sofa, staring into the fire and lost in his thoughts. During the past month, as he had come to set his heart upon joining the Union Army, he had not given any mental attention to the uniform. He had caught sight of Federal soldiers in Boston and, latterly, in Baltimore, but it had taken Missus Rutherford's words to unlock and suddenly make sense of what the old gypsy had told him five years ago.

"Breakfast, sir." The words drew no response. "Excuse me, sir, but breakfast is ready." William came to his senses with a jolt. He looked round to see young Clara peering round the door and the figure of Mister Meredith passing beyond her towards the dining room. He immediately heeded the young maid's beckoning and hurried to the table. He needed a hearty breakfast to sustain him during the day ahead.

★ ★ ★

Eleven o'clock. Having thanked and bade farewell to Missus Rutherford and paid his dues, William clambered into the buggy alongside Gideon. It was a mild enough morning with a fine drizzle in the air that had wetted the leaves underfoot, heightening their colour. Momentarily, as he sat himself down, William wondered when he might again experience such homely comforts. Yet it was a thought that failed to bother him for now he was beset with the excitement of knowing that in a very short time he should fulfil his long-cherished ambition. Today he would become a soldier.

Gideon cracked his whip. The horse, a stout, grey mare, proceeded at a trot, her withers and hindquarters already sheeny from the exertion of two jaunts to President Street Station.

"So, it's West Baltimore Street, is it sir?" said Gideon in his rich voice.

"Yes," replied his passenger, not knowing whether the butler's mistress had been specific about the actual destination. "The recruiting station," he added for good measure.

"Ah, yes, I think I know of its whereabouts." In refraining from soliciting an explanation, the negro displayed a degree of politesse and sensitivity not normally expected from his kind. Yet he had been schooled well by

Missus Rutherford and, putting two and two together, was minded not to cause his passenger any embarrassment. In William's case, however, there was no discomfiture in admission that he was intent on entering the ranks. Indeed, he was more than proud to declare as much.

"I'm off to join the Army," he exclaimed, gleefully, as they rattled their way west along Pratt Street.

"Well, sir, I reckon you've come to the right place. I've seen more troops in the city these past weeks than I knew existed. They come in on the railroad, camp down and get knocked into shape, then they get shipped out on transports like sardines in tin cans. A young gentleman like yourself, in good physical condition, should have no trouble enlisting, especially as some of the newly formed regiments are still looking to fill their State quotas. And, of course, there's bounty money to be made in signing up."

"I'm told the money's good."

"Yes, very good, but I'm thinking Baltimore's not the place to strike it rich. No new Union regiments are being raised here. You see, Baltimore's a southern city which the Federal Government was swift to occupy to prevent secession. Now, if your interest had been simply pecuniary, you'd have been better placed this past summer clerking in Philadelphia or spending your days tending the fields of rural Pennsylvania. You see, the President called for three hundred thousand more troops to serve three years. Well, my understanding is that each State had a quota to raise and various districts in each State had the responsibility of creating its own regiment. And all manner of little towns and communities took responsibility for raising one of ten regimental companies. I suppose it must have engendered a lot of pride for some remote community to put its name to a company of soldiers...encouragement enough for some young fellows to sign the roll and proudly march off to war."

Gideon fell silent for a moment as he concentrated on applying the reins, for he needed to slow the pace of the animal in preparation for turning out of Pratt Street and heading north on Carey. He held back awhile to allow an approaching horse-drawn street car to pass, then completed the manoeuvre before resuming his discourse. "Well, apart from the whole process of kindling pride and trusting the actions of some young men might trigger the desired repetition in others, there was a significant inducement in the form of bounty money...County, State and Government bounties, no less. Which brings me back to my earlier point. Here in Baltimore I'm assuming you'll only qualify for Government bounty...maybe fifty dollars...

unless perhaps a recruiting officer admits to still falling short of the War Department's original State quota."

"Fifty dollars is handsome enough," said William, impressed by the negro's eloquence and knowledge. "And you appear to be so well acquainted with the ways of the military."

"It's just what I hear…and I suppose I hear plenty, for my employer, Missus Rutherford, is an influential person among the Union Ladies of this city," admitted Gideon. "I'm constantly conveying her to meetings of the Union Relief Association and I'm privy to much of the discussion while waiting around to take her home.

"So what exactly is the business of these Union Ladies?"

"They seem not to trust the War Department to look after its troops… self-appointed proxy mothers and benefactresses, I guess. They engage in a lot of fund raising and provide meals in the Relief Rooms for hungry regiments newly arrived in the city…oh, and some of the ladies spend time visiting soldiers in the city's hospitals…consoling poor, wounded fellows who lie moping far from loved ones. And they seem most diligent about taking all manner of gifts and comforters to the camps…from so-called 'housewife' sewing kits…to molasses candy…to little religious tracts and such like."

Gideon again fell silent as, once more, he applied his mind to the reins, easing the animal's trot to a walk in preparation for turning into West Baltimore Street. "No, as I say," he continued, once set on his new course, " a young gentleman such as yourself, sir, in possession of all your faculties, will have no difficulty enlisting. On the contrary, they'll snap you up. You see, the Government is crying out for more recruits what with the Union having had a bad year. Shiloh…the Peninsula Campaign…Cedar Mountain… Second Bull Run…so many setbacks, but Christmas approaches and there has to be optimism for the New Year. It's eagerly awaited by my black brethren, in bondage, throughout those occupied parts of the Confederacy…what with Mister Lincoln's proclamation…but let's hope '63 also augurs well for the Army, by bringing a change of fortune. Now…if I'm not mistaken, that's the recruiting office just ahead…the low, brick building, smothered in billboards."

Gideon drew the buggy to a halt outside the establishment. William immediately alighted, clutching his drawstring bag. As his feet met the sidewalk, it was to the gushing sound of the grey mare emptying her bladder. Both men laughed, amused by the timing and irony of such an inauspicious parting signal. William sifted a quarter from among the few coins he had left and handed it to the affable negro, drawing profuse thanks in return.

"Godspeed, Mister Reynolds, sir. May the Good Lord cherish and protect you." And with that valediction and a wave of farewell, Gideon goaded the horse into action and William turned to face the recruiting office. A small group of young men lingered nearby, perhaps hesitant about enlisting, perhaps making small talk before one or more of their number went forth to enlist. Spirals of smoke rose from their huddled midst, as several drew upon cheroots, to the exclusion of much discernible conversation. In contrast, a young fellow, who seemed but a boy, strode purposefully up to the office door and, without pausing, passed through.

For a few moments William ran his eyes over the many notices peppering the front of the building. *Volunteers wanted...Opportunities for patriotic young men to serve their Country...Rally Round the Flag, Boys...The Union must and shall be preserved ...Bounty money to be had here and now: don't wait for a draft...Pay and rations immediately available on enlistment...Help reinforce your brothers in the field.* Such announcements were embodied in an eclectic mix of black and white posters. Above them, fixed to the roof parapet, rose a stout, colourful sign bearing the image of a handsome liberty maiden who brandished a sword and bore Old Glory aloft.

A formidable-looking sergeant now filled the doorway. Beside him, on the sidewalk, was a spittoon, since smoking or chewing plug-tobacco was prohibited in the recruiting office and it was necessary to discard the fag-ends of cigars and expel one's plug-filthy spittle before entering. Just now, a stray dog ventured by, lingering briefly to sniff the receptacle. Losing interest, it looked set to move on, but instead stopped and crouched to defecate, only to feel the weight of the sergeant's right foot in its straining buttocks. William winced, feeling sorry for the poor creature as it squealed and scuttled away, its bowels already pressed into action.

The sergeant, noticing William's reaction, tried to make light of his cruelty. "For a moment, seeing its grey coat and its willingness to empty itself on the sidewalk, I guess I mistook the critter for an ill-mannered Reb." The soldier roared with laughter, such was the amusement he derived from his remark. Then, composing himself he called out to William. "If you've a wish to fight for Uncle Sam, young man, just step inside here and we'll make a soldier of you." And with that he withdrew into the building.

A minute later William pushed open the recruiting office door and went in. There was a distinctive smell about the place…beeswax polish, its scent exuded by the glistening pine boards beneath his feet.

"At your age, boy, you can't sign the roll without your mother's or father's permission." Hardly had the words been uttered than the youngster – who, full of optimism, had strode resolutely into the recruiting office – pushed his way past William, his eyes welling, his features wracked with disappointment. It clearly signalled the end of his immediate wish to become a soldier.

William stepped forward. The sergeant who had kicked the dog was nowhere to be seen but across the room two line officers sat behind a long deal table, one a captain, the other a second lieutenant. To their left, a man wearing a sergeant's chevrons sat poised with pen and ink and a wad of enlistment papers. To their right, a corporal stood easy beside an inner doorway, a flagstaff propped up in the corner – to the man's left – carrying the 'Stars and Stripes.' Behind the officers hung portraits of Abraham Lincoln and of a gentleman William thought might be George Washington. A third portrait, that of General-in-Chief Henry Halleck, was understandably beyond the scope of his recognition.

"Your name?" barked the second lieutenant.

"William Reynolds, sir," said the prospective recruit, haltingly, being somewhat unnerved by the officer's curtness.

"And you're wanting to join the Army…to enlist as a soldier?"

"Yes, sir."

"Do I detect from the few words you've uttered that you're not from these shores?"

"I'm English, sir."

"English, eh? So how have you come to find your way to Baltimore?"

"I worked my sea passage from Canada."

"Where in Canada?" interjected the captain with a withering look in his eye.

"Halifax, Nova Sco…"

"Halifax, indeed! Sounds as though you might be late of Her Majesty's Navy, young man. Deserter are you? Do you know what we do with deserters if we catch them?" continued the captain, without waiting for William's reply. "Well, they're likely to be shot."

"I'm not proud of what I did, sir. I was harshly treated but, for all that, I admit I was wrong." William felt he needed to appear repentant before the officers, yet, inwardly, he had no regrets about jumping ship.

"Harshly treated, were you? Well don't expect serving in the Union ranks to be a bowl of cherries."

"So what is your purpose in wanting to join the Army?" resumed the lieutenant, as he took advantage of a fleeting lull in the flow of words.

"I've always wanted to be a soldier, sir."

"A *fighting* soldier? Or do you just like the uniform?"

"A fighting soldier, sir." William's reply was emphatic, his earlier faltering tone having vanished.

"So why did you not attest in one of Her Majesty's regiments?"

"My uncle made arrangements for me to join the Royal Navy. It was not what I wanted."

"Ah, a wicked uncle," murmured the lieutenant, a disclosure which caused both he and the captain to smile. "It's not the money...the bounty... that attracts you then but a genuine desire to be a soldier? And I presume you're willing to swear allegiance to the United States?"

"Let me explain why we may appear so touchy and need to press you about such matters," said the captain, again disinclined to wait for the young man's reply. "The Army is sick and tired of what we call bounty jumpers. Often former sailors, such as yourself, they join the Army in one place, pocket their bounty money, then, after a few days, disappear. They then turn up elsewhere and repeat the process...sometimes more than once."

"I'd not do that, sir. My interest lies in soldiering, not in making money. I'll willingly swear allegiance to the Union and be committed to whatever regiment permits me to sign its roll," said William, with a heartfelt and earnest ring to his words.

The two officers turned away for a few moments and murmured to each other, the sergeant having remained impassive throughout the earlier exchanges. The captain then confronted William.

"Young man," he said, "being a former deserter we clearly have grave doubts over your reliability, but I am prepared to give you a chance...subject, of course, to passing your medical. Just don't let me down."

"Yes sir. I won't, sir. Thank you."

"The fact is, we can't afford to turn away able-bodied fellows. For one thing, the War Department is insistent that the Army does its utmost to enlist more men. That aside, the lieutenant and I like the look of you. Now, the regiment we represent...*our* regiment...is the One Hundred and Fourteenth New York State Volunteers. We were raised in the summer, across three counties, at the time having no difficulty achieving our full complement and meeting our district's contribution towards the State quota. In September, once mustered and organised, we left home soil and travelled to Baltimore on the railroads. Here we remained at Camp Belger until a month ago, when we received orders to be in readiness to leave on distant service. Within two or three days the regiment was on its way. Together with other units, it embarked on board a number of steamers which conveyed us down the Chesapeake as far as Fort Monroe. It is there, on the wretched transports, that the regiment has been kicking its heels for the past few weeks."

William's thoughts strayed back to the several hours – only a few days before – when the *Snowgoose* lay at anchor in Hampton Roads and the sight of the multitude of ships assembled off the fortress.

"Although by day the men are constantly sent ashore to drill, the living conditions aboard the crowded steamers are not good and sickness has taken a heavy toll," continued the captain. "A significant number of men have been sent to hospitals ashore and it is reasonable to suppose that a large proportion will be unfit to travel with the regiment when we do put to sea. Now, Reynolds, it should be a measure of your resolve if that doesn't deter you. But, in all honesty, the picture is not as black as it might seem. You see, word is that within a few days we expect to be under orders to proceed on the mission that awaits us…and putting to sea will disperse the miasma and have a beneficial effect on the regiment. However, the scale of the sickness has necessitated the lieutenant and I having to return to Baltimore…a mite unusual to be frank, but considerable importance is being attached to getting the regiment back to strength before we are directed to move. So we have been busy recruiting more men these past few days and our work is all but complete. Monday is December the first and we'll be returning to Hampton Roads with all the new recruits. Now…just one thing, Reynolds," said the captain. "The bounty money for enlisting is nowhere near as plentiful as it was when the summer sun rose high over Chenango County and the boys back home rallied to the flag. You'll get your twenty five dollars Government bounty and my understanding from our State Paymaster's office is that there may still be some State and County money in the coffers…sufficient, I reckon, to raise total bounty to fifty dollars a man. In addition you'll get a month's pay…that's thirteen dollars…in advance. All in all, still a decent bit of cash, so I've arranged for one of the allotment commissioners to talk to all the new recruits about the wisdom of putting aside some of their bounty, as well as a regular portion of their pay. There's no sense in squandering good money." The captain paused for a moment, then fixed a piercing eye on William. "So what do you say to all that young man? Do you still wish to become a private in the One Hundred and Fourteenth?"

"Definitely, sir." It was a swift and unqualified response.

"Did you hear that, sergeant?" remarked the captain.

"Yes, sir."

"Then proceed to attend to the paperwork." Having so instructed the sergeant, the captain again addressed the emerging new recruit. "Step aside, Mister Reynolds, and assist the sergeant. He'll need particulars from you to help complete a certificate of volunteer enlistment. When he's finished, take it across to the corporal and he'll escort you to the medical room to see the assistant surgeon. When that officer's done with you, bring the form back and we'll see if we can swear you in as a soldier of the United States."

A few minutes later William sat upon a rickety bench outside the medical room. The occasional exchange of words from within suggested that an examination was still being conducted. As he mulled over what had gone before, he moved his feet in a backward motion, encountering, in the process, an obstruction to free movement. This proved, on close inspection, to be a pile of discarded newspapers and other sundry periodicals. William reached down and drew forth the top publication. It was a magazine titled the *Scientific American* and soon he became engrossed in one of its principal reviews, a critique upon the development of rifled artillery since the days of Waterloo. As he studied the article, mention of the British Armstrong gun took him back to those distant days on the *Excellent*...of experimental firing across the mudflats into a burgeoning Hampshire sunset...of the fate which befell poor Francis Boney when a shell burst at the muzzle of a gun.

Suddenly the medical room door swung open and through it emerged a ginger-headed youth clutching his certificate. He was immediately followed by a tall, bewhiskered gentleman, of middle years, who peered into the passage and called for the corporal to escort the departing man back to the captain and his second lieutenant. His expression suggested a degree of surprise in finding another volunteer already awaiting his scrutiny. William closed and returned the magazine to its resting place as the medical man beckoned him to enter the examination room. Unlike the outside corridor, it was pleasantly warm, thanks to a cheery fire of hickory logs, the heat having long since caused the assistant surgeon to discard his army frock coat.

"Sit yourself down," said the officer, gesturing towards a straight-backed chair facing his desk. "I'll take that," he continued, grasping William's partially completed enlistment certificate. There was no please or thank you as the medical man fell into his upholstered chair, donned his spectacles and proceeded to peruse the document. "Reynolds...twenty years of age... born in Malta, eh?...British...former seaman. Well, let's hope you're made of the right stuff," said the officer, as he came to his feet and strode round his desk to face the volunteer. He turned William towards the light and cupped his head. He examined his scalp and his eyes, then asked him to open his mouth wide, whereupon he poked and prodded his teeth with a narrow, metal implement. "Most important for the infantry, Reynolds... good incisors to bite through the paper on your cartridge." The surgeon returned to his desk. He picked up a pen, wiped the tip, then dipped it in his inkwell. "This examination will take longer than usual. That's why you had to wait a while outside. You see, I normally have a man with me to act as clerk. I brought a corporal back from Hampton Roads to write down all these details, but the poor fellow became badly jaundiced as soon as we arrived in the city and was taken off to the Jarvis Hospital. So now I have to do it all. Right... take all your clothes off," ordered the surgeon without further ado. He paused to sprinkled pounce powder upon his jottings. "You may wish to move nearer the warmth of the fire."

As the officer continued to busy himself at his desk, William proceeded to divest himself of his clothes and shoes until, clearly ill-at-ease and now bearing a somewhat forlorn and self-conscious expression, he stood quietly in his underpants.

"I said *all* your clothing, man," boomed the surgeon as he rose to his feet. "No need to be shy. I've seen it all before, so hurry up now and remove your drawers."

Sheepishly, William obeyed. The surgeon then instructed him to execute a range of movements to test his body's agility, interspersing them with such prodding, probing and palpation upon the torso as he deemed necessary. A close inspection of his genitals caused William to flinch.

"I fear this intrusion is a necessary one," remarked the surgeon, ruefully. "The Army has enough problems with men presenting with symptoms of gonorrhoea and syphilis. We can't afford to inherit already infected recruits."

To William, standing there buck naked in front of the fire, under the minute inspection and handling of a complete stranger was, to say the least, unnerving, but an instruction to cross the room to be weighed signalled an end to the ordeal.

"All done, except for testing your eyesight. For that we no longer need you in your birthday attire so put your clothes back on."

When the surgeon had fully completed his examination he once again sat down at his desk and resumed making notes, eventually applying his signature with a flourish upon William's certificate of enlistment.

A few minutes later William found himself sitting alone in an ante-room – into which he had been ushered by the corporal – his renewed audience with the captain being delayed until the officers had finished with another hopeful. He looked down at the document, returned to him by the assistant surgeon, and was heartened to see the officer's declaration. It was to the effect that he had carefully examined the volunteer, agreeably to the General Regulations of the Army, and that, in his opinion, the prospective recruit was free from all bodily defects and mental infirmity which might otherwise disqualify him from performing the duties of a soldier. William realised he had cleared a major hurdle and felt more relaxed when, ten minutes later, he was ushered back to confront the two officers.

"Well, the assistant surgeon's happy with you, Reynolds, so there's no bar to your enlistment," declared the captain. "You'll be assigned as a private in Company E which is currently berthed on board the steamer, *Thames*. Of course, you and the rest of the new recruits will have plenty of catching up to do, after all, the rest of the men have been together for a few months now. But don't let that worry you. We'll knock you into shape as we go, starting with drill on the beach at Fort Monroe. Now, as I say, the day after tomorrow…on Monday…we'll be returning to the point of assembly at Hampton Roads. In the meantime, you'll be quartered at Fort Belger which was our home for two months before we took off down the Bay. There's plenty to be done in camp before we leave but for now you have a few hours to yourself. Go out and take a look about the city but make sure you're back here at four o'clock sharp. The rest of today's recruits will do likewise and then you'll be formally mustered in."

"Just a moment," added the second lieutenant, correctly sensing the captain had said all he intended."You'll need to sign this declaration."

A further sheet was produced by the sergeant. In essence, this stated that William was desirous of volunteering as a soldier of the United States for a term of three years and that he knew of no impediment to prevent him serving honestly and faithfully as a soldier. The new recruit eagerly accepted the pen proffered by the sergeant, replenished it with ink and neatly added his signature.

With an intense feeling of self-satisfaction, and intoxicated with excitement, William had little time for sightseeing as he eagerly looked forward to the mustering hour. He wandered east on Baltimore Street, all the while closing upon the lofty brick landmark that was the Phoenix shot tower. Then, turning right on President Street, he soon found himself amid the teeming bustle of the docks and inner harbour. Here he wandered at random, whiling away a couple of hours watching the comings and goings, alone with his thoughts. Some time soon he would need to write home, for his mother and grandmother deserved to know of his circumstances. He missed them dearly, it having been almost eighteen months since he last set eyes upon them. Suddenly his cogitation hit upon the possibility that the *Cygnet* might return to Portsmouth ahead of a letter. If so, his folks would be mortified to learn of his misdemeanours before he could colour them, sufficient to temper the anguish. It was a prospect which troubled him. As for Uncle James, he felt the wrong he had dealt him had now been righted. He half-hoped he could be told, for his uncle would be infuriated in the extreme and the thought actually amused him. At three o'clock William spent what few cents remained of Captain Burns'gift, on bread and clam stew, before ambling his way back to West Baltimore Street.

They were clearly of disparate background and appearance…half a dozen men, one or two shuffling awkwardly, perhaps making eye contact, at best exchanging the hint of a smile. Others simply fixed their gaze, distractedly, upon some inanimate object across the room. What they seemed to have in common was a respect for the prevailing silence, a silence heightened by the perceptible tick of the wall clock which looked down from beside Abraham Lincoln's colour-tinted image.

A more resounding metallic click, peculiar to the time-piece as it struck the hour, signalled the arrival of four o'clock and heralded the return of the sergeant and corporal who took up their previous positions. They were promptly followed by the captain and his lieutenant. The captain appeared nonchalant in his manner as he resumed his seat. The lieutenant hesitated and remained standing, taking stock of the assembled recruits until satisfied he had accounted for all those expected to be present.

"Right, men," exclaimed the lieutenant, "it is time to swear the oath of muster. Line yourselves up across the middle of the room facing Captain Dederer."

It was the first time there'd been any mention of the captain's name as far as William could recall.

"Sergeant, organise the men accordingly," continued the officer, rather impatiently, as if loath to leave the new recruits to their own devices in putting his instruction into effect.

The sergeant sprang to his feet and quickly marshalled the men into a tidy enough, shoulder-to-shoulder formation and simultaneously ensured that any hats were removed.

"Now, each of you raise your right hand," ordered the lieutenant. "You are going to repeat after me words which appear on your enlistment paper and to which you will shortly append your signature. When I begin I will say 'I' which you will repeat, then state your name. I will continue, stopping at intervals, to permit your repetition. A word of warning. Captain Dederer and I do not wish to witness any indifference. We wish to see that each and all of you mean what you are saying. We need to be convinced. Then we'll make soldiers of you. The lieutenant cast a steely glance along the rank of volunteers. "We will begin."

For his part William repeated the oath with spirit and commitment…"I, *William Reynolds, do solemnly swear that I will bear true faith and allegiance to the United States of America, and that I will serve them honestly and faithfully against all their enemies or opposers, whomsoever; and that I will observe and obey the orders of the President of the United States, and the orders of the officers appointed over me according to the Rules and Articles of War.*"

"Congratulations, all of you," said Captain Dederer. "When I call out your name, come forward and sign the oath on your enlistment certificate and then, as recruiting officer, I will endorse your paper with my own signature. You can then regard yourselves as Union soldiers, albeit, in terms of appearance and experience, you remain well short of the genuine article. But that will come soon enough. When we have finished attending to this important formality, the corporal here will take you to Fort Belger in a conveyance waiting out the back. There you will encounter some other volunteers who have enlisted with us over the past few days. By the way… welcome to the One Hundred and Fourteenth Regiment, New York State Volunteers!"

★ ★ ★

Being late in the month of November, it was dark when Saturday's crop of volunteers passed beneath the painted arch which bore the name 'Camp Belger.' Skirting the parade ground, the horse-drawn wagon passed through a fine grove of white oak and hickory trees, their branches, now bereft of leaves, forming a stark, enveloping tracery against the star-lit heavens. The guard house sentinels had permitted the inward passage of the conveyance with minimal delay, the corporal of the guard being aware that his counterpart was on recruiting service for his regiment.

"You boys will need to start calling yourselves the One Hundred and Fourteenth and a Half, the way you keep recruiting," he had quipped, scrutinising the corporal's latest charges, then waving him through.

An assortment of rough timbered buildings loomed, giving way to orderly rows of tents, the majority wedge or 'A' shaped, their internal illumination causing them to glow an eerie pinkish-white amid the gloom. Within the nearest the sound of mirth and chatter rose and fell, the audibility being inversely proportional to that of the more immediate creaking and rattling of the conveyance upon the gravel-strewn road.

"That's the Quartermaster's building," shouted the corporal. "You'll be reporting there tomorrow to be kitted out with your uniform. That's the hospital," he added, pointing to a large wall tent. "You shouldn't need its services, God forbid, since we go south on Monday." Progressing towards the back of the camp, flanking the westernmost row of soldiers' tents, the corporal drew attention to a range of wall tents – which housed the commissioned officers – and to the all-important cookhouse in the distance. Shortly, he pulled firmly on the reins, coaxed the horse to the left and brought the wagon to a halt in a clearing fifty yards or so behind the hospital. Here, beneath a canopy of towering chestnuts stood three Sibley tents – bell tents – which, according to the corporal, were specifically for the temporary accommodation of the One Hundred and Fourteenth's new recruits. "The camp itself is nothing to do with us although it was our home for two months. Actually, we thought we'd be here throughout the winter," said the corporal, as he jumped off the box seat and tethered the animal to the overhanging bough of a tree. "I know for sure our boys would love to be back here and off those wretched transports. So I guess you'd best relish your brief stay." He unbolted and lowered a side flap on the wagon, thus permitting the volunteers to clamber down. In the process one man slipped on the damp ground. As he reached out to cushion his fall, in the course of which he dropped his modest valise, his palms felt the effect of being thrust into an ankle-deep carpet of chestnut burrs.

"No need scrambling down there, soldier, looking for sweet young nuts," chortled the corporal. "They've already been claimed and roasted. Anyway, we'll fill your bellies soon enough with proper army victuals.

The men here will be close to finishing their supper but we'll get you over to the cookhouse shortly. Just don't be expecting the same down on the transports...oh, no. Now, here at Belger, we are briefly imposing on the hospitality of another New York outfit...the One Hundred and Fiftieth...a good bunch of fellows from Poughkeepsie way. But then I don't suppose that means a great deal to you Baltimore folks. They've just arrived here themselves and only seven weeks mustered...so they're even greener than our boys. Now... talking of victuals...which I was a moment ago, I reckon it's time to get this horse groomed, watered and treated to a bag of oats from the grain pile."

"You go and attend to that, corporal...I'll see to the recruits." The gruff voice belonged to an approaching soldier who had just exited the nearest Sibley. As the man drew near, William recognised him. He was the sergeant who, that morning, had appeared at the recruiting station door and cruelly lifted his foot to the crouching dog "Right, men...how many has the day brought forth for Uncle Sam? Six, by the looks of you. Not a good tally, seeing as we netted two dozen recruits over the last two days. Still...that's thirty more," growled the sergeant, philosophically, "...thirty more to swell our depleted ranks and I suppose that's got to be better than nothing."

William thought the sergeant's remark a barbed, disparaging way of greeting new colleagues...but then, perhaps less barbed than the fellow's boot...the boot that had put the poor stray to gross discomfort.

"Let me introduce myself. I'm a First Sergeant with the One Hundred and Fourteenth chosen to accompany Captain Dederer, Lieutenant Gibson and Assistant Surgeon Beardsley north on recruiting service. George Zuicker's my name. *First* Sergeant Zuicker. I can't be so insincere to suggest it's a pleasure to make your acquaintance. The recruits we've enlisted these past two days seem a queer bunch, so I'm expecting you lot to be much the same. Perhaps you'll surprise me...let's hope so, but I don't see you Marylanders having the fight in your bellies like us New York boys. Now, follow me."

William's assessment was that Sergeant Zuicker was a man with neither the wish nor capacity to endear himself to man or beast alike. He raised the flap of the first bell tent and, ushering in the new arrivals, brusquely announced "these are some of your new comrades," a remark which served to inform both incumbents and newcomers. The draught provoked by the ingression caused candle flames to gutter, only for them to steady and quickly recover from their deceptive flickering once all had entered. Some cursory, yet good humoured, exchanges followed between both parties, the earlier recruits – upward of ten or so then present – being in various postures of recline and relaxation. Several were huddled around the warmth of a centrally-placed stove, chatting and clutching tin cups of coffee. A fellow of more mature years paid scant attention, lost as he was in the reek of his pipe smoke. In contrast, a fresh-faced young man, perched on a cracker box and with a short plank of wood on his knee, turned away from his letter writing and smiled broadly at Saturday's volunteers. Each appeared to have recently set aside his empty supper plate. In their eclectic mix of civilian garb they looked far removed from a group of Union soldiers.

"Three of you can lay your heads in here, three in the next tent. Sort that out among yourselves," boomed the sergeant as he gestured the visitors to leave. "Now, come and meet the others," he directed, pushing the men aside and striding off in the direction of the second Sibley. "The third tent accommodates the likes of me…and my fellow sergeant and the two corporals on recruiting duty. The officers, including the examining surgeon, have taken rooms at a nearby boarding house on Madison Avenue."

Once a similar, fleeting visitation had been made upon the inmates of the second bell tent, the sergeant took his six charges aside under the starlit sky and told them they would be relieved to hear it was time to eat. He gestured towards the distant cookhouse, which the corporal had already pointed out, this being a low and elongated wooden structure.

"Take yourselves over there and seek out the compartment with a door-plate inscribed Company F. That company's cook has drawn the short straw when it comes to accommodating the victualling needs of the One Hundred and Fourteenth. It'll come as no surprise to him, therefore, to be confronted, yet again, with the late arrival of a bunch of strangers, but make yourselves known to him and say I sent you. He'll see to it you're properly fed and don't turn in hungry. You'll need to bring your victuals back here and eat them in your tents…but wait a moment." At this point Zuicker turned on his heels and made a beeline for the third bell tent into which he disappeared. A minute later he re-emerged, now carrying a canvas bag full of table furnishings…tin plates and coffee dippers, knives, forks and spoons. "Each help yourself to a set of these," he said. "No point reporting to the company cook without the necessary tools."

"Are you from these parts?" asked William of the tousle-haired fellow at his shoulder, as the six men made their way to the cookhouse.

"Yes…Catonsville," came the snappy reply. "I can tell you're not local, for sure."

"You foreign, then?" interjected another who had overheard the exchange.

"English," replied William without elaboration.

"Thought you had your own army. Seems kind of strange you want to fight for Uncle Sam."

William was not drawn by the remark.

A fourth voice entered the mix, thereby displacing any expectation of further words from the Englishman. "I'm from a place called Gettysburg, a few miles beyond the state line…in Pennsylvania."

"So why didn't you join a local unit this summer, when Mister Lincoln called for more recruits?" questioned the man from Catonsville. "You'd have drawn better bounty."

"I wanted to, but my folks were opposed. But that bar's just been lifted as I came of age. They couldn't stop me joining up."

"So now there's bad feeling between you and your folks?"

"They were hoping that as the year progressed I would become discouraged about enlisting. Yes, they're disappointed, but they know for what purpose I've come here. They respect my decision and acknowledge it's now mine to make. At least I've got away from sleepy old Gettysburg and might just see some action."

As the little group passed to the rear of the serried rows of A tents and their dividing company streets, the drift of a plaintive tune played upon a concertina, prompted a lull in the conversation. Then, as a faint smell of food began to tease the nostrils, the two men bringing up the rear – both having been silent – chipped in with a few words.

"I'm local. Baltimore born and bred. But I firmly believe in the Union and despise slavery. I'll fight for the cause as well as any man in Mister Lincoln's army. I'm assuming the same goes for you Mister Catonsville?"

"Sure does, mister," came the unequivocal reply. "Sure does."

"I'm originally from Wilmington, Delaware," claimed the sixth man in a rather high-pitched, chirpy voice. Can't stand that bloody sergeant."

"You might have to," quipped the Catonsville fellow, "if he turns out to be in your company. By the way, any of you with me in Company H?"

There was unanimity among the six new entrants that the overcooked supper was palatable enough – even tolerably good – although with the majority not having eaten all day, or meagrely at best, the reaction was undoubtedly coloured by strains of hunger. In William Reynolds' case, the watery mix of stewed pork, beans and potatoes, consumed in the wake of Missus Rutherford's breakfast and a subsequent intake of tasty clam chowder, had ill-prepared him for army grub. He welcomed the coffee, since his salty, dockside repast had induced a thirst. Yet having neither the appetite nor relish for the victuals, he chose not to demur from the consensus, for fear of being seen as one prone to carp. He was also minded that the company cook was hardly out of earshot as he set about his tidying-up and that any derogatory remarks would be both uncharitable and ill-advised. Uncharitable, because the cook had invited the six into the back of the cookhouse where he had thoughtfully made preparations for the latecomers to take their meal immediately. Here they sat themselves down on boxes, either side of a trestle table, and consumed their supper by the light of three candles, each anchored in the bad flesh of a discarded potato. "You'd best find your way back from whence you've come, men," advised the cook when the six had despatched their food. "It's turned eight. Not long before 'attention' is sounded and the bugle will blow 'tattoo.' Unless, as fresh recruits, you're excluded, you'll need to be ready to turn out of your tents for roll call."

With these words of advice ringing in their ears and with muttered thanks to the cook for the supper, the six took their leave. In the process of retracing their steps, someone suggested that they should halt a moment and toss a coin to decide who should bed down in which tent. Another queried the necessity for this on account of "only being here for two nights, so what does it really matter?" But the suggestion found favour with the majority and so it was done; and, as a consequence, William found himself pitched into the first tent along with the Baltimorean and the youth from Gettysburg. Yet no sooner had they and the other threesome re-entered their respective shelters, than, to musical accompaniment, they were bundled out by their new comrades in readiness for the day's final roll call. It was shortly after eight-thirty and, thanks to the forewarning cook, this came as no surprise. For William it had been an eventful day. He was bound once again, this time to Mister Lincoln's Army. After tattoo the newcomers began to converse with others minded to become acquainted, until the drumming of taps brought this to an early conclusion. All lights were then extinguished and, within minutes, Private Reynolds had fallen asleep.

Sunday morning. A grey dawn. William had lain awake for twenty minutes before the sounding of 'reveille' broke the stillness and men began stirring and cursing and casting aside their woollen blankets.

"Time to sluice your face and…now, what do you English swells say?… attend to one's toilet and titivate oneself," scoffed a tall, ginger-haired Irish-

American, as he cast a dissembling smile in William's direction. "Fifteen minutes to roll call."

When that customary time had elapsed the new recruits tumbled out of the two bell tents and formed a line of sorts among the chestnut burrs. It was not a dressed line, for the men were still clothed as civilians and, being unaccustomed to army drill, were excused any call for precision. The sergeant who had acted as clerk to the recruiting line officers, a man by the name of Joseph O'Malley, proceeded to call the roll. He then reported to Sergeant Zuicker – who had seniority – that all were present and accounted for. It prompted Zuicker to stroll down the line, then turn on his heels and address his charges.

"Now pay attention men and listen carefully. I'm not in the habit of repeating myself. Today's the Sabbath. It means the One Hundred and Fiftieth will be subject to a regimental inspection…a dress parade. Captain Dederer is of the opinion that it would be good for you all to watch it. I believe it begins at eleven o'clock. They are still a green regiment…greener than ourselves, so the quality of their drill will doubtless leave much to be desired. But it'll give you an idea what will be expected of you two months hence. Prior to that and after you've responded to breakfast call you…" The sergeant cut short his announcements and glared at a gawky, cartilaginous-looking fellow who shifted awkwardly in the line and had raised his hand as if anxious to speak. "What is it man? You're not meant to ask questions, just to listen and obey."

"I need the sinks, sergeant, if you'd kindly permit me to…"

"No, I won't *kindly* agree to anything soldier…not while I'm talking. You'll stand your ground and clench your buttocks, man…until I stop talking and you're dismissed. Self-control, soldier…self-control." Zuicker's words had a sadistic ring. "Now I was about to say that once you've had breakfast you'll be taken to the Quartermaster's stores to receive your uniforms and accoutrements…the whole caboodle. So, by the time you get to watch the One Hundred and Fiftieth on parade, we'll actually have you looking like soldiers. But before then Sergeant O'Malley is going to get you learning some basic drill. Dinner will follow hard on the conclusion of dress parade and the afternoon, being Sunday, will be free time. That's all I have to say, so you're now dismissed. And that includes you, long-shanks," bellowed the sergeant at the scrawny fellow. "Be off and empty your bowels if they're not already spilt." As he scurried away, without further encouragement, the poor fellow was oblivious to Zuicker's broad grin.

That first army breakfast was taken huddled about the comfort of tent stoves, newly kindled. Hash, pork and the ubiquitous soldier's coffee comprised the day's initial fare, supplemented by a wedge of crusty bread, freshly baked in the cookhouse ovens. One of the inmates of the first Sibley remarked that the bread was "as good as any my dear Aunt Ada bakes," and while others remained silent or indifferent – being unqualified to draw such comparison – the eager despatch of the bread by all and sundry seemed to suggest a consensus upon its enjoyment.

"What's that telling us to do?" enquired William of one of Thursday's recruits as another call was sounded soon after breakfast.

"That's sick call," replied the sallow youth, his pallid complexion suggesting he might himself warrant a visit to the surgeon for a dose of his quinine.

A short while later the tent flap was raised and in peered the flaxen-haired corporal who, the previous evening, had brought Saturday's recruits into camp.

"Twenty minutes and I'll be taking all of you to be kitted out. Assemble outside your tent at eight-thirty with both your woollen and rubber blankets. They're borrowed goods and need to be returned. I've just instructed your colleagues to do likewise," he added, in reference to the inhabitants of the second bell tent; and with that he was gone.

The Quartermaster's building of rough-hewn timber lay on the opposite side of the camp – on its east side – behind the sutler's shop and within sight of the two storey guard house and camp entrance. As the phalanx of new recruits made their way along the gravelled road, to the south of the main encampment, a tranquillity seemed to pervade the A tent community in contrast to the previous evening's cacophony.

"The One Hundred and Fiftieth are busily preparing for dress parade," explained the corporal, an affable fellow by the name of Rees. "An inspection and parade before supper is the usual routine but on Sundays the regimental dress parade is in the morning, along with knapsack drill. The men are busily engaged burnishing their buttons and muskets and brushing up their uniforms. Their Adjutant won't be much pleased to witness any slovenly turn out. By the way, we're meeting the Captain shortly. You're not in uniform yet but be sure not to slouch in his presence…be lively now."

As the men approached the Quartermaster's stores they were distracted by signs of activity to their right, on the approaches to the guard house. The leading vehicle in a convoy of five open wagons, each pulled by a six-mule team and each in the custody of a negro driver, had drawn to a halt alongside the guard house. Two sergeants were in earnest conversation until their attentions were drawn to the arrival of Captain Dederer and the lieutenant from their private accommodation. There followed some discourse between the line officers and the two sergeants, one of whom was the sergeant of the guard, the other, the quartermaster sergeant. Exchanges concluded, the officers proceeded on their way along the camp road as, simultaneously, the new recruits and Corporal Rees continued to advance upon the same destination. The converging parties arrived at the Quartermaster's building together, which was to the credit of the corporal's timekeeping since the officers had risen from their breakfast table earlier than intended. It meant the time was still ten minutes short of nine o'clock when Rees had been instructed to present his charges for outfitting.

"Good morning Corporal," snapped the Captain as he returned the man's salute. Lieutenant Gibson refrained from offering the same greeting, feeling perhaps that repetition was unnecessary in the company of subordinates and the Captain's words were quite sufficient. More significantly, he was silently wrestling with indigestion and, being out of sorts, was in truth a mite peevish. .

"G'd mornin' sir," barked the corporal in a clipped tone that might have graced the lips of a seasoned drill sergeant.

Back at the guard house the quartermaster sergeant had swiftly concluded his business and was hurrying in the wake of the line officers. In little time he arrived, somewhat breathless, at the entrance to the stores and made his apologies.

"I'm sorry, sir, but as I tried to explain, I needed to ensure that these wagons encountered no problem entering camp. Seems nobody had told the guard to expect five wagons loaded with timber. Without it the carpenters wouldn't have been best pleased when they arrive tomorrow to start work on the new barracks."

"That's alright, sergeant. I said I was in no desperate hurry." The captain's voice was raised of necessity, since the string of lumber wagons, heavily weighed down with sawn timber, had begun noisily wending their way along the camp road. "New barracks, you say! Well, well...if you're here for the winter you boys may well get a taste of home comfort before the really cold weather sets in."

"We hope so, sir. The levelling of the ground is complete and while the clement weather continues the men have held off from stockading their tents, for fear of it being energy expended for little purpose."

"Well, talking of purpose, man, we are here for just that, our particular purpose being to get these recruits of mine clothed and equipped like soldiers," said the Captain. Here is my requisition certificate, sergeant, or should I hand this to the Quartermaster himself?"

"He's attending to business in the Colonel's tent at present, sir, and I'm not expecting him to return within the hour. But not to worry, Captain. I can deal with this matter if you'd kindly leave the certificate in my keeping." And with that the sergeant set about organising a couple of the Quartermaster's clerks to attend to the issuance of army clothing which they did to speedy effect and with consummate efficiency. The recruits were ordered to line up outside the stores, then to filter in one at a time, the trigger to ingress being the re-emergence of the last fellow to enter, the poor man weighed down like a beast of burden.

When it came to William's turn he was asked to state his name to the seated clerk, who, pen poised, lent across some form of heavy ledger into which he was supposedly recording particulars of returned bedding and newly supplied items.

"Please place the returned blankets on that table," he directed. "You'll be getting your own in a moment." As he spoke, his colleague glanced fleetingly in William's direction. Yet it was enough. There was no call for taking measurements. Instead, the combination of experience in doing his job and the limited range of clothing size enabled the clerk to have already made a cursory assessment of just what was required. He disappeared, only to return a few minutes later with new blankets and whatever a soldier requires to clothe himself, the towering pile before him topped with a pair of brogan shoes, a neatly coiled buff leather belt and a forage cap.

"I'm told you'll be returning shortly to receive your rifle, together with such other accessories a soldier needs," said the seated clerk. "Try on your uniform before you come back. If there's anything not up to the mark then return it and we'll see if we can find a better fit. But just remember…Uncle Sam's garment makers aren't in the same league as your fancy London tailors. Oh…and by the way…if you need suspenders, the army stops short of supplying them. You'll need to buy them off the sutler."

"Suspenders? What do you mean?" enquired William.

"A question often posed by fellows from across the ocean and I'm assuming by your accent that you're British. That being the case, I believe you know them as braces."

"Fits to a nicety," exclaimed William. It was a remark made to nobody in particular as those already returned to the bell tent were fully pre-occupied discarding civilian clothes in favour of their new uniforms. The Englishman only wished for the full-length armoire mirror by which he had attended to his appearance the previous morning. Instead a cracked and diminutive shaving mirror had to suffice, reflecting no more than an image of his face and forage cap.

"Suits you, William," opined the Gettysburg youth as he struggled into his sky-blue pants.

"What does?"

"The cap. Sits well with your features."

"These shoes are grim," growled the red-headed Irishman. "Both want to live on my right foot and neither on my left."

"This flannel shirt will drive me mad for want of scratching," complained a swarthy-skinned, former insurance clerk, from Glen Burnie. It feels it's already infested with lice or fleas."

"You'll know soon enough when you're being troubled by graybacks, soldier," exclaimed Corporal Rees who had suddenly raised the tent flap. "Fifteen minutes to allow all and sundry to don their uniforms, then assemble outside for a repeat trip to the stores."

Over an hour passed. Out on the camp road, in front of the three Sibleys and their burr-strewn greensward, thirty volunteers – freshly numbered in the ranks of the One Hundred and Fourteenth Regiment New York Volunteers – stood awkwardly in their pristine uniforms. Beyond them, among the tents of the One Hundred and Fiftieth, diligent preparations were afoot for the forthcoming dress parade. It meant the fledgling soldiers were spared the threat of jeering catcalls from afar as they waited to receive a gentle initiation into army drill.

Sergeant Zuicker, clutching a musket, was first to address the men, having laid out before them, on a rubber blanket, examples of the accoutrements furnished them on their second visit to the Quartermaster's stores. "Listen, men," began Zuicker, holding high the musket. "Those weapons you've just stacked outside your tents are all the same. Thanks to the Ordnance Department you each have the latest Springfield rifle musket. Look after it and it will look after you. It's a single shot weapon of point five-eight calibre, firing what we term minie balls. This is a minie ball cartridge," he continued, holding an example betwixt finger and thumb. "You'll see it's encased in paper. Which leads me to point out the cartridge box in whi…"

Zuicker suddenly ceased his elucidation and glanced along the line. "Soldier, pay attention and stand up straight," he bellowed at a fellow rapt in watching his left foot toy with a shiny sweet chestnut. "We don't like inattentiveness in the ranks and I'm not going to repeat myself. Now, I was about to say, it is in this leather box embossed with the bright brass plate that you will keep your cartridges. To load your Springfield you'll bite off the end of the paper casing, pour the powder charge into the muzzle and use this ramrod to push home the ball. You then need to place a percussion cap on the rifle cone from this little cap-box carried on your waist belt… cock the hammer, then bring the musket to your shoulder, then pull the trigger. But all that's for a later time. You'll receive proper instruction in the use and care of your musket and there'll be plenty of firing practice for you before we see action. Now are there any questions?"

"Yes, sergeant," piped up one of Friday's recruits. "How do you avoid getting powder in your mouth when you bite the cartridge paper?"

"You don't. Just spit it out. And I reckon those buck teeth of yours, soldier, make you ably equipped to taste the stuff before the next man," roared Zuicker derisively. "Any other questions?"

Not surprisingly none were forthcoming, all choosing to remain tight-lipped for fear of inciting the scornful edge of the sergeant's tongue. "Well, once you can load and fire three shots every minute you can reckon to have mastered the art of using this musket. As for the bayonet," Zuicker added, withdrawing the item from its scabbard, "its socket slots onto the muzzle in this fashion. You'll see it fits fast to the front sight," said the sergeant, raising the musket aloft.

Zuicker proceeded to introduce the men to the purpose of the canvas painted knapsack, canteen and haversack before handing over responsibility to his fellow sergeant. "For the next hour or so Sergeant O'Malley is going to give you an introduction to army drill," he informed the recruits. "Nothing too taxing, nothing involving your muskets at this stage or any of the equipment we've been getting to know. Just to acquaint you with the ways of close order drill, to get you used to dressing and marching and such like. Try to grasp the rudiments and not look like a bunch of sap-heads…not least because I see the Captain and Lieutenant approaching. You'll not want to disappoint them or give them cause to already question their judgement, will you, gentlemen? Not with them looking on and harbouring such high expectations…having presumed you all to have the making of soldiers."

Despite the somewhat unnerving, parting comments of the contemptible Zuicker and the officers' unexpected presence, Sergeant O'Malley's modest introduction to army drill went tolerably well. The recruits' dismissal was preceded by O'Malley handing out stamped brass badges for all to attach to their forage caps before setting forth to view the dress parade. It was by now a few minutes short of eleven o'clock and by the time the thirty greenhorns had found their way to a knolly vantage point lying close to the public road, the inspection was in full swing. What confronted them was a sight to impress. And it was patently one known to locals with a liking for pageant and entertainment, since several spectators had assembled upon the road verge beyond the split-rail boundary fence. It was a sight which took William back to the days he would venture up on to the Portsmouth hot walls and watch the troops go through their routines on Grand Parade.

The weak November sun glinted upon the bristling bayonets of the One Hundred and Fiftieth who were formed up four deep across the parade ground. It was an impressive spectacle, a sea of blue, the Stars and Stripes fluttering high within its midst along with the regimental flag.

"Who's the fellow way out front?" asked the boy from Gettysburg who had made a habit of remaining close to William.

"He's got to be the Colonel. Look how grand he is, surveying all."

"And those standing out in the middle?"

"Other high ranking officers that's for sure," replied William. "I think the one facing the Colonel is the Adjutant. You can see the line officers strung out to the front of their companies."

The crunch of leather brogans upon gravel, the crisp sound of muskets being shouldered, ordered and presented, served to captivate the audience, the civilian element of which quickly swelled in the wake of the band striking up. Here, indeed, was the clarion call for Sunday morning walkers in nearby Druids Hill Park, with any fondness for spectacle, to turn their gait in the direction of Belger's conspicuous parade ground and savour an impromptu treat. And so the event is enlivened with martial music, the brigade band – freshly appropriated from the routine of raising spirits in the city's military hospitals – being formed up on the right flank. In a while it wheels out from its station, marching along the line, all in slow time, finally turning at the end to a series of muffled drum rolls, then back at a brisker pace. More drum rolls follow to raise the hairs on the back of your neck.

"First sergeants to the front and centre," booms the Adjutant. Behind the group of watching recruits one of the men on guard duty, musket shouldered, makes nonchalant progress back along his beat of the boundary. Nearby a young boy, hoop discarded and perched upon the boundary fence, decides to ape the officer by shouting his own command and raising his hand in salute.

To the band's musical strains the ten first sergeants, each bedecked in dress coat and sash, march out to salute and report in turn that their company is fully present or accounted for.

Someone suggests it would be good to see their man, First Sergeant Zuicker, among those marching forward, only to fall flat on his face. What an image to relish. There is a ripple of laughter and plenty of wry smiles among the newly enlisted representatives of the One Hundred and Fourteenth.

As the commissioned officers, white-gloved and in full-dress uniform, march forward in unison to salute the Colonel, the rank and file prepare to retire back to the company streets under the watchful eyes of their first sergeants. Yet all is not over for the men. Knapsack drill awaits them back among the tented streets; and trouble is in prospect for any soldier who, having unburdened himself of his knapsack and laid it down for close inspection, is found to harbour dirt therein.

The midday sounding of dinner call came soon enough for William Reynolds and his new colleagues once they had sauntered back to their Sibleys. It effectively meant the start of free time for once the meal of salt pork, hominy, dessicated vegetables and dried peaches had been despatched, the men settled down to write to loved-ones or to read or play cribbage. Others simply slid into post-prandial slumber. William, for his part, chose to write, not to loved-ones – since he was still collecting his thoughts upon the thorny matter of broaching his changed circumstances – but to his Blue Nose friends in Lunenburg. He had promised Tom Driscoll that he would put pen to paper when the time was right. He had also assured Reuben he would do so as they hurriedly said their goodbyes on that last morning.

Providently, knowing the likely inclination of a bunch of fresh volunteers to want to write home, a selection of steel-nibbed pens, paper, envelopes and a bottle of iron-gall ink had been supplied to each tent. Having gathered up pen and paper and decanted a little ink into his tin cup, William sat himself down, his legs stretched before him, his back propped up by the bolstering support of kersey blanket and knapsack. On his lap he placed an upturned hardtack box, cushioning his writing paper from its rough surface with a discarded copy of the *Baltimore American*. It was upon this makeshift writing desk that William spent the next half hour composing his missive to Tom, Henry and Reuben. He recounted what had befallen him since setting sail on the *Snowgoose*, of how he had stuck with the old tub as far as Baltimore, of his enlistment and of what little he knew of the imminent adventure awaiting him as he prepared to go south once more. William considered it a letter not up to his usual standard in terms of neatness, this being attributable to his awkward writing position and the poor quality of his selected pen. Yet it would suffice and, as he sealed it in its envelope and addressed it to Tom Driscoll, it was with a sense of satisfaction, knowing he had discharged that commitment.

Despite its transformation into a military encampment, Camp Belger – having propinquity with Druids Hill Park – still retained much of the parkland character of its neighbour. It was, in consequence, a pleasant enough place to wander at leisure and to rid one's lungs of the unwholesome air that would soon accumulate when living with others under canvas. Being therefore desirous of some casual exercise and intake of fresh air, and the afternoon being fine, William decided to venture forth to better acquaint himself with the locale. He set his gait in a south easterly direction as if returning to the morning's vantage point. Once past the regimental hospital he veered away from the camp road, shuffling among fallen leaves, the soft rustle of which began to compete with the increasing audibility of a lone, inspiriting voice. Passing a cluster of stark hornbeams, William came upon a pleasant clearing which, by all accounts, had become a favourite haunt of successive army chaplains when taken to addressing troops on the Sabbath. Yet never before at this time of year. However, with the weather being remarkably and unseasonably mild, the regimental chaplain had today chosen this outdoor location in which to give his customary Sunday afternoon sermon.

A timber rostrum, to serve as a pulpit, had been placed on the high point of the clearing. Stretching back before it, a modest-sized congregation of soldiers appeared to be listening attentively to the clergyman's pronouncements upon patriotism and courage. William recognised him as the chaplain who had briefly appeared during the morning dress parade to say a few prayers. On parade he had worn an army forage cap. Now bare-headed, a black felt hat lay before him on the makeshift pulpit. He looked resplendent and distinctive in his dark, black-buttoned frock coat, standing collar and mutton-chop whiskers. And not a whisper fell from the mouths of the heedful soldiers – with one exception – as their minister concluded his sermon by turning to the book of Deuteronomy. His voice was cultured and reassuring, his diction crisp…

"When thou goest out to battle against thine enemies and seest horses and chariots and a people more than thou, be not afraid of them; for the Lord thy God is with thee, which brought thee up out of the land of Egypt. And it shall be, when ye are come nigh unto the battle that the priest shall approach and speak unto the people. And shall say unto them, hear, O Israel, ye approach this day unto battle against your enemies: let not your hearts faint, fear not and do not tremble, neither be ye terrified because of them. For the Lord your God is he that goeth with you, to fight for you against your enemies, to save you."

The chaplain closed his bible, straightened himself and cast a stern yet merciful eye upon the assemblage before him. "Let us pray."

William, having halted in the rear of the congregation, removed his cap and bowed his head in orison. Minutes later, prayers concluded, the chaplain opened his eyes and immediately addressed a young man, who, unlike the vast majority of listeners, had appeared distracted throughout the communion and as such a disturbance to others. "Soldier," he said firmly, fixing his eye upon the culprit. "I have noticed during our communion this afternoon that you have paid scant attention and been bent on entertaining… nay, irritating, those around you. That is behaviour unbecoming of such occasion. What do you say for yourself?"

The young private seemed transfixed, his face contorted, his colour heightened with embarrassment.

"Well, answer me, man," implored the clergyman.

"Yes, sir…sorry, sir," spluttered the humiliated youth. "If I'm honest, sir, I'm not one to dwell on talk of battle and death."

"You're afraid, boy?"

"Yes, sir, I'm afraid alright."

"But it's a soldier's work to fight and defend his country. Why did you join up if you feel this way?"

"My folks, sir…they insisted. The neighbour's boys were eager to sign the enlistment roll at the first War Meeting and then it emerged my cousin had put his mark to the roll. My folks said I had to go or they said I'd be osticised and so would they."

"Ostracised."

"Yes, sir, that's right, sir."

"Your folks knew of your fear?"

"Yes, sir."

"Are they God-fearing folk? Do they trust in the Lord?"

"They do, sir."

"Then I'm sure your folks will be praying for you as you prepare to go forth and fight the good fight. The fifth book of Moses tells us to be strong and of good courage. It tells us that the Lord thy God goes with thee and that He will neither fail thee nor forsake thee. Put your faith in the Lord, soldier, say your nightly prayers, pray for that strength and courage to face adversity. Have you written to your folks recently?"

"No, sir. We did not part on the best of terms."

"Then when you return to your tent take up pen and ink and write them a letter. Tell them of your concerns and ask them to pray that you shall show courage and steadfast resolve. Do not harbour resentment towards them. Let them know where you are. Write often. It will be a great comfort to them and I say this not simply to you, soldier, but to all of you assembled here. It is most unlikely your own kin will forsake you but in that sad, unfortunate event not all is lost if you trust in the Lord. The Book of Psalms states that when our father and our mother forsake us then the Lord will take us up."

The chaplain's words pricked William's conscience. "Let them know where you are. Write often. It will be a great comfort to them..." He determined in that moment he would later attempt to pen a letter to his Mother and Grandma. He had last written before his incarceration in the Halifax Penitentiary. They would wonder at not hearing from him for so long and could be sorely worried over his well-being. If the *Cygnet* had returned to Portsmouth they might already have learned the truth.

"Now, soldier," continued the chaplain, looking directly at the youth in need of courage, "you will be aware that beyond imparting spiritual guidance to you all as an ordained minister, I also have responsibility for discharging my duties as regimental postmaster. In those circumstances you will not be surprised to hear that I expect you to present yourself at the post office tomorrow armed with the said letter you are about to write to your folks. Do you understand?"

"Yes, sir," replied the youth, sheepishly.

"Very well, enough of that then." The clergyman immediately diverted his gaze and nodded towards four members of the band who had been standing patiently below the rostrum with their bell-up horns and cornets. The four proceeded to seat themselves before stands bearing sheets of hymnal music as the chaplain addressed his congregation.

"We will conclude this afternoon by singing two hymns. You should know the words to both. If not, then those of you who have shown sufficient foresight and prudence to bring along your little red book…your *Soldier's Pocket Book*…should find the words to the first hymn on page thirty-nine. Now, raise your voices and let us sing *Nearer, My God, to Thee*."

As one of William's favourite hymns he was in no need of the printed word. Yet the wistful sound of that group of soldiers stirred his emotions to the point of stifling his own ability to sing. The music drew thoughts of home, thoughts already kindled by the chaplain's pronouncements upon letter writing, thoughts now inextricably tangled with feelings of guilt. An eerie atmosphere fell upon that peopled clearing as the November sun began to set, the low, late afternoon sunbeams filtering through the adjacent cluster of trees to throw a soft, milky light upon the heads of the congregation. Once the hymn had run its course, William turned away, his eyes dampened by the evocation of nostalgic feelings, his mood sad and reflective. He suddenly felt homesick, the first time he had truly felt homesick since entering the *Excellent* as a fifteen year old.

William had intentions of completing a circular perambulation of the camp before darkness closed in, having incurred unintentional delay while he stopped to listen to the chaplain. But it wasn't to be. Once he reached the parade ground he was distracted by the tail-end of a contest he took to be a game of rounders. Among the spectators William spotted his fellow Saturday recruit, the rather overbearing, cocksure fellow from Catonsville.

"Who are the teams playing rounders?" enquired William of the other.

"Rounders? What's rounders, mister? By the way, the name's Ezra Wilson, Company H."

"William Reynolds, Company E. Looks like an English game called rounders, that's all."

"It's baseball," said the American. "I gather the teams have been drawn from Companies B and F of the One Hundred and Fiftieth. It looks like the men from F are the likely victors with the score standing at twenty points to twelve."

"How many to win then?"

"First to twenty-one."

"Have you heard what's happening tomorrow?" enquired William.

"No idea. Doubtless we'll be told at roll call. All I know is that we're to be shipped down the Bay to link up with the Regiment."

"Sounds as though it's none too healthy or comfortable down there."

"Well, hopefully our time off Old Point Comfort will be short-lived. I'm inclined to think that…Oh! Lucky man, soldier! Did you see that? He should have been caught on the fly but for the bungling fielder…but watch him run! Wow…that's got to be it. Well done Company F!"

"Just as well. I suspect the twilight hampered the fielder," opined William.

"Yes, I daresay you're right, Reynolds. Do you think between us we can find our way back to dear old Camp Sibley?"

★ ★ ★

William's good intentions to write home failed to materialise that evening, despite the tent being far better lit after supper and as such more conducive to letter writing. Two kerosene lamps were the source of improved illumination, brought from the main encampment by three fellows from the One Hundred and Fiftieth. They had befriended the red-haired Irish American who had decided to invite them to join him for some hands of whist and euchre. And, being of similar character to their host and of brash disposition, the relative tranquillity which pervaded the tent was soon lost to noisy and ebullient raillery. Disappointedly for William, this undermined his earlier proclivity to put pen to paper, for it severely hampered his need for clarity of thought.

At Sunday's final roll-call the men were told they would depart Camp Belger shortly after dinner the following afternoon. Sergeant O'Malley would again instruct them in drill after breakfast. Thereafter, arrangements had been made for all to receive their first month's pay and, more significantly, their bounty money. And on that occasion the opportunity would arise to talk to one of the allotment commissioners, there being merit in making arrangements to set aside a portion of one's income, to save it – as Sergeant Zuicker put it – 'from being squandered, lost or appropriated'.

And so, come Monday morning, O'Malley had the men formed up three deep, their Springfields stacked behind them. The day had dawned bright and crisp, with a dew chilled close to freezing, yet the recruits had been well fortified with a breakfast of fresh bread and hot pea soup. They had then collected their muskets and proceeded to the parade ground where the sergeant began by instructing them in stacking their weapons in a neat and stable fashion.

"Bloody cold, sergeant," grumbled one of the men. It was if, in his naivety, he felt such a remark might prompt O'Malley to forget about drill and send his pack of greenhorns back to the comfort of their tent stoves.

"Be quiet, soldier. What did Sergeant Zuicker tell you? You're just meant to listen and obey. If you're cold, then we'd best get you all moving. Now, do you remember what you learnt yesterday? The essence of drill is that it will instil discipline into you and discipline is so essential in the life of a soldier...your modus operandi. It will serve you well, believe me. Yesterday you learnt about routine marching and of keeping in step with one another and of how to face properly and dress the line. You were taught how to stand to attention and of the need to remain motionless on parade unless directed to do otherwise...the importance of keeping heels together, shoulders square, head and body erect, legs straight." The sergeant hesitated a moment and looked along the front line. "You, soldier...the English fellow. What's your name?"

William's heart was suddenly in his mouth, wondering why he had been singled out. "Reynolds, sergeant."

"Yes, that's right...Reynolds. Now, Reynolds...where are your arms meant to be when you're standing to attention without your musket?"

"By your side, sergeant, hanging normally."

"And your hands?"

"Little fingers behind the trouser seams, sergeant."

"Good, Reynolds. We call them pants by the way."

"Yes, sergeant."

"You, man," exclaimed the sergeant, switching his attention to another in the front rank. "What's your name?"

William inwardly sighed with relief, feeling he had acquitted himself well enough.

"Simpson, sir."

"Well, Simpson, what are your eyes doing when you're standing to attention?"

"Looking straight ahead, sergeant."

"Not quite, Simpson. I'm looking for more than that," said O'Malley. "Anything to add?"

The sergeant proceeded to reposition himself in front of the men by marching forward a certain distance from the front rank and manoeuvring to directly face Private Simpson. "Now Simpson, what are you meant to be looking at?"

"At you, sergeant." It was a reply which suggested Simpson had been far from attentive the previous morning.

"At my *feet*, Simpson. These things at the end of my legs, man, because they're fifteen paces in front of you. Fix your eyes on the ground fifteen paces ahead."

"Right, without more ado we'll spend some time going through all you learnt yesterday. We'll get you marching and marching some more and introduce you to double quick time to get those feet aching. We'll raise a sweat alright despite the morning chill. Then when we've had enough of that you'll retrieve your muskets and I'll school you in the art of shouldering, ordering and presenting arms. I'll also introduce you to the commands and motions for loading your weapon and fixing bayonets. Any questions before we begin?"

The sergeant looked at the faces confronting him. There were plenty of forlorn expressions, little hint of enthusiasm, a wealth of furrowed brows.

"Just remember an appointment with the paymaster awaits you and think of all those spondulicks. Surely that'll put a spring in your step. Now we'd best get started," declared O'Malley.

For the next three hours the crisp, gritty sound of marching feet and later, the metallic noise of muskets being handled, was peppered by O'Malley's barked orders, and his repetitive "left…left…left" as marching feet were brought down in unison: sounds later magnified across the parade ground as three companies from the One Hundred and Fiftieth separately went about their own routines. At ten-thirty the new recruits were dismissed, told where to present themselves to receive their money and instructed to take their haversacks with them when reporting to the cookhouse after dinner call.

"You'll be taking two days rations with you when we depart this afternoon and they will need to find a home in your haversacks," explained the sergeant. "We leave at two o'clock for the docks but don't worry, for although you've done well enough at your drills this morning, you'll not be expected to march there. You are far too removed from being well-drilled soldiers. That'll take some weeks of drilling and more drilling. In the meantime, it would neither be in the regiment's interest, nor your own, to subject you all to the discomfiture of marching through the city streets. Instead, the Quartermaster of our host regiment has kindly consented to three of his wagons with drivers being placed at our disposal. Consider yourselves fortunate in that respect, because, since it was decreed by General McClellan, soldiers are not allowed to ride in army wagons without special dispensation. But all that's for later…you'd better be off to meet the paymaster."

It was with eager anticipation that the men congregated outside the paymaster's wall tent waiting for their names to be called. When it came to William's turn he gave his name to the paymaster's clerk, only to be instructed to sign a receipt for one month's advance pay of thirteen dollars. Then he was called upon to add his signature to a further document before being handed twenty-five dollars of Government bounty and twenty dollars of State and local government bounty. It occurred to William that, in total, this was less than the fifty dollars initially estimated by Captain Dederer, yet not far short of it, and, combined with his advance pay, he was clutching the princely sum of fifty-eight greenbacks. Almost immediately he was asked to step aside to sit before a somewhat flabby-looking gentleman wearing thin metal-rimmed spectacles, his upstanding collar struggling to cup, and barely restrain, a combination of double chin and luxuriant side-whiskers.

"Have you folks at home?…family, I mean," asked the overweight commissioner. "If you have, then I am here to tell you that you are well-advised to consider the prudence of regularly setting aside an element of your monthly pay for their benefit."

"I have folks, sir, but they are in England and not reliant upon my support. But, yes…I would like to put money aside. You see, I wish to accumulate sufficient to pay my passage home once I leave the Army and hopefully to set me up in business back in the Old Country. What should I consider setting aside, sir?"

"Well, those of a thrifty disposition, and especially men with wives and children to support, are often happy to place as much as ten dollars in safe keeping, leaving three for incidental expenses."

"Then I'll do the same," said William emphatically. "And I also wish to invest my bounty."

"Very well," said the commissioner. "You'll need to complete this document, then you'll be signed up to an allotment plan authorising ten dollars to be placed, every month, in the Government Bank."

"Is it in order, sir, that this regular arrangement commences in January and, for now, I open my account with fifty dollars? Only I need to visit the sutler and equip myself with a few essentials."

"Perfectly acceptable, Reynolds. Perfectly acceptable."

And thus, with eight dollars in his pocket, William exited the tent with a sense of satisfaction. He felt he had been astute in accepting the commissioner's advice and that, once the war was over, he would be financially well-placed. Perhaps by then his desire to be a soldier will have been indulged to the full and he will be ready to return home with good money in his pocket and thoughts, however fanciful, of becoming a gentleman.

The Quartermaster's wagons were due to draw up on the north side of the parade ground and a hundred yards short of the guard house at a quarter to two. Other than a few stragglers, only now departing the sutler's shop, the majority of the men had assembled at the designated meeting point by one-thirty, their stomachs full, their haversacks stowed with army rations, their canteens filled with coffee. After receiving his money, William had found time to visit the camp post office, to hand in his letter to Tom Driscoll and to acquire postage stamps. Then, after dinner, he had joined many of his fellow recruits in paying a call upon the sutler whose gingerbreads, pies and molasses cakes proved popular supplements to the cook's rations. And, with that letter home in mind, William had satisfied his stationery needs as well as purchasing such other commodities a man needs to keep himself respectable, notably a comb, mirror and toothbrush and a razor and strop. He had also treated himself to some new pairs of socks, of superior quality to army issue, as well as a quaint little cutlery combination of knife fork and spoon that folded away to neat and quirky compactness.

And so the men waited patiently for the three wagons to arrive and, back in his shop, a highly contented sutler – fresh from assisting an unexpected influx of new recruits to part with newly acquired cash – set about finishing a dinner that had suffered a most profitable interruption. Over at the guard house, a brougham had drawn up momentarily and was being waved through. Shortly it was pulled up on the camp road nearby and, having clambered down from his raised seat and tethered the horse to a bough of a tree, the driver proceeded to open the carriage door and assist two middle-aged ladies to alight. Outwardly, from the quality of their attire, they were ladies of not insignificant means. Their contrasting feathery and florally decorated bonnets were especially striking, their dresses both fashionably colour-matched with winter mantles.

"Gentlemen, gentlemen," screeched one of the ladies, as both made their way towards the assembled men, "are we right in presuming you to be newly recruited soldiers of the One Hundred and Fourteenth New York Regiment…and that you are about to depart Camp Belger?"

"You are ma'am," confirmed Sergeant Zuicker who had just strolled up from the opposite direction in company with his fellow sergeant and Corporal Rees. "Well, we're mighty pleased to have waylaid you in time," said the second lady. They both arrived somewhat breathless, closely followed by an equally short-winded driver, his exertion multiplied by having to carry before him a small, yet heavy, tin trunk.

"Let us introduce ourselves," said the lady with the feathery bonnet, the babble of the men having fallen to silence. It was a quiescence born of curiosity and politeness, yet one which promised to be shackled and maintained by the emergence of the odious first sergeant. "My name is Rose McKinney...my good friend and companion, Cora Sallis. We are representatives of the Maryland State Bible Society, gentlemen, and are here to make you a little gift to carry with you throughout your service and until the Good Lord sees fit to bring this conflict to a close."

As persons bent on bestowing kind deeds upon the soldiering fraternity, it occurred to William that these two ladies were of the same sort of age and kidney as the kindly Missus Rutherford. He wondered whether she was known to them.

"Mister Laman, will you kindly...," said Missus McKinney. It was a sufficiency of words – when coupled with a simultaneous nod in her driver's direction – that had him decanting lots of little books from the tin trunk. In turn, Missus Sallis began filling a wicker basket with a manageable quantity of the little volumes for distribution to the soldiers.

"You will find two books we propose to leave in the safe keeping of each and every one of you. Cora, my dear, will you hold a copy of each aloft please?"

Missus Sallis proceeded to comply with her companion's bidding.

"The first, that on the left, is a copy of *The Soldier's Prayer Book*, published last year by the Protestant Episcopal Book Society. It should be invaluable when time is of the essence, yet there is call for worship, however brief. Secondly...oh, do hold it a little higher, Cora, my dear, if you'd be so kind," implored Missus McKinney, noticing that several of the men in the rear of the group were straining to catch sight of the volume. "The second is a testament of compact proportion which we are sure you will cherish and will be a comfort to you in the field and on the march. But one thing to which I would draw particular attention is the information sheet inside the front cover. You'll see there is room for your name and your regimental details. Importantly, there is a place to inscribe the identity of whoever you would wish to be notified in the unfortunate event of your death, as you go forth to defend the Union. Let us pray to the Almighty that this will not prove necessary but it is as well to be prepared."

Missus McKinney proceeded to join her companion in distributing the prayer books and testaments. When Missus Sallis came to hand William his copies he thanked the lady for her kindness, then posed a question.

"Tell me, ma'am, are you acquainted with Missus Rutherford?"

"Rutherford, you say, young man?" The lady turned away momentarily to speak to her friend. "Rose, do we know a Missus Rutherford? The name sounds familiar."

"Jane Rutherford, do you mean?"

"Yes, ma'am," confirmed William.

"Yes, of course, we do, Cora. You know Jane Rutherford. The lady who keeps a boarding house on Hanover Street and who exercises some authority in the Union Relief Association. Our paths cross from time to time when visiting the camps."

"Yes, indeed, Rose. Now you mention that, I do recall the lady. Silly of me. My memory is not what it was," reflected Missus Sallis.

"When you next see Missus Rutherford, please tell her that William Reynolds achieved what he set out to do...that he enlisted in the One Hundred and Fourteenth New York Volunteers and left Camp Belger on December the first. We are to join a flotilla of transports lying off Fort Monroe, Virginia. Beyond that it seems our future movements remain a mystery. It's just that I recently stayed a night in Missus Rutherford's establishment and she was aware of my interest in joining the Army."

"We certainly will young man...if that memory of mine holds up," chuckled Missus Sallis. "I guess I'd better jot down the substance of your message and your name. William Reynolds, was it?" continued the lady as she made a few pencilled notes on the back of a surplus copy of the little prayer book.

"Yes, ma'am...I'm grateful, ma'am"

Missus McKinney gave a parting wave in Sergeant Zuicker's direction. "Thank you, sergeant," she exclaimed, seeing that all the recruits had now received copies of the little books and were beginning to stir at the sight of three approaching covered wagons. "Godspeed and God Bless you all," she continued, her voice now straining with emotion. "And just remember that the prayers and blessings of those who love and cherish you will sustain and comfort you wherever you lay your heads."

With that the ladies returned to their carriage where Laman, the driver, was already untethering the animal.

Once the men and their baggage had been loaded on the wagons, the journey to the docks was uneventful, albeit highly discomforting. For the vehicles were built to carry army baggage, not troops, a factor that became only too obvious as even the smallest of irregularities upon the road surface seemed to be magnified; and in consequence, harsh joltings and pummellings were constantly suffered. It prompted one the fellows to quip that, had he known how uncomfortable the ride would be, he would have sought out the hind axle slush bucket and greased his buttocks before setting off.

To William the dockside activity seemed as lively as ever. With all having alighted from the wagons and baggage unloaded, Sergeant Zuicker ordered the men to stack their muskets on the quayside. There they were to wait patiently, while he and O'Malley sought to locate Captain Dederer and the lieutenant. William spent a moment taking stock of the location. They had been brought to one of the piers across the inner basin from the Light Street Wharf. Moving away from a neighbouring wharf was a lighter crammed with troops. In the other direction a derrick was in use, hoisting animal carcases on to a stationary lighter. To William they looked like sides of beef and for a moment he shuddered at the thought that, seventy-two hours ago, those same carcases might have belonged to his charges on the *Snowgoose*.

After a few minutes the captain and lieutenant appeared in company with the two sergeants.

"Now, men, if you'd pay attention to what I have to say," said Captain Dederer, raising his voice above the norm to ensure he was heard above the dockside's eclectic sounds. "We are to board that vessel moored out in the stream, just east of Federal Hill." It was a statement that caused everyone to peer into the distance through an intervening jumble of masts and rigging. But the old steam transport was discernible well enough, her visibility aided by her jet-black hull and twin stacks. "She's the *Louisiana* I'm told...an old Bay Line vessel requisitioned by the War Department. She's been taking on troops since one o'clock, along with fresh meat, commissary stores and munitions. Hopefully we'll get the nod to embark pretty soon. I'm informed the ship's captain will instruct one of the returning lightermen when he's ready for us to go aboard. Then we can take our turn. In the meantime all we can do is wait. Just don't wander off."

Forty minutes elapsed with no sign of clearance to proceed. The lighter which had gone out laden with troops returned to its pier of departure only to be tied up and secured, its labours – for the time being at least – seemingly complete. By this time most of the men had settled down on the quayside seated on their rolled blankets. A few groups amused themselves with cards, others dozed, several chatted. On the whole the men's demeanour seemed to be upbeat, despite the talk of dire conditions on the troopships off Old Point Comfort. That, after all, promised to be a mere temporary inconvenience with the fleet expected to depart, for God knows where, sooner rather than later. And so there was a blithe mood of expectation abroad on that chill quayside as authorisation to embark upon the *Louisiana* was eagerly awaited. William, being in more pensive mood and, for obvious reasons, far less excited than most about putting to sea, took his recently acquired prayer book from his knapsack and perused its contents. Half the little volume was devoted to hymns. As he turned the pages, wondering how many he would recognise, his eyes fell upon the opening verse of a hymn with which he was unfamiliar...*Return, O wanderer – return! And seek thy Father's face! Those new desires, which in thee burn, Were kindled by his grace.*

The words caught his breath. Although a stanza patently directed at a lost and spiritually wayward soul, here nonetheless was a sobering reminder to the reader that he had strayed in the material, earthly sense. They were words apposite to his circumstances, words which like the chaplain's, the previous afternoon, sorely pricked his conscience. They shook William and, for a while, he became saddened as his thoughts strayed back to King Street. The smiling features of his mother and grandmother waxed and waned in his mind's eye...then those of dear old Uncle Charley, bless him... someone he could talk to in confidence, someone who would understand.

"On your feet men. Retrieve your muskets and line up two deep over here. And be sure to have all your baggage to hand." The barked words of Lieutenant Gibson drew William out of his thoughts with a jolt. An empty lighter was approaching the pier, a fact which raised expectation in the minds of Captain Dederer, his lieutenant and those not otherwise absorbed.

As the men formed two ranks those expectations were fulfilled. A fustian-clad lighterman bawled at the soldiers as his vessel came within hailing distance of the pier.

"Captain Dederer's men?" A hearty and corroborative cheer rang out from the assembled men on the quayside, rendering superfluous any need for spoken affirmation. "Then kindly ready yourselves for conveyance to embark upon the *Louisiana*," yelled the lighterman.

A fresh adventure was about to dawn.

Two

In Transit

December 1862

The master of the *Louisiana* wasted little time weighing anchor once Captain Dederer's men had come aboard and a final consignment of commissary stores and gun carriages had been committed to the hold. The new recruits were directed to lower deck bunks ranged along the ship's sides, just for'ard of amidships. Here they were swift to make casual acquaintance and exchange friendly banter with a gaggle of Maine troops who ostensibly had already settled in and begun to relax. As to Captain Dederer and the lieutenant, they had both been assigned cabins aft... pleasant enough rooms, except for a persistent mustiness; also the presence of tired-looking furniture with tarnished fittings and warped mouldings that told of better times. Elsewhere, in the vessel's after-part, a modest-sized stateroom was allotted to First Sergeant Zuicker to share with his non-commissioned comrades.

While waiting upon the call to supper, most of the One Hundred and Fourteenth's newly enlisted men – together with a fair sprinkling of other troops who had embarked at Baltimore – spent the mild, early evening chatting and smoking on the upper deck. Despite the late time of year, the day's brightness had seemed long to fade in the western sky, silhouetting to starboard the occasional skein of snow or brant geese above the darkening wetlands. Eventually nightfall swallowed up the far horizon, snuffing out any passing interest attributable to the Bay's waterfowl. Little noise intruded upon the calm of the upper deck save for the murmur of gossiping soldiers and the wash and tumble of water off the *Louisiana*'s cutwater...little until a sudden barked order rent the air.

"Men of the One Hundred and Fourteenth pay attention," bellowed a voice that in its stridency might have carried to Main Street in nearby Annapolis, for the entrance to its harbour lay off the starboard beam. It was the bullying Sergeant Zuicker, his figure faintly illuminated by a lantern close to the main hatchway. "Captain Dederer wishes to speak to you before supper," he continued. "You're to follow me below immediately. I've already roused those in their bunks."

Without further ado the sergeant turned on his heels and entered the door amidships through which he had recently emerged. The regiment's new entrants obediently followed in his wake, taking a short, laddered descent through a hatchway, into which wafted the smells of galley cooking. At the bottom of the ladder, in a narrow passage running fore and aft, stood the handful of men Zuicker had drawn from their repose. Directing these fellows to join the snaking line of men behind him, the first sergeant turned left towards the after-part of the ship. The aromas of lingering cigar smoke and of furniture polish displaced the galley smells. Mahogany furnishing and brass plating was now in evidence. Yet the most noticeable feature, through a dimness twilit by the occasional flickering lantern, was the relative quietude of this part of the *Louisiana*, compared with its more populous space for'ard. Sergeant Zuicker halted outside a door leading to one of the more spacious staterooms and one specifically designated for the exclusive use of the ship's captain and the commissioned officers. He knocked boldly and the occupant called upon the men to enter. Inside, behind two cabin tables spread with the master's charts, sat the captain who promptly rose to his feet and cast the remnants of a cheroot into a nearby cuspidor.

"Now, men. Before we arrive at our destination tomorrow I thought it apposite to call you together, briefly, to avail you with a little more information upon what awaits you at Hampton Roads. Firstly, if you're not already aware, our commandant is a much revered gentleman from Chenango County in New York State, Colonel Elisha Smith, our Adjutant, the equally well regarded Lieutenant Colonel Samuel Per Lee of Norwich. These are gentlemen and officers to be shown the utmost respect. Remember that at all times. Now, when you enlisted in Baltimore I told each of you where your company is presently accommodated...on one of three transports, the *Arago*, the *Atlantic* and the smaller vessel, the *Thames*. Personally, as Captain of Company E, I will be returning to my cabin on the *Thames*."

William Reynolds was cheered by the news that Captain Dederer was in command of his company since it seemed to him that here was a fair and decent man.

"So," continued the Captain, "you'll find that we are sharing our transports with other regiments with which we are brigaded…three further New York infantry units in addition to the Thirty-Eighth Massachusetts. Brigadier-General William Emory has command of the brigade although more recently that responsibility has devolved upon Colonel Littlejohn of the One Hundred and Tenth New York. This has permitted the General to assume control of all the Union troops presently in transit at Hampton Roads." Captain Dederer hesitated and cleared his throat before proceeding. "Now, are there any questions?"

There were none, probably the product of nervous reticence rather than any disinterest in the minds of the officer's audience. In consequence, silence reigned in the stateroom for a few seconds. Only the creaking noise of warped deck timbers beneath the footfall of scurrying, tray-laden cabin waiters in the outside corridor had the temerity to invade it.

The Captain resumed. "I sense that supper is beckoning but lastly I must tell you this. There is a significant flotilla assembled at Hampton Roads and there is all likelihood that orders to set sail will not be long in coming. That said, I know nothing of the intended destination, for there is great secrecy about our expedition. People are formulating their own views. All I do know is that a large body of troops is being assembled at New York under the command of Major-General Nathaniel Banks and word is we are destined to link up with those men. Also, when we do put to sea, we expect to depart with sealed orders with only the regimental commanders and ships' captains privy to knowledge of the initial port of call. That's all, men. Away to your supper."

★ ★ ★

Armed with hindsight, and once conducted to their new floating homes, the regiment's recruits were swift to appreciate the relatively spacious, if not commodious, conditions they had experienced in their brief stay aboard the *Louisiana*. The requisitioned vessel had dropped anchor in Hampton Roads, late on Tuesday the second of December, after an uneventful journey down the Bay. Being an advanced hour, the ferrying of the men to their designated vessels would normally have been conducted the following morning. However, orders had been issued on the Monday which required troops on the assembled transports to remain onboard and to no longer be permitted ashore. It seemed this order was the harbinger of the long awaited voyage to places unknown and nothing, in terms of the increased industry which prevailed throughout the day of the *Louisiana*'s arrival, had dispelled such conclusion in the minds of ordinary men. It had, by all accounts, been a day of toing and froing, as the transports were coaled, watered and provisioned and, given these signs of imminent departure, it was felt appropriate to get the recruits aboard their new homes post-haste.

In consequence, after supper had been taken and with darkness having enveloped the assembled fleet, it was to the *Thames* William Reynolds was rowed late on the second of December. With him in the ship's boat were, among others, two fellows known to him who'd been assigned to Company H: Ezra Wilson, with whom he'd briefly passed the time of day while watching the Belger baseball contest and the tousle-haired man from Catonsville – a youth by the name of Sam Butler. Also in the sternsheets sat the boy from Gettysburg, bound, so he said, for Company K.

Once aboard the *Thames* a corporal from each of the occupying companies – namely E, H, I and K – was directed to show the new men to their sleeping quarters. In the case of Company E, three recruits were called forward by its non-comm: William, together with two of Friday's volunteers who had been tented in the second Sibley back at Belger. The three followed their corporal – a fellow called Will Jackson – for'ard on a poorly lit lower deck. In so doing it proved necessary to step gingerly over various equipments strewn across a narrow passageway which coursed between flanking tiers of sawn-timber bunks – three deep – en route to a dingy fo'c'sle. Men lounged in many of these bunks. Arms and legs hung limp from some, partially adding to the obstructions within the dividing thoroughfare. Few seemed pre-occupied in leisure pursuits or in reading or writing, for the intense gloom that prevailed between widely dispersed ship's lanterns was hardly conducive to such. Some men chatted, a few appeared to doze. There was no laughter, no apparent joy. William wondered whether the putrid smell which pervaded the lower deck had begun to instil a kind of torpidity into the very sinews of these poor fellows and dulled their senses into the bargain. The stale air was more mephitic than anything he had had to endure on the *Excellent*'s gun deck, even in the height of summer: a feculent blend of human sweat and exhalations from men confined like sardines – that and the stink of fetid bilge water rising from below.

Once well for'ard, Corporal Jackson halted on reaching a cluster of empty bunks. "Isaiah Bryant, you bed yourself down over there," he said, directing the man's attention to a lower bunk. "William Reynolds and Caleb Trask…each of you take one of these," he continued, pointing to two adjoining upper tier berths. The corporal then proceeded with some cursory introduction of the new recruits to a few of the men who reclined nearby. As for reciprocal preliminaries, he refrained, telling the new arrivals that it was pointless since there were too many new faces. "You'll get to know your brother soldiers soon enough," he suggested, "and, by the way, apologies for the stink down here. Once you've lived with it for a while you become insensible to it. I worked in a dry goods store back home in Norwich. We used to roast and grind coffee beans. A fine piquancy it was, a delight to inhale. But when I'd worked there a couple of months, I had trouble detecting the smell of freshly ground coffee. It's much the same with this shitty smell, except we look like putting to sea shortly and that should clear the air soon enough." And with that the corporal disappeared aft.

"Guess he's right to some extent." The gruff voice emanated from one of the upper berths in the opposite range of tiered bunks to those of Trask and Reynolds. "You do get used to it, until you leave the old tub for a while and then come back to her. Then it hits you."

"So you spend time ashore?" asked William.

"We've been ashore alright…most days, drill and more drill. Not so easy on the beach but it gives us some exercise and a good dose of fresh air… and what with a recent spell of unseasonably fine weather, some of us got to wash our shirts in the briny and drown a few graybacks. That was a bonus and even more of a relief. You see, most of us are lousy with the little critters. Incidentally, I take it you're English from that dainty accent?… by the way, my name's Charley Ellis."

William nodded in response to Ellis's question. "From Portsmouth."

"Portsmouth, indeed…that's queer. We were tied up in Norfolk for a few days only last week…a right old shit-hole of a place, the way the war has treated it, but we crossed the Elizabeth River and came upon a neat little town which is called Portsmouth. Not that we saw much of it. We were drilling most of the time in some farmer's field…literally up to our ankles in Virginian mud. Now we're confined onboard, waiting, it seems, to set sail…good in some respects but I wonder about the seaworthiness of this old tub. I'd sooner be on one of the bigger transports if we're putting to sea."

A young fellow in a nearby bunk, hitherto having been motionless and seemingly asleep, suddenly jumped down into the passage and scurried away as if caught short. As he hurried off he gratingly burst into song.

"*Bobby Shafto gone to sea, silver buckles at his knee, he'll come back and marry me, bonny Bo…*"

"Shut up, Corbett. Christ, I swear that fellow's soft in the head."

"So where d'you reckon we're bound?" chirped Trask, who had taken the bunk next to William.

"They haven't told us. Mind you, most of us don't care. Notwithstanding my own misgivings, I suppose we just need to get moving…get some ventilation in this rat-infested old bucket."

"Why don't you go up on deck? I noticed there were a lot of men up there getting some fresh air."

"Oh, I do man. Only thing that keeps you sane, getting up there to clear your lungs. But if I'm honest…and I'm not especially noted for my honesty…I got a little business down here this evening. But, yes, most of these empty bunks belong to boys who are taking the air up top and having a smoke."

"So are all these bunks taken?" enquired William.

"Beyond the three you boys have laid claim to, precious few are not spoken for. But it's nowhere near as crowded as when we first embarked at Baltimore. Then it was a case of grabbing whatever bit of floor could be found. It was bloody murder, I can tell you, what with having the weight of the next man's boot in your face or the stink of his hairy ass. Well, since then, many of the fellows have succumbed to all manner of ailments because of the crowded conditions…jaundice, typhoid fever, the ague… and the measles have taken a heavy toll of late. There are a lot of men… and I mean a lot…holed up in the hospital over at Old Point Comfort… the Chesapeake General, over on the foreshore, just alongside the fortress. Most of them won't be well enough to come away with the regiment. It's this atrocious overcrowding, you see, and having to make do with raw meat and hard bread and the like. None of that good cookhouse grub they serve up at Belger, I can tell you. Even ashore, although the niggers provide good value, those bastard sutlers' prices are extortionate. Three cents for a bloody apple that's a shadow of those from my uncle's orchard back in Broome County. But don't worry," continued Ellis, observing the forlorn expressions on the faces of the new arrivals, "things are a trifle improved. At least they've had the carpenters onboard this past week installing these bunks and we've now got a cook-galley set up on deck. And, though you may find it difficult to believe, conditions here are better than they are for those bunked down in the hold. So, all in all, things…" Ellis halted in mid-sentence as his attention was taken by an approaching figure. "Aha," he continued, "here's my little bit of business."

Charley Ellis removed some small change from his pocket and handed the few coins to the visitor who disappeared as swiftly as he had arrived. In exchange, the fellow had passed a lumpy, muslin-wrapped bundle to Ellis, having furtively drawn this from the confines of his tunic.

"One of the cabin waiters," explained Ellis as soon as the man had withdrawn. "We have a little arrangement. He brings me choice snippets of the officers' victuals, you see." There was a smile on the soldier's face and a wink in his eye. "Mind you, as I say, what with the newly-installed galley, the eats aren't as bad as they were. At least we can now expect cooked food, even if it falls well short of a darkey's breakfast."

"So what's a darkey's breakfast?" enquired Isaiah Bryant, now prostrated on his lower bunk.

"Well, by jiminy, I'd say it was the best thing around in these parts. We've spent a lot of time ashore, mainly at Newport News, more recently at Norfolk and Hampton and, from time to time, over by the fortress, drilling on the beach. Everywhere there are negro shanties where the darkeys sell you cheap oysters but they'll also do you a grand breakfast... mutton chops, onions, griddle cakes, warm 'pone and a mug of coffee and all for a quarter. Bloody good...wouldn't you agree, Lawrence?" bellowed Ellis, mockingly, as he suddenly raised his voice to address a brother soldier reclining silently at some distance.

The remark was met with a grunt of contempt from afar.

"My good friend over there enjoys indulging in what the darkey huts have to offer, don't you, Lawrence? The other day he had fifty cents worth off a nigger in Newport News."

"A good appetite then," observed Trask.

"Excepting it wasn't a double portion of mutton chops and onions, was it Lawrence?" chortled his vexer. "The fact is, while the darkey was busying himself cooking breakfast for a long line of soldiers, Lawrence was round the back of the poor devil's hut mounting his woman across a pile of discarded oyster shells. And all for the price of two breakfasts. Well, needless to say, poor Lawrence is now annoyed we're confined onboard and there won't be any further jaunts to Newport News...and just when he's found a coon's buxom woman to..."

"Shut up, Ellis, you bastard. Go boil your shirt! Go to hell!"

"The fellow's getting abusive. Perhaps it's time to take you fresh fish up on deck," chuckled Charley Ellis, "and show you a bit more of this old tub before it's time to turn in."

★ ★ ★

"Christ…General Emory's steamers should have enough fuel on board to take us around the world at this rate," shouted one of the privates, as yet another load of coal clattered through the hatches. The men in the hold and in the lower deck berths had partaken of breakfast in their bunks, there being no alternative space in which to consume meals. Back amidships, cabin waiters scurried aloft on their way between the shabby main stateroom – which served as the commissioned officers' mess – and the galley, clearing away the aftermath of breakfast.

William Reynolds tilted his head backwards to gain a view through the porthole that lay just above his bunk. The scuttle glass was spattered with drops of water which might have been cast up from the waterline, for a noticeable swell had developed and the wind was up. Yet the morning appeared grey and murky. It was rain. A steady precipitation ensured that Rip Raps and the more distant Sewall's Point were lost to view while the conditions threw a wraithlike appearance upon those assembled ships which lay close by. A few scavengers' bumboats plied between the transports to collect and carry rubbish ashore while quartermasters' boats busied themselves conveying yet more hardtack, together with fresh meat and vegetables, to Emory's steamships.

"Trask, Reynolds and Bryant. You're to report to the quarterdeck at ten o'clock sharp with the other new recruits for arms drill. Make sure you're not late." The order, brought by Corporal Jackson, drew William from his pre-occupation with the scuttle's window upon a dreary vista.

"So you fresh fish sound as if you're in for a soaking this morning," observed Charley Ellis, without, in fairness, any sarcasm in his voice.

"Can't be helped," said Bryant. "After all, we need the instruction, that's for sure."

"He's right," said Trask. "Being less than a week in uniform we've a lot to learn when it comes to drill."

"Well, be it company drill, regimental drill, drill in the manual of arms, even brigade drill…don't wish for any of it, man. It'll catch up with you soon enough and in time you'll be sick and tired of it," scoffed Ellis. "As to the quarterdeck, you really need to be aboard one of the larger vessels if you're going to stand much chance of finding room to swing a cat, let alone

57

a musket. That's the trouble with this damn old tin dipper. Too small, too crowded, too worrying when it comes to seaworthiness."

"There can't be more than ten or more of us new boys between the four companies onboard," said William. "They wouldn't have ordered us onto the quarterdeck if there isn't room for arms drill. Anyway, why do you speak so disparagingly about this ship? Conditions are atrocious, I'll readily admit, but are they likely to be any better on the *Arago* or *Atlantic*?"

"Damn sure they are. Much bigger vessels, you see. We've spoken to our boys on board them when we've been ashore. The accommodation's much better, they're far less crowded and they've had cooked meals since we left Baltimore. It doesn't require a sage from Harvard to work out why we've so many men in the Chesapeake General! But what concerns me more is the physical state of this old tub. She's rotten, yet she's expected to put to sea with four hundred men on board." As if it were a reflection of his contempt for the vessel, Ellis cleared his throat and spat a globule of phlegm into his tin cup. "Christ," he added, staring down at the slimy gob of yellow mucous, "if I could collect a bit more of this spittle and show it to the surgeon, he might just commit me to hospital before we set sail."

"Wishful thinking, Charley, except I don't think you've got the makings of a hospital rat." The words came from a burly fellow in one of the lower bunks who had been pre-occupied chewing on a tobacco plug. "The old girl can't be that bad. She must have passed muster by the inspecting board of officers."

"Well, pray tell me, Otis Browne, what do the army skunks know about the condition of ships, for God's sake? I would wager it's no more than I know about the works of Cephalus the Greek...and that's nothing at all, man."

"They say the board is thorough in its scrutiny. It usually includes an officer from the inspector-general's department and another bent on sailing in the vessel. That must count for something, Charley."

"Balderdash, man. Just mark my words. I fear they might come back to haunt us all."

Thursday the fourth of December dawned bright and cheerful in sharp contrast to Wednesday's gloom. Yet it was not the weather which captivated the majority. Early in the day the assembled fleet was ordered to make ready to put to sea, causing much excitement among sailors and soldiers alike.

Soon after ten o'clock the Hampton Roads anchorage rang with the sound of anchor chains rattling and clanking through hawsepipes as sailors heaved upon capstan and windlass bars. Soldiers thronged the decks and cheered. Hot water vapour blew and hissed as the engine room stokers worked up good heads of steam. Fo'c'sle decks throbbed with the tramp of anchor-weighing sailors and the sounds and rhythms of their repertory of old shanties. On board the *Thames*, William Reynolds jostled with the crowd on the upper deck to get a glimpse of other ships, now readied for sea, beginning to make their way out across the lower reaches of the Chesapeake Bay. Meanwhile the old *Thames* trembled, its sides straining to the vibration of boilers long in want of an overhaul. For'ard, the deck-hands laboured to complete hauling in the anchor to the entertaining chant of a favourite old capstan shanty…

From Boston town we're bound away,
Heave aweigh, heave aweigh,
Around Cape Horn to Frisco Bay,
We're bound for Californi-o!

So heave her up and away we'll go,
Heave aweigh, heave aweigh,
Heave her up and away we'll go,
We're bound for Californi-o!

"Bound for California, indeed! That'd suit me fine," quipped a high-spirited private from Company K. "I could lay down my rifle and go a'prospecting. If I couldn't get flush by finding any of the yellow stuff I'd still have thirteen dollars a month courtesy of Abe Lincoln!"

"We'll be lucky enough to get to the Carolinas in this old wreck, let alone California," shouted a fellow of like mind to Charley Ellis.

"Well that might just be enough," retorted another soldier. "After all, some are saying we may be bound for Charleston to try to break the rebel defences."

Within half an hour the *Thames* departed Hampton Roads, steaming between the fortress and Rip Raps to take her place in line. In time the cheering and tomfoolery of the soldiering men on deck began to subside, this rendering audible the repetitive throb of the ship's engine and the cries of encircling gulls. Some men, unaccustomed to life at sea, began to feel queasy after the relative tranquillity of the anchorage, since the approach to the ocean brought forth a lazy, gathering swell. It was a problem set to worsen. Off the neighbouring Cape Henry headland the ships were required to stop in line ahead on account of an unexplained delay to the flagship, the *Baltic*. It was an interruption which meant the vast majority of Emory's men were left to suffer the repetitive rise and fall of the uneasy swell for hours on end. And no more uncomfortably was this felt than upon the little *Thames*. Some hardy souls were swift to find their sea legs, while others – such as William Reynolds – blessed with past experience of living afloat, were used to coping with such complications. It was these men – who were in the minority – who were able to while away the afternoon hours leaning upon the *Thames'* gunwales, watching the skittish ways of flying fish and porpoise.

As to the remaining soldiers, some, in their discomfort, were huddled below in their bunks, willing themselves to sleep. Yet such was their inner turmoil and feeling of wretchedness that sleep was not a practicable option. Inevitably the sudden sensation of rising vomit would, in time, grip the sufferers, prompting in some an attempt to scurry aloft and puke overboard. Yet for most this proved too much of an undertaking and the passage between the lower deck bunks and its equivalent down in the hold, were soon slippery with obnoxious stomach content.

The promise of some respite came at the start of the first watch, at around eight in the evening. By then the *Baltic* had finally taken her place at the head of the line and lights signalled the order to proceed; and so the fleet got underway at last with the gunboat *Augusta* bringing up the rear as convoy. Not many had partaken of their suppers on account of their ailing condition. Those hardier fellows with their constitutions untroubled, including the crew of the *Thames* and the likes of William Reynolds, were inclined to consume their suppers alongside the galley, on the upper deck. Here there was an evening chill to contend with, but this was to be preferred to going below where the smell was so intense, so intolerable. Indeed, it was quite ironic that, having waited so long to put to sea, to rid the ship of its Hampton Roads stench, circumstances had conspired to make matters worse. Sadly, conditions were now set to deteriorate markedly. Although the *Thames* had rid itself of that gut-wrenching rise and fall associated with a stationary, wallowing presence in an uneasy swell, this brought no dramatic respite for those prone to sea-sickness. Overnight and throughout the following morning many continued to suffer. Then, as the afternoon of the fifth unfolded, the glass began to drop with some rapidity. The wind veered westerly and strengthened until it blew a formidable gale off the land and rain fell in torrents. The sea frothed and boiled and, in its confusion, cast sheets of spray across the forecastle, tossed high from waves that crashed repeatedly against the ship's weather bow. The noise became deafening what with the thunderous sea, the screech of the wind and the groans of the old tub's strained timbers as she rolled and pitched, a cacophony which drowned the moaning of a multitude of souls who felt their stomachs in their mouths and continued to drench their sleeping quarters with whatever spew was left in their guts.

Those more accustomed to riding out storms did what they could to ease their colleagues' discomfort. These were, notably, the sailormen themselves, together with a sprinkling of soldiers. As far as Company E was concerned, those soldiers numbered three: William Reynolds, Jack Chidester and Duncan McKeller, themselves all former bluejackets. In William's estimation, this was by far the most prodigious storm he had encountered at sea, a tumult of frightening proportion, yet his several years as a sailor had braced his vitals to cope with this sort of thing. The effect of the elements upon frail and unaccustomed stomachs, was, of course, no respecter of rank, yet, by dint of cooperation between the three men and a collective willingness to do what they could – rather than through any instruction from above – they set about easing the plight of their comrades on the lower deck. It was what Chidester and McKeller called a right hurrah's nest of confusion – everything thrown about and just where it shouldn't be – and, amid it all, the recumbent bodies of the afflicted, some lying on bedding saturated in their own vomit. As to a few of the unfortunates occupying lower bunks, involuntary vomiting from above had at best spattered them and their blankets and, at worst, drenched their heads as they, themselves, lent from their beds to heave on the deck.

"I'll try to find the ship's carpenter," screamed Jack Chidester, "to see if I can lay claim to some sawdust."

Chidester staggered away on his mission. In so doing he was tossed like a rag doll by the ship's motion, lurching between one tier of bunks and the other, his body weight slamming into a forearm that hung limp from a middle berth. Its owner yelled in agony as his arm felt the crushing force, a piercing scream which, for all its harshness, was lost in the bedlam that prevailed. As Chidester offered a cursory apology, hesitating momentarily before pressing ahead, William's attention was drawn to a couple of metal cuspidors, one of which brimmed with vomit, the other less so.

"I'll get rid of these," he shouted.

"I'll take one of them," bawled McKeller. "Of course, the hatches are all battened down, man. We'll need to use one of the doors amidships."

"I reckon we'll need the port side door," screamed William.

"You bet, lime-juicer. I doubt we could open the weather-side door. And if we did, there's every chance these pretty packages would be tossed back all over us. Christ, man, the stench is vile."

William Reynolds and Duncan McKeller made their way aft. Beforehand, however, they chose to equalise the levels of vomit between the two spittoons, mindful that that containing the more copious amounts would inevitably suffer spillage, however hard its carrier tried to maintain his equilibrium. It was a precursory exercise which made both men feel nauseous, simply because of the intensity of the stench at such close quarters.

"Here's the lee-side door," shrieked William after the two former sailors had successfully negotiated the laddered climb to the upper deck. William placed his cuspidor down and opened the door for McKeller to pass through. Outside the noise levels rose several notches. Here the tumult was deafening. McKeller looked for'ard. Two deckhands battled against wind and rain as they attempted to move aft, grasping hold of the capstan's drumhead to steady themselves and avoid being sent tumbling. Everything seemed to merge in confusion, noise and opacity, great drifts of spume and spray being tossed high by the raging sea's constant assault on the starboard bow. The wind howled in the yards and rigging, the masts creaked and groaned, water roared and growled through hawsehole and scuppers while the foaming caps of great waves came streaming over the knightheads.

Duncan McKeller saw no need to step into the maelstrom but cast the contents of his cuspidor out on the deck. Within seconds it was swept up and washed through the lee-side scuppers. Gone for fish food so he said. William stepped forward to the threshold and repeated the procedure. Then, as both men returned for'ard, they were suddenly halted in their tracks by a thunderous, discordant, crashing sound from somewhere deep in the bowels of the vessel. Immediately, a vibration took hold of the old *Thames*, a frightening sort of tremor and one altogether different from the ongoing reverberations attributable to the storm's fury. Was the vessel now doomed? William and Duncan McKeller staggered for'ard to discover a changed mood among the rank and file of Company E. A minority of the afflicted still groaned in their discomfort and remained indifferent to what had just happened; yet many of the sufferers had found the inner strength to raise their weighty heads to question the cause of this sudden loud grating noise and vibration. .

"Holy Moses, has the old girl broken her back?" asked one poor fellow.

It was a question overheard by Jack Chidester who had suddenly emerged, hot on the heels of Reynolds and McKeller, carrying two buckets of sawdust.

"I've just run into one of the men from the engine room," he said. "These past few hours they've had an uphill task nursing the engine, what with the heavy sea running and the ship being overloaded. Well, the poor old engine's now given up the ghost. Broken it is…come to a grinding halt."

"So that explains the almighty noise," said the white-faced occupant of one of the bunks. "What do you think this means for Christ's sake?"

"The engineer said they'd tried to coax the engine as best they could but it was hard going what with the vast sea running and the heavy cargo," replied Chidester.

"Then we'll now be drifting without power and at the complete mercy of the hurricane," suggested another fellow, prompting others to pour forth words of dread and hopelessness.

"Christ, I reckon we're doomed…God help us, we're doomed!"

"If we are to face our Maker, let it be quick!"

"I'm not ready to die. I'm a fucking soldier who's yet to fire a shot in anger. Shooting wild turkey is the only killing I've ever done."

"I can't face drowning. If we look like going down I want some hard liquor…then someone to run me through with my pig sticker. I'll offer ten dollars to anyone who can sell me a bottle of strong red eye."

"I told you so," roared Charley Ellis, his voice showing despair rather than any sense of elation at proving his point. "All the while I've maintained we were courting disaster, having to go to sea in this old wreck. But it gives me no satisfaction to tell you I told you so. Christ, no. I don't mind catching a bullet but I don't want to die like this."

The *Thames* continued to roll and toss violently. Hitherto, running by Cape Hatteras, she had generally held to her southward course but now things had changed dramatically. A gathering dusk, coupled with the opacity of driving rain, spume and sea fog had descended across the watery waste, adding to the sense of despair. Now, being utterly out of control and bereft of forward motion, the *Thames* was perilously close to foundering as the mountainous sea constantly threatened to swamp her. She wallowed and swung about wildly in successive troughs as all the while her heavy load served to impair her capacity to surmount the next, towering, oncoming wall of water. The severe gale, meanwhile, showed no signs of abating. If anything it blew the more and while one or two of the accompanying vessels had, until now, occasionally remained in sight, that was no longer the case because of the darkness and the fog. Distress flares were sent up in the earnest hope that someone would be gimlet-eyed enough to spot them and realise a vessel was in distress. Meanwhile, the ship's master conferred with the regiment's senior officers regarding the need for urgent disposal of a good part of the cargo, in a desperate attempt to try to save the old ship. They needed little persuading and the first mate immediately hurried for'ard in search of volunteers to help put the plan into action. William, together with Jack Chidester and Duncan McKeller, along with a number of tars and a handful of privates from the other three companies, were keen to put their energies to the task. In consequence, under the first mate's direction, they immediately began carrying items of stowed cargo up from below. These were then cast over the gunwales during those fleeting moments of respite between the drenching, stinging flight of great volumes of water cast over the bows and weather-side bulwarks. However, while this desperate work proceeded apace there came news of the most heartening kind.

A young sailor, one of several who had shown the temerity to venture on deck to obtain a better sense of the *Thames'* predicament, had suddenly lost his desperate grip upon the foremast. The stem of the ship had reared up against an advancing wave and the resulting violent motion ensured he was swiftly separated from his shipmates. He was sent tumbling aft, ultimately crashing into the legs of one of the first mate's volunteers and sending him sprawling on the deck. Remarkably it had been sheer joy and excitement, as much as the boisterous conditions, which had caused the surrender of the seaman's grip on the mast. As both men staggered to their feet, their demeanours were in sharp contrast. Whereas the felled volunteer's face spoke of surprise and irritation, the tumbling sailor, whilst bruised, drenched and bleeding, wore the broadest of grins.

"We're going to be saved, thank God," he screamed.

"What's that, man?" hollered a soldier who stood ready at the port side door, his arms girdling a cask of molasses. "What's that you say?"

The bruised sailor squeezed past the private on the threshold. Here, in the less deafening confines of the vessel, he again gave vent to his excitement, punching the air as he shouted wildly. "We're going to be saved. There's one of our ships off the starboard quarter heading this way!"

The few men in earshot, themselves weighed down with items of freight, cheered rapturously in realisation that when all seemed lost, divine providence was about to show its hand. Within minutes the news had spread like wildfire through the *Thames* to the sound of great exaltation. Even the afflicted, weakened by constant retching, summoned some cheers at the thought of salvation. In the forecastle a few terrified sailors, convinced they were bound for a watery grave – and already well imbibed with liquor – put their tar water aside in realisation that there was now every good reason to put their shoulders to the wheel once more.

It transpired that the brigade commander, Colonel Littlejohn of the One Hundred and Tenth New York, had been standing in the stern of the *Ericsson*, sweeping his telescope across the boiling seascape that lay in the paddler's wake. The fogginess had lifted a mite and, in that moment before it closed in again, the colonel was convinced he saw a distress signal. He immediately sought out the ship's captain but had great difficulty in persuading him he'd not imagined what he'd allegedly seen. After a few minutes the captain relented and ordered the *Ericsson* to be put about. It was the sight of its ghostly, distant approach in the advancing twilight that had caused such elation among the handful of men who had ventured onto the *Thames'* upper deck. Yet at first the *Ericsson* made no attempt to venture too close to the little screw-propeller. Keeping its distance, its upper deck swarmed with Union soldiers eager to witness the rescue mission about to unfold. Beneath its wheelhouse lanterns the master appeared, clasping to his mouth a flared hailing trumpet.

"What's troubling you…what's the matter?" bellowed the captain of the *Ericsson*. In failing to receive a reply, he reiterated his question.

"I can't hear you," came the answer from the skipper of the stricken vessel, who, clutching a similar mouthpiece to that of his counterpart, lent his wind-battered frame against the wall of the temporary cook galley.

"What's the matter?" repeated the master of the *Ericsson*, this time taking greater care to enunciate his words.

"We've a broken engine."

"Then throw out a hawser and we'll take you in tow."

"I can't do it. We haven't got any."

"Then to hell with your cracker box," screamed the *Ericsson*'s captain in his frustration. "How come you've put to sea without a hawser?" And with that the rescue ship turned away as if to resume its journey.

"Christ, she can't do that," shouted an onlooking soldier on the *Thames*.

She can't leave us to the mercy of the ocean. Her master deserves to be hauled up to the maintop by his ballocks."

Others who had chosen to risk the fury and dangers of the storm-swept upper deck were struck silent in disbelief. Yet their horror was short-lived for the *Ericsson* was simply in the throes of giving the *Thames* a wide berth as she commenced to circumnavigate her and come up on her windward side. Once the manoeuvre was complete she stopped her wheels rotating and came to a smart halt, in true paddle-steamer fashion. Then, after well-intentioned, yet ultimately futile attempts to lower a lifeboat and to use wooden casks to float lines across to the *Thames*, the master of the rescue vessel attempted a more ambitious plan. Having pulled away from the screw propeller, the *Ericsson* got up steam once more and set her course full speed ahead to run past the *Thames* as if close enough to graze her. The purpose of this manoeuvre was to throw a rope to the foundering little steamer on which deck soldiers and deckhands watched in awe and trepidation at the approaching giant. Its wheels thrashed into the foaming, boiling brine as it appeared to bear down upon its little cousin. Hearts were in mouths among the onlookers. Some turned away and waited with bated breath for the sound of splintering wood. Yet the plan worked, albeit at the cost of inflicting a broken leg upon the master of the smaller vessel. The *Ericsson* ran alongside the *Thames'* starboard side, close enough to cause great rejoicing as the rope came across and fell into eager, grasping hands. However, as the big paddler's stern ran past the propeller's poop deck and thus almost clear of the *Thames*, one of her overhanging boats made contact with the adjacent ship and was pulverised in the process. The incident, in turn, caused the *Thames'* spanker boom to be carried away, striking the unfortunate captain.

With the rope made fast, a substantial hawser was hauled across from the *Ericsson* and likewise secured, enabling the paddle-wheel to significantly advance her rescue operation by taking the *Thames* in tow. Yet the fate of the little propeller remained on a knife edge during the unfolding hours of darkness. The hurricane continued to blow, reaching new heights of fury until midnight had passed. The poor *Thames* lurched and rolled like never before. Those soldiering men, who – on account of the gravity of the situation and being bolstered by sheer curiosity – had ventured on deck, had since scurried back to their bunks in the wake of the excitement. Here they languished, sometimes being tumbled out of their retreats by the force of the ship's movement, sometimes spewing forth yet more portions of vomit until the spittoons were once more awash. The stench was again intolerable but at least now, in the knowledge that salvation was in his grasp, many an ailing fellow thought to drag himself out of his torpidity and go up on deck. Here he was able to clear his lungs and nostrils but, more importantly to put himself to good use. Yet it was a tricky business, for wind and motion had the propensity, that night, to conspire to rid a man of his mortality; and so the recklessness of committing cargo to the deep, or of bailing out unwelcome water, was only undertaken by men whose torsos were already tied to masts or stays or ratlines.

The early hours of the sixth of December began to bring respite, but not before the master of the *Ericsson* – on three separate occasions – had believed the *Thames* to be so inundated with water that she was in the throes of going down. Thankfully, each time, he had withdrawn from the brink of ordering a man to lay an axe upon and cut the hawser. And so the storm gradually abated throughout the day, although not without incident. While the hawser had held firm throughout the height of the tempest, fatigue appears to have been the cause of its parting early in the afternoon of the sixth – an event that necessitated a repeat of the *Ericsson*'s perilous exercise of getting a line to the *Thames*. Mercifully that repetition was again marked by a favourable outcome.

Sometime after midday on the seventh, under greatly improved conditions, the *Ericsson*'s wheels slowed and stopped. Astern, upon the screw-propeller, much industry in repair and cleaning-up proceeded apace, this undertaken with renewed vigour by a multitude of overjoyed, good humoured men, newly spared a watery grave. Almost unnoticed, one of the *Ericsson*'s boats came alongside, bringing Colonel Littlejohn, and the master of the paddle-steamer, to visit the captain of the *Thames*.

Private Charley Ellis had been on deck and witnessed the two gentlemen step aboard. "Good grief, boys, you should have seen the expressions on the faces of those big bugs as they were led to the Captain's quarters," said Charley, who had gone below with others for a deserved interval of rest and a dipper of coffee. "I guess our man is getting some harsh words about putting to sea when ill-prepared and in a wreck like this."

"Well, we had plenty of time to get our own hawser on board, let alone overhaul the engine, when we were just sitting around in Hampton Roads," said another.

"I reckon Littlejohn and the *Ericsson*'s skipper must be furious that so many lives were put in jeopardy…not only ours but theirs as well," opined Otis Brown.

"Well, the old man, as the deckhands call him, will just have to sit tight and face the music," suggested Charley. "After all, he can't make off, what with his broken leg. Perhaps they'll end up breaking the other one for him." It was a comment that caused a ripple of laughter which was interrupted by the emergence of Corporal Jackson.

"Now listen, boys," said the non-comm. "Our visitors are about to depart and Colonel Smith is keen to ensure we give them a grand send off to show our great appreciation…for what the crew of the *Ericsson* did for us in our hour of need. So without further ado, get yourselves up on deck. Oh, and by the way…before you do, word is we are to be towed into Port Royal. Furthermore, the cat is out of the bag concerning our destination. We're bound for Ship Island."

During the latter part of sixty-one and the early months of sixty-two – being attached to the North America and West Indies station – the *Cygnet*'s base in the Caribbean had been Port Royal, Jamaica. Jackson's mention of being taken to Port Royal served momentarily to give William Reynolds a jolt. His thoughts triggered a picture that made him shudder as it flashed through his mind's eye: the irony of the *Thames* being tied up alongside the *Cygnet*, the horror of being spotted, the prospect of his recent past catching up with him. Of course, when he thought about it, it became patently obvious that Corporal Jackson must have been referring to a totally different Port Royal. Then all became clear, as, emerging up on deck, William overheard two fellows from Company K talking about the *Thames'* interim destination.

"If I'm not mistaken, Port Royal lies between Charleston and Savannah," said one.

"You're right," said the other. "It's got a good, deep harbour and, if my memory serves me correctly, it was a squadron under Flag Officer Du Pont which captured it towards the end of last year. His naval gunners did a good job on the forts and left them in the hands of Sherman's troops."

William had cause to breathe more easily. He wended his way through milling soldiers to gain a vantage point to see the departing visitors. As he did so, he stumbled into a fellow who seemed oblivious to where he was going. As they glanced off each other there was mutual recognition: it was Sam Butler, the man from Catonsville. He looked drawn and heavy-eyed in contrast to the character with whom William had enlisted only a week since.

"Hello, there, Reynolds. How did you fare during that ordeal?"

"Much like most of us, I suppose," said William, not wishing to draw attention to a stained naval career, which, if nothing else, had at least conditioned him to eradicate feelings of seasickness.

"Bloody awful business. This is the first time I've felt able to get up here and swallow some fresh air," said Butler. "Can't say I've slept a wink since leaving Hampton Roads and as for my innards…they're so strained from retching it hurts to breathe, man." Apart from looking gaunt, Sam Butler wore a saturnine expression and there was little hint of the cocksure youth who breezed into Camp Belger the previous Saturday.

"I've just been speaking to one of our sergeants…O'Malley…the guy who took us for drill in Baltimore, last Monday morning," remarked Butler.

"God forbid," said William, only too aware that so much had happened in the interim "Was that less than a week ago? So he's in Company H, eh?... and what of that beastly first sergeant? I haven't seen him around."

"Zuicker? I think he's on the *Arago*. Anyway, Sergeant O'Malley tells me we're bound for the Gulf. By all accounts Ship Island is off the Mississippi coast, quite close to New Orleans. To be honest, I don't care where we're going. I'll just be glad to get off this damn ship."

At that moment a jostling for position told of the visitors' imminent departure. William and Sam Butler found themselves pressed against the starboard bulwark and in sight of the boarding ladder. There was no sign of the captain of the *Thames* bidding farewell, ostensibly on account of being indisposed with his broken tibia. However, as one private was overheard to facetiously remark, "after the chastisement he's probably suffered he's thought better to remain in his cabin and lick other wounds."

Instead, as the master of the *Ericsson* followed Colonel Littlejohn down the boarding ladder, released his grasp on the manropes and settled into the sternsheets, the bearded Colonel Elisha Smith hailed the departing duo from above. Resplendent in his dark blue coat with its double row of gold buttons and its distinctive silver eagle shoulder straps, the field officer removed and held his hat high. Such was the gesture which instinctively prompted one of the first sergeants – already perched precariously upon the roof of the cook-galley – to lead the onlookers in a heartfelt and most ardent rendering of three cheers. It was a sincere expression of thanks to the departing visitors and the crew of the *Ericsson* for the deliverance of some four hundred souls from a premature and watery grave.

★ ★ ★

"Land ahoy!...land ahoy!

With the wind having fallen light beneath a clearing sky, it had been an unruffled twenty four hours that followed in the wake of the visitors' return to the *Ericsson*. Now, in the early afternoon of Monday the eighth of December, those assembled on deck could just about discern the distant South Carolina coastline. Port Royal beckoned. At dusk the two steamers made their way into harbour between the flanking promontories of Hilton Head and Bay Point where Forts Walker and Beauregard proudly flew Old Glory. In a short while, with night having fallen and her lifeline to the *Ericsson* slipped, the *Thames* dropped anchor in Port Royal harbour.

William Reynolds, detached in thought, looked out towards the several lights which marked the village of Hilton Head and its jetties. It prompted him to recall the waggish exchanges among fellow soldiers as the *Thames* weighed anchor in Hampton Roads. One had quipped that we – meaning the passengers and crew – would be lucky enough to reach the Carolinas in the old wreck in which they found themselves. Well, the fellow had been eerily correct, yet, for all that, William felt sympathy for the old tub's master. After all, he had allegedly taken a tongue-lashing from his opposite number and Colonel Littlejohn. Yet was the poor fellow so culpable for the dire peril into which four hundred souls were thrown? What of the so-called inspecting board of officers...and what of the vessel's owners? William had seen their nameplate on the wheelhouse...Hubbell and Sturgess of New York.

The following morning, buoyed by having narrowly cheated death, many of the soldiering men aboard the *Thames* lazed on deck, smoking and relaxing in the relative warmth of the South Carolina sunshine. Some sucked upon juicy local oranges brought out in bumboats from timber stagings along the palmetto-fringed shoreline. Others simply marvelled at the sight of placid, blue water...water that, at most, merely rippled against the hulls of the many craft which lay at anchor in the bay. A far cry from those angry, tumultuous walls of water that had rent their full energy against the poor *Thames*.

During the afternoon, a party of surveyors came on board to conduct a detailed scrutiny of the vessel at the behest of Colonels Smith and Littlejohn, who had gone ashore in the forenoon to secure the necessary arrangements with the Post Commandant. It was an exercise which proved both alarming and illuminating. No hawser. No chronometer. No steam pump or log book. A defective compass and a chart room in dire need of a chart of southern waters. A vessel with a carcass in such a state of rottenness as to be capable of being run through with a soldier's bayonet. And so, in consequence, the old cracker box was pronounced unfit for further service. A replacement ship was to be sought and, once this was available, the *Thames* would be sent packing, back to her New York owners.

The men, on hearing this news were overjoyed. Once more Charley Ellis launched into such remarks as "I told you so," yet, unlike before, in the midst of the tempest when all seemed lost, his words rang, not with despair, but with a mix of cynicism and elation.

Over the next few days, these being generally bright and mild, the men of the One Hundred and Fourteenth were ordered ashore, disembarking at the jetties near Hilton Head and making their way to the firm sandy beach which fringed the village. The first day they spent leisure time bathing and having their fill of fresh food – including fine oysters – at the little settlement's eateries. It was a delight to the palate to consume fresh meat and vegetables after having endured days of living on weevil-infested hardtack and raw pork. Yet that delight was surpassed by the sheer joy of being alive, of feeling the earth beneath one's feet, the sand beneath one's toes and the sun on one's face. Thank God for Colonel Littlejohn's spyglass and the blessed *Ericsson* without which four hundred souls would have been pitched into old Neptune's lair.

As William emerged from the foam's edge, dressed in nothing but his flannel drawers, he inwardly reflected upon the previous week's close brush with death. While retracing his steps up the beach, alone in the wake of other dripping comrades, he recalled one of Parson Veck's sermons based upon the teachings in the Book of Exodus. In some respect he could see recent events as having been analogous to aspects of the parson's story. He pondered upon sharing his thoughts with others with whom he had enjoyed a relaxing swim and attended to some much needed laundering in the brine; for the stench of stale vomit was rife and permeated many a man's uniform.

Reaching a grassy hummock at the back of the beach, William lay down upon the greensward with several fellows from his berthing area. Some sat quietly, composing letters home. A greater number had set about mending clothes with the assistance of their little housewife sewing kits, presented to them back in Greene by the Ladies' Aid Society. Behind them, those garments already treated to a wash – William's included – lay strewn on the grass beneath a warm sun and drying breeze.

"Do you think Colonel Littlejohn's a God-fearing man?" William's question broke the silence that at the chosen moment dwelt among the writers of missives and those who laboured with needle and thread.

"I've no idea," said a swarthy-skinned fellow who, possessed of aquiline nose and goatee beard, answered to the name of Clem.

"Why would you want to know?" asked Otis Brown.

"It just struck me that we were rather blessed in being delivered to this place out of that dreadful tempest. It has echoes of the Israelites' deliverance from Egypt into the Land of Canaan, if you know the story. I can't help thinking the power and will of God were at work."

"I know the story alright," said Jed Little, the son of a Calvinist minister from Otsego County in New York State. Moses caused the waters of the Red Sea to part, allowing the children of Israel to escape the Pharoah's soldiers."

"Well, yes, he caused the sea to part by stretching out his rod over the sea but it was at the Lord's command that he should do so. It was by His decree alone and His influence that the waters divided."

"Are you saying that the Colonel must be a staunch believer, otherwise his chance sight of us and his ability to persuade the master of the *Ericsson* to turn about and rescue us would not have happened?" enquired the bearded Clem.

"Perchance. Who knows?" replied William. "To be honest I'm more inclined to believe in the power of prayer. Think how many distraught and fear-stricken men turned to prayer in their desperation after the engine broke and in the height of the maelstrom. That itself...that call for mercy and expressed trust in the Lord could have caused His heavenly protection to work through the actions of Colonel Littlejohn. Added to which God would have been aware that our military quest was for the good. After all, in it is a will to release poor blacks from slavery. Moses' quest was not dissimilar. The Lord had called upon him to deliver the Israelites out of Egyptian bondage."

"Very profound," interjected a bystander who had overheard the conversation as he stooped to rearrange his drying shirt and underclothes. "I'd sooner believe in the power of the Colonel's spyglass and of human will than that of God or prayer."

"Well, I suppose we can't all think al..."

At this moment the conversation was interrupted by the sudden arrival of two privates from the direction of Fort Walker, the existence of which had sparked the village's recent growth. Both men appeared dishevelled and the worse for drink. William recognised one as Tobias Lawrence, the fellow Charley Ellis had taunted over his mounting of the nigger's woman at Newport News. The other he did not recognise as one from Company E.

"So what have we here?" sneered Lawrence. "A bunch of idlers, no less. You should be enjoying yourselves, what with today being free time." Lawrence's companion said nothing, the effect of drink having rendered him torpidly uncommunicative.

"We've been making good use of our time," said one fellow, a mite incensed. "Attending to personal hygiene, Lawrence…de-lousing ourselves in the briny and washing and mending our duds. You'd do well to follow suit." It was a remark which drew a muffled oath from beneath the recipient's breath.

"So how have you and your friend, here, been occupying your time, Toby?" enquired another, his less condescending tone of voice succeeding in eliciting a reply.

"We met up with a couple of off-duty Zouaves from the fort," said Lawrence, his voice decidedly slurred. "Genial company. We shared a good few glasses of red eye and they introduced us to two firm-buttocked mulatto girls who were even better company."

"Well, lads," exclaimed Corporal Jackson who had inconspicuously appeared on the scene, "with Lawrence and his companion having got their whorin' and carousin' out of their systems, thanks to their fancy Zu Zu friends, I would have thought it opportune to guarantee them a sobering and much-needed wash. So what do you say, men, about tossing them into yonder briny?"

Some of the men needed no further encouragement. Springing to their feet, they dragged the unfortunate Lawrence and his companion to the ground, lifting them both, spread-eagle fashion, each suspended between the clutches of six of their fellow comrades. The Hilton Head foreshore was rent with expletives as, squirming and cussing, the tight couple were transported down the beach destined for a ducking and dousing. Behind them, those who chose to refrain from such coltish behaviour, William included, allowed themselves to be distracted from any pre-occupation to engage in high-spirited badinage. And so a cacophony of quips and hearty cheers accompanied the carriers and their writhing burdens down the beach, only to reach a crescendo as crashing spray and flailing limbs signalled a completed mission.

Such was the relaxing nature of the first day on dry land. The next two days saw a different regime. Once taken ashore the men were formed up on Hilton Head beach and put through their paces with arms and company drill. William Reynolds and the remainder of the Baltimore recruits, being green, were taken aside and given tutelage by an assortment of drill sergeants, only to be pitched into the company ranks at the eleventh hour on the third day. Subsequently, as darkness fell and the men returned to the *Thames* – feet aching and throbbing from the effects of marching on sand – it was to find a newly arrived vessel tied up alongside their decrepit and condemned, floating home. This was the barque *Voltigeur*, a sleek three-masted sailing ship which, in its equipage and seaworthiness, coupled with the assiduities of its experienced master, was to prove the very antithesis of the wretched *Thames*. It was, therefore, with vigour and some enthusiasm over the next three days, that the men of the One Hundred and Fourteenth were happy to trade the tedium of drill for the physically demanding transfer of the *Thames'* cargo into the adjacent barque. Either that, or assisting a gang of ships' carpenters in fitting out the *Voltigeur's* hold with rows of bunks; for being a deep-water cargo carrier, she was not generously appointed to meet the sleeping needs of an army of passengers.

It was with no regret, whatsoever, among her erstwhile lodgers, that late on the sixteenth of December, the *Thames* – in possession of such makeshift repairs as had been deemed necessary to get her back to New York – took her leave of Port Royal harbour. Good riddance was the sentiment of some – as she stole away under cover of darkness – since the damned old tub had nearly been the death of them. Yet now the tendency was to look forward, hopefully to an uneventful remainder of the voyage to Ship Island. The following morning a steamer appeared and quickly set about taking the *Voltigeur* in tow. Soon, with the steamer's work done, the barque was standing out to sea, where, in favourable airs, a goodly expanse of canvas was hoisted and sheeted to the wind. In no time she was out of sight of the South Carolina coast and making steady progress on a southward course.

What a difference from being on board the ill-fated *Thames!* The men revelled in their new-found surroundings. Above all, they appreciated their decent sleeping quarters and the absence of that perpetual stench, reinforced, as it became, with the nauseating reek of vomit. Yet it took several days at sea for the men to clear it from their nostrils, for there the smell continued to linger, despite repeated applications of vinegar upon the ship's timbers; and after all, they had remained on the hapless old cracker-box until her day of departure. On the *Voltigeur's* upper deck it was a revelation to most, the sheer experience of looking aloft at the magnificence of billowing sails and the agility of the seafaring men as they scrambled on high upon yards and rigging. For William, it reminded him of his spell on the *Edgar*. Recollections of his former ship, in favourable weather, running with a wind abaft the beam, the spread of canvas being a sight to behold…a powerful sight, matched by the magnificence of the several consorts astern…*Trafalgar*, *Algiers* and *Diadem*…all in station and under full sail. Yet, unlike many a ship-of-the-line, the *Voltigeur* was no vessel of staid, matronly appearance. She was altogether a more elegant ship. There was almost an arrogance about her, what with her sleek lines and rather stately bearing; and she was rigged with such efficiency as to warrant a crew numbering a mere fifteen souls.

Such recall waxed and waned in William's mind as, three days out of Port Royal, he chatted with Trask and Bryant on the upper deck, it being a particularly fine and bright day with a good breeze astern. Overhead the sight of sun-kissed white sails, straining and cracking, each harnessing the wind to full advantage, might have been the envy of many a washerwoman. This, and the occasional scurrying of a man aloft, drew the men's attention from time to time, although the lazy contemplation of the comings and goings of the Gulf Stream weed that lay upon the ocean was less demanding upon neck muscles.

"What a contrast with that wretched existence aboard the *Thames*. Quite invigorating, don't you think? Makes you feel good to be alive." The approaching voice from behind was not a familiar one to the three greenhorns but, as they simultaneously turned around, it was to unanimously recognise their Company's First Sergeant…an affable fellow, according to Jack Chidester, by the name of John Reynolds.

"I understand we share the same name," said the non-commissioned man, addressing William with a smile, "but being told you're English, I'm inclined to the acceptance that we're unrelated."

"It's a common enough name, Sergeant, so I guess it's a safe presumption. By coincidence my late father also shared your Christian name," said William, refraining from actually stating the name for fear of it being construed as over-familiarity.

"Well, John is a mighty common name, soldier…so much so that it might be over-stating things to label it a coincidence, don't you think?"

William felt edgy. He was reluctant to dwell upon family and background for fear of drifting into the sensitive matter of his former career. He changed tack. "You're right, Sergeant. We were only saying how good it feels to be rid of the *Thames* and out of the clutches of that hurricane."

"Sure thing. I think we can all feel lucky to have escaped death by the skin of our teeth." First Sergeant Reynolds looked pensive. "I guess that's the truth of it, alright," he continued. "Let's hope that same luck sees us safely through what remains of this war. Christmas is coming and our thoughts will inevitably turn to home, sweet home. It would be grand to think we might all be back at our firesides and with our loved ones come this time next year."

It was a comment which provoked sadness in the heart of the first sergeant's namesake, so unattainable a prospect did it seem to him. The sentiment troubled him for the rest of the day and led to a fitful night's sleep.

★ ★ ★

Two or three days saw the *Voltigeur* amid the Bahama islands and into the green shallows of the Great Bahama Banks where caution and the taking of regular soundings was of the essence. It was a seascape familiar to William Reynolds since he had passed this way on the *Cygnet* only some six months earlier, calling at Havana on the journey north to Bermuda, then Halifax. The subsequent half year could hardly have been more eventful for him, a fact that had not escaped his thoughts. By the twenty third of the month Cuba was in view and, by Christmas Day, the Dry Tortugas light and the coral-reefed coast of southern Florida were well astern as the *Voltigeur* cut her way through the waters of the Gulf of Mexico.

The general mood among the men on Christmas Day was not a joyous one but one which heightened thoughts of home, of loved ones and of Christmases past. The chaplain, a man by the name of Callahan, held a Christmas morning service on the waist of the upper deck for those inclined to participate. Of those, there were a goodly number, for what better day to call upon the Lord to bring conflict to an early end than on Christmas morn. Yet there was no obligation to attend. Some lay in their bunks writing letters home, feeling perhaps that that was the way to moderate their feelings of homesickness and to temper, in the mind's eye, images of last year's joy and gaiety about a familiar hearth-side; of family games and laughter, of mince pies and eggnog.

For William Reynolds it had been during his days as a Boy RN on the *Excellent* when he last spent a Christmas at home, yet his own mind's-eye images were no less sharp. He attended the service on deck, then went below, where he spent time mending some of his underclothes with the aid of Ellis's little sewing kit. Like many of his companions he was distinctly maudlin. Inwardly he constantly rebuked himself for how he had conducted himself during the past year. So much had transpired but nothing of which he could remotely feel proud. He had let himself down. He had let his family down. Yes, he had become a soldier…but at what cost? He was thousands of miles from his native land. Yet, while circumstances had conspired to set him on a course to take Uncle Sam's bounty money, rather than the Queen's Shilling, he remained convinced he was destined to be fighting for a good cause. At least he felt committed.

Christmas dinner materialised in the form of wormy crackers and a pint of beans. Even a cook's galley upon one of Her Majesty's men-of-war – an austere enough place – would serve up something special on Christmas Day: a sea-pie, perhaps; a hearty plum duff. And the Captain, if worth his salt, would order a splicing of the main brace. Thereafter, fortified with an intake of grog, the men's light-heartedness would slip into merriment as singing and dancing – invariably bolstered by the presence of the ship's band – graced a candle-lit lower deck. Yet there was no such merriment and good cheer aboard the *Voltigeur*. Only on the twenty-seventh of the month did the men's general mood promise to lighten somewhat as Ship Island was sighted, fine on the starboard bow.

The presence of strong head winds necessitated the soldier-laden barque having to engage in a prolonged series of tacks which meant the vessel only arrived off the island during the following forenoon. There was an eeriness about this barren, sandy bar off the Mississippi coast, probably as much attributable to there being not a single transport in sight as to any topographical blandness. The expedition had moved on. The only sign of life as the *Voltigeur* prepared to drop anchor off the point of the island, was a rowing boat putting out from the shore. In time the open boat drew alongside, carrying in its sternsheets a gentleman who announced himself as the island's Post Adjutant. He had orders, he said, to convey to the ship's master and promptly came onboard to be escorted aft to speak to the same. The visitor's presence was brief enough and no sooner had he departed than the order was given to put about. Yet any intention to set sail once again was thwarted. What light airs had prevailed soon fell away. The *Voltigeur* was becalmed.

During the middle part of the afternoon it was announced that the

Colonel would shortly be addressing the men on the upper deck. There was no compulsion to attend. This was on account of there being insufficient space in the waist of the deck for the assembly of some four hundred and more souls. It was also appreciated that whatever the Colonel chose to impart would be promptly conveyed to absent colleagues. By three-twenty, those who had chosen to listen to what Colonel Smith had to say had squeezed and jostled themselves into place as latent interest in the nature of the regimental commander's words had revealed itself significant among the four companies. On the half hour the Colonel appeared at the break of the quarterdeck, flanked by Adjutant Per Lee, a number of commissioned officers – including the four company captains – and Captain Blye, master of the *Voltigeur*.

"Soldiers...soldiers of the One Hundred and Fourteenth." Amid the peacefulness of the dead calm the Colonel's voice rang out with clarity. "You have endured much hardship and torment already," he began, "having, through a combination of unfortunate circumstances, been on the brink of being cast into a watery grave. But the Psalter tells us the Good Lord is our Shepherd and, with the *Ericsson*'s assistance, He chose to deliver us to a safe haven and into waters of comfort. Now Captain Blye and his doughty crew have brought us to the threshold of whatever awaits us... and for that I thank you, Captain, with all sincerity and indebtedness. And, being confident that my sentiments are keenly felt by all, I tender them on behalf of the many soldiers of the One Hundred and Fourteenth who you have conveyed to this place with such assuidity."

The Colonel's words drew forth a mix of applause and effusive cheers from his audience, the seemingly heartfelt nature of which caused an emotional response...a hint of awkwardness and embarrassment...in the demeanour of the normally crusty old Blye. Yet, in the presence of a vast crowd of soldiering men, the Colonel's words did not escape the odd witty retort.

"I'll wager that so-called assuidity was wasted on the Colonel himself and the rest of the big wigs," whispered Duncan McKeller in William's ear. "I doubt they had to settle for a Christmas dinner of crackers and beans."

"I am sure it did not escape attention, earlier this afternoon, that the Post Adjutant from Ship Island came on board," continued Colonel Smith. "He brought word that all is well with the expedition. The fleet assembled here two weeks ago, some ships arriving as early as the eleventh, although most of the large steamers appeared on Saturday the thirteenth. These included our old friends, the *Arago*, and the *Atlantic*, bearing our other Companies and the dear old *Ericsson*, bless her."

Mention of the *Ericsson* caused a further ripple of cheers and applause from the assembled throng.

"Now, quite apart from the vessels emanating from Hampton Roads... ourselves apart, of course...the ships assembling here a fortnight since also included a flotilla which had sailed from New York. These vessels carried troops under the command of General Nathaniel Banks who travelled here on the flagship *North Star*. The Post Adjutant said it was a quite a spectacle...the sight of so many ships in the anchorage with twelve thousand troops aboard and the sounds of regimental bands playing patriotic tunes. Well, it appears General Banks was not prepared to dally because, soon after arriving here, he promptly issued orders to get steam up and set sail once more. And it will not surprise you to learn that the expedition's destination was New Orleans. Now, you will glean from this disclosure that the Post Adjutant has conveyed to Captain Blye and myself, orders to follow in the wake of the other ships. He also brought word, received from New Orleans, that, upon arrival there, General Banks replaced General Butler in taking command of the Department of the Gulf. Some of you will be aware that it was General Butler's forces who secured our military possession of the Crescent City earlier this year." The Colonel hesitated a few moments to draw breath and stroke his beard. "So that's it, men. We are initially bound for New Orleans. Beyond that I cannot say what is likely to await us although there's no disputing it will be hot and important work. Yet, as you are only too aware, for the moment we remain becalmed, with not the lightest of airs to give us steerage way. As soon as the wind picks up Captain Blye is intent on weighing anchor and we will make for the Mississippi River's South West Pass."

The stridency and clarity of Colonel Smith's voice faded towards the end of his last sentence as he suddenly became distracted by a matter of some gravity. Captain Bullock of Company H, his face telling of shock and sadness, had passed the Colonel a note from the Assistant Surgeon. The recipient hesitated a moment to digest the surgeon's words before continuing to address his men.

"Soldiers...it is incumbent on me to impart some sombre news to you all. It seems we have arrived at Ship Island not entirely unscathed. Word has just reached me from the sickbay that Private Thomas Dolan of Company H has this afternoon departed this life. The poor fellow had been stricken with fever for several days but is now at peace."

The Colonel broke off from addressing the men, who, beyond exchanging some initial whispered words of surprise and dismay, now stood in shocked silence. He turned round and, for a few minutes, conferred with several of his fellow officers, notably Captain Bullock and Chaplain Callahan. He also spoke with the master, Captain Blye, before returning to face his audience.

"Listen now, men. Arrangements are to be made for the funeral of Private Dolan at midnight. Our brother soldier will be committed to the deep with military honours. Any man who back home has sung in his local church choir, or considers he has an aptitude for vocal music, is asked to inform his Company's First Sergeant before supper."

With that the Colonel turned away, his saturnine mood, attributable to the unexpected announcement of young Dolan's death, mirrored in his features. He was followed aft by Captain Blye. The commissioned officers proceeded in their wake.

★ ★ ★

The midnight hour passed unnoticed to many, the still of the breathless anchorage being conducive to slumber. In consequence, by mid-evening, a good number of those minded to pay their respects to poor Dolan, being already in their bunks, had succumbed to the soporific effect of being afloat in placid waters. William Reynolds was among them. Yet, unlike most, his slumber was not attributable to the clement nature of the Gulf waters, but to the sleep-inducing effect of trying to read a small-print dime novel he had borrowed from Jack Chidester. .

"Stir yourself, Willie." It was a hushed tone of voice from the mouth of Caleb Trask as he shook his comrade in an endeavour to rouse him. It was a shade before midnight. "Time to go aloft."

William sat up and wiped the sleep out of his eyes. He noticed that some bunks had already been vacated but the majority were still occupied by a wealth of snoring comrades.

"We'll need to exit via the fore-hatchway and find a spot to stand in the fo'c'sle," said Trask, as William jumped out of his bunk and grasped his sky-blue pants. "Corporal Jackson says the funeral will take place amidships. The cortege will accompany the body from the after-deck."

Simultaneously slipping on his brogan shoes and tunic, William tossed his forage cap and *Soldier's Prayer Book* at his comrade for safe keeping while he fumbled to secure his buttons. Meanwhile, Trask began to lead the way up on deck from where carried the voice of Chaplain Callahan, signalling that the ceremony was about to begin. William and Caleb emerged onto a crowded fo'c'sle as, poignantly, the solemn cortege progressed to the sound of muffled drumbeats. The deceased, poor Dolan, sewed up in a blanket and weighted at the feet, was borne on pine planking and carefully set down beneath a newly-lashed spar from which, in the still night, limply fell Old Glory.

Witnessing a burial at sea was as new an experience to William – notwithstanding his former career – as it was to his soldiering comrades. The Chaplain spoke kind words upon the character of the deceased. The service followed that set out in the *Soldier's Prayer Book* which William recognised as a shortened version of the order for burial contained in the *Book of Common Prayer*. Several hymns were sung, adding to the solemnity and touching nature of the moonlit ceremony. They were delivered by the newly assembled choir of volunteers who acquitted themselves well, their final hymn proving especially moving. As they fell silent after the first verse, poor Dolan's corpse was released into the deep. Thereafter the remaining verses were sung; then came three volleys of musket fire and Chaplain Callahan's invocation of the benediction.

It was widely agreed by those who attended Dolan's service that it was a very touching affair. William returned to his bunk soon after twelve-thirty. He found sleep hard to come by, only succumbing some two hours later. Yet it was an uneasy sleep, culminating, towards dawn, in a deeply unsettling experience from somewhere in the labyrinthine abyss of his unconscious mind. A nightmare gripped him. Duncan McKeller said he was woken by William's agitation and a piercing scream. He saw his arms flail. He saw his body flex and twitch. Then William emitted a shrill cry and sat bolt-upright, in the process grazing his head upon the base of the overhead bunk.

As a precursor to finding sleep, William's thoughts had dwelt long upon man's mortality. The funeral had unsettled him. He could not picture poor Dolan in his mind's eye. He hadn't known the fellow, what with his being in another Company, yet were he to be shown an image he would have doubtless recognised it, for they had been housed together within wooden walls for nigh on a month. Ezra Wilson and Sam Butler would have certainly known him, being of the same Company. With the ship becalmed it chilled William to think of the deceased nearby, wrapped in his weighted grey blanket, somewhere just below the *Voltigeur's* hull. Then restless sleep engulfed him until thoughts of Dolan welled again in his remote, inner world. He pictured the blanket shrouding the corpse…

twine was unravelling…William was in the water. There was warmth on his back…it was enjoyable, like it had been bathing in the shallows off Hilton Head beach. But he was not amid shallow water…suddenly it was intensely cold water and William was sucked down…he could no longer feel sand beneath his feet. Familiar sensations…he had been here before, except now there was the blanket again…but just an empty blanket. The twine that had bound it lay suspended vertically before William's eyes, wriggling as if a living creature. It multiplied and thickened until it resembled an enveloping curtain of mucilaginous Gulf weed. Suddenly, before him, the weed-like substance parted to reveal a terrifying apparition…a blanched, wraithlike cadaver, its head featureless. In his bunk William moved in violent jerks and emitted utterances that told of agitation deep in his unconscious. Within seconds the corpse had spiralled away, the weed-like curtain closing behind it. The vision came again, but not from behind the weedy veil. Now it popped up beside him, the face, such as it was, turned away. Slowly it revolved to face the dreamer…would Dolan's dead features now be revealed? No!…within a foot of William's face was the marbled visage of the drowned waterman he had helped the sick berth attendant lay out on the *Excellent*. Familiar images…except, as his mouth opened, there was now nothing left of the partially eaten tongue which appeared in the Penitentiary nightmare. William was gripped by fear…he emitted a shrill scream…his body went rigid, his arms flailing. It had been then that McKeller began to stir and was soon awake. The apparition, like the first, receded but then a third broke through the drape of weeds, the cadaver's hideous, contorted features spewing blood from its gaping mouth, its glazed eyes distended…the unfortunate Francis Boney revealing himself once again. In his bunk William let out another shrill and piercing cry and lurched forward into a sitting position, his shirt drenched in perspiration. He didn't feel the contact with the bottom of the upper bunk but, once fully awake, he was soon aware of his head beginning to throb.

"Are you OK Willie?" said McKeller from his bunk across the aisle. "I thought you were having some kind of fit."

"Yes, I'm alright thanks." William's reply was long in coming. It was as if he still needed time to wrench his thoughts away from events haunting the deep recesses of his unconscious mind. "I had a vivid dream…a nightmare."

"What about?"

"Bodies…dead ones. In the water."

"That's because you witnessed poor Dolan's funeral."

"You're probably right…but I've had much the same nightmare before."

By mid-morning a gentle breeze had picked up and, with plenty of canvas aloft, the *Voltigeur* had weighed anchor and lost sight of Ship Island. Two days later – having been delayed somewhat by strengthening headwinds – the haughty-looking barque began to approach the delta front of the great Mississippi, in a sea stained brown with river sediment which lay suspended in great bands. It was New Year's Eve and the *Voltigeur* shortened sail and threw some of her canvas aback. Now, hove-to and in sight of the conical brick lighthouse marking the South West Pass, she signalled for a pilot to take her to New Orleans, a request which drew a swift response. Within minutes there appeared a small sailing vessel which, once close to the barque, lowered a rowing boat for the pilot's use; and with him safely aboard and shouting orders, the *Voltigeur* moved the short distance to the Pass entrance which lay between narrow, projecting mudflats strewn with low weeds and rushes. Here the ship dropped anchor and, with all canvas furled, awaited the arrival of a tugboat from New Orleans.

Throughout the forty-eight hours which had elapsed since William's unpleasant experience he seemed dispirited. The euphoria which had gripped all since the *Ericsson* delivered them safely to Port Royal, had – quite understandably – diminished with time, diluted by the impact of daily routine and the very human tendency of taking matters for granted. Nonetheless, William had felt blessed, he had sought answers through his faith to explain the *Thames'* deliverance and seen God's providence at work: and silently he had continued to offer up thanks in his nightly prayers. Yet it was William, more than most, who felt downcast. His terrifying nightmare had left an impact upon him, a nightmare much akin to that he had experienced in the Halifax Penitentiary. It had doubtless been triggered by Dolan's burial and, during the following two nights, had provoked, in turn, bad images of that wretched prison in the deepest layers of William's mind.

The night of New Year's Eve brought little solace to the Englishman for sleep was both fitful and interspersed with troubled dreams. And despite the time of year – the ushering out of the old and the welcoming of the new – there seemed a dearth of collective merriment onboard. As he lay awake, unaware of the time, William recalled the Royal Navy tradition of striking the ship's bell sixteen times and having the band march round with renditions of *Auld Lang Syne* and *God Save The Queen*. Sadly, New Year's Day brought no cheer aboard the *Voltigeur* as she lay off the South West Pass: quite the contrary and not least for the men of Company E who, to a man, were quickly plunged into a state of despondency and grief. Their comrade, Private Martin Skillman, had been taken during the night, another victim of typhoid fever.

Another funeral. William had known Skillman well. He had found him an affable fellow. Now he stood with others of Company E on the barque's foc's'le, watching the receding ship's boat. Chaplain Callahan had conducted a touching ceremony on the waist of the ship and Captain Dederer had spoken well of Skillman. Now both officers accompanied the deceased and the guard to a little muddy islet in the mouth of the Pass. A grave-digging party could be seen in the distance, clutching the shovels with which they had just finished excavating a waterlogged grave in the cold, rich delta mud.

"Seems death is dealing us what it considers to be a good hand at present, what with Dolan and now our own Skillman," remarked William, mournfully.

"You might say that," said Charley Ellis. "A good fellow, was young Skilly. It's always the good 'uns that get taken. Perhaps the Good Lord has had time for reflection and considers we got off lightly when on that old cracker box. Perhaps he's redressing the issue."

"How are you feeling, Willie?" interjected Isaiah Bryant, pulling him aside and knowing him to have already been in low spirits before this latest visitation by death.

"This certainly doesn't help, does it? More sadness…and right in our midst. I've got a feeling I could end up with another bad night and a sore head," said William. "But to hell with it," he suddenly exclaimed, after pausing briefly. "After all, I'm alive and shouldn't be so damned melancholic."

"Strange though that you should get a recurring nightmare. Perhaps it's telling you something."

"That my turn's coming soon?" said William, his words laced with a hint of sarcasm. "No, not exactly" he continued, reflectively. "But it certainly appears to be about man's mortality. Perhaps such images of death in my dreams simply underline the fragility of life and my concern for the distant lives of those dear to me." He refrained from any elaboration, not wanting to disclose any particulars of his recent history. Yet, in that moment, he inwardly resolved that writing home could be delayed no longer.

The men on the fo'c'sle fell silent as attention switched to the mud islet off the port quarter. The deceased was being lowered into the earth as Chaplain Callahan prepared to deliver the final obsequies and the guard, its volleys of musket fire. Meanwhile, on the starboard side a deckhand,

84

acting as side-boy, helped the pilot aboard from his rowing boat. After the *Voltigeur* had dropped anchor to await its tugboat, the pilot had returned to his nearby home which was set on marshy ground to one side of the Pass. It lay among a handful of dwellings – collectively known as Pilot Town – which were raised above the level of the marsh, uniquely built upon poles driven into the mud and inter-linked by timber boardwalks. Now the fellow had rowed back to the barque, to impart important news from Virginia.

"I'm told General Ambrose Burnside has suffered a heavy and bloody defeat at the hands of General Lee," reported the pilot as he clambered aboard. "It happened on the thirteenth day of December at a place called Fredericksburg on the Rappahannock. The General had hoped to advance on Richmond. It is said there were heavy Union casualties."

It was sickening news to digest, deepening the gloom and despondency which prevailed upon the *Voltigeur*. Such was New Year's Day 1863.

Three

PORT TOBACCO, MARYLAND
CHRISTMAS 1862

A cold sleet had begun to drive into the face of the rambler before he had strayed too far from the comfort of his hearth. He had turned his back on the town, early in the afternoon, taking the road north towards Pomfret. After half a mile he left the highway by cautiously negotiating a rickety stile. It brought him to a poorly defined, mudded path which led across a succession of dank fields, where patches of gluey mire chilled and sucked at his boots and slowed his pace. Such was the exposed nature of his chosen route that he pulled his coat tightly about him. Then he lifted his moth-eaten muffler up over his mouth, leaving only nose and eyes barely visible below his slouch hat.

Ahead, through the grey, driving precipitation, the ill-defined bounds of a clump of woodland began to loom. George Atzerodt cursed his luck. He should have found time to venture this way earlier in the day, before the weather closed in. George had a natural tendency to stoop, and now, as he reached the edge of the wood, he bent his frame yet further to follow a path through fringing dogwood which soon gave way to chokecherry thicket. It was a familiar spot where, in season, he had been known to bring Rose to pick fruit for her chokecherry pies. Now it served to offer some shelter from the inclement conditions; and, in consequence, here he lingered a few minutes until detecting some respite in the weather.

Twenty minutes later, having skirted the wood, George reached his intended destination, a jumble of dilapidated timber buildings including a covered sawpit. It was the workplace of an elderly woodcutter, one Cornelius Smith, an acquaintance of George by reason of his inclination to down the occasional whisky in Brawner's. On this wet and gloomy, fourth Sunday in Advent, the place seemed a lonely spot in the failing afternoon light, the damp reek of decay and fallen leaves mingling with the resinous smell of freshly cut timber and of yesterday's waste wood ashes. Today, being the Sabbath, the woodland clearing and its eclectic collection of lichen and moss-covered shacks had fallen silent, save for the noise of the wind in the neighbouring oaks. George jealously pictured old Smith where, in all likelihood, he might be found: with his feet up by a cosy fire fuelled by his own logs. Back in October, in exchange for work on a cart and wagon, Cornelius had supplied George with a substantial load of cut timber for winter fuel. More recently, in response to the carriage painter's expressed wish to obtain a Christmas tree, he had mentioned that he was about to cut some softwood and would leave, rather than burn, any piney tops which might suit his purpose. George was to help himself.

Once George had selected what might suffice as a Christmas tree for Greta, he set his gait back in the direction of Port Tobacco. It seemed to be getting colder, for the icy rain was turning to wet snow but at least the keen blast was now at his back. By the time he reached home the snowflakes had lightened and were swirling and dancing in the wind. As George set his little tree down in front of his modest cottage and applied his boots to the scraper, he noticed that the broken, tan-coloured ferns – which bordered the copse across the road – were beginning to bear a white veil of snow.

"If I'd have known it was going to turn out like this I'd have gone this morning," grumbled George as he removed and shook his coat and muffler in the little front passage.

"I kept telling you the sky was looking threatening," said Rose Wheeler, his common-law wife. "Anyway, did you achieve what you set out to do?"

"I did. I've left the tree outside. I'll put it in the outhouse until Christmas Eve. I've also picked some sprigs of richly-berried holly to freshen up the Adventskranz."

"Well, you'd better carry it to the outhouse now, before it's buried under snow. But bring the holly in and I'll replace the shrivelled berries in the Advent wreath. Which reminds me…it's the Sunday before Christmas. We must light the fourth candle. Oh, and when you've put the tree in the outhouse you should go and thaw yourself by the fire and I'll bring you a glass of warming gluehwein. But be quiet as you enter the parlour. Greta nodded off on the sofa while you were out and she needs her sleep. I think it's partly the excitement of Christmas. It'll mean something to her this year, being two and a half."

"The other day I told her about Sankt Nikolaus and of the tannenbaum being trimmed with apples and candles on Heiligabend…and of the thrill of Besherung…the exchanging of gifts. I think she understood. For a few minutes I was back in Prussia as a young child," said George, reflectively.

"Well, I trust you didn't confuse her with all those strange German words. After all, this is America and she will be growing up a young American. And I certainly hope you didn't frighten Greta with tales of that malevolent Grampus fellow."

"Krampus…Knoct Ruprecht."

"Yes, him," said Rose.

"No, I didn't. But I know what you mean, Rose. I was indulging my sentimental side, that's all. Greta will be growing up as an American… whatever that will mean. I feel for her future. God knows what will become of this Country and her old ways and traditions if Richmond falls." George Atzerodt wore a glum expression.

"I thought you were only saying on Friday that the tide might be turning for the Confederacy. Your cheerfulness seems to have quickly evaporated."

"Things looked bad after September's setback in western Maryland but, yes…I'll admit I was cock-a-hoop to hear of the recent victory at Fredericksburg. The Union got a bloody nose alright and with it Richmond should breathe more easily. But what did that Greek fellow say about seeing a single swallow?…that it doesn't make a…"

"Oh, for goodness sake, George. You're such a pessimist. Go and sort out the tree, then sit yourself down and I'll bring you that glass of mulled wine. By the way, are you working this week, only money's getting tight?"

"I've got a small job to finish tomorrow morning. But that's it before Christmas. By the way, I'm half expecting some night work sometime during the festive period. If so, I'll get a message from Captain Cox. One of his niggers will bring word."

"Trust your wretched underground work to interrupt our Christmas," said Rose, indignantly. "What's going to happen to Greta and me if you're caught?"

George offered no comment. It was not the first time Rose had expressed her resentment over the impact and potential danger of his clandestine activities. Yet it was the more immediate concern of a dwindling household budget that presently caused her greater worry.

"Just make sure you stay well clear of Brawner's this side of the New Year. It really annoys me when you slink away to that awful tavern. The trouble is, George, you're irresponsible. You're never satisfied with a single drink, preferring to spend time and hard earned money we can ill-afford. The truth is our coffers won't stand the cost of your favourite tipple. You'll have to make do with Rose Wheeler's homemade gluehwein."

★ ★ ★

"I do miss my childhood Christmases, Rose...back in Dorna. They were really special." It was Christmas Eve. George Atzerodt was sitting at the table in the parlour, sifting through a bag of sweet chestnuts in search of the best to roast. Rose busied herself trimming the tree.

"I'm sure this time of year is special for most children of Christian families all over the world," said Rose, "but clearly far from special for many American families this year as the war drags on and keeps menfolk far from home. For many it will be a Christmastide blighted by bereavement. Just think of all the sad homes with wet-eyed young widows and fatherless children. And what of the soldiers themselves, encamped in the cold with meagre rations and deprived of home comforts? Poor wretches deserve better at this time."

"I agree with you Rose. Do you know, they're saying many of the wounded froze to death in the snow and cold after Fredericksburg. Thank God most were Union men."

"That's not very charitable George. The men on both sides are simply doing their duty, fighting and dying for their cause. And it's sobering to contemplate, not least at Christmas, that they are all God's children."

"Hmm. Thank the Lord you're not a Richmond politician or a Confederate general my dear," opined George as he made a wry face. "By the way, where's Greta? Asleep?"

"You don't pay attention to things I say," said Rose with mild irritation. "I told you a half hour since that young Ella, next door, was looking after her while I trim the tree. She loves being with Ella and, when I fetch her, it'll be a wonderful surprise for the little darling to see the tree adorned with its candles and baubles. Oh, and by the way, here's a surprise for you, my dear. I've made some of your beloved iced lebkuchen... gingerbreads... into which I have set cotton loops so I might also hang them upon the tree."

"Thank you, Rose. Now that will take me back to my childhood, seeing the tannenbaum bedecked with lebkuchen. You know, Holy Eve was such a joyous time. After supper Mother would call us into the parlour to see the tannenbaum all lit and decorated. We would then exchange our gifts before trudging off through the snow to Mass in our little church. I can hear the choir singing *Stille Nacht, Heilige Nacht*. I remember the last occasion before we set sail to make our home in Maryland. It was snowing hard as we stepped out of church into the village street. The night was truly a silent one…it was as if you could hear the hush, the stillness, amid the tumbling snowflakes. It struck me as magical."

"Well," said Rose, "I'm sure it'll be magical this evening when you see little Greta's face. I think she'll love the tree. But tomorrow will be soon enough to exchange our presents. By the way, we must wrap her gift from that kind gentleman down in Bel Alton."

"That's true. I'd quite forgotten about it. I put it in the little pine closet in the bedroom. I'll fetch it now."

George had been touched by the kindness of the old gentleman from Bel Alton. A few weeks previously, when he had called at the 'Chimney House' to collect his buggy and settle his account, he had presented the carriage painter with a Christmas gift for his daughter. He had previously met the little girl when, in November, he had chanced upon George and Rose one market day. The elderly gentleman had been quite taken, quite entranced, by the child, explaining later that, while blessed with two sons, he had lost two infant daughters to diphtheria. Perhaps this part-explained his subsequent kindness but George also saw it as being indicative of the old man's satisfaction with his work That was pleasing in itself, since the carriage painter very much relied upon recommendation and work was becoming increasingly scarce in these troubled times. The actual gift, which appeared most apt – given the nature of George's trade – was an exquisitely carved model of an open carriage and pair. It had, according to its giver, been fashioned and painted by a long-serving house slave adept in working with wood. In the rich, blue carriage with its gilded detail sat a newly betrothed couple. It was pulled by two greys. Its liveried driver, with stove-pipe hat, sat upright on the box.

George had been profuse with his thanks but the old gentleman had dismissed his own generosity as of no great import. "After all," he said, "like me, old Clarence is in his sixties. He's been with the family since he was a boy and gone are the days when we worked him hard. Now, with more time to himself, he is permitted to indulge his liking and aptitude for carving such trinkets."

"I'm just about finished now," exclaimed Rose, with satisfaction evident in her voice, as George returned with the little wooden present for Greta. "What do you think of our Christma...of our *tannenbaum*, George?"

"It looks grand, my dear. You've done well."

"Good. Now, I'll find some paper and string and we'll wrap Greta's gift. Then I'll go and fetch her and we'll see what she makes of the tree." There was excitement, a sense of eager anticipation, in Rose Wheeler's words.

As George bent to stoke the fire and add a fresh shagbark log, there came a determined thud upon the front door.

"That could be young Ella with Greta," exclaimed Rose. "Perhaps, bless her, she's become difficult or maybe she just wants to come home. But that's fine. It saves me going out and the tree is ready."

Struggling to his feet, George picked up his glass and swigged the last vestiges of his mulled wine before venturing out into the passage. As he opened the front door, fully expecting to see Greta in Ella's arms, it was with some surprise he found himself confronted by a tall negro.

"Mas'r...compliments of Cap'n Cox," said the visitor, thrusting a wax-sealed envelope into George's hand.

George knew what was coming and must have looked downcast as he opened the envelope and sidled back into the passage to angle the letter beneath the spreading light of a paraffin lamp. It wasn't as if he didn't want the expected assignment but he balked at the thought of having to turn out on Holy Eve. After a minute or so digesting the missive's content, George turned once again towards the negro. "Tell your master that it will be done and I will see him at the 'Chimney House' on Thursday."

"Yes, mas'r." And with that the negro turned away and made off. George noticed that what was left of Sunday's snow was eerily illuminated beneath a moonlit sky; and the crusting effect of an early frost was evident from the snow-crunching noise of the negro's retreating steps.

"I gather I was wrong...it wasn't Greta, then," said Rose, as George returned to the warmth of the festive-looking parlour.

"It was Cox's darkey. I should have realised. I half expected it as I said before."

"So what is required of you and when?" asked Rose, dejectedly.

"Not tonight, thank God, but late tomorrow night and into Thursday. One in the morning. But don't worry, Rose. I'll not be crossing the river. It seems a courier is bringing over an important package from Richmond. I'll be taking a storm lantern to aid the boat's entry into Pope's Creek.

The Captain says he wouldn't have troubled me but for the fact that Mister Jones, his foster brother, is away from home at present."

"Jones?"

"Yes, you remember. The fellow who was arrested last year for so-called disloyal practices. He was thrown into the Old Capitol Prison for several months. Well, he's an important agent in Charles County. According to the Captain, had he been at home, Mister Jones would have wanted to see this package safely ashore himself. Now I'll take delivery of it and pass it to the Captain on Thursday."

"There's the door again," said Rose, reacting to yet another knock. "I'm sure this will be Ella with Greta."

As Rose surveyed the tree and made some final adjustments to the placing of the gingerbreads, George returned to the entrance passage and opened the front door. Rose listened carefully.

"Papa! Papa!," came the shrill and excitable young voice on the threshold. "Christmas, papa…it's Christmas!"

"I've just been reading a Christmas story to Greta," said Ella in explanation.

"Yes it is, Greta, dear. It's Christmas Eve. Say thank you and goodnight to Ella, my child, then I'll carry you into the parlour. But remember to keep your eyes closed until I tell you to open them," whispered George. "Your mama and I have a surprise for you."

Four

From Railroad Duty To Port Hudson
January To July 1863

Boutte Station, New Orleans, Louisiana
February 6th 1863

Dear Mother,

I would like to think that sight of my handwriting will lift your heart when the postman drops the envelope containing this missive upon the passage carpet. You will not have received word from me since I penned a letter in St John's, Newfoundland, which left with the mail steamer for Halifax. That would have been in the early part of September last and would have crossed with yours, which I received at the end of that month.

Oh, Mother! Just where do I start? I have delayed writing long enough… too long. But you will see shortly, as you read on, why this has proved such a distressing task for me to undertake. I hardly know where to begin but, suffice to say, I have parted company with the Cygnet and now find myself a soldier of the United States of America. I say I have delayed too long and, yes, I am only too aware, long enough for the Cygnet to have returned to Portsmouth. I just hope it has not, since, in those circumstances, disclosure of my desertion will not be news to you. Instead, you will have already learned of my erring ways and doubtless formed your own opinions. Otherwise, this will come to you as a complete shock and for that, dear Mother, I can but tender my profuse and heartfelt apologies.

I suppose my problems really only began on the Cygnet, although, as you know, I was never enamoured about joining the Navy, notwithstanding Uncle

James' insistence that I should. Well, to be honest, I adapted successfully enough to life aboard the Excellent and Edgar. Yet the Cygnet was altogether a different kettle of fish. I suppose, in part, my troubles were of my own making. I made careless mistakes – not least, on one occasion, spoiling a significant amount of fresh meat – and before long I found myself an unpopular steward. And I soon discovered, Mother, that to alienate superiors and be a target of antipathy upon such a modest vessel as a gunboat, can make for a most uncomfortable existence. Well, my life became so wretched that, last September, when on shore leave in Halifax, Nova Scotia, I seized the opportunity not to return to my ship. However, I was insufficiently vigilant and was picked up by a party of Royal Marines from the Nimble. On being returned to the Cygnet, I was sentenced to four weeks in the local Penitentiary. There, with the assistance of others, I hatched a plan to try again to part company with my ship. Well, to cut a long story short, the plan met with success and, by late November, I had found my way to Baltimore with the resolve to enlist in the Union Army. There I joined a regiment of New York State Volunteers and, after an eventful journey south, we arrived, on New Year's Eve, at the mouth of the great Mississippi River.

Since then we have entered upon a landscape of most singular character and where water rules supreme. Our handsome barque, the Voltigeur, was towed up river behind a labouring tugboat which initially led us through a watery land of low, broken mudflats and swamp strewn with sedge and canebrake. Here wildlife flourished and pelicans and alligators were the source of entertainment for those unaccustomed to such creatures. That, I might add, was most, for the regiment is largely comprised of fellows who hail from remote rural communities in northern New York State. And all the while our enjoyment of the scenery was hindered by smut-emitting whorls of black smoke belched forth by our intrepid tug. Magnolia forests and cypress swamps were soon in evidence, later displaced, behind the levees, by fields of corn, sugar cane and fruit-laden orange orchards, where parties of negroes watched in awe as we drifted by. Well Mother, those oranges were heaven-sent, so sweet and juicy after ship's rations. I purchased some from a huckster who came out to us in his open boat when we dropped anchor a short distance below the city of New Orleans.

Well, when we got underway once more, it was to marvel at the passing sight of that grand city, a city now firmly in the grip of military occupation. Men crowded the starboard side of the ship and clung to shroud and ratline to absorb the sights. The old city's stretch of river teemed with vessels of all description, its levees crammed with ships of war and ornately timbered side and stern-wheel paddlers as far as the eye could see. In contrast, the dockside manufactories, the warehouses and cotton presses appeared down at heel, such has been the effect of the war upon New Orleans' trade. In time we reached the village of Carrollton, a few miles beyond the city, where we left the Voltigeur and were re-united, in camp, with three of our companies who had sailed in another transport. There we pitched our wedge tents and were soon immersed in the monotony of daily drills and parades. Yet we had barely begun to settle in than we received orders to pack up and be ready to march.

Well, we moved out in the early hours of the seventh of January. We made for the river where we embarked upon a fine old Mississippi steamboat, an ornamented side-wheeler with twin smoke-stacks and such a low hull and lofty proportion to suggest she might keel over in a stiff wind. Upon this we were conveyed to Algiers, a settlement located across the river from New Orleans and from where a railroad (strangely the American people don't speak of railways) runs west to Brashear City. This is known as the New Orleans, Opelousas and Great Western Railroad. We were under instruction to guard the track and, as soon as everything was loaded upon the carriages (the Americans call them cars), we headed out into the countryside. It was proposed that each of our companies be camped at a different station along the railroad from where we would undertake picket duty. You know, Mother, for a while the track outside Algiers ran close to the levee and, at intervals, groups of little negro children (they call them pickaninnies) stood in awe of the passing steam engine with its cars crammed with blue-coated soldiers. Seeing those poor mites on top of the levee through our swirling, smoky emissions, fondly took me back to school days at Forton. In that moment I was standing upon old Parson Veck's spoil heap, below his vegetable plot, watching the Royal party steam towards the Clarence Yard jetty. To think how life is so different for me now.

My particular company's duty is to guard Boutte station and to patrol between picket posts in both directions such that, collectively, our companies patrol the whole track. It is a desolate little place comprising a few rough-timbered houses on the fringe of a cypress swamp and we have pitched our tents alongside the track. Well, at present we have encountered no rebs and life is altogether far from irksome. With my comrades being largely country boys they have fared well in the art of snaring wildfowl, rabbits and cat-fish, all of which has served us admirably when cooked on the fry-pan or cast into the camp-fire mess kettle. And those exquisite oranges remain plentiful. Oh, and yesterday, when off duty, I was one of a handful of men permitted to visit a nearby plantation and its sugar-mill where we came to appreciate the rudiments of growing and processing sugar cane. And on the last Sabbath, several of us, including two of the commissioned officers, attended a negro prayer meeting. Such a revelation it proved, what with their strange songs and incantations. As for the swathes of bald cypress swamp, they are a most peculiar feature of this land. The trees rise out of the water itself where the trunks are strangely thickened and fluted, their overhead canopies weirdly draped with Spanish moss. One of our sergeants warned me against venturing into or around these swamps since, by all accounts, they harbour some deadly water snakes.

So, Mother, that is enough of my present situation. I dearly hope you will find it in your heart to write me a reply and, longingly, I will wait for it. But as one guilty of such errancy and imprudence I can understand should you find it difficult to do so, after all, I am swift to acknowledge that I have acted most improperly. In consequence, if God spares me through the coming trials and tribulations, that will surely test me in this conflict, I need to return home and do whatever is required of me to earn the forgiveness and respect of my kith and kin. I am not proud of what I have done, yet, in all honesty, I do not feel ashamed, for in this army I know I am fighting for a good cause, which is to free the hapless negroes from the shackles of bondage. Do you remember Missus Stowe's book, 'Uncle Tom's Cabin' that dear Uncle Charley gave me on my thirteenth birthday? Well, in my short time in this country I've already seen the reality of it – the effect of slavery upon the blacks. It's true enough. I've seen the wretched system in practice and, although I may have disgraced myself and brought disgrace upon my family, I feel I am beginning to tread the road of redemption so long as I remain steadfast to this cause. And, Mother, my enlistment has permitted me to place money in the National Bank which should enable me to return to the Old Country should I emerge unscathed from this war.

Now, Mother, please give my love to dear Grandma and to Uncle Charley and my kind regards to any enquiring friends. How is dear Grandma? I often think of her sitting by the fireside with Palmerston, her black cat, asleep on her lap. I hope she won't think too ill of me and, Mother, if you cannot bring yourself to write me a lengthy missive then a short note would suffice, just to tell me that Grandma, Uncle Charley and yourself are all in rude health. Is Uncle James still at sea? Knowing he is such a dedicated sailor and steward I *fear my actions will be viewed as so grave, in his opinion, as to be unforgivable. Bearing in mind his aspirations for me I fully expect him to be enraged and to feel personally slighted by news of my desertion.*

I will now conclude, dear Mother, for I am shortly to commence a spell of picket duty. I will close with kindest love from your erring yet ever affectionate son,

William Reynolds

P.S. I still carry the little palm cross given me by Parson Veck on that last Palm Sunday at Forton. It is now somewhat broken but I constantly keep it close, tucked inside my tunic.

Direct. William Reynolds
Co. E 114 Regt. N.Y.S.V
Department of the Gulf
19th Army Corps
Louisiana

William returned to the top of the first page and added the day's date. He had refrained from doing so earlier since it had taken him three sittings to complete his letter. He sat on the edge of the wooden platform, outside and beneath the timbered canopy of the little station house, the ubiquitous cracker box top on his lap supporting his final page. Throughout the morning the sun had gathered strength in a cloudless sky producing a warmth to rival that of an English summer's day. William lifted his forage cap and, in the same movement, used his cuff to wipe his sweaty brow. From the edge of the nearby cypress swamp something croaked. There came a croaked reply and then a flurry of other weird and unrecognisable noises from within the rank and fearsome habitat. The writer cleaned his pen with a piece of rag and drained what fluid remained in his well back into the Company ink bottle. Then he corked the receptacle. The sun glinted on the rails below and upon shards of iridescent glass, the remnants of an inkwell he had accidentally let fall upon the track amid the emotional distraction – three weeks ago – of attempting to start his letter. He winced. The dazzling light was fleeting. Now it had gone. Gone also was something which had troubled William since he left Halifax: the need to grasp the nettle…to write to his mother, tell of his whereabouts and make known his misdemeanours. Well, he had done it. It had been an accomplishment and, as such, lifted a weight from his shoulders.

★ ★ ★

It was the middle of April, three and a half months after the regiment had arrived in Louisiana. In January, while on railroad duty, it had been disclosed that General Banks' Army was to be known as the Nineteenth Army Corps within which the One Hundred and Fourteenth was to be brigaded with, among others, two New York infantry regiments – the Seventy Fifth and the One Hundred and Sixtieth. This brigade, the second among the three brigades comprising the Corps' First Division, was placed under the command of Brigadier-General Godfrey Weitzel, a young, yet very experienced officer, who was soon to earn the respect and devotion of those who served beneath him. Weitzel's Second Brigade also numbered the men of the Eighth Vermont and Twelfth Connecticut within its ranks and from the ninth of April it began a marched advance westwards along the course of the Bayou Teche in pursuit of Richard Taylor's retreating Confederates. Accompanying the brigade were those of Brigadier-General William Emory's Third Division.

On the morning of April the nineteenth, the One Hundred and Fourteenth found itself mopping up after a night of torrential rain and thunderstorms. The previous day the troops had bivouaced upon open prairie, a few miles beyond and above the meanderings of the Teche and not far from the village of St Martinsville. In the early dawn, as the men of the regiment dried and rolled up their rubber blankets, it was in expectation of pushing on up country, towards Opelousas, that occupied everyone's thoughts. But it was not to be. As the expedition moved off, at around five in the morning, it was without the One Hundred and Fourteenth. Colonel Elisha Smith was in receipt of fresh orders for the regiment to turn back and retrace its steps to Brashear City from where it had commenced its push up the Teche, one of the principal backwaters of the great Mississippi. Its new mission was to confiscate what cattle might be rounded-up across the plains and to drive these – together with horses and saddlery seized from local planters – back to Brashear, for the Army's use.

This proved extremely arduous work. Despite some of the men being proficient enough on the backs of requisitioned ponies, here was a regiment of foot soldiers having to act as drovers to several thousand head of cattle; and, at night, despite posting ample guards upon the livestock, many animals managed to escape, necessitating efforts to retrieve them the following morning. Yet, come the twenty eighth of the month, the regiment moved to within sight of Brashear City. Tired in body, their uniforms frayed, tattered and dust ingrained, the men had, by midday, disembarked from the steamboat transporting them across Berwick Bay and entered their former camping ground outside Brashear City.

In camp little had changed since April the ninth when the regiment departed. The company streets and standing tents were as the men had left them. Yet arrival back in camp for the exhausted One Hundred and Fourteenth brought no immediate respite. After a delayed dinner call and a sating of craving stomachs with salt horse and hard crackers, orders were given to all companies to busy themselves in a range of fatigue duties, not least the procurement of fresh water and kindling wood and the sprucing-up of the camp. Interspersed with such labours, numbers from each company, in turn, were directed to attend the Quartermaster's stores to draw new uniforms and shoes. Once the whole of Company E had done so and the men had returned to their tents, there was much good humour as some fellows strutted about in their new duds. Yet the cheerfulness was not so much triggered by the issue of fresh garments as by the realisation that they had made it back to Brashear City with the prospect of a less trying time in camp.

"Thank Christ that's finished with," exclaimed a weary private. Perched on something resembling a milking stool, the fellow struggled to remove his shoes which seemed loath to part company with the inertial fusion of worn leather, army socks and hot, blistered feet.

"Once you've got those off you'll find difficulty fitting into new brogans," remarked another. "What with your feet being swollen, that is."

"Sergeant Stoughton has lent me this pot of emollient," he replied, pointing to a little jar of ointment. "Says he swears by it for chafed feet. Well, if there's no improvement by morning I'll just have to answer to sick-call and try to appeal to the better nature of Mister Surgeon to get me excused fatigue duties and drills."

"I wish you luck," chuckled the other. "As you say, man, it's good to get that done with. I can't see me ever wanting to be a cattle drover."

"I'd have preferred to stay with Weitzel and Emory, chasing those darned skedaddling rebs."

"So would most of us I guess. Trouble is we'd still be on the march and think of your feet. Think of it that way."

"Hmm," mused the footsore soldier. "Right enough, I guess. And, when there were no opportunities for foraging, the victuals…such as they could be called victuals…were mighty grim."

"Mighty grim when driving back them beeves, if you ask me, soldier. Fresh beef can be mighty fine…yet day after day for breakfast, dinner and supper…oh, no, I soon began hankering for camp grub."

"Sure enough, same thing day after day and it gets…" The footsore soldier's words tailed off, to be quickly superseded by a wincing groan that signified extreme discomfort. He had by now taken to applying the blade of a bowie knife to one of his stubborn shoes. While this had made short shrift of ripping open the worn leather, the piece which he prised from around his heel dragged with it a weeping, agglutinated blend of blistered skin and matted sock.

A few tents further along the company street, while this conversation and discomfort was being played out, amid other proximate banter and peacocking, William Reynolds paid scant attention to his pile of new garments and shoes. Instead, he sat pre-occupied, beset with thoughts which mixed joy and feelings of trepidation. A bag of mail had arrived in camp a few days before Company E's return and with it came a letter, its envelope bearing a Portsmouth postmark and the stamp of the transatlantic Black Ball Line packet boat. William had been in possession of the letter for all of ten minutes. Now he sat upon a barrel, eyeing the envelope and vacillating at length upon its opening. Would it be damning of his past behaviour? Might there, just conceivably, be any words of endearment? Given that seven months had flown by since he last received word from home, might it carry unwelcome news? Such thoughts waxed in William's mind until, finally, he summoned up the courage to slit open the envelope. Whatever the letter contained, his mother had at least been prepared to write to him.

31 King Street
Portsea
Hants

20th March 1863

Dear William,

What have you done, son? Just what possessed you? At first it thrilled us to hear from you and to learn that you are well after such a long time. Your Grandma and I have been most anxious at not having had word from you and we assumed a letter had gone astray. Yes, sight of your handwriting did, indeed, lift our hearts. Nevertheless, as I read your letter to Grandma, our joy was swiftly dashed on learning of your recklessness and of the undoubted disgrace you have brought upon this family. I have to judge it a blessing that your dear father is not around to learn of your iniquitous and unforgivable behaviour – and to think, William, you have proceeded to place yourself in the utmost danger as a soldier fighting in a foreign conflict. Since hearing your news I have noticed that your Grandma has become fretful and is finding sleep difficult. I thought she had been truly inured to coping with kin being placed in great danger, what with seeing all three of her sons go off to war but, being so fond of you, and what with your transgression – well, it's hit her hard. So yesterday I called upon the Queen Street pharmacist who has mixed her some herbal calmative. I'm hoping it will have the desired effect.

Your Uncle Charley was shocked by your news but has not voiced to me any condemnation of your actions. He is loyal, of course, and has always been full of regard for you, but I sense, William, he is quietly very disappointed. As to your Uncle James, he is back home from sea. He has taken up residence with us here in King Street and taken over the lease, thus relieving Grandma of such responsibility. Alas, I cannot begin to describe his chagrin. My disclosure of your news left him, at first, dumbfounded, then furious, since when he has become withdrawn and irascible. It has clearly had a profound effect on him and during the height of his fury he vowed never to speak to you again. You will doubtless find that upsetting, William, but I suspect your uncle will mellow with time – for time, they say, is a great healer.

Now, I cannot recall whether I told you in my last letter that your Uncle John – my eldest brother – returned from military service, in India, in February last year. He served there a total of thirteen years and brought home with him a young wife, Jane, and a baby daughter who I was delighted to hear they had named Charlotte. Poor Jane. She is but a child herself and had lost her first husband – a colour sergeant in your uncle's regiment – to dysentery. With his time in the regiment having expired, Uncle John and his wife have settled in Hatfield where he has joined the staff of the Hertfordshire Militia. As instructor to the regimental drum and fife band I imagine he is in his element once again, added to which he has recently written to say they have just been blessed with a second daughter.

So, William, it has been of great cheer to us here in King Street to have had two of your uncles return safely from foreign parts, not least for your dear Grandma. Now we somehow have to absorb the shattering news that you have needlessly placed yourself in grave danger, a worry greatly exacerbated, should I say, by the manner in which you have gone about becoming a soldier and with it wreaking ignominy upon our good name.

I have to admit, however, notwithstanding your serious transgression, that I do not lose sight of the fact that I am your Mother and, whilst this is all very distressing, I implore you to remain alert at all times and to do your utmost to keep yourself safe. Under no circumstances forget to say your prayers and put your trust in the Lord. And, son, write to us often, to help allay and temper our concerns. That would be a great comfort. Your Grandma and I will steadfastly pray for your safety and for an early end to this rebellion you have committed yourself to help quell. I will now close, Willie, with tender and warm-hearted wishes from your ever loving, yet heavy-hearted Mother,

Charlotte Reynolds

William raised his eyes from the letter and looked straight along the company street. The footsore private, grim-faced, still sat on the squat stool as he now applied Sergeant Stoughton's emollient to bare, blistered feet. Nearby, Isaiah Bryant, adorned in his new pants and tunic, aped one of the brigade's drill sergeants to the amusement of two comrades. Both little cameos lay in William's line of sight, yet he registered neither, such was the engrossing force of his immediate thoughts. The letter's content could have been worse in its condemnation. His Mother had not considered him so unworthy as to disown him. Neither had his Grandma nor Uncle Charley. As for Uncle James, it was he who had been responsible in the first place for setting him on this course in life. It didn't bother him that he had reacted in the way he did. What did trouble him, however, was the hurt his actions had caused to those dear to him. He always knew that running from the *Cygnet* would be greeted with a mixture of shock, dismay and anger among his nearest and dearest yet it was not until now, seeing such expressed in his Mother's hand, that William began to appreciate the gravity and selfishness of his actions.

Supper was taken that first evening back in Brashear City around a multitude of camp fires, there having been insufficient time to organise the company cooks' kitchens. Yet this was the cause of little displeasure since many preferred to attend to cooking their own rations which were doled out under the watchful eyes of the orderly sergeants. During the afternoon the issue of new clothing, the washing of sweat-stained, unsavoury bodies and visits to the camp barber's chair for long overdue shaves had taken precedence over afternoon drills. Fortunately, the supply of new shirts and underclothing served to nullify any requirement to sit and skirmish for graybacks or to plunge lice-ridden garments into mess kettles of boiling salt water. Instead, great delight was taken that evening in setting aside much of the newly-gathered firewood in favour of discarded and infested flannel. In this way was helped kindle many a little pile of river birch logs over which kettles of simmering coffee began releasing wreathing columns of steam into the early evening sky. As to the day's distributed victuals, most seemed thankful to have bidden farewell to what had become the recent customary – albeit wholesome – supper of fresh beef. For once the proffered pork rations seemed inviting, the majority opting to commit these to camp fire fry pans. The cooked meat was then consumed with a boiled broth conjured from dessicated vegetables along with the ubiquitous hardtack biscuits, now rendered more palatable from being fried in hog grease. With tin cups re-charged from coffee-boilers, some simply sat, talked and smoked within the glow of dying embers. Others withdrew to engage in leisure pursuits. Yet given the fatigue exacted by days of cattle driving, these were pursuits of an essentially passive nature with most – Private Reynolds included – choosing to seize an opportunity to write home.

In William's case it was imperative to put pen to paper sooner rather than later. While back in camp, with a greater prospect of finding time for letter writing, he knew only too well that circumstances could change in a trice. Ashamed and angered, his mother had, nevertheless, asked him to write often and this he resolved to do, for he was eager to commit to anything that might help make amends for his misdemeanours. Reconciliation with his loved ones, after all, must be his ultimate goal, albeit that atoning for his actions in the eyes of Uncle James had to be considered a lost cause. But with that he could cope.

William returned to his tent and gathered from his knapsack what could be recovered from the stationery supplies he acquired at Camp Belger. These amounted to a bone-handled pen and a few envelopes, plus a small roll of tinted letter paper, now a trifle grubby but impressed with the mark of a Massachusetts paper mill and evidently of good quality. He then picked up a little bottle of ink and some fresh nibs, newly acquired that afternoon from Parce, the sutler, together with a short piece of planking. This he had salvaged from the woodpile, for use as a lap-board. Outside his tent he pushed over the hogshead cask on which he had earlier perched and proceeded to sit upon its hooped staves, thereby placing within easy reach, his inkbottle, which he'd steadied amid the lush clover lapping his feet. Finally, having tucked a piece of cleaning rag beneath his right thigh and treated his pen to a new nib, William lost no time in putting ink to paper. Having already laid bare his transgressions and thus lanced and expelled the reticence which had delayed that first letter home, his words – perhaps not surprisingly – flowed with a greater briskness than they had at Boutte.

Brashear City, La., USA
April 28th 1863

Dear Mother,

I received your letter this afternoon following my regiment's return to Brashear City where we are now encamped and felt overjoyed that you had considered my own worthy of a reply, despite my wayward behaviour. Yet I am alarmed and remorseful that, in writing my letter, I caused you and Grandma such undeserved distress and trust, henceforth, I will have the self-discipline to conduct myself in a fitting manner, sufficient to help expiate the wrong.

You say, Mother, that it would be a great comfort to you and Grandma to receive regular word from me and, with this in mind, and suddenly finding myself back in the relative quietude of camp, I am seizing the opportunity to promptly put pen to paper. I will begin by recounting what has happened to me since I wrote to you last. Well, within a day of finishing my letter at Boutte station, we were relieved of our railroad duty, the Regiment moving to Brashear City where it was re-united for the first time since we came south. We finally settled where we find ourselves once again, on a pleasant enough site overlooking Berwick Bay – pleasant enough, that is, excepting for the country being a veritable waterland, much of it stagnant and a breeding ground for countless mosquitos which prove a bane once the sun has gone down. Back here now, I am again aware of the little pests' presence and suspect, come the order for lights to be extinguished, they will once again become a nuisance. Previously, this, and especially the absence of fresh water, seemed to contribute to a high rate of sickness and we were issued with a whisky ration and quinine to help combat local ailments. I'm just hoping they reinstate the ration, since, although I never felt queer, it was grand to have a regular wee nip.

Well, Mother, things became a trifle monotonous in camp last time, or, should I say, the endless drill practice did, but at least I began to feel I was becoming proficient enough in the routines. There was little excitement, save for occasionally catching sight of some enemy pickets across the Bay and then, for a spell, pulling back from Brashear in an attempt to deceive the rebels. Anyway, in time, preparations to make an advance against the Confederate forces began to gather pace, culminating in our being issued with three days' rations and sufficient ammunition to fill our cartridge boxes. Then, on the ninth of April, the Army was transported across the Bay, by gunboats, to Berwick City. We left there two days later, marching along the shore line, then along the dusty banks of the Atchafalaya River. And we marched with a jaunt and a swagger, uplifted by the thought of excitement ahead and by the music of the regimental bands. Ahead we could occasionally hear the sounds of skirmishing and rebel artillery, before, late in the afternoon, we reached a place called Pattersonville where we made camp. The next morning we ceased following the Atchafalaya and began moving along the banks of the Bayou Teche until, again, with the afternoon well advanced, we found ourselves within a few miles of a heavily manned Rebel fortification known as Fort Bisland. By now we were pushing on through a field of sugar cane in battle formation, when, all of a sudden, the air was filled with the scream of shot and shell. Well, Mother, despite my time with Excellent's gunnery school, I had never heard the likes of such a thunderous noise and of attendant flame and smoke as our batteries, in the rear, began giving the Rebel artillery a good taste of their own medicine. Fortunately, in due course, we were ordered back, beyond the range of the Rebel fire, where we bivouaced for the night amongst the cane. Next day we advanced once more, only for the artillery to open up again with little work for us infantrymen to do; and, as soon as our gunners – now occupying a more forward position – were spent of ammunition, they would limber up and gallop by, amid much noise and dust, to replenish their caissons. Meanwhile, our regiment did come under fire from the cover of nearby woods but another New York unit successfully flushed the Rebels out – yet not before we suffered some casualties. A highlight of the afternoon – greeted by a big cheer – was when one of our batteries took the roof off a distant sugar mill from where Rebel officers were surveying the scene of the battle. Then, the following morning, as we anticipated moving forward to undertake an infantry advance on the pulverised fort, there came loud cheers *from the front as a column of our men went over the breastworks unopposed. The enemy had fled overnight.*

William's eyes were beginning to feel strained, this, in all probability, more the product of extreme tiredness than the effect of fading light. It was turning eight o'clock, a half hour before assembly would be sounded to signal evening roll call. William placed his writing materials aside, rose to his feet and turned away. In a few moments he had returned with his bayonet and a candle. Keeping hold of the latter, he pushed the point of the weapon's blade into the ground, to the side of the hogshead, then ambled across to the remnants of the camp fire around which he and several comrades had partaken of their suppers. Having ignited the tallow's wick among the glowing embers, William returned to his makeshift seat, cupping his hand about the flickering, young flame as he did so. He firmly secured the candle in the shank of the bayonet, then immediately sat down and resumed his letter.

So, Mother, although the artillery did most of the work, our regiment was commended for the manner in which it conducted itself under fire and for showing unflinching bravery. I suppose I've now seen the elephant, as they say here when an untried or green regiment first sees action. Well, after the battle's conclusion, we pressed on in pursuit of those Johnny Rebs and, all the while, our numbers swelled beneath a withering sun, our dust-dried vocal organs helping to sustain us with rousing Union songs. As we passed each grand plantation house we were joined by joyful slaves – men, women and children – most carrying their bundles of mean possessions on the end of sticks and shouldered in the manner by which we carry our muskets. And so we tramped on in the wake of the enemy and ahead of our negro followers who regarded us bluecoats – Mister Linkum's sojers they call us – as their blessed liberators. Then, some eight days after leaving Brashear City, beyond a place called Martinsville, we came upon some prairie land where cattle grazed in great number. We camped there for two nights, taking some much valued respite from the hot march and grasping the opportunity to bathe and cleanse our weary bodies. Come the nineteenth of April, as the Army moved on, it was with surprise and no little irritation that our Regiment was ordered to round up and confiscate much of the local cattle. Evidently, our mission was to drive the beeves back to Brashear City where we eventually arrived, earlier today, after corralling the livestock on the other side of the

Bay. Now the poor beasts will swim across and be transported to Algiers for slaughter to help keep the Army supplied with fresh meat. As for me, I sit here, footsore and tired, outside my tent, digesting my supper of camp victuals. It's a balmy evening by English standards and, as the darkness intensifies, the mosquitos and moths are especially active in the little pool of light cast by my candle. And such is the stillness of the air that my flame has not guttered but remained steadfast.

I will now set about finishing this letter, Mother, since, in about ten minutes, we will be called to what is termed tattoo, the day's final roll call. Thereafter we have half an hour to ready ourselves to turn in to bed and extinguish all lights. You know, in times of solitude, I will frequently recall Home Sweet Home. Sometimes, in my mind's eye, I picture the springtime daffodils upon the glebe land at Forton, their pretty heads tossed in the chill March breeze. And there, wending our way among them, on the way to church, are you and me and Grandma. At other times I find my thoughts among the shops in Queen Street, on Christmas Eve, all gaily lit for the festive season, the mingling street smells from food vendors' trays and stalls, the latter eerily illuminated by candles flickering behind murky tubes of oiled-paper. The general merriment of the festive season is a fillip to all – barring, sadly, the more destitute – while Dodds, the poulterer, tries to entice passers-by with knock down prices for what remains of his geese and turkeys that hang plucked and limp over a blood-stained pavement. Such modest yet treasured scenes, Mother, which, if God is merciful to me through this conflict, I would hope to experience once again. In the meantime, I keep my portraits of you and Grandma and Uncle Charley in my knapsack and look at them often.

I will now conclude, Mother, by sending my love to you all and will write to you again once in receipt of what will be your anxiously awaited reply. I close with fondest love from your repentant and affectionate son,

William Reynolds

Direct as before.
William Reynolds
Co. E 114th Regt. N.Y.S.V.
Department of the Gulf
19th Army Corps
Louisiana

William determined, in referring to his family portraits, to refrain from any mention of Uncle James; after all he no longer had his photograph, having resolved to leave it upon the *Cygnet*. Yet it wasn't simply that. Omission of his name was telling in itself and, as such, the source of some personal gratification. He was also careful not to mention too much about Bisland…the fear when pinned down in the cane, the roar of grape and the hiss of countless minie balls overhead…the sound of bursting shells, some coming to ground and showering the concealed infantry with ripped up stalks and dirt…battle wounds and, in particular, on the return cattle drive, the sight of enemy dead in and around the hurriedly abandoned fort – poor wretches hastily left in the fields with barely a spadeful of earth to cover them. Rotting flesh. Squirming, bloated maggots.

Lights out and sleep was swift to embrace the weary Englishman. The sound of that distinctive rattle of drumsticks, which was taps, had barely faded when he succumbed to slumber.

★ ★ ★

It was probably true to say that quiet optimism pervaded the minds of the vast majority of the men of the One Hundred and Fourteenth that they were now truly destined to rejoin their brigade. Recent experience did nothing to support this view, yet perhaps it was simply time to expect a change of fortune, there being a widespread sense that the steamship *Cahawba* was carrying the regiment to a brand new chapter in the campaign.

It was early in the evening of the twenty-ninth day of May. A few hours had elapsed since the regiment clambered off the cars at Algiers station, marched through the docks and joined the Ninety First New York aboard the steamship. The vessel throbbed. Escaping steam hissed. The *Cahawba* cast off from her riverside berth, her cork-stuffed, canvas fenders emitting a discordant, creaking sound as they grated against the wharf's resilient old timbers. Once underway, soldiers crowded the vessel's sides to smoke and jaw and to watch, with great curiosity, the big city slip by beyond its levee. William found himself leaning against the starboard bulwark next to Ezra Wilson, his old friend from Belger days. "I had a feeling we'd end up joining the rest of the brigade" said Wilson.

"I think most of us were under that impression once we boarded the train to Algiers…and this seems to confirm it now we're heading up river," observed William.

"Yep…guess we're bound for Port Hudson."

"Well, let's hope it doesn't turn into another wild-goose chase," chirped a cynical bystander from Company K, as he nonchalantly tired of a plug of tobacco and spat it into the gliding waters below.

"Won't be a wild-goose chase," countered Ezra. More a big turkey shoot with those grey-panted, feather-assed Johnnies ripe for plucking."

"You know what I mean," remarked the onlooker. "After Bisland we thought we were set to stick with the brigade all the way to Opelousas and beyond. Instead we got turned back as a bunch of fucking drovers. Then, within a few days of getting back to Brashear, it happened all over again. We got ordered to New Iberia…but , oh, no…that's not enough. We press on another hundred miles to Cheneyville only to be told that Banks, damn him, has quit Alexandria and we've got orders to march back to Brashear yet again. That's what I mean by wild goose chases. Goddam it…let's hope they don't come in threes. By the way…if we end up picking a fight with the Rebs at Port Hudson I'm not so sure they'll end up the turkeys in a shoot. They say the Confederate stronghold there is a formidable one up on a bluff so we could end up the turkeys, or, God forbid, sitting ducks."

It was now dusk along the river. Insects were biting and feasting on Yankee blood. Ahead a brown heron rose from a reed bed, soon to cast a primeval shape in its silhouetting against the sun-shot western sky. Minutes later a fellow from the Ninety First discharged his firearm into the margin of the adjacent levee swearing he'd seen an alligator slithering into the water. The man's action was met with derisory jeers, from those known to him, with chiding remarks for not recognising an old piece of timber, eased off its perch by the wash from the Cahawba's bow.

"Never seen a 'gator splinter so much," roared one comrade.

"Can't you recognise a dead bit of live oak, if you'll excuse the contradiction?" screamed another.

In a short while, rounding a bend in the river, the sound of old plantation songs could just be heard rising above the noise of the steamer and the hubbub of its passengers' idle chatter.

"Hey, look at those niggers on yonder levee." It was a loud utterance, tinged with scorn and aggression, and one emanating from within a group of rank and file gathered in the port side waist of the vessel.

From his starboard position further forward, William Reynolds – now sharing experiences with a soldier from the Ninety First – recognised the port side gathering as men from Company H.

"For a minute I thought I'd seen a swarm of fireflies in the twilight but it seems it's the whites of those coons' eyes," continued the raised voice of disdain. "That guy firing his musket must have drawn them all down to the levee. Well, the bastards can't latch onto us this time unless they jump in the river and swim for it. I wonder whether them 'gators like nigger meat."

"That man from your regiment sounds as though he takes exception to blacks," suggested William's companion.

"Maybe. Some of the men became irked by the behaviour of many of the negroes that fell in with us or were confiscated during endless marching up and down the Teche country. Thousands of contrabands, there were, stretching miles to our rear, most with all their worldly goods and chattels... and, invariably a good deal of their owners'...piled high on rickety old plantation carts. If there'd been room to carry it, they'd have emptied the many gin houses which were awash with cotton."

From out on the western levee the singing became louder. William and others sauntered over to the other side of the vessel to take a look. Ahead and to the left, a grove of pecan trees stood behind the levee. A long and low sweeping branch, of the like peculiar to that variety of nut tree, swept down to almost kiss the top of the embankment. Astride this perched a young black who played upon a banjo. Beyond him, and strung along the bank, stood many of his fellow slaves who sang and crooned to the youngster's melodies. Men, women and children swayed and tapped their feet in unison but, as the *Cahawba* approached, the singing ceased, feet stopped moving to the beat and the banjoist put aside his instrument. A mangy dog raised its haunches to stand and bay at the sight and sound of the approaching steamer full of bluecoats.

Grinning faces, several chewing on roasted sweet potatoes, greeted the troops as they drifted by. Old straw hats were lifted high above shiny and woolly pates. Women in gunnysack shifts and brightly coloured bandanas waved handkerchiefs. Picanninies remained impassive and wide-eyed. Occasionally, discernible comments could be heard by the soldiers.

"Whar y'gwine, Yankee sojers?"

"Gawd bress Massa Linkum."

"Which way to de promised land?"

Generally, however, little of what was shouted from the levee could be understood by the Union soldiers.

"Sounds like double Dutch to me," exclaimed one of the bluecoats.

"Gibberish, if you ask me," said another.

"Louisiana Creole," suggested a sergeant from the Ninety First who seemed to know what he was talking about. "Creole sugar joint by the look of that raised plantation house and the big sugar-mill in the distance. Quite common in these parts by all account. Their master will have been one of those uppity peacocks who speak French and I reckon those niggers, or their forbears, were originally shipped from Senegal."

"Where's your master?" shouted the aggressive fellow from Company H, noticing that no lamps had been lit in the big house.

"Gawn t' N'awlins," came a lone reply.

"From that damage to the roof, I suspect Farragut's gunboats and mortars caused the planter to take fright," piped-up one of the ship's crew as he wended his way aft. With the *Cahawba* leaving the plantation's frontage in its wake, William couldn't help notice – just visible in the gathering gloom and perhaps two rods behind the levee – the figure of an old slave sitting beneath a gnarled mulberry. The curds of blue smoke that rose stealthily from his corn-cob pipe seemed to underline a consummate sense of satisfaction, sufficient to ensure total disinterest in the excitement just played out along the riverfront. It was as if all was well with his world and William suddenly had a mental picture of Missus Stowe's Uncle Tom – although then a younger man – sitting in his garden patch on the Shelby estate, contented in his life with Aunt Clara. In William's mind's eye there was Tom, not smoking but, for relaxation, imbibing a glass of peach brandy and glorying in the visual delight of his multiflora and the bright scarlet bignonia festooning his log cabin. Again, within the context of a shackled existence, all was well with his world, yet how life had a habit of turning sour. Deliverance was yet to come but it was good that right now, amid the ravages and deprivations of this war, an old man, subjugated beneath the yoke of bondage, might already seem at peace with his lot.

The following morning the idiosyncrasies and distinctive character of the Louisiana countryside continued to captivate the attentions of the Union soldiers as the *Cahawba* made steady progress up river. Yet, in its intensity, it was a captivation which fell short of that experienced by the many blacks drawn to the levees by the sight and sound of the passing steamer. They mostly stood silent, seemingly in awe of the northern liberator slipping by before them, impassive compared to the merry group of Senegalese slaves the men had encountered downstream.

"Perhaps the heat of the day subdues these niggers," remarked one of the soldiers from the Ninety First.

"Guess they come alive after sundown," said another.

"Don't you believe it," was the adamant comment of a private from the One Hundred and Fourteenth. "Them contrabands who fell in with us along the Teche were never short of plenty to say. Once they're free of their masters they soon get lippy."

On both sides of the mighty Mississippi, grand plantation houses shadowed by majestic live oaks gave way to colonies of lowly slave cabins and loftier sugar mills. Here and there intervening groves of magnolia dappled the river's surface. Blossom petals flew and wafted fragrance in the breeze. Sleepy villages, including Plasquemine, slipped by, all seemingly beset with somnolence beneath the burgeoning heat of a late May morning. For a moment the war seemed a world away. An erstwhile farm boy called Cyrus from Cortland County quietly drank in the experience as he sat deep in thought, perched upon a coil of hemp by the port gunwale. Emerging from his muse, it was to abruptly declare that what lay before reminded him of a few days he spent with pals – in the summer of sixty-one – messing about in boats on the Susquehanna, west of Binghamton. It was a remark he quickly regretted, since it sparked endless banter from several of his comrades in Company H.

"You know, Cyrus, I can see nothing to liken this to Tioga County," barked one of the Company sergeants. "Strikes me that you and your fellow pie-eating country-boys must have been wallpapered on State cider to have come away from Binghamton thinking it was just like this."

"I hear them New York State 'gators devoured all the bass and walleye on that stretch of the river back in sixty-one," joked another man.

And so the quips came thick and fast.

"P'rhaps it was the constant sight of them Northern nigger slaves weeding cabbage-patch greens under the cruel gaze of those ruthless Tioga County overseers."

"Or cider-mill niggers, tight on apple juice, snoozing upon beds of Spanish moss."

"Maybe a Mississippi steamboat took a wrong turning and ended up on the Susquehanna. Now that might have confused young Cyrus here and his Cortland County country boys."

The attention of those who found such badinage entertaining was soon distracted by a new urban landscape. The *Cahawba* had by now arrived at Baton Rouge which teemed with occupying Union soldiers, its riverside buildings, pitted and scarred by war, presenting a forlorn appearance. After a stop here, to take on board ammunition and provisions for the front, the steamer pressed on up river, until, early in the afternoon, she arrived at Springfield Landing. This was the supply depot for Port Hudson – which lay some ten miles or so to the north – being a clearing at the edge of extensive forest, on the east bank of the Mississippi. It lay opposite Prophet Island which here split the river into two channels. With the *Cahawba* tied up to the river bank, the New Yorkers waited patiently to disembark while members of the ship's crew erected a timber staging for that purpose. It was a task they performed with such speed and efficiency as to surely warrant admiration from the army's own engineers. Once this was achieved the soldiers marched ashore, across the intervening slough of river mud, only to then encounter a lengthy wait while the vessel was unloaded.

Springfield Landing presented a purposeful, bustling appearance, the intensity of activity – and the multitude of stores and army conveyances – having an incongruous effect against the propinquity of its afforested backdrop. Along the river bank, several steamships were in course of being unloaded. Others lay idle, having already been disgorged of supplies or human cargo destined to reinforce the besieging army. Another, being specially adapted to convey the wounded, was receiving a fresh batch of passengers to be transported down river to Baton Rouge. Of these, the less severely injured tended to make their own way on board, although there was often a need for assistance. This left the more seriously wounded to the guardianship of a gang of negro stretcher-bearers who, it should be acknowledged, performed their duties with the utmost care and compassion.

Once off the *Cahawba* the Union troops made for the cooling shade beneath a clump of retained trees, towards the central part of the clearing. Here piled boxes of dried food also offered shadow and hence, relief, from the afternoon sun, plus support for the backs of those who chose to sit upright. Arms were first stacked before many lay down to sleep, in anticipation of refreshing themselves before receiving the expected order to march to the front. Some seized the opportunity to write to loved-ones or to play cards, while, in the distance, rumbled the sound of the big guns at Port Hudson. A train of covered wagons attracted some attention as it was being loaded with ordnance and commissary stores in readiness – later in the day – to be hauled to the front by six-mule teams. Then a certain amount of commotion signalled the emergence from the forest of a long convoy of ambulances. All were four-wheeled carriages which collectively brought three dozen or so sick and wounded fellows. Negro stretcher-bearers – four to a stretcher – hurried from the direction of several hospital tents that lay over to the right. The poor victims appeared to act with great dignity as they concluded their bumpy ride across a long, hard road and were transferred from ambulance to stretcher under the watchful eye and instructions of an ambulance corps sergeant. Many of the men were gravely wounded from the appearance of blood-caked swathings that encased stumps where an arm or a foot used to be. Some would need immediate attention from the surgeons at Springfield Landing before being placed upon a steamer and taken downstream to the hospital in the old Baton Rouge Arsenal. A few might reckon to leave almost immediately upon the hospital ship being readied along the river bank and it was in this particular regard, a private, newly arrived with the convoy, made a beeline for the vessel. The man's instruction was to convey to the captain an assessment of the number of newly arrived sick and wounded considered capable of onward travel and to establish whether berths could be made available. His route brought him close to the resting men of the two New York Regiments, prompting several from the One Hundred and Fourteenth – identifying the soldier from his green cap band and half chevron as one attached to the ambulance corps – to pepper him with questions of a like ilk. The gist of these was to establish the whereabouts and well-being of Brigadier-General Godfrey Weitzel's brigade.

"They're at Port Hudson alright," confirmed the private without any hesitation. "Been there about ten days I reckon. As far as I know they came across from Alexandria with General Banks by way of Simsport, crossing the Mississippi at Bayou Sara."

"How are they getting on?"

"Having joined up with Auger's Division they took on the Rebs and got badly knocked about. That was on Wednesday. It was hot work there with plenty of metal flying but they've now got the Johnnies penned up and laying siege to their earthworks. These poor fellows we've just brought in are some of our casualties."

"What of General Weitzel?" enquired one bluecoat, a reflection of the regard the men had for their brigade leader. .

"He's okay, to my knowledge," shouted the now receding, green-banded private. Pressing ahead, he was reluctant to permit the conversation to interrupt his mission.

By late afternoon orders were given to get into marching formation and move out into the forest. The corps supply wagons were still being loaded, so the way ahead was clear as the men marched off. Yet, before darkness began to envelope the forest and the regiment encamped for the night, further ambulances were passed, transporting casualties to the Landing. The men eventually halted in a grassed clearing just off the dirt road, by which time most of the trek to the front had been completed. Blankets were spread after a hurried supper and, once pickets had been posted, the men lay down on the ground beneath a moonlit sky. Most succumbed swiftly to slumber, yet, for whatever reason, a small minority – William Reynolds included – found sleep elusive. William tried to focus on the stars speckling the night sky yet this was no ordinary sky. Across it rolled the occasional noise of Parrott guns and bright flashes of light, the noise now so much louder than it had been at the Landing. Left to the imagination, it was as if some mythical old world Gods were venting their anger at the brotherly strife tearing this land apart. In between these thunderous roars could be heard the snores of more fortunate comrades and the mysterious noises of the forest. William had found the unfamiliar, yet natural, sounds of rural Louisiana, very disconcerting on his arrival in the State, but now, after four months, they held no fear for him. Twice before midnight the rumble of carriage wheels and the whinnying of horses signalled the passing of more army ambulances. As the conveyances approached and ran past the encampment, the moonlight revealed their presence on the road. When it came to the passage of the second convoy, William fancied he heard the groans of one or two of the wounded as the carriages lurched and jolted across the rutted dirt track. His thoughts immediately returned to an April afternoon in Portsea. He recalled his conversation with the severely wounded private who had sustained a deeply lacerated thigh at Inkerman and had lost a hand in the trenches before Sebastopol.

"...if I were you right now, I wouldn't touch the army with a pair of tongs," the invalid had told him. "I've seen too many brave young men perish...too many coffined long before their time...dreadful waste of young lives...get the soldiering life right out of your mind, boy."

The fellow's words came back to him as clearly as if they'd been uttered yesterday. Amid the loneliness from which sleep seemed unwilling to release him, William heard them yet again in his thoughts and in his mind's eye he pictured the old soldier. Now, in this remote spot beneath the stars, seeing and hearing the passing ambulance train – coupled with the imminent prospect of reaching the front – those words sounded uncannily predictive and disturbing. Another groan broke the relative silence as if fortuity had called for an encore to underline William's thoughts.

"Sorry, Sergeant," shouted the driver of the rearmost ambulance as it passed from view beneath the moonbeams. "I'm doing my best but this road is in a bad state and it's far from easy at ni…" The driver's fading words were cut short by another earth-trembling roar from the Union batteries at Port Hudson. By the time the noise receded, all trace of the ambulance convoy had been swallowed up in the forest.

By six o'clock the men had packed up and departed their grassy, clover-strewn clearing and once more were back on the march. The forest's tree canopy was a godsend in shutting out the full effects of the sun, for the morning temperature was already soaring. The dirt road was of varying state, this largely dictated by the prevailing nature of the tree canopy. Thus, it was invariably baked and rutted where the overhanging foliage was broken or sparse, or alternatively, inclined to be sloughy beneath the denser foliage or where tracts of marsh and mire were encountered. It was not long before the column began to approach the rear of the Army, a propinquity noisily highlighted by the roar of a Confederate field-piece. To the confusion of all, the shell hissed and tore its way through the forest until it took out the top of a mighty pine, the bulk of which, amid shards of lesser pieces of timber, fell but a rod to the left of the column. "It was," someone observed, "like watching a man-of-war being deprived of a topmast." With calm quickly restored, the march resumed. Soon the men found themselves being hailed by other bluecoats.

Here, towards the edge of the forest and less than a mile from the nearest Rebel embrasures, the column fell upon clearings containing the encampments of Union troops attached to Dwight's Brigade. Its passage generated plenty of welcoming cheers from men delighted to witness the arrival of more fellows to swell the ranks of the besiegers; and although this boisterously expressed welcome lifted the spirits of the New Yorkers, it was tempered by disclosure that a four or five mile march remained ahead of them.

"Brigadier-General Weitzel?" repeated a sergeant belonging to a Maine infantry regiment when asked about the location of that officer's headquarters. "Keep heading north under cover of the forest, especially over the next mile or two while passing our boys and those of General Augur's Division. I say that because once out of the forest you'd be exposed across the cotton fields to a string of Rebel gun platforms. Further on, the terrain gets more difficult when you get to pass by Paine's and Grover's boys… you know, hilly ground with plenty of gullies. By then you'll be turning west beyond the north side of the Rebel garrison. If your feet start to get wet and you're stuck in a quagmire you'll soon enough know you've gone too far. You see, there's an impassable swamp this side of the Bayou Sara road. Above all, stay concealed within the magnolia forest, otherwise them Johnnie sharpshooters could get trigger-happy."

Armed with the cheery sergeant's good advice, General Weitzel's headquarters were safely attained before midday. With Colonel Elisha Smith indisposed through illness and at the time languishing in a New Orleans' hospital, it was left to Lieutenant Colonel Per Lee – the former Adjutant and now acting commanding officer – to report to Weitzel. This done, the men were supplied with additional ammunition, then marched off to take their position in the forest where they had to endure a baptism of shelling from some of the enemy's heavy guns. The next day, the first of June, the Regiment was ordered forward to the relative shelter of a ravine through which coursed the briny waters of Sandy Creek. Here, being within much closer proximity to the Rebel lines, it settled in for several weeks.

As time advanced the men gradually became indifferent to the noises and flashes of the opposing heavy artillery and, to an extent – and as far as the relative confinement by the terrain would allow – soldiering life assumed some element of normality. Boredom was interspersed with picket and guard duties while turns were taken in the trenches and rifle pits which had been excavated upon the crest of neighbouring high ground. Here, for hours on end, the men – along with their counterparts in the enemy works – would act as patient marksmen waiting to discharge their muskets at the slightest movement.

On the night of June the fifth, William Reynolds was among a party from Companies E and F to relieve a group from a Vermont unit who had completed their allotted time in the trenches. It happened that no lights were permitted along Sandy Creek for fear of attracting the attention of those employed at pouring shot, shell and canister into the Union lines. The prevailing moonlight was, in consequence, a blessing, since it provided the relief party with a modicum of faint light to guide their crawl up and into the rifle pits. But, as much as it was a blessing, it was also a peril in aiding the opposing sharpshooters to spot their prey. William found himself in a pit with two others. One was his old friend Jack Chidester. The other was a young farm boy from Sherburne village, New York, attached to Company F. He answered to the name of Orrin. All three had inclined themselves against the relative comfort of sacks stuffed with cotton, their rifles directed through a matrix of sticks and brush that lay upon the edge of their pit.

After an hour of inertia and no discernible movement in the rebel lines, the boy Orrin became restless and decided to elevate himself with the aid of a sand-filled box, one of a number of such items littering the trench.

"Careful, young feller," whispered Jack, such was the proximity to the concealed Rebel marksmen and the stillness of the night...a stillness punctuated from time to time by the discharge of the enemy's pivot guns and the returning roar of the Union artillery. "Don't be fooled by the lack of movement. Those Johnnie Rebs are lurking there, just like us. If you give them a glimpse of yourself they'll surely open up."

"I'm fully aware of that," said Orrin. Being whispered, his reply gave little hint of the indignation he felt in being spoken to in this way by the older man. At seventeen he considered himself invincible and no callow rustic. "Trouble is, my rifle arm's gone numb and I need to reposition myself." Given this temporary hindrance he experienced some difficulty in employing his bayonet to excavate a shelf in the soft, yellow clay. Here he proposed to anchor the box. "Since the moonlight has dimmed, courtesy of that bit of cloud cover, I reckon it's time to shift. And, if I shave off another two inches of this clay, I reckon I can get a clear line of fire without showing myself. But yes, man...I'll be careful." Orrin's last sentence, although still hushed, was delivered with a shade more emphasis to reflect the youth's displeasure. It didn't go unnoticed by Jack who, in turn, raised a knowing and sardonic smile.

Sadly and ironically, young Orrin was not true to his words. Puffs of smoke and yellow flame signalled the discharge of a volley of bullets by a party of Rebel sharpshooters positioned no more than six rods from the Union rifle pit. To William's and Jack's horror the youth reeled backwards – his face contorted as he fell – then slid head first down the slippery, clay slope. In an instant it was agreed that Chidester would remain at his post and return the enemy's fire, while Reynolds would clamber down to see if he could aid the unfortunate Orrin. William expected the worst and, on reaching the lad, his first impression seemed to confirm his fears. The left side of his face was drenched in warm, syrupy blood. He was conscious, although in shock and trembling. Nearby was a cotton-sack, one of many prepared by the infantry for use in bridging ditches. William gathered it up and, lifting the injured man, used it as a pillow to support his head. Having made him as comfortable as he could, he whispered some words of reassurance about seeking help, then scrambled back down into the Sandy Creek encampment.

Amid the darkness William made for the dull, oil-papered lamplight which marked out the Surgeon's tent, there being no other lights or campfires permitted during the hours of darkness for fear of drawing attention to the Regiment's position. Once arrived, he acquainted the Duty Sergeant with the wounded man's predicament, the non-comm immediately ordering two cornet players to take a rope and pole stretcher and return with William to the rifle pit. They were to bring the casualty back down to the hospital tent where his injury would be assessed and treated. Then, should circumstances require, he would be taken to the Division field hospital, to the rear of the line, by stretcher-bearers from the ambulance corps.

Poor Orrin. He was still conscious. Having placed their man on the stretcher, the two young cornet players soon found it impossible to get their burden back down into the ravine in this fashion, such was the gradient of the bluff upon which the rifle pits were excavated. Were they to persevere it was William's opinion the problem might worsen, since failure to secure a firm footing in the dark could well see the wounded man pitched out of the litter. Instead they had little alternative but to spread the poor fellow's outstretched arms across their shoulders and – with William's guidance – to slowly and gingerly carry him down the slope where he was delivered to the care of one of the meds.

★ ★ ★

Life in and around Sandy Creek and, for that matter along the Union lines, continued in such monotonous vein. Sharpshooters on both sides spent countless hours playing cat and mouse, while, on the broader stage, the Union batteries relentlessly poured grape, shell and canister into the Confederate fortifications. Along the waterfront, the Navy's mortar boats inflicted significant damage to the Rebel batteries' heavy artillery, including their eight and ten inch columbiads. Ashore, detachments of sailors relentlessly pounded the Port Hudson defences with their mighty Dahlgrens, ably supplementing the army's siege howitzers and mortars, their Parrotts and Napoleons.

And all the while, in their forward positions, the Union men – the One Hundred and Fourteenth included – were massed in their ravines and among the magnolia woods, often within a stone's throw of the Rebel lines. Here monotony and deprivation sorely tested patience and fuelled a burgeoning desire for orders which might bring about a sea change in circumstance and an end to the boredom.

"Seems as though we're getting off lightly at the moment," said Caleb Trask as he sat with William and others, engrossed in a game of four-handed euchre. "Those rebel guns seem much quieter than they did." Ironically his words coincided with a roar of cannon from a nearby Union battery.

"They say it's because they're running short of ammunition," retorted one of the opposing partners, a Private by the name of Knapp.

"I can well believe it," remarked William. "After all, the Navy seem to be in control on the river and we appear to have the Rebs well and truly pinned down elsewhere. Sergeant Stoughton says they are now very short of food and have resorted to eating rats and mule meat."

"Now that sounds most appropriate victualling for those fucking Gray Backs," quipped Shaw, the man partnering Knapp and a fellow Private from Company F. "Don't you believe it," said Trask. "Word has it that mule meat can be mighty palatable and comparable to venison or beef. And they say that rat meat, nicely broiled, can rival a sweet spring chicken. So I'm thinking they won't be on starvation diet while mules and rats are plentiful and after that, well...there are plenty of snakes and other critters."

"Talking of snakes, did you hear what happened to that nasty blowhard of a First Sergeant in Company C?" queried Knapp.

"Not Zuicker?" replied William in a trice and at a loss to think of any other First Sergeants in the Regiment so obviously deserving of Knapp's description.

"Yes...Zuicker. Well...I was earlier talking to two fellows from his Company. It turns out, a couple of nights back, Zuicker was overseeing some men clear a swathe of undergrowth. They were at the head of a gully which runs south westwards towards the enemy lines, about twenty rods east of here and beyond the cook shanties. The objective, by all accounts, was to clear the ground in preparation for cutting a new sap towards the Rebel breastworks. Well, apparently, in Zuicker's opinion, his party were making too much noise for his liking, his fear being that enemy sharpshooters would hear and discharge a volley of rifle-balls in the sappers' direction. Anyway, while he cursed and swore at his subordinates in whispered tones, he took insufficient care to watch his step and tripped headlong into some low briars, disturbing a snake in the process. It seems the reptile was not much pleased and took its fangs to Zuicker's forearm. The fellow yelled out, ironically causing the commotion he was so keen to avoid. Seconds later there was a roar of musketry from the Rebel fortifications and the men were forced to terminate their labours and retreat to safety."

"What kind of snake got him?" asked William.

"I doubt anyone knows, including Zuicker. After all, it was dark. But there are some nasty critters in these woods. Corporal Sumner of Company B narrowly avoided treading on a cottonmouth moccasin a few days back and I'm told there are black snakes and king snakes…oh, and one of our Sergeants has seen a rattler."

"So how is the bastard?" enquired Trask.

"What Zuicker or the snake?"

"The snake of course, poor thing," interjected William, to the amusement of all.

"Well, I can't speak for the critter," continued Knapp, "but I'm told Zuicker has yet to breathe his last and, in fact, is making a good recovery. It turns out, that, against their better judgment, his men took him promptly to the Surgeon's tent. There Mister Sawbones quickly applied a tight tourniquet to Zuicker's upper arm and, according to the fellows from his Company, he scarified the wound with a fleam and drew off the venom with a cupping glass."

"I bet having tasted Zuicker's blood the serpent will be feeling nauseous," observed Shaw.

"By the way," said William, adopting a more sober tone of voice. "How's that lad, Orrin, from your Company? He was with me and Jack Chidester up in one of the rifle pits about a week ago and got in the way of a Rebel ball."

"Word is our First Lieutenant paid him a visit yesterday in the Brigade hospital," said Shaw who tried to hide his disappointment at having just been euchred, with Trask marking two points. "Seems as though he was a lucky fellow. The ball kind of scalped the left side of his head down to the bone…an inch to the right and he'd have been a goner. But he's making good progress and, according to one of the hospital orderlies, should be back with us soon."

"That's grand. In the dark I feared the boy was done for. There was blood everywhere, as evident from all these stains on my tunic," said William, the relief showing in his face.

"Oh, so that's another feller's blood, Willie," quipped Caleb Trask. "We'd assumed you'd taken Rebel lead in the chest and simply shrugged it off."

"OK, time to cut for deal," said Knapp, amid a round of laughter.

★ ★ ★

The thirteenth of June arrived in the wake of several days of bombardment from the Union batteries, sometimes incessant and in full fury. In return came scant response from the enemy's gun emplacements. At eleven in the morning, an hour of intense cannonading poured forth from all the batteries as a prelude to General Banks demanding the garrison's surrender. This was refused: and so the Federal bombardment resumed and continued throughout the day.

The sense that such constant artillery assault would, sooner or later, carry the Rebels' endurance to beyond breaking point was a burgeoning one and hopes were high in the Union ranks that weeks of monotony were drawing to a close. The fact that major plans were afoot became evident as the infantry were supplied with something akin to marching rations as well as sixty rounds of ammunition to fill their cartridge boxes. Added to which, the men of the One Hundred and Fourteenth had recently had their spirits raised by the reappearance of their beloved commanding officer. Colonel Elisha Smith had arrived at the front looking pale and gaunt, having discharged himself from hospital in New Orleans, contrary to the good advice of his medical practitioners. He had been bravely insistent that his place was beside his men at Port Hudson, rather than biding his time amid the comparative safety and boredom of a General Hospital.

Midnight on the thirteenth. The men were drawn from the comfort of their blankets and quietly assembled to receive instructions while the cooks and camp servants circulated with hot coffee and warm corn-meal mush. Company E, together with four other Companies – B, D, F and G – were instructed to move out under the direction of their ailing Colonel. The Regiment's remaining five Companies, under the command of Lieutenant-Colonel Per Lee, were ordered forward to the trenches where, in due course, they would engage in heavy firing upon the fortifications. This was intended to be a distraction from planned major assaults upon a formidable section of the Rebel works located on the left of the Union lines; and it was towards this objective that Colonel Smith's detachment made its nocturnal progression. Through fosse and trench the men slowly trudged, sometimes stumbling over protruding snags and roots, unseen in the darkness. And, as they pushed on, the five Companies were gradually joined by other Regiments of the Brigade. Later they halted to await the arrival of further troops, including units from Morgan's Brigade.

"Bet your life we're going to advance on the enemy and hope to overrun them," whispered someone in the ranks.

"It doesn't take much between the ears to reach that conclusion, man," countered another bluecoat sardonically. "Everyone's under arms. It's just a matter of when. Do we surprise them under cover of darkness or wait until sunup?"

"Ours is not to reason why…or should it be *when?*" crowed Isaiah Bryant, as if out to make an impression. "Ours is but to do or die."

"*Their's.*"

"What's that Willie?"

"*Their's*, not *ours is.*"

"Who said that?"

"Tennyson…about the noble six hundred." William recalled the time he'd had to memorise *The Charge of the Light Brigade* and recite it before his class and the odious Jenkins.

"General Weitzel's in the saddle over yonder," shouted a man in Company D. "He's conferring with other officers…just this side of the Eighth Vermont." It was a remark that carried along the phalanxes of assembled troops in a pig's whisper. And such was the enthusiasm with which it was received that it was both swift and effective in snuffing out hushed discourse upon all manner of diverse subjects, including any further deliberations upon the poet Tennyson or the events at Balaclava. The General, after all, was held in high esteem throughout the Brigade and for some time hitherto, during the cannonading, had been much preoccupied with the batteries. Now, at what promised to be a pivotal moment, the General was back with his foot soldiers. It was news that greatly heartened his men and raised self-belief in achieving success in whatever they were called upon to do.

"Colonel Smith is to take command of the Brigade," was the next announcement to spread like wildfire.

"Poor fellow. It looks as though he needs his sick bed. What a brave and honourable man to have forsaken it in favour of this." Such were the sentiments and remarks which greeted the news.

"Major Morse will lead our Companies." These words were well received by the men of Company D, in particular, since the Major had been responsible for recruiting those men and had fleetingly served as their Captain before being promoted.

In due course the Brigade was ordered to march off. Its destination lay a further two miles to the left of the Union lines, the place from where the assault upon the enemy would be launched and where further troops were already assembled. It remained dark, but the eerie light of dawn would soon bloom. A damp fog hung among the woods and lingered along the ravines. Beyond the massed and secreted Union soldiers, the enemy lay behind well-constructed fortifications. In front of these an impressive ditch and a haphazard abatis of felled timber presented significant obstacles for advancing troops. And, although a battle plan was swiftly devised, it was not until deep into the early hours that it began to be put into effect, ruling out any hope of a surprise attack under cover of darkness. Instead, behind the earthworks, the Rebels readied themselves to repulse the now anticipated Union assault.

The devised strategy for an advance relied upon the troops filing, under cover, through a deep ravine, to then secure more open ground. From the head of this gully they would emerge some three hundred yards closer to the Rebels' earthworks, then to immediately adopt battle formation and advance upon the Confederate positions. The first to go would be the Twelfth Connecticut and the Seventy Fifth New York, these Regiments to act as skirmishers ahead of Morgan's Twenty Fourth Connecticut and Ninety First New York. The men of the Twenty Fourth were each to carry two bags stuffed with cotton, the intention being to toss the cotton bags into the defensive ditch to aid its crossing by the men in the rear. As for the Ninety First, they were armed with hand grenades to rough up and strike terror into the enemy sharpshooters manning the Port Hudson breastworks. It would then be the turn of the Eighth Vermont, followed by the One Hundred and Fourteenth and the One Hundred and Sixtieth New York, these Regiments to advance in line of battle. In the rear would come the remainder of Morgan's Brigade.

The assault commenced in accordance with this strategy. Dawn had broken before the word was given to open the ball. The early fog had thinned. A strange pink light permeated the mist. At the western head of the ravine the Union skirmishers led the advance into the more open ground. Overhead, the tumultuous sounds of Union shot and shell from the artillery in the rear was returned with equal force from the Port Hudson guns. Muskets along the Rebel ramparts incessantly spewed lead ball into the advancing bluecoats. Down in the gully, the One Hundred and Fourteenth waited for their turn to climb up the stony path ahead. The noise of musket volleys beyond and of the trading of screaming shot above was deafening. William Reynolds, with others of his Company, crouched and waited.

"Frightened, men?" shouted some noisy braggart, clearly out to impress comrades with his supposed nonchalance. There was no longer, of course, a need to whisper. "Let it rip," he continued. "Sooner we get started the sooner it's done. After all, it's Sunday and we're due our free time after dinner."

Most chose to ignore the fellow's comments. A few chuckled.

"I'm bloody well petrified," said another, as he crammed some plump, juicy blackberries into his mouth. The men of Company E were for the most part gathered in a forward part of the ravine where fruiting brambles presented a distraction for those partial to their sweet, ripe berries.

"I thought the bastards' artillery had been silenced by a lack of ammunition. Seems we were lulled into thinking this would be a turkey shoot," shouted someone dispiritedly. Overhead the air continued to be rent by the hiss and shriek of projectiles. A young fellow in Company D was openly admonished by one of the non-comms for his slovenly eating habits.

"Look at the state of your tunic, son…smothered in blackberry juice. You clearly don't know where your mouth is. Are you sure you'll be able to bite on your cartridges? Some distance to the rear, a middle-aged private in the One Hundred and Sixtieth, of portly frame and a good baritone, chose to compete against the noise of the gunfire with his rendition of Lyte's *Abide With Me*. Many, including William Reynolds, remained silent and contemplative, some having drawn forth their little red *Soldier's Pocketbook* to dwell upon hymns and psalms and scripture selections. Of these, most eyes fell upon comforting words intended to be read and uttered with the impending prospect of battle. Dry lips silently mouthed the printed words…*O Lord God, from whom I have received life and by whom that life has been preserved until the present moment I would humbly and confidently commit myself to thy holy keeping in the prospect of coming battle…I would desire to feel the courage and determination of a loyal soldier and to perform my duty faithfully… If it be thy holy will may my life be preserved while I remain steadfast to my post and let all cowardly fear be banished from my heart …should it be thy purpose that I fall, may the sting of death, which is a sin, be taken away…To thee, O Lord, I now commit my soul and body and may I not forget thee amidst the roar of battle. This I earnestly ask for Christ's sake; and to the Father, Son and Holy Ghost shall be all the praise. Amen.*

Ahead, the boys from Vermont now began to clamber up the bank and out of view to the encouraging cheers of some of the less preoccupied New Yorkers. Pocketbooks were tucked away. Men and boys tried to steel themselves. A few felt a final need to empty their bladders and pissed into the adjacent undergrowth. The call came to move out and the men began to follow the Vermonters into the fray.

Out on the open ground all was commotion and mayhem. A pall of smoke hung over the land: no longer the ethereal fog, suspended in dawn's limpid air, but swirling curds of sulphurous white and grey smoke. For what seemed an eternity the men of the One Hundred and Fourteenth felt like sitting ducks as they waited for the One Hundred and Sixtieth to move out of the ravine and complete the battle line. In front, little could be seen of the skirmishers, the cotton-baggers and the Ninety-First. In the still stationary line, William Reynolds saw a comrade slump forward but half a rod to his left. Now, with the battle line complete, Colonel Smith gave the order to charge. It was an order the men seemed to relish, if only to experience the perceived feeling that being on the move, and all the while ducking and weaving, markedly diminished the chance of being hit. As they pressed forward, lurching and scrambling over tree stumps, logs and bushy debris, they were met by a rain of minie balls which left their points of discharge amid spurts of yellow flame and billowing vapour. For a while, as they moved onwards into the lead storm, the men were aware of litter-bearing ambulance men moving in the opposite direction. Cursing and hollering, the bearers were intent in making known their whereabouts for fear of their wounded charges being tossed aside by advancing comrades. As the line of bluecoats moved forward, it became increasingly fragmented as men were hit by the withering Rebel fire. Men fell on all sides. Bullets whined. Soldiers yelled in pain and screamed obscenities. The smell of burnt powder infused the air. Balls tore bark off tree stumps or lacerated flesh and shattered bone. The sight of dead and wounded was everywhere.

Through a void in the curtain of smoke, William Reynolds glimpsed an uprooted base of a large tree, just ahead and to the right. Turning momentarily, he caught sight of Isaiah Bryant at his shoulder and shouted to him to make for the cover it offered. In so doing, he took his eyes off the ground ahead, caught his foot on a snag and tumbled headlong into a briar.

"Christ, are you hit, Willie?" screamed Bryant.

"No, no," came the quick reply. "Don't wait for me. I'll catch up."

As William retrieved his rifle and disentangled himself from his brambly bed, he heard a whimper to his right. Although his immediate impulse was to retrieve his situation and rush forward to gain the cover of the uprooted tree, his eye caught sight of the source of that sob. A callow youth, perhaps the witness of no more than sixteen summers, sat upright against a stump, his feet stretched out before him. He was all of a tremble and blabbering to himself. Beyond his feet, a cotton bag lay torn, its spilled contents stained blood red and strewn with grey matter. Close by, William noticed a soldier lying on his front, his forage cap gone. The tragic reality was that the top of his head had been carried away. The shock of witnessing a comrade meet such a gruesome end had clearly had the most profound effect upon the young soldier. William drew himself close to the boy from Connecticut. He uncorked his canteen, encouraged him to take a swig and then sluiced the boy's face with water to rid it of clinging morsels of scalp and hair and brain tissue.

Anxious to help the youth and rid him of the constant sight of the dead man, William coaxed him to his feet. Then, taking hold of his left arm, he took it across his back, inclined his own frame to the left and so gained purchase by using his right shoulder to take much of the boy's weight. In this manner his right arm remained free to carry his musket and he successfully gained the shelter and greater safety of his earlier goal.

"Thank God you made it, Willie," exclaimed Bryant. "You did well to spot this place. It offers good protection and when the smoke clears I get a good view of those Rebel sharpshooters. There are some loopholes through these tree roots and with all those hours in the rifle pits I'm reckoning we're proficient enough to bag a few Johnnies."

It was only as he turned to face William, cartridge paper poised between his teeth, that Isaiah Bryant realised his comrade was not alone. "Christ, what are you doing? Taken to acting as ambulance man, eh?…as if storming the enemy position is not enough."

"He's not wounded, Isa. The boy's in extreme shock. Seen his friend brutally cut down with, literally, his brains blown out. I'm just going to lay him down in the lee of this big, old root ball where he'll be out of sight of those Johnny Rebs but in full view of any following stretcher bearers. They may or may not feel inclined to help him. William proceeded to lower the boy down, so that he was seated in much the same manner as before, with his back now propped against the vertical, earthy face of the matrix of tree roots. "That's about all I can do for you soldier," said William to his young acquaintance. "You should be safe enough here." The boy continued to tremble with emotion but his erstwhile rapid breathing appeared to have slowed and he raised a faint smile of appreciation. "Now I've got work to do," and with that William took up his musket once more, withdrew a cartridge from his box and found a niche alongside Isaiah Bryant. Both men hoped they might pick off a few enemy sharpshooters before attempting to move forward once more.

There was little or no respite from the fusillade of lead ball the Rebels pumped into the advancing Federal troops. Many had fallen and, therefore, the line had broken and fragmented. In consequence, and on instruction brought by one of General Weitzel's staff officers, Colonel Elisha Smith halted the Union push, such as it was. The intention was to enable the reorganisation of the Brigade for a final advance on the enemy position. In the lull that immediately followed, while the Colonel and his officers conferred over tactics, the men prostrated themselves upon the ground. This action took advantage of an element of protection offered by a gentle cresting in the topography ahead and was met by a reduction of activity along the Confederate ramparts. William Reynolds and Isaiah Bryant, meanwhile, being aware of what was happening, and eager to rejoin colleagues who had pushed forward of their own position, made a dash for the line.

With the men on the ground, the whine of flying minie balls from the fort had all but ceased but a short hail of lead greeted the two infantrymen in their flight. Unscathed, and reaching their procumbent comrades, they hurled themselves upon the earth. Seconds later a familiar voice rang out to William's left.

"Christ, Reynolds, where have you suddenly come from?" William turned to face the voice. It was the cheerful, straight-talking Charley Ellis sporting a broad grin. Beyond him several other familiar faces were pressed against the dirt. More by luck than judgement, they had found their way back to their own Company.

"Seems these fuckin' Rebs are intent on putting us through the mill," continued Ellis. We appear to have lost a good few. And what the hell became of our skirmishers? Sergeant Tombs says he saw G's Captain Tucker go down. It looked bad."

"Pay attention, boys," screamed a fellow down the line. It was the voice of Jed Kendall, a Corporal of two weeks' standing. "We have to remain alert to receive fresh orders. Seems the Colonel is already instructing the men over on the left as to what he requires."

With the firing having diminished, the palls of milky smoke had dissipated markedly but, overhead, the artillery fire was unrelenting as projectiles were traded by the opposing batteries. Suddenly, however, spurts of yellow flame could be seen along the Rebel ramparts as sharpshooters discharged a hail of bullets towards the left of the Union line. Among the two New York Regiments occupying the centre and right, little significance was paid to this incident. Little significance, that is, until word passed through the ranks like wildfire. The Colonel had been hit, felled by a Confederate bullet. Moments before, when Corporal Kendall had shouted out, William had been aware of the distinctive figure of Colonel Smith. He had been standing tall while directing the men of the Eighth Vermont as to what he required of their formation.

"Let's trust he's not badly hurt."

"Goddam it. I thought he was being rash and making himself too much of a target."

"If only he'd stayed with us and not been given the Brigade."

"He should have laid low like the rest of us. He should have kept his head down."

"Let's hope it's just a flesh wound and clear of his vitals."

"Inwardly let us all say a little prayer for our dear Colonel."

"Brave man…but so much for dedication. Damn it, he was ill for God's sake and should have still been convalescing in New Orleans."

Such were the anxious remarks spoken along a shocked line concerning the fate of the One Hundred and Fourteenth's beloved Colonel. Nobody seemed to know the severity of the officer's injuries or, indeed, whether he had been mortally wounded. In fact, he had been hit in the stomach by a ball which shattered his spine on exit. Those who immediately attended to him swiftly lifted the poor man out of the line of fire, made him as comfortable as possible and, much to the Colonel's protestations, arranged for him to be taken to the rear.

Despite this most unsettling of incidents, the Brigade received orders to advance once again. The several Companies of the One Hundred and Fourteenth gained the shelter of a gully, perhaps twenty five yards from the breastworks. Resting here for a short time, they pushed on once more with the intention of reaching the ditch that fronted the enemy position. Now the leaden rain, into which they advanced, was so intense that only a handful of men attained this ditch, only to realise the hopelessness of trying to cross it and scale the earthworks. Several men were lost or wounded in the action, the number of officers in the field now being severely depleted. Lieutenant Longwell, who had assumed command of Company E, was hit and retired from the field along with Major Morse, who, for some while, had been suffering from a serious wound. With the Regiment's strength seriously undermined, further adjustments were made, with Lieutenant Searle of Company G assuming command and Lieutenant Colonel Van Patten of the One Hundred and Sixtieth New York taking the Brigade.

Now came a final, desperate push, with Lieutenant Searle leading his Regiment at the head of another charge. In turn, the confronting enemy responded by pouring more and more lead into the path of their advancing assailants. It was a heady, intoxicating experience for many of the bluecoats: one that threatened to spawn foolhardiness as they seemed drawn into a vortex of emotion and a frenzy to succeed in their quest. On this occasion many more, William included, reached the ditch which had become a maelstrom of desperate activity wreathed in billows of Rebel smoke. In the struggle to reach and mount the earthworks, men tumbled in the ditch amid yells and curses. Others succeeded in crossing and attempted to scale the works, yet it was an impossible task. That sense of infallibility had now crested...had now reached its zenith and was set to decline. William lost his footing for the second time since the day's action began, this time stumbling over a prostrated comrade who had gone before. On this occasion he fell heavily, badly jarring his right elbow as it came into contact with the ricocheting butt of his rifle. But perhaps being stalled in this manner was a slice of good fortune. Ahead, the several brave fellows who still tried desperately to make inroads into the entrenchments were getting savagely repulsed. As William tried to struggle to his feet to meet the challenge, his progress was once more interrupted. He was immediately sent flying again, this time by a yelling soldier who fell back from the face of the incline above, his collar bone shattered and what remained of his left ear bleeding profusely. As William and the fellow pinned down below him attempted to extricate themselves from beneath the wounded man, William witnessed a sight that would haunt him thereafter. It was a fleeting, gruesome experience. Looking up and to the right, as he eased the badly injured man aside, he found himself peering through a hole in the smoke. He could see a young officer mounting the embrasure, perhaps four rods away. Suddenly the poor fellow's head recoiled violently, the top of it appearing to explode in a rain of blood, bone and gore. The hole in the smoke closed as if the observer had seen enough. William was physically sick, spewing regurgitated corn-meal mush, darkened by blackberries, down his tunic. For a moment he could fully understand how the youth from Connecticut had reacted as he did.

The repulse was complete, the action calamitous. Their final flush of courage now expired, those men capable of doing so turned and fled to seek cover from the ever vigilant Rebel sharpshooters. Most were forced to lie low throughout the hours of daylight, surrounded by the dead and dying and those lying in agony with unattended wounds. At least darkness brought respite and William Reynolds, together with five comrades – bruised and blood-spattered to a man – retraced their weary way back to the Sandy Creek camping ground.

★ ★ ★

Dejection gripped the men of the One Hundred and Fourteenth in the aftermath of this most resounding defeat. It was a mood that reached its nadir on the nineteenth of the month when the revered Colonel Elisha Smith passed away in the Brigade hospital. Gone already was the intelligent, theological graduate, Captain Charles Tucker – shot through the chest – a most genial and popular officer. Gone also was Second Lieutenant Henry Corbin, the poor fellow who William had seen so brutally slain during the brave attempt to scale the Rebel earthworks. It had been a most horrific little cameo which William would have been spared but for a contrivance between fate and the flighty transitoriness of drifting gunsmoke.

Now and into July the melancholic Army of General Banks saw their lives return to the tedium of siege warfare. The burial duties which were interspersed with spells in the rifle pits were a sad and sickening reminder of the Union setback during the days following the fourteenth of June. Meanwhile, the life of inertia in the woods and ravines, dampened by heavy storms, roasted under a scorching sun and chilled under clear night skies, was a recipe for sickness and disease. The hospital tents were, in consequence, full to overflowing. Scurvy and diarrhoea were commonplace. Pediculosis was rife. Rations dwindled and, with clothing supplies hard to secure, the men looked increasingly scruffy and bedraggled.

For a short spell on the Fourth of July there came some relief from despondency, boredom and routine: several bands struck up a medley of rousing tunes and a thirty-four gun salute was fired. Yet, unknowingly, there was already emerging a good deal more for celebration. Further up the Mississippi, the siege of Vicksburg ended with that garrison's surrender. However, several days elapsed before the news of this momentous event was delivered to the Union forces at Port Hudson. When it came, the disclosure sparked great excitement and yet more bands struck up their patriotic tunes. Great joy prevailed among the besiegers and, come the following morning, flags of truce raised by the Rebels were a precursor to the opposing Generals partaking in discussions. And, throughout the eighth, with hostilities suspended, the rank and file on both sides appeared to enjoy each others company between the lines.

Evening brought the joyous news for which all on the Union side had hoped. Port Hudson had surrendered. The fall of Vicksburg had hastened its own capitulation. The garrison had realised its time was up, for now there was the prospect of having to face the combined might of Banks' and Grant's Armies. The formal occupation of Port Hudson was duly undertaken by the Union troops amid much joy and emotion. Ragged and depleted they were, but not in spirit. With a spring in their feet and the bands playing the likes of *John Brown's Body* and *The Battle Cry of Freedom*, the bluecoats blithely marched into the fort to observe the ceremony of surrender. And once formalities were completed and the Rebel flag lowered, the Stars and Stripes were proudly hoisted on the bluff above the waters of the great Mississippi. No longer tainted or fettered by siege warfare along its course, no longer *hors de combat*, it was as if Old Glory was reassuring the river that its waters were now open to the sea.

Five

SURRATTSVILLE, MARYLAND

JANUARY 1864

The early evening was fine but chill with the heavens star-studded and a frostiness in the air. The traveller dismounted from the saddle of his chestnut gelding. He loosened the girth, led the animal to a water trough by the tavern's woodpile, then tethered him to a nearby rail. The man was of raddled appearance, his coat well-worn and scruffy. Beneath its heavy collar he had a grey woollen muffler which was drawn tightly about his chin. He wore his hair long, a grimy, slouch hat pulled down to within an inch of his eyebrows. It was good to be out of the saddle for a while, good to feel terra firma rather than stirrup irons beneath his feet. The man coughed to clear his throat and spat a globule of viscid mucus into the dirt. He patted the animal's withers and muttered to him endearingly. His breathe vapourised in the cool air and mingled with the horse's steaming perspiration.

The traveller crossed the porch towards the bar room door. Its knotty pine timbers creaked beneath his tread. He tried the door. It was locked. Few passing customers called at the Surratt Tavern after dark during the height of winter but this was not the principal reason for the door being bolted. Since the landlady had lost her husband, she had felt it prudent to make a habit of locking up when her son was away from home. After all, these were troublesome times. A few moments later the curtaining was pulled aside and a black, fleshy face emerged behind the window alongside the entrance door. The whites of the girl's eyes were vivid, like watery marbles, as they caught the light from the candle she carried. It was a play of candle-light which, in combination with the window pane's eerie refractive effect upon the young woman's face, momentarily took the visitor by surprise and caused his heart to skip a beat.

"G'd evenin', suh. De missis says wot zackly is yer bisniss?" enquired the peering face.

"I'm riding to Charles County. I've broken my journey in the hope of being re-acquainted with Mister John Surratt and to fortify and warm myself with a glass of your whisky," replied the caller in a thick and decidedly guttural voice.

The face at the window retreated. A pause ensued before it re-appeared. "De missis says she'd 'preciate if you's 'dentify yerself."

"My name's George Atzerodt. I'm on my way to Port Tobacco."

A further delay was followed by the sound of bolts being drawn back. The door swung open revealing a handsome, matronly woman of about forty or so, attired in a chartreuse dress which complemented her colouring rather well. At her shoulder stood a younger woman, about half her age. Their features bore a striking resemblance, a likeness heightened on account of both choosing to wear their brown hair in that neat, fashionable style, drawn away from a central parting. Behind them hovered a frizzy-haired, coloured servant girl, her eyes and visage now released from any highlighting and distortion, her bearing suggesting she was nothing short of personable and cheery and not one to instil fright.

Mary Elizabeth Surratt was cautious about who crossed her threshold, yet not on account of diffidence, for she was no shrinking violet. She was, however, wary and inherently suspicious. She spent a moment taking stock of the newcomer with a gimlet eye. The man had removed his hat and loosened his muffler, revealing, beneath the scant illumination from the porch light, a bedraggled head of hair and an untidy goatee beard. His face was swarthy and it struck Missus Surratt that his eyes were furtive-looking.

"George Atzerodt you say?" The name struck a chord with Missus Surratt. She recalled her son having spoken of a man with a German-sounding name whom he'd met in Port Tobacco. That, in her estimation, had been at least a year ago, shortly after John had returned home from seminary college and become the Surrattsville postmaster. He had described the fellow as a most useful ferryman loyal to the South and had since been influential in ensuring his use as a reliable night courier between the Potomac shores. "In what way are you acquainted with my son?" enquired the tavern keeper, anxious to establish that Atzerodt was, indeed, who he claimed to be.

"He called by to see me back in the fall of sixty-two on the recommendation of Captain Cox of Rich Hill. It's been a year since I last saw him. He was returning from a visit to Richmond. I brought him back across the river from Matthias Point."

This disclosure was sufficient to put Missus Surratt at her ease. "Do come in Mister Atzerodt. My apologies for being so inquisitive but I'm sure you'll understand."

"I do, ma'am."

"Only one can't be too careful these days and John has already got himself into some trouble."

"Trouble?"

"He's no longer the postmaster here. They took his job from him... accused him of disloyal practices. As a matter of fact you've called by at the wrong time. He's spending a few days in Washington looking for work. Now, come on in and sit yourself down." The landlady paused before addressing the servant girl. "Rachel," she continued, "take the gentleman's hat, coat and scarf and hang them up."

"This, by the way is my brother, John Jenkins," said Missus Surratt, turning her attention once again to the visitor and pointing towards a seated fellow across the room.

George looked up. Until now he had been too preoccupied in divesting himself of his outdoor clothes and hadn't noticed the middle-aged man sitting by the bar-room hearth.

Missus Surratt's brother, a balding, bespectacled gent with bushy sideburns and whiskery cheeks, grunted as a form of acknowledgment. A large Kentucky whisky stood within his reach on the low mantelpiece. He had dispensed with his shoes, choosing to gently toast his stockinged feet before the maple wood fire.

"Good evening, Mister Jenkins," murmured the visitor, notwithstanding the terse nature of the other's initial reaction. After all, George Atzerodt, as a somewhat sullen and retiring character himself, was not unaccustomed to being treated offhandedly. Such treatment simply washed over him.

"Rachel, fetch that chair for Mister Atzerodt and place it beside Mister Jenkins," interjected the girl's mistress. "He'll be wanting to warm himself after his ride. Oh, and Anna," she continued, turning now to face her daughter. "There's a loaf and some pickles on the table in the back parlour... also a ham in the kitchen, wrapped in a piece of crash linen. Be a dear and fetch them. Mister Atzerodt may like to eat someth…"

135

"No…no thank you, ma'am. I've no wish to put you to any trouble and besides, I only broke my journey on account of passing this way and in the hope of renewing acquaintance with your son."

"Are you, sure?"

"Certainly, ma'am. I had a good plate of oysters before leaving the Pennsylvania House…but I'll trouble you for a stiff whisky please."

"Anna, my love…kindly bring Mister Atzerodt a whisky. So you've come from Washington have you?"

"From Baltimore actually. I'm a carriage painter by trade but the war has sapped my livelihood. With little work this week I took the opportunity to go and see my mother. A customer who owes me a favour lent me his horse. I broke the return journey in Washington, staying at the Pennsylvania House"

"Not the most wholesome of establishments," mumbled Jenkins. "I stayed there once myself. It was always known as Kimmels. I believe young John may also have stayed there."

"Yes, but once was enough," confirmed Missus Surratt. "It was while he was studying. At the moment he's staying with an old college friend who's recently secured a clerking job with the Commissary General of Prisoners. His friend obtaining a job seems to have been the impetus to find himself a position."

"Well, from what I recall of that hotel, I warrant there are nearly as many rogues resorting there as in that ignoble, fag-end of a Washington Government," proclaimed Jenkins with some fervour. "The blackguards seem intent on destroying the Old South and that will certainly be the case the longer this damned war drags on."

"Your whisky, sir," said Anna, handing the visitor a glass of bourbon.

George fingered for some coin in his vest pocket.

"No, Mister Atzerodt," exclaimed the landlady. "As a friend and associate of my son and a supporter of the Confederacy you may treat it as being on the house."

"It's my earnest hope, as I'm sure it's yours, Atzerodt, that this New Year brings forth some better fortune for the South," said Jenkins. After a guarded silence, in the immediate wake of the stranger entering the tavern, Missus Surratt's brother had clearly satisfied himself that George Atzerodt was friend, not foe. In consequence, he had already confidently dispensed with his oft-used pretence about being loyal to the Union and was now speaking openly upon his politics. "Sixty-three was a bad year for us, what with the blockade and losing control of the Mississippi. Then there was Gettysburg and Chattanooga…"

"We were victorious at Chickamauga," observed George.

"Not if you consider the amount of Confederate blood spilt. It was a hollow victory. And now we've lost any momentum we might have had to bring an early end to this war. The way it is, our life blood's being drained… and if it's not the damned Yankee blockade it's the damned Yankee bayonet."

"Still," interjected Mary Surratt, "this year brings forth an election, albeit not until November."

"And therein, I suppose, lies our best hope," said Jenkins. "To get a Democrat in the White House. That's our best chance of peace."

"Yes, but there are Democrats and Democrats. No point ending up with a Douglasite," opined George.

"You're right, of course," said Missus Surratt, "We need a Copperhead in the White House. We need to see the likes of Mister Vallandigham back."

"Hmm," murmured Jenkins, reflectively. "I suppose that while there may be a strong Democratic opposition in Congress, the party's fractured and, as long as that evil rail-splitting bastard keeps defeating our boys in the field, then his popularity will inevitably soar. In all honesty, the way things are going I reckon Lincoln will be returned yet again in the fall. As for seeing a Copperhead nominated and ending up in the White House," groaned Jenkins, derisively, "well…I think there's a greater chance of the sitting tyrant and his lady inviting you and I to take tea there on the Fourth of July."

"I think we have to be patient and trust in the Lord," observed Missus Surratt, philosophically. "Mister Lincoln will reap what he sows. The Old South will survive."

"Patience and reliance upon God's guiding hand may number among your virtues, sister dear, but they'll only help precipitate the loss of the old ways and customs. They'll bring forth the death knell and cast us into oblivion. The war needs to end mighty soon and so does Lincoln's tenure as President. Someone needs to wring his neck or open him up from neck to navel. What say you, Mister Atzerodt?"

George lent forward, grasped his glass of whisky and took a gulp. He was by nature a retiring man. He did not court violence. He was cheered when hearing of Southern victories and saddened by news of defeats; and he cherished the old ways of the upper South. But, listening to John Jenkins, it was clear to George that here was a man who expressed his views with fervour, with passion. And George was fickle. But for the money it earned him, he would not have ventured on his nocturnal missions on behalf of the Southern cause. There had even been a couple of occasions – unbeknown, of course, to others active on the Confederate underground route – when he had accepted payment from Union men to ferry them across the Potomac.

"I'm quietly confident that things are about to turn to our advantage, Mister Jenkins," said George, blandly and without being drawn about gruesome deeds being exacted upon the President. "Like you, I have every hope this New Year will bring a change of fortune." He took a further swig of liquor, emptying his glass. "I suppose I'd better take to the road again, only I've a lengthy ride ahead of me tonight."

"Oh, there is one thing before you go," said Missus Surratt, sensing that her visitor was quickly tiring of her brother's somewhat fervent views. Either that, or he was simply lacking any appetite to engage with him in further conversation – conversation which looked set to waver little from an unrelenting castigation of the incumbent Federal Government. "When John left for Washington three days ago," she continued, "he told me to expect a gentleman…a Confederate agent…to call here to collect a package bound for Richmond. The gentleman was supposed to be travelling south from Montreal and was expected to arrive the day before yesterday. Well, he has yet to appear…indeed, I thought it might be him when you knocked on the door. The thing is, the gentleman's crossing of the Potomac is being arranged by Mister Thomas Jones but I doubt his own journey is constrained by time. The package, on the other hand, is a different matter. John said there was some urgency in getting it to Richmond. It is perhaps fortuitous, therefore, that you have seen fit to interrupt your ride home by calling here this evening. You see, I'm beginning to wonder, Mister Atzerodt, whether I might prevail upon you to at least deliver the package into the hands of Mister Jones. John says he is aware of its importance and the urgency involved. If need be, he can arrange for another courier to take it on to Richmond."

George Atzerodt smiled meekly. He had little time for Jones. The man's closeness to the influential Sam Cox – although understandable, what with them being half-brothers – irked him somewhat. It meant that more nocturnal ferrying work was put his way…work which George would have welcomed. Yet he had no intention of spurning the tavern-keeper's request. After all, he wanted to keep on the right side of those who held sway along the underground route through Prince George's and Charles Counties, and that included the Surratts and Jones himself. If he showed himself to be uncooperative then, inevitably, it would not be in his long term interests.

"I will certainly take the package to Mister Jones, ma'am," said George with little hesitation. "His residence near Pope's Creek is known to me."

"Thank you Mister Atzerodt…John will be pleased when I tell him." Mary Surratt turned towards the coloured servant girl. "Rachel, please go into the front parlour and fetch me the valise on the low chair by the fire… and while you're there check the coals."

The girl promptly obeyed her mistress and shortly returned. The landlady proceeded to extract a number of sealed, brown paper packages from the travelling case and simultaneously beckoned to her daughter. "Anna, my dear. My sight gets no better, especially in the absence of daylight. Can you look at these parcels and establish which one we require. You know how John marks those urgently destined for Richmond."

Ten minutes later, when the noise of departing hooves on the road south had melted away, Mary Surratt sat herself down by the fireside alongside her brother.

"I must be on my way shortly, my dear," said Jenkins. "I'm tired and will not be long out of my bed."

"Will we see you tomorrow, John?"

"I doubt it. I've business to attend to over near Piscataway. I'll be late back."

"Well, being here this evening you've got to meet one of your nephew's friends on the underground route, albeit his presence was short-lived."

"Hmm, can't say I was impressed," muttered Jenkins. "Not much to say for himself and I wouldn't be inclined to trust the fellow…what with those shifty eyes."

"Well, I have to admit…he seemed a strange sort. He struck me as unsavoury and of slovenly appearance. His clothes were in need of a good wash and he reeked of perspiration and liquor."

"If the truth be known he'd probably downed a few glasses at Kimmels before taking to the road."

"Yet it was providential that Mister Atzerodt's appearance presented the opportunity to get that package further down the road to Richmond. At least John will be pleased."

Six

THE RED RIVER CAMPAIGN, LOUISIANA
MARCH / APRIL 1864

Bayou Rapide, Alexandria, La.
March 27th 1864

Dear Mother,

I currently find myself in camp along the banks of the Bayou Rapides where it meets the Red River, outside the city of Alexandria. Darkness has fallen, Mother, so kindly excuse what will doubtless be an untidy letter, penned beneath poor candlelight with inferior ink and with the distracting hindrance of high-spirited soldiers laughing and joking on all sides. Our purpose here is to be in readiness for the army to push north into Louisiana's Red River country, but more of that later.

I last wrote to you before Christmas while the Regiment was in winter quarters at New Iberia in the Teche country, an area of which, to be honest, we are glad to be rid. Familiarity, they say, breeds contempt, and it was calculated that between last April and the turn of the year we had marched almost a thousand miles in three expeditions through that same country. But I digress. My own letter followed quickly upon my receipt of yours which came by steamboat from Brashear City. Well, perhaps you failed to receive that missive but, ever hopeful that you did, I have waited constantly for a reply. That expectation has faded with time although I permitted it to become re-ignited as we entered Alexandria, thinking that a mail steamer might have brought it up river from New Orleans. Alas, my re-kindled hopes were swiftly dashed.

Surmising – as I am now inclined to do – that my last letter must have failed to reach you, I will attempt to re-cap a little of my history I would have recounted therein. I will then bring events up to date. My recollection is that in an earlier letter I had told you about the arduous and hot work which culminated in our capture of Port Hudson. That was written while in camp near Thibodeaux during early August. Well, our time there was all too short, for it was a pleasant place, a deserted plantation home where, fleetingly, life was comparatively sweet. We were permitted time to visit the local town and would seek out ample supplies of fresh fruit, milk and other local produce from neighbouring plantations. We were also supplied with long overdue and much needed new equipments including tents and clothing. Our camping ground was known as Camp Hubbard which I found amusing and thoughts drifted back to my childhood when Grandma would read me nursery rhymes. A favourite was Old Mother Hubbard. Ironically, the old lady's cupboard was bare which could hardly be said of Camp Hubbard's plentiful larder.

Long before August had run its course we were back in a malaria-stricken Brashear City and, by early September, were conveyed by railroad to Algiers. There, strange to say, we were re-united with our old friend the Cahawba to which we had bade farewell at Springfield Landing at the end of May. With two other Regiments on board, we steamed down river to the mouth of the Mississippi. Here we lay at anchor while a large fleet assembled, this comprising a most eclectic mix of vessels, each packed with soldiers or horses or artillery. Well, we set sail for the Texas coast and reached a place known as the Sabine Pass where our several gunboats fared badly against a small rebel fort. In no time we had turned about and were on our way back to New Orleans without a Union soldier having stepped ashore. Yet on no account was this in response to the repulse of our gunboats. The fact was the expedition had been poorly planned and, by the time we had reached the Texas coast, fresh water and victuals for ten thousand troops was already in short supply. Had we pressed on, starvation would surely have proved our undoing. Instead we survived, but, needless to say, the whole, wretched affair was the cause of much discomfiture to the Army of the Gulf.

Soon enough we were back in Brashear City where an overland incursion into Texas was being planned and, shortly, we were again marching across familiar ground, through the Teche country. That was in the middle of September but, come the end of October, our efforts were, yet again, foiled. This time navigational problems put an end to matters, as low water prevented our intended supplies base being reached; in consequence the expedition had to be abandoned and we withdrew to New Iberia. As I have earlier stated, it was while there I last received word from you and I reciprocated with the letter which seemingly, Mother, has failed to reach you.

So let me now bring you up to date. December was dismal, wet and icy, a month of clinging mud and plenty of it. We were told the weather was unusually cold for the time of year. Christmas, itself, brought little cheer, except we were afforded a whisky ration and a friend of mine was generous with some boxed food his mother had sent him. I would never have thought that a stale mince pie could seem such a luxury! Well, a week into the New Year we began moving back down the Teche. The mud and water was so dire as to cause many wagons to be abandoned. As for our horses and mules, the demanding conditions so consumed their strength that some of the poor beasts fell dead from exhaustion. After a couple of days we reached a place called Franklin where tents were pitched and, shortly, the weather improved. Here we remained until the middle of this month when we marched north to Alexandria, arriving here two days ago. What an idyllic day as we made our way towards the city, past opulent plantation houses, the sun all the while warming our backs; and ahead the already occupied settlement encircled by the tented presence of encamped Union soldiers. We entered it to the strains of the Brigade band, with State and regimental colours streaming in the breeze and all under the watchful and, I suspect, impressed eye of our commanding officer, General Banks.

So here we are gathered with the rest of this army, waiting to move out tomorrow. What lies ahead of us I cannot imagine, but let us trust it brings good fortune. We have had a restful two days here, Mother, after ten days on the march and I have had the opportunity to venture into Alexandria, a quite pleasant city situated on the south side of the muddy Red River.

Earlier today, whilst taking a turn about the place, I came upon a photographic studio just off the main public square. It appeared to be doing a brisk business, so much so that I suspect the proprietor was inwardly overjoyed that Alexandria's occupation seemed set to butter his bread rather well. The studio window displayed signs advertising the production of tintypes and cartes-de-visite at most reasonable prices, so I strode in and took my place in the seated queue behind perhaps six or eight other soldiering men. I had occasion, before being seated, to speak to someone in the waiting room. The man I sat next to, a lieutenant from the 156th New York, had overheard my words and, recognising my English accent, engaged me in conversation. He was a most affable officer. He explained that he was of Irish descent and had been educated in Dublin – I sensed to a high standard. I said we had something in common, explaining that both you and Grandma hailed from Erin's isle. The lieutenant, who gave his name as Charles Kennedy, a family man from Staten Island, New York, spoke candidly to me, notwithstanding my lowly rank. I gathered he had first entered the Army as a member of the rank and file which perhaps explained his cordiality towards the likes of me. I, in turn, felt rather guilty in my reticence about disclosing details of my former career. But we talked at some length about England's supposed neutrality in this war, cloaking the British Government's undoubted wish to see the Confederacy succeed and, with that success, a lessening in the growing power of the United States. I ventured to suggest, from papers I have read, that public opinion at home is deeply divided, irrespective of class. I proffered the view, however, that since late sixty-two, when the Union had placed its cards on the table regarding the abolition of slavery, British support for the Union would have strengthened, particularly among the working classes. Poor Lieutenant Kennedy actually spoke of division within his own family, having been drawn into some harsh arguments over his father's unwavering support for the South, a stance that has left the two men somewhat estranged for the time being.

Anyway, before he was called forth to sit for his portrait, the lieutenant and I had fallen into discussion about the forthcoming campaign. It emerged that the Brigade of which his regiment is part has been detailed to remain behind and help garrison the city. Yet he was not exactly cock-a-hoop at the prospect...yes, he did not envy us the march, but I sensed he harboured more than an inkling of desire for the excitement of setting off tomorrow with the rest of the Corps. And thus ended a most congenial twenty minutes or so of conversation. We bade each other farewell and Godspeed in dealing with whatever might rise up to test us during the remainder of this war.

Well, Mother, in fifteen minutes attention will be sounded, then assembly and it will be time for tattoo, so I will conclude this letter without much more ado. We will move out tomorrow morning in the direction of Shreveport which they say is a well fortified Rebel town about two hundred miles further north, up the Red River. In all, the army on the march will probably number around thirty thousand strong, so, if and when we encounter resistance, we should be capable of giving a good account of ourselves. In due course, when my card portrait catches up with me, I will send it to you and perhaps, Mother, you will reciprocate by sending me photographs of yourself and Grandma. That would be greatly appreciated. The photographer said he will be despatching *my carte within a few days, packaged with others. Seemingly, many a soldier in this army has sought a portrait in uniform to send home. As to your own portraits, I am now missing those I always carried with me right up until we left camp for Port Hudson. Sadly, they were then lost through no fault of my own. I kept them in my knapsack which, among other things, was left at Brashear City, since we were required to leave there in light marching order. Unfortunately, while we were away, the rebels took control of that place and, with their occupancy, our possessions were lost. So to obtain replacement portraits would give me great joy, enabling me to look at you both once more. Is Uncle James still mad at me? I can't imagine he would find it easy to excuse my past behaviour and I can understand that he may feel I've been disloyal and reckless. Perhaps, when the opportunity presents itself and I am in the right frame of mind, I will write to him and tell him my side of the story. I now conclude in haste. I send my enduring love to you and Grandma, from your errant but affectionate son,*

William Reynolds

PS. Please remember me to dear Uncle Charley. In my mind's eye I often picture him at work in the 'Sheer Hulk'.
Willie

Direct. Wm. Reynolds
Co. E 114th Regt. N.Y.S.V.
Department of the Gulf
1st Brig, 1st Div, 19th AC

The previous evening's roll call had brought news of marching orders: the Nineteenth Army Corps were to move out on Monday the twenty-eighth of March. This came as no surprise, since word had gone round, earlier in the day, that a mounted orderly – hotfoot from General Banks – had ridden into camp with a dispatch tucked inside his tunic. Sunday morning had, in consequence, seen preparations for breaking camp. Now, at company tattoo, before dismissing the line, Sergeant Stoughton announced to the men of Company E the timing of their departure on the morrow. After breakfast, tents would be struck. The men would then proceed to draw their marching rations and forty rounds of ammunition to fill their cartridge boxes.

Monday morning. Any observer engaged in night-fishing the bayou, believing himself to be well removed from human habitation, might have been excused thinking the transformation was a violation of the natural way of things. An ethereal mist, which accompanied the day's beckoning dawn, hung eerily over the tributary where it was about to enter the Red River. Shortly, through this grey murkiness and beyond the opposite bank of the watercourse, an extensive military encampment was vaguely discernible to the perceptive eye. It was a scene cast in monotint: varying shades of grey. Silence prevailed until the Sergeant of the Guard had called up the bugler to stir the men out of their blankets. Soon muffled voices were detectable and, as the camp beyond the Bayou Rapides gradually sprung to life, that noise became a burgeoning one. By seven o'clock, a soft drizzle contributed to the dampness of the misty air as the men of the Nineteenth Army Corps busied themselves in readiness to break camp and proceed westwards along the banks of the bayou.

Just before nine o'clock all was in a state of preparedness. Brigadier-General Emory and the Headquarters staff began to move out as attention was sounded and the men took their places in the column and awaited the bugle call to move forward. The bands began to play and the day's march got underway. Farewell Alexandria. Despite the drizzle having intensified, the river mist had lifted. No longer were the troops and their paraphernalia cast in the amorphous, shadowy grey of a murky dawn. Instead, all had come alive, both colourfully and tunefully, as thousands of feet took to the road along the bayou. Above the dark blue tunics were borne flags of all types: the Stars and Stripes at the head of the column, brigade and divisional flags, the State colours and battle flags of individual regiments. There was a jauntiness to the many tramping feet as they responded to the music of fife, drum and cornet. Men raised their voices or whistled to the sound of Root's stirring song, *The Battle Cry of Freedom*. Yet, inevitably, that spring in the feet, that enthusiasm, was to diminish as the miles were eaten up. The bandsmen, having given their repertoire of patriotic tunes a good airing, ultimately lowered their instruments. Fatigue took hold. Feet began to blister. At least the column was spared the ravages of a withering sun. Instead, a darkening cloud base had lowered and the early drizzle was replaced by a heavy rain drawn in from the Gulf.

Rubber blankets about their shoulders, the soldiers of the Nineteenth Corps continued to follow the bayou, through flat, cotton growing country. The discomfort of having to march in a drenching downpour – rain constantly thrumming against rubberised ponchos – across a featureless terrain, only served to wreak tedium upon the men. Just occasionally the monotony was relieved by the sight of some imposing plantation house nestling within a sprinkling of live oaks or beside a grove of pecan trees. And still the rain teemed.

"Can't see none of those sugar mill chimneys," chirped someone in the ranks.

"That's 'cos cotton is king in these parts," remarked another. "Just the odd field of corn to feed the farm animals and the niggers. This is cotton gin country."

"You're darned right," quipped a third fellow. "And does anyone know who invented the gin? Well, it was not some damn secesh. No, it was a feller from the North... Connecticut if I'm not mistaken...feller called Eli Whitney."

"Connecticut? Never!" scoffed a soldier from the ranks of the Thirtieth Massachusetts. "The Bay State can take credit for Whitney and his gin. My old grand-daddy's brother was well acquainted with his mother's family, the Fays of Westborough."

"Well, that's as may be," added another man, clearly unimpressed by the connection. "But what is a fucking cotton gin? I've a liking for gin-slings served up by some of those fancy city bartenders but I'm sure at a loss to know what gin's got to do with cotton."

"It's a piece of machinery which makes separating the seed from the cotton fibre a lot easier," said the fellow who had had the temerity to suggest the gin's inventor hailed from Connecticut.

"And the fact is the gin's made cotton production a very profitable business in the South," claimed another voice from the Bay State.

"Has it indeed!" They were words laced with derision, uttered by the man with the taste for gin-slings. "Well, it looks like your feller from Massachusetts has only gone and lined the pockets of those rich Rebs and got them needing all these poor nigger slaves to work their grand plantations. Not a lot to be proud of, I'd say..."

Late afternoon brought relief from the downpour but not before the column encountered a mud bath. Hitherto it had been a dry spring but the day's rains had greatly softened the road surface flanking the Bayou Rapides. Well in advance of the infantry, mile upon mile of covered baggage wagons plied this same road and, before the Corps had completed its day's march, it began to get bogged down on a surface severely cut up by the preceding supply train. The army wagons and the hooves of their slithering six-mule teams had, in their struggles, left tracts of rutted dirt that only served to dam pools of liquid mud: sloughy hollows, which, in the train's wake, drenched and sucked at the chafed and blistered feet that now fell into them. And so it was a relief to all when the foot soldiers, weary and bespattered, were ordered off the bayou road to make camp. It had been an unpleasant and sometimes arduous eighteen mile march.

"This kindling's as dry as newly picked oakum," exclaimed Caleb Trask as he finished coaxing and fanning an infant flame into something that might realistically make a difference. There was satisfaction in his voice. What had hitherto been a smoking pile of damp wood now began responding to the dancing, orange flames beneath. Soon the timber was hissing and crackling. The prospect of being able to dry out after the day's toiling march and to brew a kettle of hot coffee immediately lifted the mood.

"Where did you find it, Cal?" asked William, recently returned from being part of a detail gathering fence railing for firewood.

"In some secesh farmer's barn, just beyond that brow," said Trask. "There's a good deal of hay stashed there, so Jim Corbett and I are going back to help ourselves once we've had some hot coffee. We can sleep on the stuff. Otherwise we'll have to put those wet ponchos on the damp ground."

"You've done well," remarked William. The two shared a friendship forged since the days they were allocated adjoining bunks on the *Thames*. After Port Hudson, they'd taken to tenting together, buttoning up their cotton drill shelter halves to form the customary dog tent. On this occasion, in the absence of something suitable to use as tent poles, William and Cal had turned to the popular contrivance of sticking their upturned, bayoneted rifles in the ground and stringing rope between the trigger guards. And, as was often the case, they had agreed to share their fire with Otis Jones and Jim Corbett who, likewise, were tenting chums.

When on the march, Jones and Corbett each made a habit of carrying a hardwood split stake, suitably fashioned to thrust in the ground either side of a camp fire. As a consequence, with a stick bridging the two uprights and a mess kettle to suspend from it, an early supply of brewing coffee was always guaranteed when sharing a fireside with this pairing of friends. And now, in a gathering twilight, as a damp, evening chill hung over the encampment, dippers were frequently replenished from the kettle of steaming, generously sweetened coffee. The four had already despatched a fried supper of sow-belly salted pork, supplemented by skillygalee – wetted hard bread, browned in the meat fat. Now they all sat comfortably, each on a thick wad of the seized forage brought by Trask and Corbett from the farmer's hay barn. With empty supper plates put aside, four pairs of bare feet were pressed towards the fire, their day's chafings drawing some comfort from the warmth of the embers. Above, and dangling from slender switches cut from a cluster of nearby saplings, wet and mud-caked brogans bobbed and twisted at the end of their arcing supports. Weather permitting, they would be more serviceable on the morrow.

"A penny for your thoughts, Cal," demanded William, as he half raised himself to a standing position and refilled his dipper.

Caleb Trask looked William in the eye, his erstwhile pensive expression – which had prompted the comment – now transformed into something which conveyed bafflement.

"Sorry…it's an old English turn of phrase. I simply want to know what you're thinking."

"Well, to be honest I was thinking how we have all been closely courted by the shadow of death these past fifteen months and how the time has flown since we reached Ship Island."

"Flown in part, except when we were cooped up for weeks on end in the gullies at Port Hudson," interjected Otis Jones. .

"I think on the whole you are right, Cal…and you, Otis," opined William, as he settled back upon his cushion of hay. "What I find more thought provoking are the changes we have witnessed since the beginning of sixty-three. To think that those regiments brigaded with us back then are with us no more. We are all that is left of what comprised Weitzel's Old Brigade and gone are some fine men, not least dear Colonel Smith… brave man that he was."

"When he left for the North, before Christmas, General Weitzel said he would be back," observed Jim Corbett, reassuringly.

"Perhaps he might choose to be but that won't be his decision, Jim. I doubt we'll see the General again, more's the pity," said William. "I can't imagine there being a more loved and respected commanding officer."

"You're right, Willie," added Caleb. "Everyone misses him. Now… even closer to home…we're told the Company's losing Captain Dederer… resigning his commission because of disability."

"That's how we lost your namesake last summer, Willie…through disability. And don't let's forget Jack Chidester. Poor Jack had to go because of those wounds he received at Port Hudson." Otis Jones hesitated for a moment and appeared reflective. "I thought First Sergeant John Reynolds was a very good man…perhaps we'll see a Sergeant *William* Reynolds before we're done with this war."

William chose to ignore the remark. He had always said he had no wish to become a non-comm. "The Captain's been a constant presence since the day we enlisted. He's a fair and most approachable officer and likewise, we'll all regret his going," said William, inwardly recalling his first encounter with Captain Dederer in the Baltimore recruiting office. Perceptive enough to conclude he was a naval deserter, the officer had told William there must be grave doubts over his reliability but he was prepared to give him a chance. "Just don't let me down," he had said, to which the new recruit assured him he would not. William felt he had kept that promise.

★ ★ ★

William Reynolds was right. Much had changed, but then war is an uncertain business. Originally placed in the Second Brigade, First Division, under General Emory, with young General Weitzel commanding the Brigade, the One Hundred and Fourteenth was the sole survivor of what became known as Weitzel's Old Brigade. Now, in the early spring of 1864, the regiment found itself brigaded with three other New York outfits, the One Hundred and Sixteenth, the One Hundred and Fifty Third and the One Hundred and Sixty First. Along with the Twenty Ninth Maine and Thirtieth Massachusetts, they collectively comprised the First Brigade, First Division with Brigadier-General William Emory leading the Division and General Dwight in command of the Brigade. At the end of March the Nineteenth Corps – with the exception of Brigadier-General Grover's Second Division which remained on garrison duty – had marched out of Alexandria behind a vast army supply train. The cavalry had already left, as had a large body of Union troops, some borne upon river steamers. They comprised three further Corps that had served with Grant at Vicksburg.

★ ★ ★

In view of problems encountered ahead by the wagon train, the next two days saw the Nineteenth Army Corps make tardy starts when marching off from its overnight encampments. Its progress, such as it was, took the men away from the bayou onto relatively higher, sandy ground and into a land of pine forest. On the morning of April Eve they reached and crossed the Cane River, by way of pontoon, then followed its course northwards in the direction of Cloutierville.

"Well, this wretched wind's got a will of its own but it sure beats that damn mud and rain we had to suffer a few days back." So exclaimed a private, hurrying back into line. As he spoke, he thrust his recovered forage cap back on his head with a determination that it should not again be taken by a gust off the fields.

"This road dust is a fucking nuisance," remarked another, indignantly. "Keeps getting in my eyes, damn it."

"It's not so much off the road, man, but off them dry fields."

"Some of it's smoke, not dust...can't you smell it?"

"Wow, look at that fine plantation house over yonder!"

"Where?"

"To the right, beyond that grove of fig trees."

"Look at that thicket...as snowy white as dogwood blossom."

"That's stray cotton fibre, soldier, blown about in the wind."

Such was a sample of the banter as, suddenly, the column was drawn to a halt. A roadside trough had presented an opportunity to water the officers' horses. Shortly, two mounted non-comms galloped to the rear to goad any stragglers to catch up and get in line. The clattering hooves spawned clouds of dust to the discomfiture of rank and file who swore and cursed in the riders' wake. In more sedate fashion, those officers in the saddle at the head of individual regiments, began moving forward to obtain refreshment for their steeds. Meanwhile, having previously spotted the approaching column of Union soldiers, two field slaves had abandoned their heavy hoes to stand by the roadside and gawk at the bluecoats. Soon they were eagerly fetching pails of fresh water from a nearby wash-house to replenish the horse trough. It was a task they appeared to relish, clearly pleased to be helping Mister Linkun's sogers.

Further down the column, some of the men of the One Hundred and Fourteenth New York had halted but a stone's throw from the entrance drive to one of the locality's more modest plantation homes. The farmhouse could be glimpsed behind its enclosing picket fence and crepe myrtle shrubbery, in front of which an old man sat upon a burlap sack of cotton seed. Ostensibly watching the Cane River world pass by, he relaxed beneath a spreading chinaberry tree where he spooned crawfish stew out of a hollowed-out gourd. A piece of crash was tucked into the top of his shirt to catch any gobbets and drips. On the ground beside him was a tin cup of corn beer. His wrinkled skin and close-cut white hair, drawn to a cowlick over his forehead, told of his advanced years. His skin was sun-cured and swarthy, a complexion as dark as that of any tawny mulatto; yet there was something about his demeanour and appearance that set him apart from the negro. Nearby, the Federal infantrymen paid scant attention to the old man. Many prostrated themselves at rest on the road margin. Others attended to chafed feet, drank from their canteens or, with the help of cupped hands, expended frugal amounts of water swilling dusty and sweat-beaded faces. The old man, likewise, seemed to pay meagre attention to the huge phalanx of soldiers until he had finished his stew. Meticulously he gathered up whatever morsels clung to the inner surface of the gourd with a wedge of soft bread. Once that was consumed he drained his cup of its beer and dabbed his mouth and jowls with his crash napkin.

"Where you soldiers heading?" the old man shouted. It was a question met by a quick volley of answers, mostly disrespectful in content.

"Mind you own business, grandpappy."

"That's not for you to know, old man."

"We don't talk to secesh or lazy niggers."

For the moment the old man said no more, seeing that it might prove easy to provoke these men from the North. However, having already engaged the bluecoats in conversation, some of their number now seemed interested in prolonging the dialogue, if only to antagonise the old-timer.

"No work today or are you too old to weed the fields?"

"I'm turned sixty, so, yes, I suppose I'm old…but I've got hands to tend my land. I'm no nigger slave if that's what you think."

"You've got land?…and slaves?

"I'm free coloured, soldier. Seven slaves…not nearly enough to exempt me from joining the army had I been young enough to follow the call. But from what I've seen of the Confederate Army I'm not so sure I'd want much to do with it."

"Are you saying you're a Union man, then?"

"I'm my own man, soldier. Cane River man, born and bred…not forgetting my West Indian roots. Born, raised and farmed land this side of Monett's Ferry like my folks before me and their folks before them. It's just that my neighbours and I have been sorely treated by the boys in grey. Yes, I'm a Southerner for sure and I kind of supported Louisiana's secession from the Union but I'd say it was an overstatement to call me

151

a dyed-in-the-wool secessionist. And the way things have turned out, the war hasn't been kind to us along the Cane River.

"So what's the gripe with your Johnnie Rebs?"

"I'll tell you what's my gripe. Do you get a whiff of that smell in the air?"

"I can detect a waft of freshly prepared hoecake," chirped a joker, wishfully.

"Then you've got a keen sense of smell, soldier, seeing that what I'm referring to is strong and all pervading. Cotton...that's what it is. Burning cotton. Dick Taylor's men came by and helped themselves to everything in the way of food. Left us precious little to eat and incinerated our cotton. Said they didn't want you Yankees to get your hands on it. Look at that drifting smoke over there," said the old man, pointing a gnarled finger at a smouldering ruin in the middle distance. "It's what's left of a large barn which was packed tight to its timbers with cotton bales until the Confederate Army came along. It belonged to a Creole French neighbour of mine who's away fighting. Well, the soldiers arrived and frightened the womenfolk and torched their cotton. In this stiff wind the charred timbers still keep smoking."

"So why was all this cotton stashed away, mister?"

"Can't sell it. There's a voluntary embargo in force and the Union blockade has taken its toll. Our crops have been stockpiled and now the State government wants us to grow corn and beans 'cos food is getting awful scarce and costly. Seems Richmond is only too happy to see the likes of England and France starved of cotton so they might take arms with the South against you boys."

"So is that what you're doing, mister...growing corn and beans?" Those soldiers in earshot of the old farmer had begun to gain respect for this free man of colour. They were impressed by his openness and honesty: some even felt sorry for him.

"Well, there's been no point this past month or two preparing cotton beds. You can see what's happened to my cotton seed. Nothing. I'm sitting on a sack of it. Instead we have little choice but to turn our hands to corn and the like 'cos food is scarce. But we have precious little confidence growing food for our own households when the likes of our army come by and plunder it. Everything seems to be against us at present, not least a very dry spring."

"Then you could have done with some of the rain we encountered along the Bayou Rapides," remarked one soldier, his voice somewhat impaired by the wad of black navy plug he had just tucked inside his cheek.

"Well, we certainly saw no sign of it this far north. Most of the men are away in the army, so running the plantations is largely left to the womenfolk. Not surprisingly, negroes are becoming restless and inclined to take liberties in the absence of masters and overseers. I wouldn't mind betting that some of the local slaves will have already followed your wagon train or will choose to run off now you fellers have arrived. At least I think I've no fears there. My wife and I have treated our slaves well and they've all been with us for years. The house slaves are like family. So I can't see any of them wishing to follow your army. Now, tell me…are you soldiers also intent on helping yourselves? If so, you'll find that I, for one, ain't got much left to steal."

"We can't deny, mister, that your secesh farms and plantations are fair game for plunder. We have to eat and need to supplement our rations."

"After your prairie schooners rolled through, just around sunup, I noticed my corncrib had been raided."

"Did you lose much?"

"No, but then there wasn't much to lose."

"Doubtless an individual or two hankering for a few ears to roast. But, I'm thinking, mister, other than suffering such minor privations you should get away lightly as far as this Corps is concerned. You see, I know for sure we sent out a foraging party early yesterday, ahead of the column, and gathered in several days' forage to supplement our provisions. The officers in charge would not have encouraged the sort of destruction and burning engaged in by your boys in grey. However, some of those farms south of Monett's Ferry would have suffered some serious pillage in the course of replenishing our larder."

"Well, I thank you if I'm to be spared any further loss," said the old man as he turned his head to the north and squinted towards the front of the column. "Seems like some of the slaves belonging to my Creole neighbour, Monsieur Durand, have abandoned their field labours to carry water and ingratiate themselves with your officers. He's a hard taskmaster is Durand who's away in Natchitoches. He's exempt from enlisting on account of possessing so many negroes but I'll wager he'll lose a few today in the ranks of your camp followers."

Shortly there was a call to attention. The few seconds it took for the Union soldiers to rise to their feet were marked by a melodious rattle of accoutrements in collision – a cacophony heightened by the metallic cadence and chink of tin coffee cups grazing the likes of belt and cartridge plates, musket nosecaps and trigger guards. Before the instruction to move forward was sounded, the ageing free man of colour had vacated his makeshift seat beneath the chinaberry tree to retrace his steps home. His receding, hunched figure, arm raised to signal adieu, was soon lost to view behind the crepe myrtle shrubbery.

★ ★ ★

Two days later the Corps marched into the quaint little town of Natchitoches. As the men passed down Main Street, it was a scene reminiscent of entering Alexandria, with flags drifting in the breeze and patriotic martial music to stir the blood. Except this was a truly dignified little place of a character strongly influenced by the Louisiana Creoles. In particular, its elegant, galleried buildings were overhung by balconies adorned with ornate railings, much in the style of New Orleans' French Quarter. For William Reynolds and his regimental comrades, going into camp on the northern fringe of Natchitoches ushered in a welcome break of a few days from being on the march.

For Company E, the comparative restfulness of that time was only interrupted by the tedium of picket duty and the digging of trench latrines. Meanwhile, a couriered package from nearby Grand Ecore – where it had arrived by boat the previous day – brought a spell of excitement to the recipients of its contents, William included. Here were three copies of his carte de visite portrait. He spared himself a little time to derive a modicum of self-satisfaction from studying his uniformed image. It exceeded his expectation and pleased his eye; and so he added the cartes to the little treasures he secreted inside his tunic, including what remained of Parson Veck's palm cross and the little whalebone buttons that came as a parting gift from Reuben Miller. It was during these several days' respite that an amusing little incident occurred. Relieved at his post from night picket duty, a young private attached to William's Company was determined to retrace the steps he had taken when making for the station where he stood sentinel. His route took him along briary paths through a piece of woodland which, along its inner edge, skirted the distant camp clearing. He recognised none of the paths or their bordering vegetation, after all, it had been dark when he ventured in the opposite direction. Yet he felt confident enough that he could put his trust in his innate, good sense of direction. It was a confidence soon shown to be justified.

Late the previous evening, as he traversed the wood, the soldier's attention had been drawn to a lighted room in what was no more than a modest timber shack nestling among the trees. An old sulky stood just inside its fenced bounds. Its gate marked the beginning of a green lane that showed signs of scant use and which ran away southwards through an enveloping, sylvan canopy in the direction of Natchitoches. The pool of light cast beyond the little abode was sufficient to outline nearby outhouses, including a short run of stables and a hen roost with its pitted, earthen run. As the soldier pressed on, he conjured up thoughts of a meal of roast chicken with the skin done to a crispy turn. It was common enough fare for the soldier in camp or on the march – the foraging parties saw to that – but this private had latterly seen too many meals of salt horse and his taste buds hankered for a fresh, juicy, campfire chicken.

During his several hours stint on picket guard that thought had drifted back to him from time to time. Now, while the surroundings he encountered on his way back to camp failed to draw recognition, that innately sound sense of direction bore fruit. Once again, the soldier found himself looking at the drab sulky beyond the wicket gate. All seemed quiet in the early morning light. In the chicken run, several plump dominique hens scratched at the ground and pecked at some scraps and grit. Leaving his rifle propped against a tree just inside the gate, the soldier stole across the yard and gently slipped the bolts that secured the run. He then proceeded to grab two of the birds and, with an air of nonchalance imbued with enthusiasm, made light work of wringing their necks. Shortly, however, a feisty old rooster emerged from the hen house. Seeing what the intruder had exacted upon two of his hens, the cock bird flew into a seething rage. The soldier was thrown off his stride by the ferocity of his adversary's aggression, the altercation sending him tumbling in the dirt. In turn, the noise of it all attracted the attention of the elderly owner who came scurrying out of her home to see what all the commotion was about.

Horrified to see the sprawling Union soldier in the chicken run, with the irate rooster dancing about him, and black and white feathers swirling around, the old widow took a few moments to take heed of what was happening.

"You thieving varmint," screamed the old woman, seeing the hen carcasses still within the soldier's clutches. She entered the run, shooed the big rooster away and began beating the intruder about the head with an old broom handle. The soldier cowered beneath his new assailant's beatings and her tirade of abuse. He uttered no words of remorse but spluttered a few oaths as he took the blows, eventually managing to scramble away and get to his feet while still clutching the dead hens. As his forage cap lay in the dirt the old woman noticed the thief's regimental and company numbers.

"I want to speak with your Captain, you scoundrel. Now hand over those birds, damn you, you chicken-livered Yankee!"

The soldier, clearly loath to relinquish all of his booty, dropped one of the hens at the feet of its owner and, gathering up his rifle, made a dash for freedom. His hope was that this partial surrender might help pacify the woman and that would be an end to the matter.

An hour or two later, a rusty, creaking old sulky, pulled by an equally enfeebled grey nag, drew up before the encampment of the Nineteenth Army Corps. The elderly woman at the reins demanded of one of the second relief guards to be granted an audience with the Captain commanding Company E of a certain New York regiment. After rather protracted exchanges concerning the nature of her grievance and involvement of the corporal of the guard, the visitor, still seated in her conveyance, was escorted to see First Lieutenant Rorepaugh.

"And what can I do for you, ma'am?" enquired the First Lieutenant, dispassionately, as if he had not already been briefed upon the substance of the woman's complaint. "The Captain of this company is currently indisposed and I fear you will need to make your representations to me."

"Well, Lieutenant, earlier this very morning I heard an almighty uproar coming from my backyard and, upon investigation, found one of your men in my chicken run. I have five hens and a rooster and by the time I had confronted the thief he had already wrung the necks of two of my birds. Well, when I demanded him to hand them over, the wretch made off. Perhaps he had a twinge of conscience, for he dropped one hen, as he hastened away with the other."

"So you've come here to retrieve your missing hen?"

"Yes, Lieutenant...and to see that the culprit, who killed and stole it, is duly punished."

"I have to say, ma'am, that you need to appreciate that we are an Army which finds itself on the move in hostile country. Our rations need to be supplemented..."

"What, at the expense of a destitute widow? What sort of Army is this?"

"Well, ma'am, it is a legitimate practice to live off the land in enemy country. That is a fact. But we send forth organised foraging parties, each under the command of an officer who will always ensure our appropriation of food..."

"*Thieving* of food. Call it what it is," said the old woman, indignantly.

"Well, I was about to say," continued the Lieutenant, "that an officer leading an authorised foraging party will brook no gratuitous damage to property and will always be heedful of the importance of not leaving folk totally devoid of food."

"That's as may be, Lieutenant, but this man of yours was alone and would have made off with all my birds had I not disturbed him."

"Well I'm afraid, ma'am, this State of yours has decided to place itself in rebellion against the Union and has to face the consequences. There is no way that foraging by individual soldiers can be stamped out. Yes, it is frowned upon and certainly not encouraged, but we would not punish a man. Some would not consider taking provisions or livestock on account of having their own misgivings...from a moral or religious standpoint, you understand. But this war has dragged on for three years and such is its artificiality...its defiling effect...that few retain such high scruples. And so, both on the march and in camp, many will have an eye to securing the occasional tasty fowl for the pot. Now, if you can identify the man you discovered in your backyard, I will ensure he looks you in the eye and apologises for his actions. If it is also possible to deliver up and return to you the carcass of your hen then this will be done."

Twenty minutes later the woman goaded her old grey mare into action and passed out of camp. She had been taken along the line of Company tents by Corporal Laman and invited to identify the culprit. Some men were away on fatigue duties but those faces she saw failed to prompt any recall. In truth, the old woman quickly came to appreciate that, in her mind's eye, she had not been left with sufficient image of her intruder's features to facilitate his recognition – an undoubted consequence of the trauma and fleeting nature of what had occurred. And so, with bad grace, the old woman took her leave, without her hen and in the knowledge that her thief had got off scot-free.

Later, as the men attended to cooking their suppers, First-Lieutenant Rorepaugh took a stroll past Company E's tents. He halted by one camp fire. A pile of newly plucked black and white feathers lay nearby. The fire hissed merrily beneath the falling juices of a plump, spitted chicken.

A short distance down the Company street, William Reynolds and Caleb

Trask, busily attending to their own, more modest preparations, overheard the words of the First Lieutenant.

"I'm assuming, Private, you heard about that old secesh widow paying us a visit earlier today?"

"Yes, sir. I was here and darned scared when I saw her approach with the Corporal. Then, to my amazement, she walked right by and I was mighty relieved."

"Well, soldier, that hen looks real tasty and I'm thinking, as just reward for getting you off the hook with that old woman, I'd better unburden you of those two crispy drumsticks."

"Yes, sir."

★ ★ ★

After several days at rest, a renewed ardour among the men of the Nineteenth Army Corps helped quicken their step as they took to the Shreveport road. Their jaunty gait was assisted by a spirited delivery from the bands; and a sense of well-being was fostered by the invigorating intake of fresh, morning air imbrued with the resinous smell of the forest. It was the sixth of April, two hours after sunup and a large column of Union troops had left Natchitoches in its wake and rudely entered upon a land of silence. Under the overall command of Major-General Franklin, the Army's advance was headed by Lee's Cavalry Division followed by two divisions of the Thirteenth Corps. General Emory's men of the Nineteenth had been next to take the road, then a brigade of coloured troops.

These piney woods had already witnessed the passage of General Dick Taylor's retreating Rebel Army which, only recently, was believed to be concentrated at the village of Pleasant Hill, further up the Shreveport road. Now it was the turn of Franklin's bluecoats to snake their way through the unbroken pine forest, the din of march and music deeply penetrating its dark recesses. Seen through the borrowed eye of some raptor gliding effortlessly amid the high thermals, the column might have appeared as a vivid blue stream, meandering its course through the forest. Otherwise, where the tall pines rose like sturdy sentinels set back from the narrow road, as a congregation singing to the strains of martial music between the supporting columns of some lofty nave.

After a stiff march of about fifteen miles, its completion slowed by artillery and infantry on the road ahead, the Corps bivouacked that night along the Bayou Dupont. By late afternoon the next day, having advanced

158

a further twenty miles, Emory's men trudged into the village of Pleasant Hill, where Ransom's Thirteenth Corps had arrived a few hours earlier. As for the cavalry, they had sometimes been hotly engaged, throughout the advance, skirmishing with the enemy in the woods. It was work which continued to engage them several miles beyond the village, in the direction of Mansfield.

Pleasant Hill amounted to a dozen or so properties bordering upon an extensive green clearing that interrupted the monotony of the forest. Here the infantry proceeded to pitch their tents. As evening approached a steady rain began to fall, precipitation that hampered the rear of the column, including the wagons, which continued to labour on the road from Natchitoches.

"Looks as though the Rebs just keep on retreating," said Caleb Trask, who, along with William Reynolds and others from Company E, had been detailed to fetch drinking water from the village cistern.

"Yep...guess they skedaddled out of this place knowing we were on their tail," remarked a newly recruited man by the name of Rogers. "That young darkey back there says they've been gone a few days."

"According to Corporal Delamarter, talk is that General Banks doesn't expect those Johnnies to stand and fight," added Will Fuller, a young man who had done well to recover from a head wound received at Port Hudson. "He thinks they'll lead us on a merry march all the way to Texas."

"Well, that's remarkably considerate of them," opined William, "but I suppose we can be thankful we're not following the Teche. At least it's all new to us around here."

"That must be the cistern...a short distance beyond the stage coach station," exclaimed a fellow called Post, as the fatigue party approached the centre of the village. Straight ahead a large and weary gathering of men were queuing with pails. "But I'm thinking we'll have to be patient and take our turn."

It was a particularly wretched, stormy night. Although content in the knowledge that Company E had been spared picket duty in the dark and inclement conditions, William and Caleb found sleep hard to realise. It was, after all, a night when the disruptive sounds of the elements were augmented by the often unremitting and noisy arrival of those other regiments and trains comprising the rear of the column: men, mules and conveyances severely delayed by what had become a heavy, muddied road. Eventually the activity subsided and the weather relented, only for disturbance to be revived at four o'clock as an infantry brigade from Ransom's Thirteenth Corps prepared to march out. None of this was conducive to equable slumber under canvas.

★ ★ ★

"This damn trout is artful. It sure ain't for tickling." Such were the exasperated words of a pre-occupied country boy from Cortland County. Trousers rolled up to reveal scrawny white calves, the youth crouched on his haunches in a leat upstream of the mill wheel, the seat of his pants but an inch off the water.

"For Christ's sake get out of there and get your shoes on," bellowed a friend. "Didn't you hear the bugle call us into line?"

"I kinda heard it…but I'm also kinda partial to a nice trout."

"Well, get a move on 'cos I reckon we've got ourselves some marching orders. McNeil says a mounted orderly just rode in from the direction of Mansfield. I'll wager that means only one thing."

"Christ, man. We've only been bivouacked here a couple of hours…"

"Just hurry up, Ben…otherwise you'll be in trouble."

It was now around four in the afternoon on the eighth of April. The One Hundred and Fourteenth New York, along with the rest of the Corps' First Division had left Pleasant Hill at about eight in the morning, three hours beyond the departure of Ransom's troops. After tramping some eight miles they reached a clearing alongside the Bayou Saint Patrice, in the vicinity of Carroll's Mill – a deserted saw mill – the chains in its hoist tower having long since fallen silent. Here they stacked arms and bivouacked, thinking they were finished for the day. Then a horseman rode into camp carrying General Emory orders from General Franklin. Since dawn, supported by the Thirteenth Corps' First Brigade – which had left Pleasant Hill long before sunup – the Union cavalry had succeeded in pushing back the enemy to Sabine Cross Roads, some three miles short of Mansfield. Come early afternoon, about the time Emory's troops reached Carroll's Mill, General Ransom had arrived at the cross roads with his Second Brigade, intent on relieving the First in its support of the cavalry. Here a large Confederate force now occupied the wooded crest of a substantial green clearing that straddled the Shreveport road.

Back at Carroll's Mill, seven miles to the southward, frenetic activity now gripped the men of Emory's First Division. The orderly had ridden in with a despatch from General Franklin instructing Emory to move up his infantry immediately. Although the opposing forces had continued to skirmish throughout the day, the battle scene was now set. It was clear the retreating Southern army was ready to stand and fight and, as matters stood, the Confederate force assembled at Sabine Cross Roads greatly outnumbered the opposition. Ordered to be ready to leave within ten minutes, Emory's men set about striking and rolling up their dog tents, tossing kettles of coffee aside and dousing their fires. Into haversacks was stuffed two days' supply of hard bread, sugar and coffee and, within the allotted time, the column was responding to the bugler's call to move forward. Soon all were setting a tidy pace.

In the ranks of the One Hundred and Fourteenth New York a young soldier muttered disconsolately. "Given time I'd have surely caught myself that fine trout."

"Put it out your mind, young 'un, we've got bigger fish to fry," chirped someone nearby. "Just think of those tasty sheet iron crackers you've tucked into your bread bag."

The quip raised a few laughs. To most chuckles there was a muted, nervous edge. An hour or two before no one had truly expected to be pitched into some violent conflict before the day was done. Yet the sound of distant artillery spitting anger spoke differently. The Thirteenth Corps and the cavalry were hotly engaged at the front and, as the noise of battle increased, so the marching men of the Nineteenth's First Division were spurred to greater efforts. Gone was the familiar route step. Now the men advanced at double quick pace…now at a run. The rub of brogan upon blistered feet cut into the raw flesh of many a fellow as the men moved forward, four abreast, across the narrow, dusty road. And all the while came the shout – as some faltered in their strides – of "close up, now…close up."

"This bloody dust is choking me," groaned one of the men. Together with many of his comrades he was beginning to flag.

"Give us a rest," pleaded another, his dust-powdered face streaked by the passage of tiny trickles of sweat. "We need a break and a stiff whisky to cut this fucking dust."

As the pace quickened, few men held their muskets to the shoulder, it being a good deal easier to carry them at arms length.

"I'm dropping out of line in a minute and taking a rest," grumbled Isaiah Bryant, despairingly, his blistered feet testing his resolve in the extreme.

"Try not to, Isa," said William. "If you do you'll not catch up again."

"I'll just have to join the stragglers."

"I'd think twice about that. This wretched dust will be a darned sight worse back there, what with all the movement ahead. You'd do better to drop out for as long as it takes to remove your shoes. It'll be a good deal more comfortable to march in your bare feet."

"Guess I'll do that Willie...you're right."

"Well just be quick about it and choose a spot where you can get in under the trees. If you sit on the grass beside the column you're just as likely to get trampled on, what with all the mounted aides and orderlies riding by."

Within a short while Isaiah had taken his friend's advice. Ahead, the raging sounds of battle, marginally cushioned by the intervening buffer of piney woods, continued to intensify. Minutes later, William was aware of Isa's re-emergence. Once he had stumbled back into line, he appeared to move with greater ease and less discomfort. From the muzzle of his now shouldered rifle dangled a pair of old brogans. What remained of his army socks was meagre, leaving his toes fully exposed together with raw, blistered heels that wept and oozed blood.

"Well, Isa, is that any easier?" enquired William.

"It was sheer agony removing my shoes but thank God, with my feet set free it's already a great relief."

With a short lull in the delivery of calls to close up or to hasten, the ranks had lapsed into a pace more akin to the universal route step. Yet all was to change. An aide-de-camp had arrived bearing orders to hurry forward. The Thirteenth Corps and the cavalry were now in dire straits and being overrun by the enemy.

"Close up, men...close up." Once again the familiar call rang out. A double quick pace was ordered, only for the column to slow to enable the passage of several ambulances proceeding from the front. One of these carried General Ransom who had been carried from the field after sustaining a shattered knee. It was from the wounded General that Emory learnt of impending disaster. Moments later, as the men resumed their hurried progress, a fractious, riderless horse galloped by, its breast and withers greasy with the blood of its missing trooper. This lone animal's appearance was the harbinger of what was to come...a chaotic exodus from the field of battle. Some forty rods ahead, where the Shreveport road disappeared over the crest of a low brow, there suddenly emerged a bedraggled and ever growing mix of human beings, horses and equipment, all in disarray.

"All is lost."

"We're done for!"

"Goddam those fucking secesh."

Such were the impassioned cries, screams and curses of terror stricken souls… infantrymen, artillerists, cavalrymen on foot, as they streamed and brushed by the advancing column…men from the Thirteenth Army Corps and from Lee's cavalry, negro teamsters and camp followers, men bespattered with blood, many exhausted, others wailing, some struck silent and bewildered in their terror. Limber ammunition wagons and ambulances rattled by, causing the men in the advancing column to duck and dive to avoid being swept aside in the stampeding retreat. And as those fleeing the rout reached and began to pass the men of the Nineteenth Corps it was with pleadings they addressed their hastening comrades.

"Hold back, boys, or you're done for!"

"Don't go forward for pity's sake. The Rebels are on our tail. They'll overrun you boys."

"There are too many of the bastards."

"Heed our words, I implore you. Keep advancing and you go like lambs to the slaughter!"

To their credit the men of the Nineteenth Corps appeared to close their minds to the chaos and terror that gripped the fleeing fugitives and which threatened to engulf them: a fear instilled through ultimate recognition by all those bluecoats engaged in the fight that they were doomed to be soundly beaten by General Dick Taylor's superior numbers.

And so it had proved. Spirited fighting, not least boldly led by the Confederate cavalry, had caused the Federal line to fall back into the woods and to adopt a second defensive position. Yet, notwithstanding gallant resistance, the line began to buckle, precipitating a pell-mell of a retreat among the terrified Union forces. It was the beginning of that flight which Emory's men were now witnessing, on the Shreveport road, about three miles south of the battlefield at Sabine Cross Roads.

As the men of the Nineteenth Corps bravely pushed on with purpose, against the stream of oncoming fugitives, more riderless horses came at the gallop. Nostrils dilated, eyes bulging, the frightened animals dashed through the low undergrowth and brambles which lay between the column and the forest. Dispirited and bedraggled foot soldiers and dismounted cavalrymen now began to spill out of the woods, forced off the road ahead into a detour by their own abandoned cavalry wagons. Tuckered out, two young artillerymen sat against the bole of a lofty pine, doubtless waiting upon a second wind to assist their flight. One was a ventman, blackened and begrimed. A sleeve torn and bloodied, the gunner had received a sabre cut from a Confederate trooper as the Rebel cavalry bravely reached the canister-spitting Union guns. The fellow sobbed, not on account of his wound, which was superficial, but because he felt deeply over the number of artillery horses he had seen cut down. The other was a musician, presumably from the same battery. He muttered something about the number of guns that had been abandoned behind the cavalry wagons, destined now to fall into enemy hands. The youngster bore no outward sign of injury but his youthful face was drawn and grey, like candle wax, his jacket's scarlet braid darkened still by fresh blood. It had been a stern introduction to battle, a tough first encounter with the elephant.

Onward surged the Nineteenth Corps to the repeated calls of mounted officers to close up. The vast majority seemed undeterred by the distracting effect and ramifications of the ongoing flight from the field. Instead, here were troops determined to cold-shoulder the palpable contagion of fear and to evince the Corps' bravery and resilience in the wake of the rout of their comrades. As they advanced there was a steely, purposeful look in many an eye. Very few men choose to straggle and dip out of line but those so inclined felt the persuasive prod of a file closer's rifle butt in their loins.

"Fix bayonets!" It was an order directed at the frontliners, including several companies from the One Hundred and Sixty First New York, who were deployed as flankers in the woods, either side of the column. Reaching the top of the cresting road, the advancing troops encountered yet more fugitives, wagons and caissons streaming by from the field of conflict. Yet it was an exodus now fully open to view, one in its last throes which petered out across a tract of farmland that fell away gently to the north. The First Division had reached a clearing named Pleasant Grove, some eighty or ninety rods deep, which was centred around a minor crossroads and traversed by a small watercourse, known locally as Chatman's Bayou. Brigadier-General Emory saw the opportunity the open farmland offered, but time was of the essence. In the distance, out of the woods, figures clad in grey and butternut were beginning their ascent towards the brow of the knoll, in hot pursuit of their fleeing assailants.

Decisive action was now taken. Emory ordered forward the One Hundred and Sixty First New York in a skirmishing role to delay the advancing Rebels. In this capacity they would hopefully buy time and enable the remainder of the Division to be deployed just behind a rail fence which ran just shy of the brow, along the south side of the clearing. Here the ground dipped sufficiently to enable the men to lie low and remain out of sight of the oncoming enemy. Of General Dwight's First Brigade, the One Hundred and Fourteenth New York was placed firmly in the centre of the line with the Twenty Ninth Maine on its left and the One Hundred and Sixteenth New York on its right. The right flank comprised the Division's Second Brigade under General McMillen's command with Colonel Benedict's Third Brigade occupying the left flank.

"My brave men of the Nineteenth Corps, we hope to take the enemy by surprise as they advance up the slope. Let your pieces remain quiet until the last moment. Then shoot low. You'll be ordered when to open fire. God be with you, stand your ground, and we shall win the day." Such were the words of Brigadier-General Nathaniel Banks as he rode at a canter with General Emory along the Union lines, pausing to deliver his words at intervals. He sat high in the saddle and spoke strongly in his authoritative and well-enunciated style. In turn, the stooping men looked up at the revered Banks, their countenances set firm, their thoughts beset with fear and apprehension, bayonets glinting menacingly where touched by misty shafts of late afternoon sun.

"Speaks well and cuts a grand figure for a former bobbin boy from Massachusetts," whispered someone in the ranks.

A severe test was in the offing. Much rested upon the men's shoulders. The Corps' honour and self-worth depended upon a successful outcome against a force which had fought bravely and seen off their earlier assailants. It appeared there was a score to settle. The men knew what was expected of them as they watched the two Generals ride off, their receding figures etched against a western sky now paled by the failing light.

"Look at our boys skirmishing on the fringe of those woods. They're giving a good account of themselves and stalling the Rebel advance." It was one of many complimentary remarks upon the resilience and determination of the One Hundred and Sixty First that were expressed among the troops as they waited nervously for the enemy's visitation.

"You heard what the General had to say, men…stand firm. Our skirmishers can only hold out for so long. They'll be beaten back soon enough…and if those sons of Southern bitches aren't deterred by our opening volleys, try tempering their enthusiasm by tickling their bread baskets with thrusts of cold steel."

William Reynolds recognised the voice that spawned these bellowed words. They came with stridency above the nervous murmurings and mumbled prayers of others...others who, pre-occupied with apprehensive thoughts, had abandoned conversation in favour of introspection. It was the mouthy Sergeant Zuicker.

"Our boys are falling back," shouted someone who had a clear view of events along the fringe of the distant woods. In truth General Emory had become aware of the enemy's incipient yet determined progress in pressing the Union skirmishers; and, while the New Yorkers had continued to show great resilience and backbone, the Divisional Commander had ordered them back before they succumbed to irresistible numbers.

As they retreated towards the higher ground, the Yankees were followed by their marauding assailants who remained unaware of the surprise awaiting them beyond the brow. The crack of musket fire and whirr of Rebel bullets filled the air as the pursuing Confederates attempted to pick off the retreating infantrymen. Meanwhile, just beyond the brow, the massed bluecoats readied themselves.

"Just listen to those approaching gray backs yelling and screaming... they sound like mad dogs, damn them," hollered Charley Ellis. "Well, just come on, my beauties, and you'll get a generous dose of Northern lead to keep your sawbones busy."

"Load, men," shouted an officer, an instruction repeated by others throughout the line. "When I give the order, rise up ready to discharge your pieces, front rank kneeling, rear rank standing. Don't fire until ordered to do so. Aim low. After we pump an opening volley of greeting into our grey-coated friends, reload and fire at will."

The men of the Nineteenth Corps went about their business, biting upon cartridges and pouring powder into their rifle muzzles. Hesitating, some cussed and cringed, as they spat forth an unwelcome intake of sour-tasting gunpowder. Musket barrels began to jangle as numerous ramrods prodded and tamped home bullets. Then, with the application of caps to firing cones, came the heavy clicking of hammers being drawn back. The men were ready for action. Meanwhile, the devilish and frenzied yelping of the advancing Confederate foot soldiers drew nearer, its fiendish and stentorian nature enough to unnerve many a Union counterpart lying in wait ahead.

"If you find yourselves in a bayonet fight, remember boys, thrust and twist...always twist." It was a final piece of gory advice from the wretched Zuicker.

Soon enough the Union skirmishers, who had so successfully kept the enemy in the distant woods until compelled to retire, began to tumble through their crouching comrades who lay in wait on the higher ground.

"Give them hell." "Give them a bellyful from us." These utterances and such-like fell from the lips of the men of the One Hundred and Sixty First as they leapt and clambered over the rail fence and encountered their friends.

A few minutes later the relative silence was broken in dramatic fashion. Driven by joyful expectation of imminent victory, the Confederate line blindly spilled over the brow of the rising ground. Instantly – still yelping and screaming in their exultation – the oncoming Rebels could be seen by those in the Union line. The bluecoats waited obediently…time seemed as if suspended…hearts beat lustily beneath tunics. The Rebels were closing in fast.

"Ready yourselves!"

The Union officer's order was out of his mouth before most of the advancing Confederates had detected the presence of their new assailants. Behind the rail fence an impressive blue line rose to full height, muskets at the ready. In front, kneeling infantrymen steadied themselves while firmly pressing musket butts into their shoulders.

"Aim!"

"Fire!"

The sound of that opening volley rent the air with deafening and astounding ferocity, causing much carnage as numerous Rebels fell victim to a rain of Union lead tearing into their midst. William Reynolds tried to close his mind to the godawful scene a few rods in front of him: a young fellow lurched forward, his grey cap spiralling skywards, his musket clattering in the dirt, his face mangled like a blood orange crushed beneath a hammer blow. Did his opening ball kill the youth? William shuddered at the thought but knew he had to retain his composure as best he could and concentrate upon what was expected of him. Kill or be killed…there was no room for anguish over what his actions might inflict in terms of loss of life and suffering. He was doing his duty. William bit upon a second cartridge, poured the powder into his barrel and rammed home another minie ball into the breech.

All along the Union line men did likewise. Hurried repetition of the procedure then continued apace…load, discharge…load, discharge; and it was performed with such a rapidity and efficiency to suggest the participants were possessed of a kind of automatism. Thus – with few exceptions – the men kept up a withering fire upon a resilient enemy. Only those truly mortified with fear fumbled with cartridge and percussion cap or mistakenly forgot, in the excitement of the occasion, to bite off the end of a cartridge paper before thrusting a bullet home.

With the incessant discharge of Union ball, swirling curds of white powder smoke began to cloud the spectacle of the oncoming Confederates who reeled and stumbled in the face of the leaden onslaught. Ultimately the Rebel line fell back, its complement greatly reduced. Yet further lines of greycoats came again…and again…each time suffering badly as men were cut down by the unrelenting fire.

"Christ, you've got to admire these damn Rebs," shouted someone just along the line from William Reynolds. "They've got spunk to keep driving in, what with so many going down like summer hay before the sickle."

William remained silent, as did most of his comrades, such was the degree of concentration. Like all around him, he went about his task with fervour and diligence, his lips now blackened by gunpowder, his right shoulder bruised and tender from the constant recoil of his rifle. Behind, above the deafening roar of the musketry, the whimpering and whinnying sound of mules signified that teamsters were busy distributing new boxes of ammunition in the rear. Out in front there was little sign of the oncoming Confederates failing to yield against the constant hail of Union ball. Their yelling and yelping was undiminished but heavily interspersed with blood-curdling screams, groans and cussing. The push against the middle of the Federal line was intense, an occasional Rebel breaking through the dividing wreaths of smoke bent on bayoneting a bluecoat. Time and again the Twenty Ninth Maine took the brunt until the pressure seemed to wane and the focus of assault on the Union line shifted to the eastward.

"They're now trying to break through on our left flank," shouted Lieutenant Searle of the One Hundred and Fourteenth. "The One Hundred and Sixteenth is having to contend with a stiff assault and seems to be falling back."

Along the centre of the Federal position the milky drifts of smoke had dispersed, revealing a pitiful scene. Confederate dead and wounded littered the field, young flesh and bone torn and mangled by Union minie balls. Blood from butchered flesh pumped and seeped into the dirt, sometimes pooling as dark as ebony in the half-light. Men moaned, screamed in their pain and cried for help. Harrowingly, some called for their mothers. From the assault on the right it was now the turn of a Pennsylvanian regiment to take a battering. Bullets whistled and hissed overhead but, at last, there was an element of respite for the One Hundred and Fourteenth.

"Looks as though our boys in the 'Sixteenth have rallied and are helping to hold the right," proclaimed the lieutenant.

"That's correct, sir," bellowed a private who had been directed to the rear to help distribute ammunition behind the right flanking regiments. "The Pennsylvanians nearly broke but our boys, bolstered by a New York outfit from the Second Brigade, have plugged the crumbling line. The Rebs have been pushed back over there and the immediate danger has passed. General Dwight has just ridden over to the left flank…seems the Rebs are about to test the Third Brigade's ability to hold their position."

Soon enough the incessant discharges previously heard over on the right were repeated to the front of Colonel Benedict's troops. Yet, as twilight progressed to darkness across the field, the struggle that flared up on the west side of the Shreveport road was to prove fleeting. The Confederate advance failed to turn the Union left flank. Instead it was staunchly repulsed by yet more rapidly repeated volleys, effectively ending the contest. Hurrah for the Union! The abject defeat that had befallen Banks' army at Sabine Cross Roads had to some extent been redeemed by the bravery of the men of the Nineteenth Corps; and this as darkness drew a veil across the day's bloodshed and quenched the spew of fire and violence upon the field at Pleasant Grove.

★ ★ ★

The great rejoicing in the Union ranks was but fleeting. Ordered to remain vigilant – for fear of a Rebel attack under cover of darkness – the men of the First Division lay down where they had fought. Beneath a starry sky, few – at least initially – succumbed to sleep, despite intense weariness. The earlier stew of fear, commotion and excitement, still imbued the taut sinews of the men in blue. What words were uttered came at a whisper. Chill hands felt the need to clasp warm dippers, dry mouths to receive hot coffee. Yet no fires were permitted in a darkness only surpassed in its intensity by the inky blackness of the high pines that stood sentinel behind the Union lines.

"Reynolds…Reynolds. Fall in, man and be quick about it." To William the terse, whispered instruction fell from unidentified lips. Whoever the non-comm, he had swiftly moved on to rouse other slumbering souls into action. Despite his sluggishness, William was aware that others were busy gathering up their equipments and belongings and quietly making their way back towards the tree line and out onto the Shreveport road. He rose up and composed himself. Picking up his rifle, he followed suit.

"What's the time?" asked William as he fell in beside Will Fuller.

"Around midnight, I'm told."

"Good gracious, sleep must have claimed me for a couple of hours. I remember thinking I must stay awake in case the Rebs came again…"

"Don't worry Willie. You'd have soon woken up if those Rebs had started yelling. I guess many of us managed to doze a bit."

"Well I sure didn't," bemoaned a private in the following rank…a fellow by the name of Cable. "I was too damn cold, what with no blanket and only a mouldy bit of hardtack to appease my guts."

"Get away with you, Theo," teased Will Fuller. "I reckon you were plain scared not to toe the line and chose to remain alert. Either that or you were being protective of the rest of us who stole the occasional snooze."

"To hell I was. I reckon I was too played out to sleep and would have given my trigger finger to have entered the land of nod. Instead I had to listen to all those wounded Southern boys lying out on the field wailing for their mothers. To make matters worse, a Reb or two over in the woods started serenading the poor bastards…"

"*Lorena*," said Isaiah Bryant who still resorted to going barefoot, such was the continued agony of his sore and blistered feet. "Yeh, I heard it too…my grandmother's favourite song. The banjo player was good, the harmonica player poor and the singing a shade worse than dreadful. Fact is, the grayback's voice did to that sweet song what commissary rations do to a man's bowels…and that ain't nice."

"Damn right, soldier," remarked the hollow-eyed Cable. "And to think some of those poor wretches out on the field may have breathed their last to that rendition. Now that sure pulls at my heart strings. Well, I was mighty inclined to join in and show their butternut choirboy how to sing in tune but, of course…"

"Thank God you didn't, boy," chortled some wit, to raised and accompanying laughter. "That would have made matters worse…a truly rude awakening for us beauty sleepers."

The guffawing within the ranks attracted a swift rejoinder from without.

"Keep the noise down." The words came from one of the non-commissioned officers. They were emphatically put, yet in a strained undertone which somehow had the ability to reinforce the need for quiet. "We're covering the rear of the column and hoping Johnny Reb remains unaware of our withdrawal. At least none of us New Yorkers are forming the rear guard…that's been left to the Twenty-Ninth Maine."

Minutes later, without the customary bugle call, the First Brigade began its march back down the road towards Pleasant Hill…an arduous shuffle of weary souls beneath the blackness of the towering forest. Few men spoke as all power of concentration was directed at putting one foot in front of another. Yet each step took the Union troops further away from the bloody field at Pleasant Grove and an unsuspecting enemy. To some, as the miles were eaten up, that effort of coaxing forward tortured limbs and feet became an exertion too much. Resolve wilted, legs buckled, men fell out and sprawled beside the road, only to be prodded and goaded by spiteful non-comms to get back in line.

William Reynolds reflected upon his lot as small distraction from the pain that assailed his feet and lower limbs. A year had passed since he first saw action at Fort Bisland but, for all that had happened there – and at Port Hudson – he had never witnessed the sheer terror of the close quarter butchery upon which yesterday's sun went down. The deafening, unrelenting crash of musketry and – amid the sulphurous smoke – the yells and screams of oncoming, grey-clad infantry, still echoed in his ears: damnable Rebels, yet brave men who seemed unruffled as they strode into the withering fire of serried lines of blue-coated soldiers, only for lives to be snuffed out in a trice by Union lead. The smell of burnt flesh seemed to cling in his nostrils while the sight of freshly spilt blood and of warm, newly-strewn viscera kept haunting his mind's eye. In that wearying nocturnal march back through the piney woods, William finally admitted to himself that he had had enough of war. His boyhood hankering for a soldier's tunic was spent…played out. So far he had survived. God willing he would continue to be spared but he had seen enough to convince him of the extreme fragility of life.

Dawn was beckoning, the soft tints of an inchoate sunrise just sufficient to conjure some better definition to the high, sylvan canopy. Suddenly the rumbling crash of distant gunfire resounded through the forest as if thunder was announcing the birth of a new day. Confederate artillery!

"Hurrah! Bully for us Union boys! We've surely duped them grayback skunks."

"Wow…just listen to them Johnny Rebs wasting their shot and shell shootin' squirrel!"

"Those dumb Rebs sure don't know we've skedaddled."

"That sure is a doggone way of cutting timber."

"Guess they're about to discover we've gone and absquatulated!"

"That'll be when the secesh guns go quiet."

"Guess those Rebel horse soldiers will be on our tail once they realise they've been bluffed...something to give our Maine boys in the rear a little more than our laggards and tardy mule teams to think about."

It was but a short while before the Rebel artillery fell silent, leaving the forest to the natural sounds of daybreak...those, together with the reverberations of a column of weary soldiers wending its way inexorably southwards: the constant tramp of feet, the chafing of equipments and leather strappings, the melodic chink of metal, the rattle of wheels bearing gun carriage and caisson. Yet the silence which had fallen upon the now distant Confederate batteries had instilled a realisation that the game was up...that perhaps an irked army of greycoats in the rear, was – to the limping Union hare – a bloodhound straining for the pursuit. It was an appreciation sufficient to inspire greater urgency to the enervated gait of the men of the Nineteenth Corps.

★ ★ ★

Pleasant Hill. Late afternoon on the ninth of April. The men of the One Hundred and Fourteenth New York, together with other regiments of Dwight's First Division, occupied an advanced position in the woods, just to the north of the village. A short distance to the west lay the Shreveport or Mansfield road. To the east, the ground fell away promptly into a wooded ravine. The troops had, since noon, been lying here in readiness for a Rebel attack. Earlier in the day the activity had been frenetic as regiments marched to their allotted positions, horsemen rode hither and thither and artillery was unlimbered for the fight. Now the noise of tramping feet and of thundering hooves had subsided and the Union men dozed on their woodland floors or nibbled at hardtack.

All the while the sporadic crackle of rifle fire told of encounters between Union pickets and rebel skirmishers deep in the woods. It had begun upon arrival at Pleasant Hill when a small group of Confederate troopers caught up with the retiring Union column and was repulsed. Now, and since mid-afternoon, the skirmishing had both returned and markedly intensified.

"I'm shit scared of all this blood and killing," mumbled a callow, freckle-faced youth. His fear was palpable, fuelled by the unattainable wish to be sowing and planting back on the family farm...that and a desire to go

172

sparking again with the compositor's daughter from Lebanon with whom he had developed an infatuation. "That's nothing to be ashamed of boy," said a swarthy, middle-aged private who went by the name of Joshua Nash and rested on his gun two rods from the youth. With his greying, longhorn moustache and goatee he looked every bit the seasoned veteran. "I defy anyone to be indifferent to all this blood letting. I often think how good it would be to be fearless for once…not to give a rat's arse. But it ain't easy just before the battle…you know…the anticipation of what could happen. Most people think of their folks. Well mine are long gone and pushing up sweet grass in the Catskills. I've got nobody 'cept my Maker to think about and if it's my time to meet Him then I guess that's it. But I still find it impossible not to give a rat's arse. It's not death, I guess…just the suffering that can go with it on the battlefield."

"I think a ball of mine killed a man right in front of me up near Mansfield," said the callow youth. "He was coming right at me through the smoke…about thirty I reckon…probably with a wife and children back home. I let him have it at close range. After the fighting I saw him lying motionless in a pool of blood, half his jaw blown away."

"Don't dwell on it young'un," mumbled the old stager. "We all had a hand in yesterday's killing. There's folk out there we call the enemy but it's only them politicians in Washington and Richmond that make them so. I often think that fellers on both sides, had they had reason to meet in peaceful circumstances, could have ended up firm friends, rather than deadly foes. As for killing that man, it was him or you, boy. Kill or be killed. He would have surely run you through with his pig sticker had you let him."

William Reynolds sat close by, half aware of the conversation between youth and veteran. He had been perusing his *Soldier's Pocketbook* and drawn solace from selected scriptures. As he closed and returned the little book to the safekeeping of his knapsack, he recognised the voice of his old acquaintance, Charley Ellis, whom he had first encountered when boarding the *Thames* in Hampton Roads.

"Not so sure that pocketbook is much good Willie. When the chaplain was reading aloud from it a while ago he spoke of lifting your eyes unto the hills from whence cometh help. Plain stupid if you ask me 'cos I sure as can't see any hills to look up to in this goddam Louisiana snake pit."

William cast a smile at Charley – being inwardly amused by his fellow soldier's wit – yet it was superficial. As a God fearing person he refrained from commenting upon what he considered inappropriate levity.

It was now approaching five o'clock. From beyond the main Mansfield road, over on the Union left, the din of battle had commenced. Word soon arrived that Colonel Benedict's men were locked in a deadly close quarter struggle with advancing Rebels. Being well outnumbered, they were getting forced back towards the blue-coated Reserves who awaited the call to become entangled in the fight. Meanwhile, with the success of their objective seemingly gathering pace, the Confederates began to press Shaw's troops from the Sixteenth Corps who held an advanced central position in the wooded fork between the Mansfield and Logansport roads. On the Union right, the One Hundred and Fourteenth, together with other New Yorkers, were promptly moved up into the cover of a pine thicket to strengthen an increasingly loose hold upon the main highway. It was a position rendered vulnerable as Shaw's troops began to buckle under the onslaught and were ordered back for fear of being cut off.

"Listen here, men." It was the raised voice of General Dwight who had ridden into the pine thicket to address his troops. "It is imperative…" His words were lost beneath the noise of screaming Rebel shells and the nearby tear and crash of falling timber. "It is imperative you hold the Mansfield road," he continued. "I put my trust in you to remain steadfast at all costs." And with that the General was gone.

From the open ground occupied by the Confederate brigades to the north there poured an incessant and heavy fire. Shell, canister and musket fire tore into the wooded apex between the two highways. The Rebels had the bit between their teeth and, having already got the better of Benedict and Shaw, were intent on pressing the advantage home.

"Take cover, men, as best you can," bellowed First Lieutenant Rorapaugh. "Use those fallen tree trunks as protection," he continued, beckoning towards a haphazard tier of mighty logs. And all the while, as the men dashed forward in abeyance of the officer's instruction, the thicket was riddled with the scream and whine of Rebel bullets and of grape and canister.

"That raucous screeching, sir, suggests to me that somewhere out there the Rebs are bearing down on us," shouted Sergeant Johnson above the din of artillery fire. It's that same blood-curdling yell they used when pouring forward yesterday."

"Fix bayonets, men," bawled the Lieutenant. "We've got the benefit of some good cover here. Chances are that if the enemy burst their way through our wooded brake we can take them by surprise and tickle them with some cold northern steel."

The clamorous Rebel yell added to the unrelenting noise of gunfire. Now crouched behind one of the fallen pines, William Reynolds, together with others from his Company – including Bryant and Trask and a fellow by the name of George Fitch – still felt the need for greater cover. Although better protected than hitherto, they remained somewhat exposed to a peppering of bullets which continued to fly into the thicket from beyond the regiment's right flank. They made the decision to move forward again. Two rods ahead a dip in the ground, fronted by some old piles of cordwood, promised to offer the greater shelter they sought.

"Wait," insisted Fitch as the group from Company E readied themselves to seize the moment and make their move. Through the trees, way over to the left, the sight of grey-coated troops pushing south prompted a need to remain quiet and concealed. The Regiment was to keep its powder dry, ready to resist any movement to its front that might threaten control of the Mansfield road. As the men of Company E crouched low, William felt a sharp, stinging sensation against his right cheek. Now the rebel movements over on the left ceased. Trask and Fitch beckoned the little group to advance. William hesitated. A warm feeling coursed down his jaw, causing him to raise his hand. Blood dripped and trickled between his fingers. He tried to staunch the flow by holding the sleeve of his tunic against his cheek. He felt something hard, something unfamiliar, something jagged. A large splinter, torn from a pine bole by a Rebel ball, had punctured and lodged in the shallow flesh covering his cheekbone.

Damn… but I have done well enough in this war. I've been lucky and if this is all I suffer in the way of an injury then I have surely experienced good fortune. Such were William's fleeting thoughts. His comrades had by now stealthily pushed forward. Rebel lead continued to pour into the thicket from ahead and from left and right. William made the move to rejoin his comrades but as he hurried forward he felt a heavy thud upon his lower left leg followed by a searing pain. He groaned, as, unable to control his movements, his frame buckled and he lunged headlong into the forest floor, his rifle set spinning away with unbridled clatter. Ironically, the luck with which he had felt blessed only moments before had been swiftly exhausted. A Rebel ball, one of a multitude indiscriminately fired into the thicket, had ripped into William's upper calf muscle.

Seconds passed. Then, looking about, Caleb Trask realised William was not among his comrades crouching in the lee of the piled cordwood.

"Willie's been hit," he shouted, recognising the wounded man stretched out among the dirt and pine needles several yards behind. Fitch and Bryant immediately scurried back to aid the prostrated figure.

"That won't kill you," remarked Fitch, jovially and with a sense of relief, as soon as he observed the cheek wound. The gory stream that coursed across Willie's stubbly chin had slowed, courtesy of the still embedded shard of wood around which the blood was already coagulating. "One of sawbone's boys will patch you up soon enough."

"My leg…my leg," groaned William, only too aware that his gunshot wound had escaped his comrades' attention.

"Christ, Willie," exclaimed Bryant, seeing the injured man's bloodied trousers and now appreciating the greater severity of his plight. "That's a mess. Let's get you out of the firing line." And, in consequence and without further delay, the two privates managed to coax William on to his good leg and to settle into a makeshift seat they created by clasping hands. With the injured man so accommodated, his comrades carried him the short distance to comparative safety, sitting him down and propping him up against the trunk of a tree in as comfortable a manner as possible. As they did so the blood that had seeped into his left brogan squelched in sickening fashion. All around, meanwhile, the cacophony of battle continued, with activity now seemingly concentrated beyond the pine thicket to the east and thus forward of the Regiment's right flank. Here, ominously and mirroring the earlier southward advance of Confederate infantry to the west, there appeared a rash of retreating Union soldiers. In considerable disarray, they were falling back in the wake of sustaining an overwhelming Rebel onslaught.

Caleb Trask was busy scrambling around in his knapsack. His hand emerged clutching a roll of bandaging which he proceeded to throw into the clutches of Isaiah Bryant. "Use this as a tourniquet, Isa, to help stem the flow," he bellowed.

"Thanks Cal," said Bryant, who immediately proceeded to use the piece of linen in an effort to constrict the flow of blood.

"We may have to leave you here, Willie," opined Isa. "It's not looking good. The Rebs seem to be gaining ground. Some of our Chicken Guts are remonstrating with the men of whatever Union regiments have allowed themselves to be pushed back beyond our right flank. If those boys are prepared to rally and fight with us then we might just push back the damn secesh. But don't you worry, Willie. You should be untroubled here until an infirmary detail comes by to aid you."

"Thanks, fellers." Benumbed by the experience, William lay back and tried to rest. Despite his injuries, he was in no great pain. Perhaps it was the effect of shock but he fell into a state of torpidity which, whilst not conducive to sleep, left him disorientated and with scant sense of the passage of time. He remained aware of the noise of battle. It had grown louder, then reached a crescendo. Now it seemed distant, deeper into the piney woods. Familiar voices had gone. At one point he wondered whether he might lose his leg. The sawbones were known to view amputation as an easy option. William felt consumed by a burgeoning chill. He remembered seeing the pile of freshly sawn limbs, raw and smeared blood red outside the field hospital at Pleasant Grove. He felt sick to the stomach.

Now there were unfamiliar voices. Two medical men…perhaps one of the assistant surgeons and an orderly…were leaning over him, blotting out what little evening light still permeated the thicket.

"Steady, soldier…a little morphine on your leg to ease the pain."

Ease my pain, thought William, cognisant of the irony. *Now I am in pain.* He cried out. His frame tensed.

"Sorry. Take a swig of this, man. You're in shock…it will help…until the morphine kicks in."

William felt a mouthpiece at his lips and a cupped hand easing his head forward. The taste of rough whisky kissed his lips. He opened his mouth and took a gulp, then another. He heard the suction of a lid being prised from a bandage tin.

"Next we're going to plug and bind your wound, soldier. Then you'll be picked up by stretcher bearers in a short while. They'll lift you on to a litter and get you back to the hospital for the surgeons to do their work."

William shuddered.

★ ★ ★

U. S. Field Hospital, Pleasant Hill, La., USA
April 27th 1864

Dear Mother,

It is nearly a month since I wrote to you from Alexandria on the eve of setting forth on our latest campaign. It has been eventful and, I suppose, none too successful in that we fell short of reaching Shreveport and, in the process, found ourselves caught up in two stern tussles with the enemy. You will observe that I write this letter from a hospital and while I fear my presence here is as a patient, my situation is improving and I implore you not to fret. I have been incapacitated since the ninth of the month with a wound to my left leg but I am beginning to feel a bit more like my old self and, so much so, that today I have contrived and felt impelled enough to ask for pen and paper. So you see, Mother, I am definitely on the mend.

My wound was sustained during a battle in this very place. Strange to say, only shortly before, I had been thinking how well I had done, hitherto, in remaining unscathed. Well, when I took the Rebel ball in my leg it was at a time when the enemy were in the ascendancy, the field of battle being just to the north of this village of Pleasant Hill. Men either side of my Regiment's position were being forced back in the face of a stiff Confederate onslaught and bullets were flying in all directions. But comrades from my Company came to my aid in altogether difficult circumstances and made me as comfortable as they could. I then lost all sense of time until the battle appeared to subside. In due course I was given further ministrations before a litter party carried me back to this field hospital in the village where I received all necessary attention and where, despite my pain and afflictions, I was given cause for some immediate joy and peace of mind.

My first cause for satisfaction was to be told we had won the day. Apparently, after I was wounded, fresh troops – our Reserves – were brought up from the rear and, together with the rest of our boys – already engaged in heavy fighting to the point of being overwhelmed – had charged into the Confederate ranks and swept them back into the woods. It was a sanguinary affair with enemy losses far outnumbering our own. My second cause for joy, Mother – indeed, for relief – was to be told by the surgeon that my injury was essentially a flesh wound. Here at the hospital I was lifted upon a large oak table and given inhalations of chloroform while the surgeon probed the wound with his finger. Thankfully there was no need to delve for a bullet with forceps and, more importantly, the missile had not broken any bone. I say, importantly, since the surgeons in this army – we call them sawbones – are only too quick to amputate shattered limbs. Well, it appears the rebel ball hit me in the upper and larger of the two calf muscles and exited on the other side, leaving a clean wound. The surgeon and his assistants patched me up soon enough with morphine applied to the injury and a wad of lint to plug it. I was then returned to the canvas litter upon which I was carried here, this having hidden legs that were drawn down to enable its conversion to a cot. So here I have rested for a fortnight and more, occasionally plied with quinine to fortify me and with regular doses of anodynes to ward off the pain.

I feel the worst is over now, Mother, and I thank God that I have made it this far. The hospital is a commodious enough building and, by all accounts, the requisitioned home of an officer serving in the Confederate Army. It's certainly a well appointed place with fine trappings. I'm in the main ward, which was the resident family's drawing room, the bulk of the domestic furniture and any carpeting having been committed to an outhouse. Sad to say, the sweet smells of yesteryear, which doubtless pervaded this grand room, have been supplanted with the most disagreeable miasma. Yes, the sashes are usually raised, for the April weather is warm and restorative but the fresh air so derived is somehow insufficient to dispel the odours which haunt the room. I swear it reaches the open window and, disgusted by the encounter, takes flight from the fetidness rather than opting to dilute it. Only the flies seem to find our open windows welcoming. Nonetheless, I have now reached a stage in my convalescence that enables me to grasp the crutch I have propped up beside my cot, and find my way out onto the open porch which is what we might term a veranda. Here I can lounge upon an easy chair, raise my leg upon a makeshift stool and lose myself among thoughts. They are invariably thoughts of home, Mother. And so I become a touch maudlin as I think of you and Grandma, and soon enough the sight of the limp, yellow hospital flag, out on the front lawn, becomes blurred before my wetted eyes. Refreshingly, I inhale good draughts of clear air – laced only by the resinous whiff of the encircling pine forest – and watch a multitude of winged insects dance in the afternoon sunlight that plays against a nearby wagon-shed. Oh, to be so agile! Then, after my fill of such detachment and being in want of a drink, I retreat back indoors to the accompanying clonk of my crutch upon the drawing room floor.

The wound itself is doing well enough after some earlier suppuration, which they say is good. It is kept damp for some reason and they say it has benefited from the laying on of bread poultices. Yet it is deep and I suppose it will take some time for the bullet cavity to gather new tissue. All in all I feel I have been well attended. I'm told the accommodation itself had to pass muster, on the morning after the battle, when the Corps' medical director cast his watchful eye over the place. As for the hospital stewards and nursing staff, I find them all of a most diligent disposition. The doctor's rounds are something of a daily ritual, morning and evening. Our usual physician appears with two medical orderlies in tow, these carrying the customary dressing and medicine trays, newly replenished by the stewards. He quietly goes about his ministrations, which, in my case, normally involves a cursory inspection of my injury and then the call for a fresh dressing. The man is not blessed with any fine skill in communication although I suspect that is part of the ritual, emitting just the occasional grunt – of which he, only, knows the meaning – or curt instruction to the orderlies. It is his way, we suppose…showing a keen and sympathetic interest in the men's afflictions yet, seemingly, but scant interest in the subordinates who carry them. I suppose he is aloof, being an officer, but then that is the way of the world. Yet he appears thorough in his ministrations and that is all that matters. And when he is gone, at night, we look forward to a cheery face who brings round a cup of good beef tea to close our day. Then the lamps are extinguished to darken our world and bring forth restorative slumber – all except for the Betty lamp that continues to emit its glow above the duty steward's desk.

I'm told the doctor is pleased with my progress although there is every likelihood my injury will put paid to my army career. But then, Mother, I feel my thirst for soldiering has been sated. I have suffered great hardship at times and I have witnessed a good deal of harrowing sights and suffering, the details of which I shall spare you. I am ready for the comparative calm of a civilian life. The prospect is that I will leave this place before long and be taken into a general hospital for a while, probably in Alexandria. Apparently, in the immediate wake of the battle, my Regiment went south with the rest of the Army – initially to a place called Grand Ecore – and I am left here to wonder whether I will every again set eyes upon my comrades in arms. It is that thought which saddens me since living, fighting and surviving a soldier's hardships together fosters strong bonds of friendship.

You will find enclosed, Mother, two small portraits of me in my uniform, one a little torn I'm afraid, what with all the rough and tumble we encounter. If you received my last letter you'll recall I spoke of having my image taken while in Alexandria. Well, here it is. Quite the soldier, don't you think? I still await hearing from you and receiving your own portrait and that of Grandma. One of dear Uncle Charley would also be well received. I think I mentioned that those I cherished were sadly lost when the rebels laid claim to our knapsacks and other equipments in Brashear City. To receive replacements, together with a missive with all your news and perhaps a paper or two, would be a great tonic. Everyday I look for them.

Now, Mother, I'm tiring and will soon need to ready myself for the surgeon's evening rounds. Give my love to Grandma and my regards to whoever, with sincerity, may enquire into my circumstances and tell Uncle Charley that I would dearly love to join him in supping a tankard of his best porter. And do remember to write to me 'ere long. To receive some word from home, telling me all the ins and outs, would be greatly appreciated. I conclude by sending all my love from your presently invalided yet recovering and most affectionate son,

William Reynolds

PS. I forgot to mention that as well as my leg wound, I also received a battle injury to my cheek, caused by splintering wood. The fragment of pine wood was removed here in the hospital once my leg had received attention and I'm told it will leave a scar, for it was a large splinter. I am extremely thankful that it wasn't a shade higher where it might have taken my eye. I can cope well enough with a scarring of the cheek, indeed, one of the hospital stewards said it would serve me well as a trophy of my involvement in this war.

Willie

Direct. William Reynolds, Co.E 114th Regt. N.Y.S.V., Department of the Gulf, 1st Brig, 1st Div, 19th AC.

Seven

Schuylkill County, Pennsylvania

August 1864

The Pine Grove Hotel, Pinegrove, Schuylkill County, Penna., USA.
August 14th 1864

Dear Mother,

It was with great delight that I welcomed the arrival of your last letter especially since it delivered me recent portraits of you and Grandma. I am heartened to see that, despite the worry and anger my actions must have inflicted upon you, neither of you has changed a jot since our last parting three years since. That may sound presumptuous, coming from the likes of me, for I can readily appreciate it being construed as a judgement to help assuage my own guilt. I apologise if you see it that way, Mother, but I mean it sincerely. Tell Grandma it is surely a reflection of the robust nature of the Black constitution!

Well, Mother, you will see from the above address that I am now parted from the Army and a long way from the strife of Louisiana. I received your own letter soon after writing to you from the Field Hospital at Pleasant Hill, which missive of mine – with my own portrait enclosed – should have reached you but a short time later. I had, at the time, been transferred to a hospital in Alexandria. In due course, when my wound was deemed to be healed, I was sent to New Orleans, where I embarked upon an uneventful sea passage to Hampton Roads. Eventually I returned to Baltimore, having officially been discharged from military service at the end of June. Now, seven weeks later,

I find myself in the Appalachian Mountains of Pennsylvania, a far cry from the war and the rigours of Army life.

I must tell you, if only in a nutshell, just how I came to be in this remote part of the country. Well, Mother, I left Baltimore for the city of Philadelphia, a vast bustling place where I took a room in a lodging house for a few days and familiarised myself with the sights of the city and with its history – which is considerable. I had a purpose in making my way to Pennsylvania. Back in the field hospital I got talking to a fellow patient whose regiment – the 47th Pennsylvania – had been this state's sole representative in the conflict at Pleasant Hill. His was a hand injury which, it seemed, would not hamper continued involvement as a soldier and, indeed, his time in the hospital proved a good deal shorter than mine. In talking about all manner of things, I ventured to express uncertainty about my own future and the need to settle into civilian life whereupon he disclosed that he came from Harrisburg, a place not too distant from where I am now situated. He told me that since the start of the war the price of coal had spiralled, on account of its critical importance to the Union's war effort, and with it there had been a corresponding rise in the miners' wages. Many of the Pennsylvanian mine workers had left to enlist in the Army and the labour force had been left wanting of fresh blood. Well, it emerged that this fellow has a relative who is an outside foreman at one of the coalmines hereabouts. Go to the coal office, he said, and if they don't welcome you with open arms and a job of work, ask to speak to my cousin and mention my name.

I arrived here by the railroad from Philadelphia the day before yesterday – today being Sunday – and proceeded to take a room in this hotel. I intend to remain here until I have fixed myself up with a job and found some permanent lodgings. The countryside is far removed from the flat, agricultural landscape to which I had become accustomed while away fighting. Looking out of the railroad car as I journeyed here on Friday, I came upon a green land of wooded mountains, of ravines and tumbling streams. It is inherently an attractive scenery but sadly blighted by randomly dumped piles of shale derived from the many excavations. The railroads and canals seem to be the life blood of the place, constantly conveying vast quantities of coal away to wherever it is required. And, despite the remoteness, the hubbub of activity is everywhere. In some respects it strikes me as a very austere place, both in its soul and its appearance, and, although these are early days, I am beginning to wonder if I shall feel lonely here. It is the sobering realisation, I suppose, that I have been parted from comradeship to which I had become accustomed and somehow took for granted. The little mining communities have a dourness about them, the clapboarded timber buildings so grey and drab in contrast to the green stands of pine and oak which cloak the surrounding hills – undoubtedly a pallid landscape when I think of the colour and vibrancy of Louisiana.

Today, it being the Sabbath, everything has fallen quiet. As I sit here in my room, the sash window thrown fully open to help relieve an oppressive heat, I am serenaded by the peal of church bells and the faint shuffle of feet. The air is heavy and rank with the smells of a local tannery. Out in the street everyone is in their Sunday best sauntering to church. Many seem to be German folk whose native tongue is widely spoken but there are also plenty of Irish. Indeed, the presence of men from Erin's Isle was only too evident from last night's rowdy noise in the bar-room below. Only their deference for the craft of a fellow accordion player occasionally brought a halt to their rumpus as the musician struck up a sentimental old tune. Tell my Belfast born Grandma that one of the songs brought tears to my eyes –' The Rose of Tralee.' As one of her favourites I can hear her now, humming the tune in times of yore.

As for me, I have hinted at the wrench of being parted from friends and comrades with whom I went through so much but I am determined to remain cheerful and not be receptive to maudlin thoughts. In truth, however, I'm pleased to be free of the Army. I witnessed too many bad sights and too much suffering and, although it is not something to dwell upon too often, I thank God that mercifully I have lived to tell the tale. Tomorrow I intend visiting the mine to which I have been directed – just a few miles from here, in a village quaintly named Molleys Town. If I am fortunate enough to be given work then I will set about finding some lodgings. Incidentally I am pleased to say that my leg is bearing up well, although it retains a dislike of long walks and lets me know soon enough.

I will now close, Mother dear, with the promise that as soon as I am settled in lodgings I will send you my address and tell you a little more of my circumstances. In the meantime, I send my love to you and Grandma and my kind regards to any enquiring friends, from your ever affectionate son,

William Reynolds

PS I was sorry to learn, Mother, in your last letter that my uncle, your brother John Black, had, in March, lost the young wife who had accompanied him home from his lengthy military service in India. As you are aware, I have yet to meet my Uncle John but let that not prevent me from tendering to him *my sincere and heartfelt condolences. Perhaps when you next write to my uncle you would convey them to him. Thank you. It is a sad business to hear that a young woman of a mere nineteen years of age has been called upon to depart this life so early yet, as you say, we must trust in it being God's wish and that He has a purpose. My poor uncle must be devastated that the damp English climate has claimed his loved one and left him alone to raise his two infant daughters. Let God give him strength.*

Willie

★ ★ ★

"Yes please!" The official behind the coal office reception counter peered over his reading glasses as he delivered this circumlocutory form of instruction to the next man waiting his turn. His was a thin, bony face, a physiological feature accentuated by it being sandwiched between thick dundreary whiskers, as thick as the cough that seemed to afflict him.

"He doesn't seem long for this world," whispered the fellow at William's shoulder as the next man in line stepped forward. "Looks to be in need of a good dose of elixir. A touch of black lung's his trouble if you ask me."

"Black lung?" whispered William in an enquiring tone.

"Asthma...from too many years down the mine. Thing is, when they get ill with the black lung it usually means putting them to work back in the breaker. There must be more to him than meets the eye if that's his ailment...intelligence, maybe...or diligence do they call it?...such as to be trusting him with the scribing that is."

William chose to remain silent, reticent as he was to encourage his prattling neighbour's baseless discourse upon the health, employment history and capability of the coal company clerk. Fortunately, only a few minutes elapsed before he was called forward.

"Your name please?"

"William Reynolds."

"What's that rather refined accent I hear, young man?...English, Welsh?"

"Right first time. I'm English."

"And I take it you're looking for work in the mine?"

"I am indeed."

"Any previous mining experience?"

"None whatsoever."

"So what was your previous work?"

"I've been in the Army. Fighting with General Banks down in Louisiana." Warily, William waited for the next question, fully expecting his interrogator to enquire of the reason for his ceasing to be a soldier; after all, the fact that he had suffered a serious leg wound might prove an obstacle to working underground. However, the question did not arise.

"Hmm. The operators of this mine like the English...and the Welsh and Scots for that matter. Hard working, dependable and not inclined to make trouble...which, sad to say, can't be said for the Irish." The poor fellow suddenly fell into a bout of wheezing and coughing as if the very mention of the latter race had been its instigator. "Well I'm sure we can offer you work," continued the whiskery clerk, once composed, "but it's not my decision, that's for others to make...once we've attended to a few formalities. There's some paperwork to complete and sign. The fact is, the size of our workforce has suffered since the War began. It wasn't too bad at first. The three monthers returned soon enough but then the draft took its toll. Now the operators are particular about who we take on. They've witnessed some of the bigger collieries having been none too careful at times and ended up courting trouble. Come and see me tomorrow, by which time the inside superintendent will have cast his eye over your paperwork, and I'd hope to have good news for you."

William felt cheered by the man's words. His hope was to acquire work without recourse to the awkward matter of making himself known to the outside boss.

"What of the wages if I'm offered work?" enquired William.

"The terms are good at the moment for the price of coal is riding high, what with the War being on and the need to fire up all those Government steamships. And there's nothing to touch our black diamond...good, clean anthracite and plenty of it."

"So what of those terms?" continued William, eager to learn of the reward for mining the product rather than receipt of a verbal exposition upon its nature and destination.

"In this mine a collier might draw three dollars fifty for a twelve hour day, a grand wage when you consider we were paying barely seven dollars a week back in sixty-two. But against that will be deducted certain expenses, such as having to purchase your own blasting powder. However, if we take you on, you'll not draw miners' wages. You tell me you've no experience below ground so, as an able-bodied fellow, the best you can hope for is to be taken on as a labourer...as a miner's butty. You'll work alongside a collier at the breast doing much of the donkey-work and reckon on pay of around ten dollars a week. But just bear in mind it's terrible hard work and dangerous down there."

William nodded, being only too willing to engage in an arduous day's work. "It's what I'm accustomed to," he remarked, "hard and dangerous work," as if constantly putting himself in the firing line had been anything but. Adding up the figures in his head, he calculated that the monthly pay he could reckon upon would far exceed what he drew in the Army.

"I can almost see your brain ticking over, Mister Reynolds…and you're doubtless concluding you'd earn a darn sight more than when fighting for Uncle Abe. A veritable king's ransom, perhaps, compared to an infantryman's wage but don't forget…there are no quartermasters or commissaries here. You're standing on your own two feet with no army to tend to your every need. Now…let's see your hands."

William duly held out his hands, palms uppermost.

"Soft enough looking, even for a soldier but that would soon change. Cut, chafed and calloused in no time. That's what'd happen to them working at the breast."

"What time should I report here tomorrow?" enquired the visitor.

"Five o'clock in the afternoon…when the day's work comes to a close. Now," muttered the clerk, dipping his pen into his inkwell, "let's just complete these few formalities and you can be on your way."

As William shut the office door behind him he felt he had cause to be reasonably confident about his prospects of securing work. High above, wispy white clouds peppered an azure sky in which eagles drifted on the thermals. Beneath the soles of his feet he could feel the heat which the morning sun's rays had imparted on the yard's compacted, cindery surface. Some thirty rods behind him could be heard the harsh, creaking sound of two waste-laden cars, their axles in need of a liberal greasing, each being hauled by a mule in the direction of the culm dump. In its shrillness the din was singularly grating to the ear, more so than the constant, crepitant noise of coal being sifted in the breaker. William stopped, screwed up his eyes and looked skywards. How fortunate to be as carefree as the eagle in its blithe routine above a troubled world of conflict and toil.

Tuesday…and once again William made his way out of Pinegrove, up towards the hills which rose in earnest beyond his destination…the village of Molleys Town. The walk was a shade more toilsome than it had proved the previous morning. William wondered whether this was because the passing scenery now possessed a degree of familiarity. However, the simple reality was that, being later in the day, it was hotter, more humid and, in consequence, the walk was more enervating in its execution than when he had passed this way before. Furthermore, his left leg was aching, chastising him for Monday's exertion; and so the upshot of a more taxing journey was to delay William's arrival at the colliery.

It was some ten minutes after five o'clock when William entered the yard. Towards him ambled a clutch of older men and boys, recently departed from the breaker, their countenances black with dust and all evincing an extreme sense of weariness. Then, reaching the timbered structure that served as the colliery office, William stood momentarily upon the threshold, distracted by the distant clatter of the cage door from which direction he noticed the appearance of a group of miners. As he fleetingly remained there, door ajar, William was greeted from within by the mutton-chopped clerk who had now moved to the front of the office where he remained motionless, peering out of the window.

"Come in Mister Reynolds. For a minute or two I was beginning to think you had gone elsewhere in search of work."

"Oh, no, sir," chirped William. "On the contrary, being still somewhat ill-acquainted with the locality, I kind of misjudged the time it would take to walk from Pinegrove. My apologies if…"

"No, no…that's no problem," murmured the clerk, whose attention was similarly focussed on outside events. As the first batch of exiting colliers drew nearer and passed within ten rods of the office, faces blackened and begrimed, they squinted to accustom themselves to the bright afternoon light. Many removed their peaked caps and wiped sweaty brows, taking care not to unseat the newly-extinguished open-flame lamps attached to their headgear. As they trudged forward, the metallic chink of empty growlers – the miners' lunch tins – was a familiar one, reminding William of the sound of soldiering men on the march.

It wasn't until the men had drawn level that the clerk abandoned his fixed gaze out of the window and turned to address William. "Now, I'm pleased to say the inside superintendent has given me authority to offer you work, Mister Reynolds. As I intimated yesterday, you seem able-bodied enough to be a labourer but lack the skills at present to become a miner. We've a few experienced colliers currently lacking a butty but there's one in particular the inside boss thinks you'd be happy to work alongside…you being an Englishman. I've just been looking out for him but perhaps he'll be in the second cage for hoisting."

"Well, I'm mighty pleased to be offered work and to accept it," said William, a cheerful inflection in his voice. "I'm grateful to the superintendent. When shall I start?"

"Next Monday morning at five o'clock sharp. We could probably find you some outside work before then…in the prop yard, maybe…cutting timber."

"Monday is probably soon enough, after all, I first need to set myself up with some lodgings…this side of Pinegrove."

"You certainly do, Mister Reynolds…nice and local. By the way, my name's Hiram. You might do well to look at the bulletin board, just outside. Local folk ask us to place their particulars there when they've got rooms to let. You'll also need to get yourself equipped with the likes of a pick and shovel, a growler and, of course, a collier's cap and lamp. We don't have a company store that would give you credit we'd recoup against your wages…like some of the bigger operators…but there's a place in Pinegrove where you can purchase…" Hiram's words came to an abrupt halt, as, with explosive effect, erupted that latent tendency to give vent to his raspish cough. By the time his fit of coughing had subsided the man's attention was once more drawn to the murky windows. "Couldn't have heard the cage that time," spluttered the clerk, "but there's our man." He strode forward and opened the door.

"Mister Pascoe!," he croaked, in his attempt to bellow the man's name, his voice still hampered by the effects of this latest tribulation. Simultaneously hailing the man with a wave, it was probably the gesticulation that caught Pascoe's attention rather than the ailing vocals. "Cousin Jack, come inside for a moment my good fellow." said the unfortunate Hiram, his greying whiskers contrasting markedly with a high colour brought about by the prolonged spell of coughing. "Have you spoken to the inside boss today about a new butty? He was going to have a word with you."

"He said he was intent on speaking to me but as it 'appened we never came together after that. Thing is, the crew found a section of the chamber roof to be pressing so I was busily involved all day setting and wedging new props. But I'd sure as welcome a new right hand man, him being a dependable kind of fellow, of course."

"Well, here he is," declared Hiram, gesturing towards William. "Fellow countryman of yours…meet Mister William Reynolds, fresh from fighting for Mister Lincoln. Mister Reynolds, meet Mister Jack Pascoe…Cousin Jack to his friends and workmates."

"Mighty fine to make your acquaintance William," proclaimed a beaming Jack.

"Likewise," replied William, shaking the other's hand which was firm and strong. From Jack's accent he guessed he was a native of the West Country. He'd heard the likes of it around Portsea, for there was many a seafaring or dockyard man in the town who was from the south west and had first entered his trade by way of Plymouth.

"I saw the boss yesterday and he's happy, given his particulars, that we should offer Mister Reynolds work as a butty. Thought you'd make a good pairing."

"I'm concluding from your accent that you may be a Devon man," said William, surmisedly.

"Devon! Good God, William, don't let us get off on the wrong foot. I don't want to be giving thee a Cornish hug," laughed Jack. "Devon indeed. By George, no. I'm a Cornishman born and bred and proud of it. Originally a tinner by trade, from a hamlet near St Just, down in the far west of the county."

"A tinner?

"A tin miner. That's why, coming from dear old Kernow they call me Cousin Jack, although in truth my name is Jack anyway. So when do you start?

"On Monday. I need to find myself lodgings before then and some tools and such like…"

"I've a spare pick and pal in the spence…sorry, I mean a pick and shovel… that you can have, gratis like, if it saves you getting yourself pennylicken," interjected Jack. "Left behind by a former butty they were, when he took to serving the Union down in Virginia. Just make sure you've a cap and an open lamp and a sturdy pair of boots…oh, and find yourself a growler. On Sunday I'll get my missus to bake an extra pasty and some nice Cornish saffron cake. There'll be no better way to christen it on your first day than by filling it with good, wholesome, Cornish fare. See you on Monday, William".

"Willie…call me Willie."

"Willie…see you on Monday, Willie. Look forward to it. Now, without more ado, I'll bid thee both farewell. I'm feeling a bit leary, as we say, and Sarah, me 'ol beauty, has promised to fit me a dinner of pigsfry which 'appens to be one of me favourites!" And with that Jack Pascoe promptly turned away and took his leave.

"Nice fellow is Cousin Jack," said Hiram in due course. "Salt of the earth, although if you're at all like me, you'll have trouble understanding his Cornish ways and sayings."

"I sure don't know what a Cornish hug is," pondered William.

"He's used that term before. Something to do with wrestling by all accounts. Apparently Jack was a good wrestler in his younger days. Now, let's take a look at that bulletin board."

Several notices had been pinned to the board under the heading of *Rooms to Let* but at first glance the choice appeared limited.

"Would I do better to buy a Pinegrove paper to get a more thorough idea of what's available?"

"Nay," said Hiram, as he squinted at the several notices, some of which were written in Pennsylvania Dutch and required some understanding. "Two of these are good on price," he continued, "but they're both over towards Ravine." A minute or two elapsed as Hiram continued his close scrutiny of the notices. "Aah…now this looks more like it, Mister Reynolds… see here. Written in what you'd doubtless term your Queen's English and right here in Molleys Town. Three dollars twenty-five a week room and board. Well, I have to say, like everything else, the cost is a reflection of the high price of coal and a flourishing economy. You'd have struggled to demand half of that for lodgings back in sixty-two, but then wages were much lower. I'd say you'd do well to make enquiries about the room, what with it being so local. The signature looks like Ferguson. Now, if I'm not mistaken, that's Tom Ferguson…"

"Does that bode well?"

"Why yes. A dourly kind of Scotsman but well meaning enough and a good family man. Nonetheless…a word of warning…"

"What's that?" interjected William, before Hiram had the chance to elucidate.

"He's a temperance man…you know, taken the pledge. Regularly attends some lodge over in Tremont. What I'm saying, Mister Reynolds, is that if you're partial to a drop of liquor then you can forget it. Abstinence is the byword in that household."

"I enjoy the occasional drink like most fellows and would never turn down the offer of a whisky, although some of the stuff I've sampled over here has been pretty rough. But I'm not the bibulous sort and can take it or leave it. If the lodgings were to meet my needs and partaking of the occasional snifter would upset the applecart, then rest assured I'd be happy not to touch it."

William duly decided to call at the Ferguson home before setting his gait back in the direction of Pinegrove. He couldn't risk losing the opportunity of securing such conveniently placed lodgings so resolved to take time by the forelock. In consequence, he took his leave of Hiram, thanking him for his assistance and – memorising the clerk's directions – made his way back across the yard and down towards the village. The meandering dirt road through the mining hamlet ran beneath the shady overhang of oak and maple. It was no starkly timbered pitch village, the likes of which was often associated with some of the larger collieries. Instead it was a settlement exhibiting some variety in the style of its modest homes and, correspondingly, a greater diversity in the nature of its inhabitants. On one side of the village street, the dwellings, mainly log built or faced with clapboard or shingles, stood on elevated ground above the road. On the opposite side, they were largely obscured from view, save for their roofs, on account of being set into a topography which continued to fall. It was on this side of the road that Hiram said the Ferguson home could be found, nestling, he thought, behind a frontage of laurel hedge. If William had ventured beyond the old eastern hemlock then, according to the coal company clerk, he had gone too far. The comment had amused him, after all, recognition of a hemlock was beyond his gift, beyond his capacity to conjure an image in his mind's eye. No matter. Rounding a bend, it was suddenly revealed to him. He had not reckoned upon the tree's majesty alone announcing its identity, rendering superfluous William's lack of arboreal knowledge. Now, some thirty rods away and out of the lower reaches of one of the house plots on the downhill side, a grand evergreen rose to a lofty height above the dirt road. Its sweeping lines shimmered with a blue iridescence where kissed by the late afternoon sunlight. Shortly, from the sylvan seclusion of the more immediate foreground, the alarmist scream of a bird startled the stranger. A flash of blue and white plumage emerged out of the midst of a dense, enclosing hedge of mountain laurel. In that instant William concluded that here was the Ferguson home, not on account of Hiram's laurel, but as if the fleeting presence of a startled blue jay from within its bounds was a foretelling marker; for, just as transitory, there flew into William's visual memory a picture of his father's miniature silk flag in which he used to wrap a few cherished mementoes for safe keeping. It was a Scottish saltire from the Maltese islands – itself a keepsake – which, in its colouration, was that of the bird's plumage.

A singular occurrence thought William as he made his way beyond the enveloping laurel shrubbery, down to the little clapboarded house. A middle-aged woman was busying herself within the shallow front entrance porch, her recent appearance there having surely set the blue jay to flight. Cupping her apron before her, she used her free hand to pluck dead flower heads from a climbing rose, staunchly entwined within the little enclosure's side timber-lattice. It was the sound of William's footfall upon the garden path which drew the woman from her rapt preoccupation. She promptly ceased harvesting and casting the gatherings into her apron and looked up.

"Missus Ferguson?" enquired William.

"Ay, that's me," proclaimed the woman rather sullenly.

In age the visitor placed her around forty, a dark-haired woman of pleasantly shaped features whose calico dress had long since seen better days.

"An' whit brings ye here young man?"

"Well," said William rather hesitantly, "I've been offered work in the colliery and I saw your advertisement. If the lodgings are still to be had I'd like to be considered for them, ma'am."

"Say na mair, laddie. It's my guidman ye want t' be talkin to. He's at his darg e'en nou. Whan he gets hame he'll be awantin his supper, than a ken he's gat a pickle troke doun at the kirk. The morn's nicht he's gat a gaitherin t' kep sae he coudna see ye than, mair's the peety. Ay, but he'll be roond aboot on Fuirsday…lat's say at seiven o' the knock. A'll mak certain he's awa by."

"That'll be fine ma'am," said William, trying to hide his undoubted disappointment at not securing an earlier audience with Ferguson. His wife's broad Scottish dialect had – in its understanding – been a challenge, yet he had spent much of his early childhood in the company of his Lowland born father and had little trouble grasping the gist of Missus Ferguson's words. "Until Thursday then…goodbye, ma'am."

"Fareweel maister," replied Missus Ferguson, who, without further ado, resumed the deadheading of her rose.

★ ★ ★

"Damnable weather for an August day, Mister Reynolds," observed the proprietor of the Pine Grove Hotel as he stood at the dining room window watching raindrops course down the glass. "But I detect it's becoming a little more intermittent. Now, are you sure I can't tempt you with a beer or something a trifle stronger to help your supper on its way?"

William's reply was slow in coming as he finished chewing and despatching a piece of beefsteak. "I regret I must refrain from any intoxicant, landlord, for fear of it being perceived upon my breath. That would be nothing short of calamitous since the gentleman I'm meeting is a fervent believer in temperance. It's bad enough tramping to Molley's Town in this weather but at least, as things are, there must be a fair chance of passing whatever scrutiny the fellow exacts upon his would-be lodgers."

"Very well. A sensible manoeuvre in the circumstances. To attempt to persuade you otherwise would be wrong of me," declared the proprietor. "Now, do you see that umbrella in the stand by the door? Take it with you. A commercial traveller on his way to Port Carbon left it here last winter and never returned for it."

A while later William stood in the little timber porch and waited for a response to his knock on the door. Casting an eye over the climbing rose, he concluded that Missus Ferguson had been meticulous in her attentions, for there was not a spent flower head to be seen.

The door shuddered upon its hinges as it was drawn open by its owner. Simultaneously, a residual waft of home cooking was released, supplanting the rose's gentle evening fragrance. A man of some proportion stood before the visitor, his own frame amply filling that of the doorway. Mister Ferguson greeted his visitor with the mere hint of a smile. Ironically, others – not being acquainted with the family's mores – might have mistaken the ruddiness of his complexion as indicative of a recent intake of firewater. William knew otherwise.

"Good evening, sir," said William chirpily. "I believe you are expecting me to call at this time."

"Yes," answered Ferguson, abruptly. "My wife seemed tae think ye war English, frae the soond o' yer voice, but she omeeted tae ask yer name."

"William Reynolds, sir."

"Weelum Reynolds. Now, A unnerstaund, Maister Reynolds, that ye hae wark in yonder pit an are leukin for ludgins."

"That's correct, sir. I start work on Monday next and am currently staying at the Pine Grove Hotel."

"Weel, without forder ado, stap inby young man, oot o' the rain. We'll discuss yer requirements an let ye ken my stipulations."

"It's stopped , sir."

"Beg yer whit?"

"The rain, sir…it's stopped. Can I leave my umbrella to dry in the porch?"

"Please do," mumbled the elder man as he ushered William into the house. "By the way, it's remiss o' me but I forgot tae introduce mysel. My name, sir, is Thomas Ferguson. Yv'e met ma guid leddy, that's Flora. She's borne me three bairns...Duncan, Ruth an Lorna an, suffice to say, ye will gather frae oor hamelt that we're Scots."

"I'm part Scots myself," professed William. "My late father came from Edinburgh."

"Edinburrae, indeed...Auld Reekie. Weel, man, we uised tae dwall in a wee village in West Lothian, but ten miles frae Edinburrae. Nou, juist ye stap in here Maister Reynolds," said Ferguson, pointing the way through an open door. "Sit yoursel doun here in the parlour. It'll be seelent here an we can talk. Supper's ower an, wi the rain haein eased, the childer have gane intae the kailyaird. Their task is tae rid the crops o' ony gaun-aboot slugs an snails drawn frae thair lairs by the damp mochiness. My wife is oot in the scullery cleanin the supper pots. Nou, haein established that ye be part Scots, part Sassenach, ye hae awready saitisfee'd ane o' my stipulations."

William looked enquiringly at Thomas Ferguson, whose high colour and thinning auburn hair seemed to sit uncomfortably together.

"Mebbe we'll deal wi those stipulations first," declared the Scotsman. "A'll pit my cairts on the table strauchtwey for that seems richt-like. Efter an aw, Maister Reynolds, to pit it bluntly, baith o' my conditions...an there are but two A regard as binding. *Sine qua non.* If ye canna stick tae baith than we canna do business. My first micht baffle ye but here ye'v naething tae fear, kennin yer breedin. A willna enterteen an Irish ludger. I haed aucht nor ocht agin Irish fowk whan livin in my native land. Och, indeed, we an the Irish hae auld affinity...oor ain fowk, some maucht say, bein juist ower the sea frae Kintyre. But A hiv tae say A hiv nae fondness for the Pennsylvanian Irish."

"I've noticed a lot of Irish folk down in Pinegrove," said William, reflectively. "My dear Mother was born in West Meath but only on account of her own father soldiering there." He thought it prudent not to mention his grandmother having hailed from Belfast.

"The Irish hae flooded ower here tae wark the mines, parteecular syne a mony o' the local laddies hae gane awa tae the war," said Ferguson in explanation. "Thay'v buid tae wark hard but thay'v received guid rewairds whit wi the wages on offer. But thay're no saitisfee'd. Thay're wirm-eaten an awantin mair. A mony hae let doun thair Old Country wi thair drunken cairy-on an rowdiness. If thare's a fecht than ye can rackon on the presence o' a twasome o' besotted Irishmen. 'Tis a vile affliction, bein addictit tae liquor. But thare's a daurk side, Maister Reynolds. Thare's a clandestine group abreed that's infiltrated the collieries. Thay masquerade unner the weel-faured cloak o' the Ancient Order of Hibernians…the Buckshots we caw thaim but thay'v an aw become faur-kent as the Molly Maguires. Tribblesome thay are…a coorse, secretive bunch, lawless tae a man, that daunten the pit awners an thair daisters. An thay dinna stap at fechtin… killin an fire-raisin is on thair agenda if thay think thay're no gittin thair wey. An thay thwartled the draft wi sic a conviction that the sodgers haed to be summoned."

"Are their activities a problem in the Molley's Town mine, sir?" asked William, his curiosity whetted, his attention heightened.

"No at aw. Thay're a guid wee company that, as far as A can unnerstaund, are jolly parteecular ower whasomiver thay employ."

William felt he could vouch for that.

"The local pit awners are verra waurie o' the Irish. The fact thay'v takken ye on is testimony alane that ye are weel seen tae be trustworthy an reliable. It's in some o' the mair muckle pits hereawa whaur mischief's mair liken tae be fund, sic as in the Lower Rausch an Lorberry. But it's itherwhaur in the coonty, like ower in Minersville an Cass Township, whaur mair bangstrie seems tae occur. We shuir dinna want thaim anes in Pinegrove an Tremont. Anti-Union, drunken tribble makkers, yon weywart Irish…thaim an thair Democrat and grog shop freends."

"In fairness I found many a staunchly loyal Irishman in the Union ranks, sir," declared William, having yet to make known his previous career.

"Och, A dinna dout it, Maister Reynolds. Bonnie fechters thay can be… juist leuk tae the wark o' the Irish Brigade at Antietam. But A hiv guid cause to pynt the finger at yon liver-faced, couartly buckshots. Thay'v disgraced auld Erin." Pausing a moment, Thomas Ferguson looked quizzically at his visitor. "In the ranks ye say? Ye didna tell me ye'v been in the Airmy."

"You didn't ask me, sir," retorted William boldly.

"Sae why did ye win oot?"

"I was invalided but didn't tell that to the colliery. I had a leg wound, received in battle at Pleasant Hill but it's healed up nicely. They didn't ask me my reason for leaving the Army, so I didn't disclose it."

"A dinna blame ye. But Pleasant Hill, ye say?

"Louisiana. Four months ago. Fighting with Banks."

"Than A guess ye must hae seen a guid dale o' action?"

William nodded.

"Whit regiment?"

"The One Hundred and Fourteenth New York State Volunteers."

"Weel, weel," murmured Ferguson, simultaneously extending his right arm in William's direction. "Dae me the honour, sir, o' shakkin haunds. Ye hae my respect. But keep mynd o'," he continued, "A'v yet tae estaiblish whether ye can yield tae my seicont stipulation."

William knew full well the substance of what was coming.

"Are ye pairtial, Maister Reynolds, tae a drink...an, by that, A mean ony bevie o' liquor?"

"In all honesty, sir, I make no habit of supping liquor. I cannot deny that I've tried a variety in my time. Indeed, when in the Army, I have...on the odd occasion...been rendered a shade tipsy while at rest by the evening camp fire. But I last had a drink of Kentucky whisky four months ago when, for medicinal reasons, it was pressed to my lips after the battle. To be perfectly honest, Mister Ferguson, sir, I can take it or leave it."

"Weel, I apprise yer honesty, Maister Reynolds, an here's mine ain, for A daed declare A wad be pitten my cairts on the table. The fact is that we, as a faimily, belang tae a society cawed The Guid Templars. It mebbe helps tae explain why A think lichtfu o drunken, tribblesome Irishmen but it gang wider than that. My faither wis whit in Scotland we wad caw a whisky bottle...a drunkart. In his drunken hame-comin, efter his tavern visits, he wad turn veeolent an, sae suin as he wis crossin the door-sole, he wad gie my mither a beatin. Tho A stuid up tae him as A grew aulder, it wis no easy, sin he wis a strang-sinewed man, hivin daen labourin aw his life an been a prizefighter in his youth. Weel, it war a merciful easement whan he dee'd o' a pickled liver an whan, in time, my mither depairted, the war naething tae stap us no bidin oor time in Scotland...Flora, hersel, bein an orphant. We decidit tae stairt a new life hereawa aboot ten years sin, faur awa frae auld memories an wi' nae bidin o' the wratchit liquor. A obteened wark as a conductor on the Philadelphia an Reading Railroad whaur a colleague, hissel a member, introduced me tae The Guid Templars an A teuk the pledge. In time A gat a guid position in a local sawmill an we flittit here frae Berks Coonty. We built oorsels this haudin whaur aw the family...mysel, Flora an the childer, are committed members o' the Templars. Short an lang, Maister Reynolds, oor commitment is tae absteenence an..."

"Rest assured, sir, I have heard enough and would readily observe your requirements. No alcohol would pass my lips were I resident beneath your roof."

"Than that is all A need tae hear. Truelins," said Ferguson, jocularly, "soundin thatwey we micht e'en perswad ye tae tak the pledge. Sairiously, houiver," he continued, "the'll be nae birse tae hing tae The Guid Templars, anely tae respect oor beliefs. Likent wi the sodger, thare is a fae to face but we dinna confront it athwart a field. Oor fae is omnipraisent...pervasive. The demon liquor is awwhaur an the greenin intense in some o thir mining touns, no least amang thae dang Irishmen. 'Tis awethegither a wider battlefield than that o' the sodger an, if the fecht is no pheesically demaunding, it can be a passionate ane."

"I would treat your beliefs with all deference, sir," confirmed William, choosing not to be drawn upon The Good Templar analogy with the struggle and perilous existence of the fighting soldier.

"Caipital! Than A think aw haes been said that needs to be said. My anely ither stipulation is the no unreasonable wiss that ony ludger sud keep hissel clean an weel-faured at aw times, his comin an gangin shoud be ithin the boonds o' acceptable oors an he shoud pay his rent on time."

"That is fine, sir."

"Than lat me show ye the room, for tae see whether it wad saitisfee yer needs," insisted Ferguson, as he proceeded to lead William out into the passage and up the stairs. "A'v three chaumers...this wad be yers," he continued, his words partly drowned by the metallic strike of the door latch in its keep.

William ventured into the room. It was a cramped little space with a trundle-type bed and tiny hearth. Spartan in its ornament and simplicity, it spoke of neatness and thrift. A small pine cupboard stood to one side of the bed, topped with a candleholder and snuffer and overhung by a nest of bookshelves – empty but for a well-thumbed copy of the Good Book. Against the opposite wall stood a modest chest of drawers and a rustic chair upon which was piled a collection of temperance society newspapers. A single framed picture hung above the tiny hearth, portraying a man in priestly garments.

"Faither Mathew," said Thomas Ferguson, observing William's passing interest in the portrait. "He wis weel-kent as the Apostle o' Temperance. Gane tae a better warld a few years 'ere now an...believe it or no, Maister Reynolds...an Irishman A respectit ...nay, revered."

"The room will suit me fine, sir," confirmed William, as he followed Ferguson downstairs.

"That's sattelt than, my dear fallae," exclaimed the elder man, "an A tak it ye're content wi the peyment…three dollars an twinty-five ilka week?"

"Yes," replied the visitor.

"Than come i'tae the scullery an renew yer acquentance wi my guidwife," declared the Scotsman, as he ushered William through the kitchen. "Flora, dearie, lat me introduce ye tae oor new ludger an, at the same time, pit a name tae him…meet Maister Weelum Reynolds…a Sassenach…ay, but a guid an kempy fallae, newlins returned frae fechtin for the Union in the Sooth.. He is tae stairt wirkin in the local winnins neist Monanday."

Missus Ferguson received William with a good deal more cordiality than on Tuesday past, although, in fairness, the visitor could understand her previous cool indifference. His unannounced arrival had clearly taken her by surprise.

"Sae whan dae ye wiss tae be flittin, Maister Reynolds?" enquired the lady, once initial pleasantries had been exchanged.

"Saturday would me most convenient if acceptable to you, ma'am."

William's words were barely out of his mouth when the scullery door burst open and in tumbled three excitable children. From the exchange of banter there was no hint of their parents' Scots vernacular, although this was not surprising, based on Ferguson's given timing of the family's arrival in Pennsylvania. The boy, Duncan and his elder sister, Ruth, were clearly old enough to have been born in Scotland but would have been of such tender years, when the family embarked upon its emigration, that they retained no hint of their birthplace. Such was William's reasoning.

"Father," chirped Duncan, much to the amusement of his sisters, who clearly knew what was coming. "Father, I'm wondering, given the number of slugs that are eating our crops, whether it would be wise to adopt a course of action which…while you might consider it at odds with our principles…could, nevertheless, prove most effective."

"Whit is'at, boy?" growled his father. In response to young Duncan's eloquent disclosure that the proposition would be at variance with the family's ethics, Ferguson's frame bristled, his visage all a glower. Indeed, he seemed as tautly prepared as the invigorated serpent – alerted and newly cast of its slough – to spit venom upon further elaboration and thus put a swift end to whatever audacious motion lay upon the boy's tongue.

"Well, it's just that Friedrich Schulz says his father is a grand slayer of slugs by enticing them with a nightly saucer of beer and…"

"Och…eat yer wirds laddie. A willna hear thattan profanity in this hoose. Absteenence in my beuk applees tae aw o'God's craiturs. A'v nae wirrie aboot killin the dang craiturs but A willna cause thaim tae waucht German beer an tae become haul-cock in deith. Be awa wi' ye!" It was only too apparent that Thomas Ferguson was unwilling to see the funny side of Duncan's words as he spoke chidingly to the boy and cast a disapproving scowl at his grimacing daughters.

"Seturday wad be fine," interjected Missus Ferguson, as if keen to deflect any suggestion – in her new lodger's presence – that her children were any less committed than herself and Mister Ferguson when it came to the temperance movement. Once he had regained his composure her husband was, likewise, prompt to change tack.

"If ye want for help transporting yer guids an gear, Maister Reynolds, A hiv a freend near aboots wi a naig an cairiage that wad bring ye an yer baggage up frae Pinegrove for a wee conseederation. A can chack in a wee whether he coud gie a lift tae…"

"That's kind of you, sir, but I have no chattels to speak of. What's more, save for a troublesome leg, I am blessed with a constitution well conditioned to rigorous marches while laden with all manner of military accoutrement. In comparison, an unhurried tramp up from Pinegrove will present no…"

"Och, Maister Reynolds please forgie me. Ye'll consideer me as bevvied as some o' the drunkarts A denunce. O coorse, bein a steenger hereawa, an newlins dischairged frae the Airmy, ye'v anely a wee bit tae lift. Mair ootower, tis wrang o' me tae suggest that ye're onything but dochtie an young eneuch tae mak short wark o sic a wee haunds turn."

★ ★ ★

It was Friday evening and William had retired early to his room. Down below, the burgeoning bar-room noise set the precursive tone for an evening of Irish crack and song, nourished inevitably by the generous flow of liquor. As he sat upon his half tester bed, William tilted his head backwards, allowing the last beads of a brandy and water to trickle across his tongue. Then, wiping his lips upon his shirt cuff, he reflected on the fact that he had partaken of his last alcoholic drink for some time to come. His single bag was packed – a leather receptacle he had bought during his brief sojourn in Philadelphia – its contents now including the several items Jack Pascoe suggested he purchase. The bulky, all-important growler he had tied to the outside.

William shifted himself into his bedroom chair to gain the benefit of the light cast by the room's paraffin lamp. His purpose was to count what notes and coin he had to last him until his first colliery pay day as the contents of his well-worn leather purse fell across the adjacent counterpane. Amongst the coinage nestled a small, broken segment of Veck's palm cross and a tiny, limp drawstring pouch. William untied the pouch string and emptied it upon the bed. Out fell the half dozen whalebone buttons he had been gifted by Reuben Miller the day he embarked upon the *Snowgoose*, the best part of two years ago. Those buttons and the little piece of palm – the latter now but a vestige of the old parson's token – had journeyed far since that time in Lunenburg. With both mementos diminutive and precious enough for secretion inside William's tunic, they had escaped being lost with his knapsack when – during the siege of Port Hudson – the Rebels had pillaged Union belongings at Brashear City. Perhaps, after all, the buttons were destined to be sewn upon a silk vest as Reuben had intended. William's thoughts returned to those days in Lunenburg, grateful for the assistance afforded him by his negro friend and by the cousins, Tom Driscoll and Henry Jackman. He resolved to spend an evening, sometime soon, writing once again to Tom or Henry – for Reuben was unable to read – acquainting them with all the ins and outs of what life had dealt him since leaving Camp Belger.

William returned the notes and coinage to his purse, along with his cherished keepsakes. He rose from his chair and proceeded to attend to such preparations as to ready himself for bed. He pulled back the coverlet and extinguished the lamp. It was ten o'clock and, as he settled his head into his pillow, the noise from the bar-room crack subsided momentarily in deference to the musician's entrance. The strains of *Kathleen, Mavourneen* began to rise through the floor timbers...sweet music...sweet, until sorely treated. Soon enough the melody became drowned by strident, exuberant voices, their owners doubtless convinced, amid the prevailing merriment, of the value of their raw accompaniment. In truth it fell well short of doing the lyrics justice. William was familiar with the tune. It had become something of a favourite, bittersweet song around many a campfire. Now, before the bar-room rendition had run its harsh course, tiredness – stoked by three brandies and water – had allowed sleep to draw him in.

Eight

PORT TOBACCO, MARYLAND
JANUARY 1865

It had been a breezy morning and a mild one for the time of year. In addition, young Greta had slept on and, in consequence, Rose Wheeler took full advantage. It was what she termed a starchy, soap suds morning, her hands still reddened from their labours in and about the wash-tub. Unlike her partner, she was meticulous about cleanliness but this particular morning, the fourteenth of January, she felt a sense of achievement in having wrested from him a generous pile of his dirty linen to cast into the tub. Now her attentions were upon applying the hot iron to freshly gathered-in clothes and fabrics as there came a series of thumps upon the front door. With a sigh Rose returned the flatiron to its usual resting place – a thick piece of discarded cork George had salvaged from the Port Tobacco River. Then, gathering up her skirt, she ambled out into the front passage, in truth a little irked that someone had shown the temerity to interrupt her chores. She opened the door, there to be confronted by a wide-eyed, woolly-headed boy who she recognised as Ezekiel, an orphaned ten year old. It was said the child's father had died of a beating after being accused of stealing a flagon of cheap taffia rum from his master's table. The episode was said to have turned his broken-hearted mother's mind. She had fled with her infant child from her slave quarters on the estate in St Mary's County and found refuge with an elderly couple of free blacks in Port Tobacco. But the slaughter of her husband had been too much for the poor girl to bear. She had wandered down to the Potomac one dark, stormy night and thrown herself off some low cliffs into a watery oblivion. A few years later the old couple had died, leaving the child, Ezekiel, to fend for himself; and this the boy had done with a great deal of success, having eluded any threat of apprehension as the child of a fugitive slave.

"Missis…Missis Atzraw…where's the mas'r?" enquired the breathless youngster, his wide brown eyes glistening like wet marbles.

"Why, Ezekiel, he's in town. He's not working so he has taken the opportunity to run a few errands for me and get his boots mended. I'm expecting him back in about half an hour."

"It's just, missis, that I was outside the Courthouse and overheard two riders enquiring after Mas'r Atzraw. They'd been to The Chimney House looking for him. Said the place was all locked up. I told the gentlemen I could probably get a message to Mas'r Atzraw. They seemed grateful and said they'd wait at Brawners until I reported back or the mas'r appeared."

Rose almost bit her tongue. It was a sore reality that times were hard and, with so little carriage work coming George's way, the last place she wanted him frequenting was Brawner's cellar bar. Strong words had left Rose's lips only a few days previously, after George had been paid for completing a rare piece of scroll work on a gentleman's curricle. His willpower had been found wanting when he promptly blew half his earnings on liquor, much to Rose's anguish. He would surely not venture into that den of iniquity so soon, thought his common law wife…so soon after her disapprobation of his conduct had resulted in the most almighty of rows.

"Now Ezekiel, did either of the riders give his name?"

"The thin one called himself Surrit…John Surrit."

Rose had heard George mention a John Surratt…a fellow who helped his mother run a tavern at some crossroads this side of Washington and a key figure in the Confederate underground.

"What did the gentleman say about wanting to see Mister Atzerodt?"

"Only, missis, that he needed to speak to him urgently. A business matter he said."

"Well, tell the two gentlemen that I am expecting him home soon and that they can reckon upon seeing him at Brawner's within the hour."

And with that Ezekiel turned and scurried away, anxious to impart the information to the two strangers and to be rewarded with a welcome few cents for his trouble.

Rose was true to her word. Fifty minutes later, George Atzerodt's newly-heeled boots trod their way crisply over the gravelled apron that fronted Brawners Hotel. But Rose had laid down the law. George was under strict instructions not to dally there: simply to hear the men out, then to take his leave. After all, it was a Saturday and on Saturday afternoons he was expected to take his turn to amuse young Greta, relieving Rose of a responsibility which at other times was hers alone. Furthermore, if these gentlemen were seeking an audience with him, then, as far as Rose was concerned, they could foot the bill for whatever they chose to swill down their collective throats. Sadly, the weak-willed George was only too often the prey of barflies to the serious detriment of the family finances. Rose had learnt the hard way. And so, on returning home from his trip into town, she had purposely relieved George of the bulk of what cash remained in his pocket, much to his chagrin, yet leaving her in the knowledge that the coming week would at least see food on the table.

George had distractedly commenced his descent into the cellar bar, his curiosity incited by reflections upon what sort of business had brought young Johnny Surratt to see him and just who was his companion.

"George up here, man…George!"

The voice drew Atzerodt from his muse. He retraced his steps, back up the creaking staircase and craned his neck backwards. In so doing he found himself gazing at the beckoning figure of John Surratt, a glass of whisky firmly clutched in his right hand. The former Surrattsville postmaster was leaning over the top balcony rail to the hotel's front porch, an ornate timbered structure which ran the length of the building and provided access to the main reception hall, dining accommodation and saloon.

"Come up here and join us, George," yelled the erstwhile postmaster, an instruction to which Atzerodt promptly acquiesced by proceeding to negotiate the porch's short flight of steps. "Good to see you, George. You're looking well," said the younger man, warmly. In contrast, his affable demeanour drew little more than a grunt from Atzerodt, so preoccupied was he with conjecture over the other's reason for seeking him out. "Come in here and meet Tom Harbin."

Surratt ushered George into the entrance hall where a porter, going about his business, glanced fleetingly at the new arrival. George seemed to notice it, since it was a telling peep, a glance of recognition. It was as if the red-vested darkey was more than a little startled to set eyes upon this rather dishevelled and dyed-in-the-wool cellar bar regular up here in the vestibule, in unfamiliar and altogether more wholesome surroundings.

In the wake of the porter scurrying away, George's eyes were drawn towards the entrance hall's grandfather clock. It had just struck the half hour after eleven and a rather stocky, well dressed man was checking his pocket watch against the lofty old timepiece.

"Tom…let me introduce you to George Atzerodt," said John Surratt, prompting the other man to turn about as he simultaneously returned the little silver-cased possession to his vest pocket.

"Guess I need to purchase myself a new watch," the stranger remarked emphatically, as if he needed to get the observation off his chest before turning his attentions to George. He then proffered his outstretched arm in the German's direction and, with George reciprocating, genially shook him by the hand. "Well, it sure is a pleasure to make your acquaintance Mister Atzerodt. John has told me plenty about you."

George felt a shade awkward, albeit in the knowledge that, whatever Surratt had said, it should have cast him in a good light. After all, he had a reputation as a capable ferryman and had always diligently gone about his numerous missions for the Confederate underground. John Surratt had every reason to portray him in a propitious way.

"Let us repair to the saloon bar," suggested the beaming Harbin. As he spoke, he ferreted within a pocket of his outdoor coat which hung to the side of the large, mirrored hall table. He took out an ornate little snuff box. He then dallied a moment to adjust his necktie before recovering a half consumed glass of bourbon he had placed upon the table. A smart, thick-set fellow, with broad forehead, moustache and goatee, Harbin struck the carriage painter as being particular – perhaps fastidious – about his appearance: in short the very antithesis of his dowdy self.

"Another whisky please, waiter," shouted Surratt to a uniformed drinks waiter who was busying himself polishing glasses.

"Yes, suh. Right away, suh," came the high-pitched reply.

The bar was deserted, save for the presence of a tobacco trader in detached and earnest conversation with a potential client. Leading the way, Tom Harbin made a beeline for a far corner of the room which seemed to offer the best prospect of privacy.

"Snuff?" proffered Tom, as he applied a pinch to the back of his hand and drew it into his nostrils. It was an offer his companions declined to accept, both choosing facial expression over words to adequately convey their desire to forego it.

The clink of a whisky glass set down by the waiter, followed by the metallic rattle of coins being cast upon the table by John Surratt seemed to inspire Atzerodt to emerge from his quietude.

"How are things at your mother's tavern, John?" he enquired. "It must have been around this time last year when I called by and Missus Surratt and your uncle made me most welcome."

"Things have moved on since then George. It no longer suited us living in the country and it made greater sense, financially, to move into the city. So the Surrattsville property is now leased and my mother runs a boardinghouse on H Street."

"What of the new tavern-keeper?"

"A fellow about forty by the name of Lloyd."

"Is he cooperative and committed to secrecy…you know…as far as our work is concerned?"

"He's no stout-hearted Southron and I sense he would do his utmost to appear to the authorities as a good Union man and strive to keep his nose clean. But…let us say we have an understanding with our tenant and the tavern remains a safe haven for our friends moving between Richmond and Canada. To be honest, George, I don't suppose Lloyd has too deep an interest in politics. He has a far greater affection for his liquor and often seems to be three sheets in the wind."

"Well," pondered George, "liquor's not a bad thing to have a liking for…just as long as your new tavern keeper doesn't let it render him loose-tongued in the wrong company." It was a sobering thought and one tinged with irony, coming from the bibulous and faint-hearted little Prussian. John merely shrugged as the carriage painter took a generous gulp of his bourbon.

"So how's your carriage work these days, George?" enquired Surratt as he watched the tobacco trader and his companion shake on a deal and take an unsteady leave.

"Dire. It's all but dried up. I can barely scrape together enough to feed the family once I've settled my dues with Mister Barton who owns The Chimney House. Thank God some ferrying work keeps coming my way, although I had a bit of a fright one dark night last month. I'd been across the river with a friend of Captain Cox who was bound for Richmond. Well, I was rowing back, a shade preoccupied with the sound of my own humming and the gentle rhythm of my oar blades in the water, when I became suddenly aware of a bright light ahead, shimmering on the surface of the river. And there were voices. I immediately shipped my oars, quenched what modest light I had and allowed myself to drift. You see, I feared it might be some Federal patrol."

"So what happened, then?"

"Once I had stopped rowing the voices became clearer as they drifted over the water. I quickly satisfied myself that they did not belong to a patrol. The fact is, they were quite rowdy at times and occasionally peppered with laughter. By the time the tide and currents had drawn me down river and away from the other boat I had concluded that its occupants were probably none other than a couple of intoxicated fishermen. I suspect there was a damn sight more weight of liquor in their bellies than of landed fish upon their foresheets."

"Well it could have been a lot worse," opined Surratt. "And...speaking of fish, we have come here to bring you news of a much bigger fish to fry... bigger than anything the Potomac can offer up."

George looked inquisitively at the younger man while Tom Harbin gestured towards the negro waiter and called for three more whiskies.

Surratt, lowering his voice, proceeded to elaborate. "Have you, by any chance, heard of a well-heeled actor by the name of Booth?"

"Booth?" responded George. "Wilkes Booth?"

"The very man. He belongs to a Baltimore family of actors and is well respected as a thespian."

"I've heard of him...yes," mumbled the German. "In fact I saw him on stage at the outset of his career. That was in Baltimore...in some Shakespearian production, which, to be frank, was not to my liking. We were spending a short time in the city with our relations who live over in Germantown. I distinctly remember because it was a clammy, uncomfortable summer's evening and, despite a lot of talk of Booth being the son of a famous actor..."

"Junius Brutus Booth," interrupted Tom Harbin. "The famous tragedian."

"Yes," confirmed George, instinctively, although, in truth, he was totally oblivious to the father's name. "Well, for all the talk, the fellow forgot his lines and received a right heckling from the audience. But that would have been the best part of ten years ago and I know he's acquitted himself well since then. Dashing, good looking bastard, as I recall."

For a moment silence prevailed between the three men as the drinks waiter appeared with the whiskies ordered by Tom.

"Yes, he's become a well-accomplished actor by all accounts...widely known to theatregoers from Boston to Richmond," added John Surratt, once the uniformed darkey had taken his leave. "But the fact is the man's heart is in Richmond. He's a good Southron, George. Now, cast your mind back to when I first met you...back in the fall of sixty-two. If you remember, I was on my way to Doctor Samuel Mudd's place with a letter of introduction from Captain Cox. Well, the fact is the doctor's proved an invaluable ally and, during the past few weeks, he has introduced both Tom and me to Booth."

"Introduced you to Booth?!" George's surprise at this disclosure caused him to raise the intensity of his voice to a level which, in the circumstances, arguably lacked good judgement.

"Sshh...man," murmured John, looking furtively about the room. With the tobacco trader and his companion gone, the bar was devoid of other customers, the price of the superior liquor up here being a cut above that of the five cent tots peddled in the cellar bar. As for the waiter, he was busying himself with chores and well out of earshot.

"So, how does your friend Mudd know this actor?"

"Mudd only got to know Booth about two months ago and since then, things...of which I will elaborate in a moment...have moved quickly. By all accounts Booth's fervent dedication to the Southern cause has, for some time now, overshadowed his commitment to acting. Back in the fall, when visiting our Confederate agents based in Montreal, he was given a letter of introduction to Sam Mudd. He made contact with the doctor last month and disclosed to him a stratagem he has to capture the President."

Surratt stopped talking, immediately aware that George's jaw had dropped open as he sought to digest what he had just heard. Harbin sat impassively watching the astounded Atzerodt and took a swig of whisky.

"The President?...Lincoln?" whispered the stunned listener. "What would he do with the President?"

"Transport the ogre to Richmond. He'd be held as a hostage...as a bargaining tool for the release of hundreds of Confederate prisoners of war. It's an exciting plan but Booth needs a lot of help to put it into action. And that's where Tom and I come in."

Atzerodt remained spellbound, having deigned – in the wake of Surratt's disclosure – to remove his old slouch hat. He proceeded to use his sleeve to wipe the sweat from a beaded brow to which lank hair clung tenaciously. Surratt seemed to visibly wince for a moment. Sitting close to the unsavoury carriage painter, he caught a whiff of his bad breath which might have been worse but for its mild tempering by the recent intake of good Kentucky whisky. Atzerodt's mouth still gaped. It felt dry. He drained the last drops of bourbon from his glass.

"Booth has used the good doctor to help recruit a loyal band of comrades who can be relied upon to put his plan into action," continued John. "Tom was introduced to him by the doctor last month and enlisted to help. A few days later, just before Christmas, I was walking with a friend...an old school pal...along Seventh Street, when, who do I spy on the opposite side of the street?...none other than Sam Mudd. He was in earnest conversation with a rather debonair fellow who I did not recognise. Well, when Mudd saw me, he hailed me. My friend and I crossed the street to be warmly received by the doctor, who, strange to say, said he was on his way to my mother's boardinghouse. His mission was to find me in order to introduce me to his companion. Well, the introduction took place there and then, with Sam's companion proving to be none other than the illustrious John Wilkes Booth. We were promptly invited back to Booth's room in the National, on Pennsylvania Avenue, where we were made most welcome and plied with cigars and a most superior bourbon."

"It was a similar experience for me," added Harbin. "When I met the man down here...in Bryantown...I sure couldn't fault him on his hospitality."

"Anyway, at one point," continued Surratt, "Booth ushered the doctor and I out into the corridor...out of earshot of my friend. He told me of the good reports he had heard of me as a Confederate courier and was impressed by learning of my contacts in Richmond. I gather the doctor had recommended me. Well, the actor proceeded to acquaint me with his seminal ideas and there and then I became his next recruit."

"Good God," mumbled George, finding words hard to come by. "Who else knows of his plans?"

"When I met him," said Harbin, "Booth mentioned two old friends who had briefly served in the Confederate Army...one at Bull Run. But he didn't elaborate. He said he was also hopeful of coaxing an old actor friend to join in, although his powers of persuasion had so far fallen short."

"Don't forget he also wants David Herold in the fold," said John.

"Herold?" said Atzerodt. "Davy Herold?"

"That's right."

"I know Davy, damn it," murmured George in disbelief. "He and I have been hunting together in the Zekiah Swamp and bagged some tasty duck. But I haven't set eyes upon him of late."

"I believe he works for a druggist in the city. Anyway," whispered Surratt, now anxious to broach the proposition which had drawn him and Tom Harbin into Port Tobacco, "this all brings us to our purpose in sitting here with you, George." As he finished speaking, John beckoned the waiter and ordered yet another round of whiskies.

"The fact, is, George, to get Lincoln to Richmond we'll need to get him across the river under cover of darkness and so a good ferryman is essential. Now, in my book, there's none better than you and I've told Booth so. There's no one so well acquainted with the river and the intricacies of its shoreline, be it over here or along the Virginia side."

"What John's saying, is will you join our little band? Will you ferry Lincoln across the Poto...?" Tom's whispered words tailed off as he caught sight of the approaching waiter bearing his companion's newly ordered drinks.

Surratt rummaged in his vest pocket and tossed several coins upon the darkey's silver tray, sufficient to include a generous tip. "Give the matter some serious thought, George," he continued, once the delighted waiter had finished expressing his gratitude in effusive terms and taken his leave. "I know your painting work is lean and money's tight, even with the funds you derive from your ferrying activities. But if you come on board with us you'll notice a difference. Booth will look after us alright. He's a man of some means...not just money of his own but he has the ability to tap into Confederate money to make his plan work."

George Atzerodt looked flabbergasted, lost for words. As a weak-willed individual his initial thought of being foisted with such responsibility – of playing an active role in the seizure and transportation of no less than the President of the United States – terrified him to the core. Yet the concept of becoming a valued member of Booth's cabal of plotters fired his imagination...especially if it also meant an end to his money worries. It was incentive enough.

"You don't have to make a decision here and now," said Tom Harbin. "We've got other business in the area and, for that purpose, have taken rooms at the Bryantown Tavern."

"Yes, sleep on it if you will, George," added Surratt. "We've got a meeting with a Mister Smoot, down at Pope's Creek, on Monday morning and can just as easily call by to see you on our return journey."

"Smoot you say?" enquired George.

"Yes. Richard Smoot. Do you know him?"

"I did a little painting and varnishing for him last year...not on a carriage but on a rather nice skiff he has drawn up in Dent's Meadow.

"Well, isn't that a coincidence?" remarked Tom.

"It sure is," observed Johnny Surratt. "You see, George, Booth has asked us to look out for a good boat to get Lincoln across to Old Virginny. Our enquiries have revealed that for a price, this fellow Smoot may be interested in parting with his craft. So we can return on Monday after our meeting with him."

"It won't be necessary," commented George, without hesitation. "Count me in. I don't want to regret turning down the opportunity."

"Grand fellow," whispered Surratt. "We'll get word to you shortly. In the meanwhile don't mention a word of this to any living soul, including family members. There's a lot of planning to do and I'll see about arranging for you to be introduced to Booth. It would probably be at the National Hotel or it could even be at my mother's place on H Street."

"I'm due to visit my relatives over in Montgomery County in three weeks time. I'll be passing back through the city on my return and if it were convenient to Mister Booth…"

"I'll try to establish his whereabouts, George," promised Surratt. "Since he's set aside his acting to concentrate on this more pressing matter he tends to base himself in the city. I'll be in touch, George. Now, before we get the ostler's boy to bring round our horses, let me get you another glass of liquor to celebrate your enlistment in a noble enterprise."

Nine

SCHUYLKILL COUNTY, PENNSYLVANIA

JANUARY – FEBRUARY 1865

★ ★ ★

RELAY HOUSE, MARYLAND

MARCH – APRIL 1865

"Happy New Year, Willie," exclaimed Jack Pascoe. It was Monday the second of January and the Cornishman's striding gait had overhauled that of his butty some twenty rods short of the colliery entrance. A chill rain, borne on a stiff breeze, stung and reddened the faces of both men while, with every step, the roll of growlers upon their hips emitted a dull and irregular metallic cadence. Their feet crunched upon the icy remnants of the last snowfall, now reduced by successive days of melt and night frosts to something more treacherous than the soft accumulations of Christmas Eve. Last night's early frost had succumbed to rain bearing, milder air and, with the rise in temperature, a heavy mist hung about the place. It was one infused with the redolence of the enveloping pinewoods, the wintry decay of the forest floor and a hint of the approaching colliery's culm dump.

"And a Happy New Year to you and your good lady, Jack," came the upbeat reply. "It sure is a pleasure to be heading back to work, old friend. Eighteen sixty-five...can you believe it and the war enters another year. A sobering thought."

"Yes, indeed," sighed Jack. "And you'll no doubt know all about that I suppose, Willie...being sober and having sobering thoughts..." He hesitated and mischievously winked at his colleague. "Being cooped up with the Fergusons all over the festive season is what I mean."

"In truth it wasn't at all bad, Jack...on the contrary, Christmas has only served to convince me the more that they are the most kindly of people. They went out of their way to ensure it was a convivial time."

"I thought Scots were more interested in Hogmanay. I said to me ol' beauty, Sarah, that you'd sure be bored to death, what with a dry and barren Christmas among temperance folk. We wondered about inviting you round but then, you couldn't have returned to the Fergusons reeking of liquor... especially with you now having taken the pledge yourself."

"I only did that out of respect for the family, Jack, and in the knowledge that, in any event, as long as I'm resident beneath their roof, there is no way I can partake of liquor. Yes, as you'd expect, they celebrated the New Year in their own way, but, of course, there were no tipples to be had. And I didn't turn in until the best part of two in the morning. I'd been recruited into a midnight first footing visitation upon some neighbours...a local couple...who then plied me with two grand helpings of homemade apple pie made with smokehouse apples. Well, I knew little of yesterday, having slept in till gone noon. By the time I did surface and had done a bit of jobbing around it was candle lighting time."

The pair slowed to negotiate the slight but salted incline which marked the entrance to the yard as, simultaneously, there emerged three other mineworkers from the opposite direction. For a moment the five halted amidst a flurry of courteous exchanges in recognition of a year newly dawned. Pleasantries traded, attentions swiftly returned to conditions underfoot and safe progress across the colliery yard whereupon William seemed keen to resume his discourse.

"I was going to tell you about Christmas Day, Jack," said William. "Well, being cooped up with the Fergusons, as you put it, wasn't at all bad. I like to think that the trouble they went to might have been, at least in part, on account of me being there.....you know, an Englishman. But I am sure it was principally because of their dinner guests. German friends they were...a neighbouring Pennsylvania Deutsch family by the name of Kitzmuller. Tom Ferguson said they loved their Christmas ...their tannenbaum...and he and Missus Ferguson went to a lot of effort to make it special. He had been out in the woods on Christmas Eve and returned with some large sprigs of juniper which he bound together to serve as a tree. That evening, as soon as the three children had reluctantly retired to their beds, Missus

Ferguson carefully adorned it with candles and sweet confectionery. Well, the Kitzmullers duly arrived on Christmas morning after attending mass at the Lutheran chapel in Pinegrove..."

"So did you manage to get to church over Christmas?" interjected the Cornishman.

"Sadly, no, Jack." Before elaborating, William was distracted by the sight of the warm glow emanating from the colliery office window: nothing unusual, excepting that the radiance from Hiram's paraffin lamp penetrated the morning's mist to ethereal effect, defining and accentuating the minute particles of water vapour as they swirled and tumbled haphazardly. Then, as his steps took him beyond the stream of light, William became aware of the imposing and monumental shape that was the breaker, its inky mass towering in the gloom like some squatting, giant beast waiting to spring into action. Ahead and to the left of the engine house rose the colliery's timber headframe, gallows-like and skeletal in the mist. William likened it to another colossal creature but, in stark contrast to its cousin – the breaker – one stripped to the bone by flesh-picking raptors. He thought it a sombre, eerie composition, all monotint, stationary and dark with the exception of a billowing white cloud of steam emitted by the engine house.

"Sorry, Jack," murmured William as he re-engaged in conversation. "You asked me about church. Well, I'd dearly loved to have attended the service on Christmas Eve, down at the Methodist Episcopal church and then, again, on Christmas morning. But my leg was still giving me plenty of trouble and I dared not have risked it in the ice and snow. Whenever I could I kept it raised up on a footstool, such as the time when I paid the price of being a shade unkind to Missus Ferguson. Mister Ferguson and I had deigned to cajole her, light-heartedly of course, while she decorated the juniper tree... such were the painstaking efforts she appeared to be taking in placing her little adornments. Finally satisfied with their disposition, she produced a rather comical, dwarfish, yet portly figure of a kilted Scotsman with an over-sized tam-o'-shanter and a large fly in his eye. Well, this little plaid figurine, I'm told, was a cherished bauble long since won by her husband at a Leith fairground. Poor Missus Ferguson strove hard to secure the novelty in as lofty and prominent place as possible. Alas! Perhaps it was tiredness on her part but, whenever she thought she had secured the little fat Scotsman in his rightful place, he proceeded to plummet to the floor. And...as the little rascal tumbled...so did mild, Scottish expletives fall from the mouth of the tree trimmer...all in good spirit and interspersed with blithesome mutterings of self-reproach. Well, Jack, I suppose now, after several months in the family's company, I have come to judge well enough when I might be in danger of overstepping the boundaries of those proprieties prevailing beneath their roof. At certain times both can be extremely tetchy in mood, especially Tom, and not least, as you might imagine, when touching upon matters pertaining to liquor. Indeed, Jack, I think I told you of the way he scolded his children when they condescendingly suggested they might eradicate their garden slugs with a saucer of beer. Anyway, at this point on Christmas Eve, the three of us found ourselves in such a state of affability that it emboldened me to suggest that the miniature Scotsman had simply been on the bottle, was inebriated and should be banished from the house. Well, I had judged it right, thank goodness, for Tom Ferguson burst into laughter and, taking the cue from her husband, Missus Ferguson promptly followed suit. For my part…well, I paid the price for my witticism…for indulging in my own quip. I had leant forward in my chair and my own laughter threw me off-balance, causing me to take my own tumble, would you believe. So the joke was rather upon me. Amid all the hilarity I had grazed my elbow upon the fender but, thank the Lord, my leg was no worse for the experience."

Jack had been listening intently to William's discourse upon Missus Ferguson's trimming of the juniper tree, only to chuckle gleefully on learning of his butty's – as he put it – 'well-deserved misfortune.'

"So what of the German folk?" he resumed, once he had stopped chortling.

"Sorry, Jack…yes, before I digressed I was about to say that the Kitzmullers arrived in fine fettle on Christmas morn, cheeks flushed and pinched by the cold, both adults bearing armfuls of Frau Kitzmuller's homemade Christmas fare. It was all great excitement as the family crossed the Fergusons' threshold and were received amid copious exchanges of the most cordial nature. Can you believe, the whole family arrived clutching victuals, the two children weighed down with baskets of Frae Kitzmuller's sweetmeats. And, no sooner had the German youngsters arrived, than they departed with the Ferguson children. Off they went with the brimming baskets to distribute their contents to some of the village old folk and the local Lutheran preacher."

"Metzelsupp, Willie. That's what they call it. Sarah told me about it. It's an old German, Christian tradition. So are the Kitzmullers temperance folk?"

"Not to my knowledge. They haven't taken the pledge as far as I'm aware.

On the other hand, they've clearly no craving for drink on the evidence of Christmas Day. Yet who knows what happens behind closed doors? Certainly, in the presence of the Fergusons, there was no call for liquor and had there been they'd have been given short shrift, you can rest assured. But no, I gather the friendship between the couples has been lengthy. Were they imbibers of alcohol then I would surmise it is something undertaken both in private and in moderation. While in the company of the Fergusons they were nothing short of model guests and respecters of their convictions... Lutheran in their beliefs, as you would assume. Tom Ferguson won't have a word said against them and, at least to my knowledge, has never tried to persuade them to join the Templars. He says they love the Union and are a far cry from the typical German Democrat landowning class, as he puts it. With hindsight, I was so glad they were invited to join us at Christmas dinner since they were good company and Frau Kitzmuller contributed some wonderful buckwheat dumplings and a goose liver pie. God, Jack, what a cook! I doubt I've eaten as well in all my life."

"Sounds as though you had a really grand time, after all, Willie."

"I sure did, Jack...and certainly when it came to food. It got me thinking how wonderful it would be to have a wife who could cook like that... someone like Frau Kitzmuller."

"Well, I can vouch for that. My ol' beauty is good with the cooking as you know, Willie, having sampled her pasties and saffron cake. And I've got a nice piece of hoggan in my growler this morning which you can share with me. But look you here, Willie, I sense you've got something of a thing for this German woman which might not simply be a hankering for her cooking," declared the Cornishman, with a twinkle in his eye and a brief chuckle.

"She's a fine looking woman, Jack, I'll not deny. Were she not wed and I were more her age I'd dream of keeping company with her...to go sparking with her, as they say in the Army. But I'll not covet another man's wife. I might have done wrong in my life, Jack, but I'd not do that. It's in the Commandments. Anyway, it's bad of me to think like that. She's a married woman in her thirties with a couple of children."

"So I'm right. I've touched a raw nerve there. But, there's no harm having a crush on someone, Willie. By Jove, no. Perhaps that's what you need... to settle down with a good wife. How old are you, man?"

"Twenty-two this year...I think," said William, with uncertainty in his voice.

"You *think?*" Why the doubt?"

"Well, to be honest, Jack, I've completely lost count since I left the Navy." William froze, momentarily, as he realised what he'd said…*since I left the Navy*. The words resonated in his head. "It reminds me that I must ask my mother my age when I write home," he continued, immediately composing himself and hoping against hope that his workmate had somehow failed to register his unfortunate slip of the tongue. But it proved false hope.

"The Navy? You told us you were in the Army, Willie, but I didn't appreciate you'd also been in the Navy. So were you one of those bounty jumpers I've heard about?

"No, Jack, I wasn't in the Union Navy…I meant the Royal Navy…but it's a long story for another time," declared William, a hint of exasperation in his voice. "Just don't mention it to anyone, Jack…just promise me that."

"You can have my promise, Willie…rest assured," said the Cornishman as the pair passed beneath the winding tower and began to exchange seasonal greetings with other inside colleagues waiting to enter the cage. "Anyway, Willie, enough of all that for the moment. More importantly, how are you? How's that leg after two weeks confined to your lodgings? The fact that your back here seems testament to it being better," suggested Jack, searchingly.

"I'll not deny it's made a bit of progress but there's room for improvement yet," said William. "The bruising was bad and, according to the Pinegrove physician who attended me, I was lucky not to have broken my leg. Missus Ferguson, bless her, was insistent upon successive applications of her hot, bran poultices and that was good for the contusion. But my main problem is the accident has served to weaken my old wound. It's still sore and weeps somewhat as if it's no longer matted together that well. But I can't delay any longer. I have to get back to work for the money, Jack."

William's absence from work since the middle of December had been due to a fall in the mine. At the time he and Jack had been part of the inside crew working at opening up a new chamber. It was wet and slippery enough underfoot on account of a surfeit of trickling water which had been troublesome enough to cause one of the men to take an early tumble. He was uninjured and immediately scrambled to his feet but he had been carrying an oil can for filling the oil wick lamps on the men's caps and his mishap caused a spillage of the fuel. Minutes later it took William's feet from beneath him while he was preoccupied overhead, prising out loose coal with a bar-down tool. He fell awkwardly, twisting his left leg in the process. To make matters worse the poor limb was immediately peppered with and buried beneath a shower of newly-freed anthracite, including some large and weighty lumps. As for the heavy bar-down tool, it had spun away, narrowly missing William's head, its ringing clatter drowning the holler and groans of the unfortunate casualty.

The door to the wooden cage clattered closed in preparation for the lowering. William grimaced as he peered out into the dank, wintry morn. Today dawn would remain hesitant about showing its hand and another two hours would elapse before sunup. By the time his day's work was done and he and Jack were back here, ready to shuffle out of that cage, what light of day had fallen across the colliery in the interim would be spent. The sun would have already set and dusk would be bringing forth yet another dark night, as dark as any anthracite yielded up by these sombre Appalachian hills. Steam hissed. William funnelled his lips and exhaled, watching his breath vapourise in the chill air. The timber winding frame shuddered as the wheel and hoisting cable sprung into life and the cage began its descent.

No further conversation passed between William and Jack until after they had arrived below and registered their presence with the inside boss. An hour or so later, as they toiled at the breast, Jack picked up again on the threads of their earlier discourse.

"You know, Willie, I'm thinking you won't find yourself the sort of wife you need in these parts. I daresay there's many an Irish immigrant in Schuylkill County who'd be keen to palm off his spinsterish offspring in your direction. But a good-looking, intelligent and hard working young man such as yourself should be casting an eye out for one of them more refined city girls with a bit of education. I'd hate to see the leaving of you but if I were in your situation I'd be setting my sights way beyond Blue Mountain and aspiring to make my way in one of the big cities…like that fine city of Philadelphia. By George, Willie, I warrant you'd have a fine wife soon enough and both of you would be warming your toes across some grand brass fender…toasting them gently by the blue light of this Appalachian coal rather than having to hew it out of the mountain to earn your bread and butter."

"That's rich coming from you, Jack. A country boy from west Cornwall with a supposed preference for the big city. So why did you choose to settle in these remote mountains?"

"That's just it, Willie. I'm from a rural background…so is Sarah. Penzance was the closest we ever got to anything like a city and that only on a few occasions. Mining's in my blood, Willie, and it was in my father's and his father's before him. Sarah's dad was also a tinner and both she and her mother were bal maidens. Cast adrift in the likes of Philadelphia, me and me ol' beauty would be like Cornish pilchards out of water."

"What are bell maidens, Jack?"

"*Bal* maidens, my friend. Well in the Cornish tin mines they employed women. Armed with hammers, they'd be…up on the surface where they'd dress the ore. You should see the biceps on some of them bal maidens," said Jack with a chuckle.

"So why did you uproot yourself? Were the prospects bad in the mines?"

"Not at all, Willie. The trade in tin was good as was our wheal's output but it was a hard life. You might think this is hard, Willie, being cold and draughty but the tin mines were wet and hot and sapped your strength like billy-o. When my old dad was the age I am now, well he was done-for… an old man he was. And we had no cage to lower us down the shaft and to raise us out. The steam driven engines we had were beam engines for pumping out the water. Oh no, we had it hard alright…hard as Cornish granite. After Sarah and I were wed, I had to walk three miles every day from our little cottage to the mine and then three miles back. The road ran close to the cliffs and often the wind would be howling and the rain skeeting down something awful. I'd often as not arrive at the wheal drenched to the skin. So I'd leave my jacket and shirt in the engine house to dry and start lowering myself down the ladder to find my day's work. Oh, God, Willie, if you think this is a tough life you should try a stint down a Cornish tin mine. But for all that it was the cholera epidemic in forty-nine that drove us out. It became rife in our nearest village and carried off several poor souls. Well, I made enquiries and arranged passage for Sarah and me on a ship leaving Falmouth. When the day came, we had to attend the emigration office to receive the medical inspector's clearance but that presented no obstacle. Soon enough we had been given our berth on board, passed out of the Carrick Roads and set sail for Philadelphia."

"That must have been an emotional time for you and Sarah."

"It most certainly was. Sarah's folks were dead…one carried off by the cholera…while mine were too infirm to travel to the Falmouth quayside to see us off. It was a tearful time alright, saying our farewells to my old folks back in St. Just, knowing it was the last we'd see of them. And as we sailed out of the Fal estuary I was again choked up with tears and melancholy as the shores of dear old Kernow receded in the twilight."

"Now that's why taking a wife does not figure in my immediate plans, Jack. I want to see England again 'ere long. I want to be able to afford my passage home and that prospect will diminish if I settle down and set up home over here. I need to cross the ocean and set up business in my native land but, above all, I want to see my kin again and to seek atonement for earlier wrongdoing."

"I see, Willie. Suddenly you keep tormenting me with puzzling mention of being in the British Navy and about past misdemeanour. And now you seem reluctant about remaining in the United States. Tell me…am I that wide of the mark in suggesting you jumped ship? You've a right to censure me if I'm wrong but, you know, I've a sneaking suspicion…"

William's expression momentarily said it all but this escaped Jack's detection as he moved slightly, only to be temporarily blinded within the shifting glare from his butty's oil-wick lamp.

"As I've already said, Jack, it's not for now but for another time," said William, curtly. "I'll tell you a little of my history when the time is right."

★ ★ ★

"Some hae meat and canna eat
Some canna eat that want it
But we hae meat and we can eat
Sae let the Lord be thankit!"

"An so say aw o us," exclaimed Missus Ferguson upon conclusion of her husband's rousing rendition of the traditional grace. She rose to her feet and gathered up a ladle. With her left hand, it being swathed in an old piece of burlap to prevent its scalding, she lifted the lid of what usually sufficed as a porridge pot, newly and gingerly carried to the table by Mister Ferguson. Immediately a cloud of steam rose out of the receptacle to the collective delight of the several diners who numbered all who resided within the household.

"Well, there's a steaming broth if ever there was," said the elder daughter, Ruth, as her mother proceeded to fill everyone's porringer with the piping-hot soup.

"Scotch broth, juist richt for Burns' nicht, an burns the wird awricht if ye bairns dinna caw cannie," quipped Missus Ferguson. "Maister Reynolds, do help yersel to breid …ay, but keep mynd o this broth's a thick one an A'd hate ye no tae leave eneuch room for some haggis."

"Maister Reynolds haes scowth in his stamack, ma dearie, efter a lang day doun the pit," declared Tom Ferguson, who eyed his lodger intently as if in search of endorsement.

"I have to admit that, although my father was Scots, I have never before tasted haggis," confessed the younger man.

"Than ye're in for a treat, man," bellowed Ferguson. "Ye're in for a treat."

Some while later, when the diners had had their fill of Flora Ferguson's broth and the master of the house had applied his crust to what vestiges still clung to the inner surface of the porridge pot, the time came to bring forth the blessed haggis. While his wife followed on with brimming dishes of neeps and tatties, Ferguson did the honours, dressed in a tam 'o shanter and holding high the platter as if he were the chef being piped in at some formal supper for the Bard. Then, having settled the dish down upon the table, he heartily quoted from Burns' *Address to a Haggis* as he took up a knife and plunged it into the thing as if smiting some wild beast.

"...an cut ye up wi' ready slight," he proclaimed before resuming his seat. "Thare ye are, young William, thare's a wairm reekin' haggis for ye."

The meal was despatched by all with an eagerness that only served to limit conversation. As he ate, it occurred to William that what he had said about never having consumed haggis was not entirely true. There had been an occasion on board the *Edgar* – it would have been Burns night, the twenty-fifth of January 1861 – when, after a Burns supper in the officers' mess, and while attending to his duties in the galley, he had sampled some of this unfamiliar, mysterious dish. He remembered the occasion well but certainly not with affection. It was while in passage to Lisbon. The wind had fallen to a fresh breeze that evening but it had been a stormy day at sea with the ships of the Channel Squadron running into a stiff south westerly gale. For William, it had been his maiden sea voyage after leaving the *Excellent* and, feeling a dash queasy and still struggling to find his true sea legs, little nourishment had passed his lips that day. Then, in the relative calmness of the evening, he had eaten what was left of the officers' haggis. He remembered it as cold and unpalatable but at the time it sated the representations of an empty stomach. In contrast, the Fergusons' warm reekin' offering was something to savour.

"Weel, ye'v cleared yer plate, William, sae A'm thinkin ye enjoyed it," said Ferguson as he lent forward and clasped a flagon of water. "Nou, afore A teuk the pledge it wis always uisual...an sadly, an misguidedly, it is yet... tae raise a tass o baurley-bree richt nou...a demon waucht aft shabbily cawed the watter o life. Nane o that, than, but lat us raise a tass o the true watter o life tae Maister Rabbie Burns for that is the mair wirthy bree wi which tae toast oor weel-kent baird." And with that the Scotsman filled everyone's glass and the watery toast was duly performed.

★ ★ ★

On Friday the tenth of February William was the recipient of a letter from England, it always being a cause of joy for him to receive a letter from his mother. Any letter from England was, without exception, from his mother. Uncle Charley never wrote. He constantly refrained from putting pen to paper since he viewed letter writing as a womanly vocation. As for Grandma Black, badly arthritic fingers were her impediment.

William had for some days been expecting a letter from Portsea, since a harbinger had arrived separately in the form of a copy of the *Hampshire Telegraph*. He had spent the past few evenings meticulously poring through its pages. Now, on the evening of the tenth, after supper, he had passed it on to Mister Ferguson, who, perhaps surprisingly, seemed to show more than a cursory interest in the prospect of perusing a south Sassenach paper. William had lit a candle and retired early to his room. He had delayed reading his mother's missive until alone, propped up in bed. Its reading would be his post-prandial treat after an arduous day down the pit and this he proceeded to do without drawing his curtains closed. It was, after all, a clear night presided over by a benevolently bright full moon which – in its effulgence – cast more light upon Charlotte Reynolds' neat handwriting than did her son's flickering candle.

The news was scant. Christmas and New Year in Portsea had been nothing out of the ordinary. Uncle James had been there, home from sea. Little had been seen of Uncle Charley, such were his commitments in running the *Sheer Hulk*. William's Grandma had been especially slumbersome, a sign of advancing years according to her daughter and an unfortunate tendency that had caused her to scald her leg rather badly. The misfortune had happened on Christmas Eve, when the onset of suspended consciousness prompted the release of her arthritic grip upon a hot cup of cocoa. So throughout Christmas and into the New Year the sight of her mother's bandaged leg, raised up upon a footstool before the hearth, had been a constant reminder of her son's own plight following his calamitous fall in the mine. *How is your leg progressing William? Have you seen the doctor again and what did he have to say? My immediate relief this summer past, on learning of your break with the hazardous work which had taken you south, was quickly dispelled when I learnt of your mining accident...*

One thing that took William aback was his mother's guarded references to his previous term in the Army. *Hazardous work that had taken you south...* why, bless her, did she flinch from mentioning the Army? Perhaps she had misconstrued his request to curb any allusion to his previous career, by which he meant his time in the Royal Navy. Instead she chose to refrain from writing freely about his spell in the Union Army, as if prying eyes might belong to those inclined to frown upon her son's involvement in the war. Admittedly, the standing of the common soldier at home was low, perhaps little higher than that of the gutter-prowler – the rascally street thief – but William knew his mother held the British soldiering fraternity in far greater regard. After all, her own father and a brother had proudly worn a soldier's tunic. Her son had done likewise, although to what extent that had any bearing upon her opinion of the soldiering man was uncertain, given the circumstances which led to his enlistment. No, it was evident to William that his mother had misunderstood what he meant by his previous career. That would need putting to rights. As he returned the letter to its envelope, placed it aside and snuffed out his candle, William resolved to find time on Sunday to put pen to paper.

Molley's Town, near Pinegrove, Schuylkill County, Pa.
February 12th 1865

Dear Mother,

It was with joy I hailed the coming of your welcome letter. I received the paper first but it acted only as a messenger, for I knew the letter was coming soon after and anxiously did I look for it.

You mentioned in your letter that you did not wish to write with freedom as the tone of my missive forbade you. You must have misconstrued my meaning. Mother, you must not be afraid to say whatever you wish in your letters for this is a free country, every person is allowed freedom of speech and old, discharged and wounded soldiers are privileged characters here. They are not looked upon as dogs, as they are in the Old Country. However, that aside, the less you say in your letters of my former career – in the Royal Navy – the better. They may fall by accident into the hands of some of the family

I am living with and that would be calamitous. I left the Army with a good character and, since I have lived with the family, I have continued to keep it unblemished. I should like that to remain the case. They are a very kind, sober and respectable Scots family. I think I mentioned previously that their name is Ferguson and I am treated amongst them the same as their own son. The whole family belong to an Order called The Good Templars which is a temperance society and, as a matter of course, I felt obliged to join it too. So all in the house, both males and females, are brothers and sisters by order. In the circumstances, I should like you to mention them in your next letter and thank them for their kindness to me.

I am sorry indeed to hear my Uncle James is still so angry with me but I know I deserve it after all his kindness. But I will write to him soon and perhaps he will forgive me, for I know he does not bear malice. You said that if I came home my Uncle Charley might let me stay with him until I secured a situation. That knowledge is a comfort to me. With Uncle James still residing with you and Grandma, it would be unrealistic, as matters stand, for me to contemplate returning to the house in King Street.

You enquired of the condition of my leg. Yes, I have seen the physician again and he was pleased with its progress, so don't fret on that account. I resumed my coalmining work at the turn of the year and while I am managing well enough I realise that such a career can only be for the short term given what my leg has had to endure over the past ten months. It is hard work down the pit but I must not complain for a close comrade, a West Countryman, tells me that being a Cornish tin miner is a good deal more arduous. At least, Mother, you can console yourself that I am no longer trading steel and lead bullets which many young men continue to do as this war rumbles on.

I have sent you a Philadelphia paper, Mother, and also my descriptive list, of which you must take great care. I tore it a few weeks ago taking it out of an envelope in which I had it sealed. Remember me very kindly to all old friends and give my love to Grandma and Uncle Charley. Tell Uncle James that I intend writing to him shortly. I will now conclude with kindest love from your affectionate son,

William Reynolds

★ ★ ★

Ten days later. For the third morning in succession William trudged up the village street earnestly hoping for a change of fortune. It had been a clear night and bitterly cold. A thick woolly muffler, loaned by Mister Ferguson, was thrown about his neck. His breath spiralled ghost-like in the chill air. Beneath his feet the earthen road felt rock hard but just occasionally, despite familiarity with his pathway to work, he would misjudge his footing in the darkness. He knew soon enough. As he trod upon the wayside's dead fronds they made a crunching, cracking sound, such was the brittleness bestowed upon them by the encrusting icy spines of a sharp hoar frost.

William began to feel optimistic as he reached the colliery gates. On Monday morning he had already encountered downcast inside-men exiting the premises. There had been unwelcome mutterings upon their breath about there being no work, as decreed by the fire boss.

Old Hiram's turned us away. The fire boss did his usual rounds at three and found traces of fire damp. Says we can't risk the gas blowing us to kingdom come.

On Tuesday it was a similar story but there was at least some dead work available in the prop yard. By then two notices had been erected at the colliery entrance, both legible thanks to the soft glow emitted by a judiciously placed hurricane lamp. One announced the continued presence of fire damp and the indefinite closure of the mine until such time as the gas had cleared. The second told of the availability of work for those interested in cutting props and collars for timbering below. Yet it was a case of first come, first served and William's promptness in reaching the yard a shade earlier than usual proved beneficial. Calling first at the coal office, he was directed by Hiram – the whiskery, bronchitic clerk – to the prop yard where the outside-boss set him to work with ten others hewing and shaping pine timbers to roof a new gangway. It was work alright but at half a butty's daily wage. Such was the nature of dead work but at least it meant some reward.

Wednesday morning seemed far more promising as William reached the yard. There were no notices outside and no exodus of disgruntled souls who had turned up ahead of him.

A call at the coal office brought welcome news from Hiram. The fire boss had filed his morning report: there was no longer any trace of marsh gas and it was business as usual. In the circumstances, it was perhaps not surprising, that, once below, the inside-men set to work with renewed vigour, buoyed, as they were, by the knowledge that the gas had dispersed quickly enough and there would be money in their hands by the end of the week. William, on the other hand, seemed preoccupied and uncommunicative, something which didn't escape Jack's attention.

225

"Are you feeling off colour, Willie?" said Jack, as he removed his cap, squatted on his haunches and reached for his growler.

William joined him, both men finally stretching their legs out before them with their backs resting against a roof-supporting coal pillar.

"Well, I've a ravenous appetite for my lunch after shovelling all that coal into the cars," quipped the miner's butty. "So I doubt that I'm sickening for anything." A touch of sarcasm pervaded William's words which, on immediate reflection, he realised was unjustified. "Sorry, Jack…being tetchy, I mean. It's just that I'm inwardly wrestling with uncertainty."

"Is it something you'd care to share with me…to help unburden your mind while we eat?"

William remained quiet as he set about eating his lunch. A few minutes passed and Jack had already assumed that his friend did not wish to avail himself of a listening ear. Then he spoke.

"It comes back to the matter we talked about some weeks ago now… your suggestion that, for my own good, I should turn my back on these hills and look to the future elsewhere. Philadelphia perhaps."

"Why yes, Willie, we were discussing the prospect of finding you a good wife as I recall." There was a sense of levity in Jack's voice, which, in the circumstances, stopped short of being inappropriate.

"Well, a week ago, Tom Ferguson had to attend Good Templars' business over in Tremont. While there, he obtained a copy of a Philadelphia paper… the *Enquirer* …which he passed my way when he'd finished with it. Well, Jack, among the welter of advertisements was a large one announcing the raising of a new regiment under the direction of the city's Union League and calling for volunteers."

"So, you're set on re-enlisting Willie," said Jack, his face a picture of incredulity in the lamp light.

"It's in my thoughts." William hesitated a moment before continuing. "No Jack. To be entirely honest I have made up my mind. But I've yet to tell the Fergusons and I'm not relishing doing so."

"Don't worry on that account. I'm sure they'll be sad to see you go, Willie, but old man Ferguson's a good Union man, so you say, and he'll surely understand you responding to the call. But why, oh why, are you inclined to go back in the Army for God's sake?"

"It's the money, Jack…the money, my friend. The bounty's generous and I'll be able to put a large sum in the bank. Crucially, it will enable me to go home in due course and to set myself up in the Old Country. It's only for a year after all and I doubt whether this war has long to run its course. Look at how Sherman has advanced through Georgia and now South Carolina. The momentum has to be with the Union with Lincoln re-elected for another term and the Rebel army in disarray. They've been suffering badly in this cold winter and the word is that men are deserting in their hundreds every day. No, Jack, I can't see the war lasting much longer."

"I'm sure you're right Willie."

"I know I'm right. But it's not just a matter of putting good money in the bank. I've found difficulty adapting to civilian life since leaving the Army and, despite a good wage here, the cost of every little thing is so prohibitive that I'm never going to accrue any savings. And I'm sure you're correct in what you said before, Jack...Schuylkill County is no place for someone like me. It's a dull, austere existence for a single fellow and I have hated this bitter cold weather."

"It has been a cold winter, Willie...I'll readily admit that. The coldest I can recall for many years."

"Oh, and something else. I've no wish to cast gloom and despondency but, as you well know, these artificially high prices have high wages to thank and our wages are based on a strong demand for coal to drive the war..."

"Which, as you say, is likely to come to an end 'ere too long. And where will that leave us?" said Jack, reflectively, a ring of disconsolation in his voice. "The demand for coal and, in consequence, its price, will plummet."

"Precisely. And with it the operators will no longer be able to pay a good wage. Mark my words, those Irish troublemakers, the Molly Maguires, will come into their own when that happens. And do you know, Jack, I was reading in the *Miners Journal* that already, and since before Christmas, the demand for our black diamond has shown signs of falling and with it the price. It doesn't bode well."

"I'd also read that, Willie. It is a worry but thank God we've none of those Buckshots in our pit. At least I'm not aware we have, yet I can foresee trouble elsewhere in the coalfield. But, tell me, will your leg stand up to the rigours of soldiering?"

"It seems to be standing up to the rigours of coalmining, despite that fall in the mine but I accept that it will have to pass muster with the surgeon. Time will tell."

"And what time are we talking about?" enquired Jack.

"The first of March. I'll need to present myself at the recruiting office in Philadelphia on the first."

"Well, by Jove, that's but a week hence, my good fellow. If you've made your mind up then I wish you Godspeed and good luck, Willie, but there's no hiding that I'll be damned sorry to see you go. Oh, and tell me this," added Jack, lightheartedly. "Will I at last get to hear of your secret past?"

"Provided others don't get to hear of it. I wouldn't want the Fergusons to know…even after I've said my farewells." And with that, William proceeded to sate his workmate's curiosity by recounting what had transpired since his time on the *Cygnet*.

★ ★ ★

It had been a difficult business, leaving Molleys Town. Bidding farewell to Jack proved a massive wrench. The Cornishman's was a truly firm embrace as William assured him he would write to apprise him of how he was getting by. As to Tom Ferguson, he seemed entirely understanding of his lodger's decision. William had sat down with him and Flora Ferguson, after supper, two days after his frank discussion with Jack Pascoe. He had been apprehensive about disclosing his intentions, half expecting that his hosts might take umbrage, leading to a strained last few days beneath their roof. He had even made a special effort to ingratiate himself with the couple in the build up to his announcement. He had spoken to the outside-boss who had looked upon William propitiously since learning of his being in hospital at Pleasant Hill with his nephew. Well, the superintendent had raised no objection these past few evenings to William scouring the dump as soon as he had emerged from the hoisting cage. His purpose was to recover pieces of coal from amongst the culm and shale, for the cold weather had had the effect of prematurely reducing the Fergusons' own coal supply. The outside-boss had lent William a pail and Hiram had supplied a hurricane lamp and so, for the third evening in succession, he had carried home a useful and free supplement of otherwise discarded fuel to his hosts' fireside.

Whether such kindness had helped soften Tom's and Flora's reaction is conjectural, suffice to say that William was pleasantly surprised by their acceptance of his plans. In consequence, the last few days of his presence beneath their roof passed without any ill-feeling and awkwardness. Then, on his day of departure for Philadelphia, he left to hugs. The departing lodger even detected a tear or two in Flora's eyes, while Tom Ferguson wished him well and asked him to let him know how he was faring back in the war. He didn't attempt to persuade him to keep in with The Good Templars. He doubtless realised that with a re-introduction to army life that would be a lost cause. It was sufficient that William had shown such courteous regard for the family's beliefs while residing with them.

At the Philadelphia recruiting office it was the examining surgeon's conclusion that William Reynolds was free from all such bodily defects that might disqualify him from performing, once again, the duties of a soldier of the United States. Importantly, his left leg passed muster and, in consequence, he was attested as a corporal into Captain Snyder's company – Company H – of the 213th Regiment Pennsylvania Volunteers. When attending to completing the necessary paperwork there was a moment of hesitation. He remembered telling a surprised Jack Pascoe that he needed to ask his mother how old he was when writing home. He had subsequently forgotten to do so, placing himself at a disadvantage when required to disclose his age. He would do so next time, settling upon twenty one years in his declaration. It was inconsequential as it happened but, in truth and unknowingly, he had already turned twenty two.

After barely a week barracked in the city, the fledging regiment was placed under orders to report to Brigadier General Morris in Baltimore. Thereafter it was divided up and detailed for duty at strategic locations along the route of the Baltimore and Ohio Railroad. In the case of William's company, this was ordered to be garrisoned at Fort Dix, near the Relay House, some nine miles west of Baltimore. The day after Company H's arrival at Fort Dix, Captain Theodore Snyder, a burly, balding, approachable kind of man – accompanied by his First and Second Lieutenants – called together his non-comms for a briefing in the officer's building. His purpose was to apprise his more senior staff of the strategic significance of Relay and what was expected of the Company during its time at Fort Dix.

"Good morning, men," began the Captain, as Sergeant Burchfield unfurled a large map which, with the aid of an attached cord, he proceeded to suspend from a conveniently placed hook. "I have just been conducted around that clapboarded dwelling which stands in front of the woods and within the bounds of this fort. Now, for the Company's information I'm told that a visiting clergyman conducts mass there on a Sunday. All are welcome but space is limited. Tell the men that, if they wish to attend the chaplain's ministrations, they should make it known by signing the book in the entrance lobby by six o'clock on Saturday evenings. Now, while in the house I was shown the basement. Take a look yourselves, some time. There's a piece of track down there dating from around 1830 over which operated the first steam engine...the Tom Thumb it was called...the forerunner of today's iron horse. Interesting. But enough of that," he continued, with a snappiness in his voice, as if scolding himself for not getting to the point sooner. "The reason we're here in Relay is not to do with the history of the B & O. It's to do with the road's strategic importance."

Captain Snyder turned towards the map and, grasping a wooden pointer, placed its tip upon the fort's location. "Fort Dix. Here's where we are, situated on a high bluff that provides a lofty and formidable situation. To the east, the B & O leads to Baltimore. Below us, on that side, is the Relay House and Relay Station. Westwards, from skirting our position to the south and following the course of the Patapsco River, the railroad runs out via Ellicott Mills and Frederick to Harper's Ferry. Now, if you've already taken a look you'll know that just below us, on that south side and between the road and the river is a gun battery. Here it is," continued the bespectacled Captain, all the time making sure that the placing of his pointer was in tune with his commentary. "The Sandbag Battery, so-called for obvious reasons when you look at the way it is fortified. You'll see it commands the road's route to and from Harper's Ferry. Now, looking south, what will have already impressed you is that mighty fine stone bridge which spans the Patapsco...the Thomas Viaduct. I'm told it's thirty years old and there's yet to appear another stone bridge anywhere in the world that is similarly built on a curve. Well, this grand viaduct carries the road's Washington Branch southwards via Annapolis Junction to the Capital and just up here, beyond the bridge, on what is known as Elk Ridge Heights, is another gun battery...the Bouquet...so positioned to protect the viaduct."

"Any questions, so far?" enquired the Captain, simultaneously withdrawing his pointer. "No? Then I'm hopeful you've already begun to appreciate the strategic significance of the locality to the Union. The fort, together with the two gun batteries were established early in the war because of the great uncertainty surrounding Maryland's allegiance. Secession would have meant Washington being isolated behind the enemy's lines, quite apart from which, it was essential to protect the railroad and at the same time to prevent the Rebel army from receiving supplies and provisions routed westwards from the port of Baltimore to Harper's Ferry. And so our newly constituted regiment has become the latest in a succession of Union regiments to guard and police the road. A highly responsible duty, you will appreciate, but one which will also buy us time to ready ourselves for duty in the field."

William fully appreciated what that meant. Primarily drill, drill and yet more drill. Most of the recruits were greenhorns. They would need to be put through their paces on the drill ground based on endless and tedious repetition…that and instruction in small arms fire and in use of the bayonet. But mainly company drill.

"Incidentally," continued Captain Snyder, "those men already billeted in the smaller of the two barrack buildings will have already encountered some of the artillery boys…those responsible for our own ordnance and those who man the two outside batteries. I don't wish to hear of any falling out. After all, we are a brotherhood of fighting men committed to the same cause and we need to direct our efforts to that end and that end alone…to defeat the Confederacy. I am not an unreasonable man but I will brook no nonsense while we are garrisoned at Fort Dix."

The Captain ceased addressing the assembled officers and non-comms to allow one of the corporals, who had raised his hand, to put a question.

"Sir, you said a moment ago that we were here to guard the railroad. What, in practice will that entail, sir?" queried the freckle-faced corporal in a soft and lilting Irish brogue.

"Good question, Corporal. Well, the fact is, we can't be too vigilant. The Rebs have inflicted some goddam awful damage along the railroad ever since the war began and it seems there's no relenting in their efforts to cause disruption. Only last fall that wily Colonel Mosby and his raiders looted and destroyed a passenger train out beyond Harper's Ferry. Well, in a determined attempt to prevent such malicious deeds, the Union have troops located at strategic positions along the track, including, as you know, others from our own Regiment. Also, the railroad has armoured cars equipped with cannon which patrol the road but they can't be everywhere at once and they are no substitute for men on the ground. Indeed, there is a constant need for pickets to be strung out to guard the whole track and its branch lines if we are to have any realistic hope of foiling, or at least minimising, Confederate disruption. So, when we're not knocking the men into shape for field service they'll be standing picket and policing the road. There's a need to keep all manner of railroad property under close surveillance… bridges, culverts, the track itself, switches, trestles, telegraph poles and wires, station houses and depots…the list is endless, corporal. And, as you can imagine, most damage occurs under cover of darkness. Anyone acting suspiciously in the vicinity of the road will require challenging. There is also the need to occasionally stop and search westbound trains and you may be called upon to keep a close guard upon cars that are left stationary overnight, especially if containing powder and munitions in transit. In summary, there is much to occupy Company H here at Relay in the coming weeks, not least in terms of shaping it into a fighting unit. The rank and file may comprise a majority of raw recruits but we need to change that. There's plenty of idle talk about the Rebels being on their last legs but there's no telling what could happen and we are committed to ensure that this Company is readied for the fray."

★ ★ ★

As the month of March ran its course and the men of Company H settled into their routines, it was generally with a singular lack of enthusiasm that they would dwell upon their day's labours. Be it at supper time, or in the barber's chair, or when donning nightcaps in the half hour between roll call and taps, such words as monotonous, humdrum and tedious were frequently bandied about to the point of causing tedium themselves through repetition. Drill was boring according to many a green private who repeatedly failed to grasp the rudiments of the procedures. In truth, it was probably a damn sight more irritating and frustrating for the sergeant who had the dubious task of trying to knock his recruits into shape. From the Relay Station platform could often be heard the drill instructor giving vent to his frustrations as he put the men through their paces on the nearby drilling ground. Such familiar shouts of "left, left, left," or "shoulder muskets," or "right face," would frequently be interspersed with abusive or belittling comments directed at what the drill sergeant regarded as inept examples of soldiery. Such mocking and invariably amusing remarks and witticisms would, in their audibility, often fall victim to a whistling, slowing, clanking locomotive from Baltimore as it ran by the drilling ground, crossed the Catonsville Road and brought its cars to rest at the Relay platform. As for picket duty the men were often scathing about the sheer boredom caused by hours of relative inactivity and lack of excitement. The resulting ennui had, by all accounts, already caused two privates to fall asleep on duty and to be hauled before the officer of the guard for their misdemeanour.

William Reynolds had quickly adopted a more sanguine attitude towards his lot. As an old soldier, drilling was second nature to him but he could empathise with the frustrations of the drill sergeant. Long gone were the days when patriotism alone spurred a young fellow to enlist in the service of Uncle Abe. Now it was a mercenary inclination – the availability of generous bounty money – that tended to hold sway. It was a poor substitute. Once it had been credited to the recruit's bank account then gone was the kind of sustaining drive previously founded upon loyalty and commitment to the Union cause. William himself would readily concede that, as far as his second enlistment was concerned, there had been a mercenary attraction to ultimately fulfil a particular goal. Yet he would not chastise himself on that account. As a seasoned veteran who had long since proved his mettle, his dedication remained undimmed. He could see that the rank and file spawned by eighteen sixty-five was of a poorer quality than the boys he had joined up with in sixty-two; and it didn't help that a greater number were immigrants who struggled to grasp the Queen's English, or, more importantly, its American equivalent. And they became easily disgruntled, whingeing at the smallest thing and causing William to wonder how many would fare if subjected to the kind of deprivations he had suffered during Banks' campaign. Yes, picket duty along the road was a far from inspiring experience. Little if anything happened, hour after hour, but this was probably because the Rebels and their sympathisers were deterred from engaging in too much mischief in the vicinity of Relay. After all, it was no soft target but a heavily fortified place thanks, in part, to the vigilance of its railroad pickets. In a nutshell, William was content. The barrack room was draughtier than his room in Molleys Town but he slept soundly at night on account of the high security afforded by Fort Dix. As to victualling, being adjacent to the railroad and proximity to Baltimore was a blessing for it ensured a constant supply of fresh meat and vegetables; and thus the company cooks were assisted in their ability to turn out tolerably good food by army standards. And when it came to hardtack, he hadn't tasted such palatable examples since those early days at Camp Belger, for they arrived, comparatively newly baked, from the Baltimore manufactories. Above all, William felt safer than he had since setting sail aboard the *Louisiana* from nearby Baltimore in December of sixty-two. For the moment the extreme danger of fighting battles in the Gulf and the precarious existence of being a mine labourer had been put aside.

On the twenty-fourth of the month, a Friday, William found himself with plenty of time on his hands. On Thursday evening he had been detailed to report for duty as corporal of the guard and had duly responded the following morning to the eight o'clock drum call for guard mount. With him to guard-headquarters he took writing paper, pen and ink together with his little 'housewife' sewing kit, knowing full well that most of his twenty four hours stint of duty would place him at a loose end. There was, after all, time between the four two-hour turns of duty that he could use productively, including attention to a piece of personal housekeeping which derived from his lack of proficiency in the art of sewing and darning. One of the corporal's stripes he had sewn upon his tunic was already lifting. Remedying this was a priority and, once painstakingly achieved, he turned his attention with greater confidence to the matter of letter writing.

Before leaving Molleys Town, William had promised he would write to Jack Pascoe and Tom Ferguson to tell of his whereabouts and of how he had adjusted to life back in the Army. It was a promise he proceeded to discharge after playing the seamstress and before undertaking his second turn of duty of the day. When, some two hours later, he was once more kicking his heels around headquarters, he steeled himself to embark upon the more exacting task of writing to his Uncle James. In his last letter to his mother, William had said he would write to him soon, knowing that his uncle still harboured anger towards him. He could not let the matter fester any longer. He needed to ask his uncle's forgiveness, and hopefully clear the air, if he was to continue to have thoughts of returning home once the war was over. Fortuitously, the sergeant of the guard had been called out to sort out a problem at one of the guard posts, in the process vacating a chair which was pulled up at a small desk in one corner of the room. Corporal Reynolds took full advantage. He had had enough of sitting cramped, earlier in the day, upon what amounted to little more than a milking stool as he penned his missives to Molleys Town. He could also discard the ubiquitous piece of box wood that had rested upon his knees and supported his sheets of paper.

William laid a fresh piece of writing paper before him and placed his inkwell to hand. He spat upon a piece of rag he had brought with him and used the wetted cloth to clean his clotted nib. He looked out of the nearby window for several minutes, as if to gain inspiration before beginning his letter. Arcing its way southwards, he obliquely caught sight of the Thomas Viaduct, its impressive bulk of brown, Maryland granite carrying the Washington Branch with seemingly consummate ease across the extensive Patapsco gorge. Beyond it, amid the still wintry-stark trees on Elk Ridge Heights, a wisp of ascending smoke marked out the location of the Bouquet Battery. From the opposite, Baltimore direction, the shrill whistle of an iron horse denoted the approach of the afternoon passenger train bound for Frederick. William dipped his nib in the inkwell and put pen to paper.

Fort Dix, Relay House, Maryland.
March 24th 1865

Dear Uncle,

This is the first time, to my knowledge, I have written you a letter. Furthermore, I am under the impression that, in the present circumstances, it is not very satisfactory to receive a letter from a soldier but, Uncle, I must inform you that soldiers are not looked upon here as they are in the Old Country. Situated as this country is at present, every man has to rally round the flag, nearly all the officers in this Army are merchants and the rank and file, merchants' sons and mechanics of all descriptions.

My reasons for entering the Army this time are these. Being a stranger in a remote coal mining community I had to go into lodgings. After buying all my underclothing, paying to get these made, paying for washing and every little item a man requires to keep himself generally respectable, it made my pay look so small at the end of the month that I could not save ten cents in a year. By entering the Army I have put $300 in the bank. By the time my term is up, which is one year, I can make it $500 which will enable me to come home respectable. I could have taken a commission on entering this time but that would have held me three years, so I satisfied myself with entering the ranks as First Corporal but, by the time you receive this, I shall hold the position of First Sergeant. I cannot then go any further without taking a commission and binding myself for three years which I do not feel inclined to do.

My object, Uncle, in sending you this letter is to ask your forgiveness for my misbehaviour while a boy without sense, since when I have seen a little of the world and felt the want of a home, both at sea and on the battlefield. I must say I am sorry for abusing my home and your kindness as I did, but I hope, Uncle, you will look over the past and take into consideration my youth and wild nature at the time. I am old enough and seen experience enough to teach me sense sufficient to keep me from any repetition of the same conduct.

William put down his pen. Despite the importance of this letter, his eyes were beginning to tire. He had made a determined start but decided he had had enough of letter writing. Moreover, there were others in the room. The privates on guard duty who were under his charge had other ideas of how to spend the time between their two hour stints of duty on post. They were now engaged in playing cards and William sensed that to ignore their coaxing to join them in a few hands might mark him out as an aloof kind of non-comm. That being a reputation with which he had no wish to be labelled, Corporal Reynolds promptly acquiesced to his subordinates' cajoling.

It was only during the half hour between roll call and taps, the following evening, that William found the inclination and a little time to finish his letter. Now he squatted uncomfortably on his bunk, in the barrack room, forced, once again, to employ the side of a hardtack box as a makeshift writing surface. He spent several moments collecting his thoughts and picking up the thread of where he left off. Then he took up his pen once more...

I hope you will not despise me because I am a soldier for I always consider, although I wear a soldier's coat, there is a man's heart beats beneath it and I do not forget it is that of a Reynolds and the descendant of a Black and, although I am a soldier, I consider at the same time I am a gentleman. And I am satisfied that while I am fighting these battles I am fighting for a good cause, which is to abolish slavery and suppress rebellion. But, if God spares me through a few more battles (which will end the war), I will come back and try to earn a respectable living in my native land.

Please give my kindest love to Grandmother, Mother and Uncle Charley and all enquiring friends, which are very few, I know. I hope you will excuse my blundering letter, for I am writing with greasy ink and in a very uncomfortable position. I hardly know which is worse – trying to write a letter in a heavy sea or in a barracks with a pack of soldiers around me. I will now conclude, Uncle, with kind love to all from your still affectionate nephew,

William Reynolds

Direct : William Reynolds.,
Co. H 213 Regt. Penn. Vols.,
Relay House,
Maryland,
United States.

William swallowed hard as he signed off the letter with the words *affectionate nephew*. It was, after all, hypocritical. As far as his relationship with Uncle James was concerned, any feelings of affection had gone out of the window when he had surreptitiously engineered his entry to the *Excellent* back in the autumn of fifty-seven. Nevertheless, William realised it was time to try to put bad feeling aside and, on the understanding that Uncle James was still residing in the family home, he felt it would ill-become him to be ungracious, especially – as seemed likely – if the recipient were to share the letter's content with his sister. Of course, Charlotte Reynolds being privy to the letter's content could, in itself, be problematical. In all likelihood, she would not take kindly, indeed be irked, to learn of William's re-enlistment from her brother. He consequently resolved to pen a letter to his mother, sooner rather than later. However, it was not until four days later – on Wednesday the twenty-ninth of March – that the opportunity presented itself between the completion of supper and the bugle soundings which heralded tattoo.

Fort Dix, Relay House, Maryland
March 29th 1865

Dear Mother,

I suppose you are rather surprised to find me once more a soldier but cheer up, Mother, it is all for the best – all's well that ends well. If it is God's will to spare me through one more year of strife I can then come straight home, whereas, if I stayed a civilian, I should not save enough in a lifetime to pay my passage. Now, as it stands, I have $300 bounty in the National Bank and, before the war is out, I can make it $500, which is not to be laughed at in a poor man's hand.

Every man in this Army has the privilege of making a will and leaving it in charge of our colonels. For any man that then falls in battle, the will is sent to wherever it is directed. I shall will my effects and money in your name. My effects such as watch, rings and clothing will be sold and added to the money in the Government Bank and forwarded to the direction left by me. But I hope to save the Government all that trouble for the Rebels are on their last legs and it is supposed two or three hard battles will bring about the downfall of the Confederacy.

We are currently situated in quite a pleasant place. We are quartered in a barracks called Fort Dix, a strong fortification on the summit of a high hill. There is nothing to trouble us here but a few mounted guerrillas who harass our pickets at night but they cannot approach our quarters unobserved.

We are to lay here until our Regiment is well drilled and prepared for field service. I am sending you another portrait in undress uniform. You can judge, Mother, by our dress, that the soldiers of the United States are not kept under thumb as the British are, there are no belts or brass plates or leather neckties to trouble us. We are as free as the eagle we fight under, except when we are in the field: then we are required to be soldiers and also brothers.

I have written to my Uncle James to ask his forgiveness, which I hope he will grant and soon write. Remember me kindly to him, also Uncle Charley. Give my kind love to Grandma and tell her we shall soon meet if God, in bounty, spares us both for one short year. Please give my respects to Mr Barnes and lady, also to Mr Williams and family. You must excuse my awkwardly written letter, for it is hard work writing in a barracks with men dancing and singing on every side. I wish, when you write, you would let me know what my real age will be next August for I have completely lost tally. Any nice reading paper you may have to send will always be acceptable. I will now conclude with kind love to all and accept the same, dear Mother, from your ever affectionate son,

William Reynolds

NB. I will be expecting a letter from you every day with your portrait enclosed. Willie.

Direct : William Reynolds
Co. H 213 Regt. Penn. Vols.,
Relay House
Maryland
United States.

★ ★ ★

William's contention that the Rebels were on their last legs and that two or three hard battles would conclude the war, quickly proved to be the case. Before his mother received this letter, Robert E. Lee and his dispirited and hungry Confederate Army, with Union forces in hot pursuit, had taken the road to Appomattox. For nine months, Grant and Lee had been facing one another in front of Petersburg, Virginia. Then, on the first of April, with Lee's army in disarray and desertion rife, a Federal force routed a Confederate division at Five Forks and, in turn, triggered the end of the Rebel resistance at nearby Petersburg. The following day, a sustained Union assault on the Confederate trenches finally drove the Rebels out of Petersburg, prompting the evacuation from Richmond of the Confederate Government and that city's occupation by Federal forces. Lee and the remnants of his Army of Northern Virginia had pushed west in a desperate search for food. It was to no avail. By Sunday the ninth of April, at Appomattox Court House, the Confederates were surrounded and greatly outnumbered. With no prospect of obtaining food supplies or reinforcements, Lee had little alternative but to surrender to General Grant.

It was Palm Sunday 1865, a year to the day since William Reynolds was wounded on the battlefield at Pleasant Hill. At Fort Dix a comparatively uneventful Sunday was played out – morning inspection and knapsack drill followed by afternoon free time. William attended the church service conducted in the clapboarded house that stood within the fortification. The significance of the date from a personal point of view failed to register in his thoughts although, strangely, he was aware that his left leg ached somewhat more than usual. Ahead lay a fresh week of routine for Company H – drill, policing the road and yet more drill. Yet once that week had elapsed it was a routine set to be rudely interrupted for Corporal William Reynolds and a handful of others...

Ten

WASHINGTON D. C. AND UPPER MARYLAND
MARCH – APRIL 1865

It was Inauguration Day. Above the city, billowing clouds coloured gunmetal grey scurried away before a stiff breeze. They were threatening enough to suggest the imminence of further rain. To the weather-wise their briskness of movement was perhaps inclined to indicate otherwise. Like ants following ants, a mixed stream of horse drawn conveyances and pedestrians made their way along a Pennsylvania Avenue already cutting up and puddled with standing water in the wake of earlier precipitation. Wrapped up well against the elements, the many wayfarers shared a common destination from which locale a military band now struck up a repertoire of patriotic tunes, the sound poignantly audible across the dank Potomac flats. There was little trace of the acrid air that often hugged this watery ground and rose from the sewage-laden Old City Canal. Fortuitously the morning's turbulence had dissipated the usual miasma, supplanting it with a fresher, gaseous mix, more pleasing to the olfactory senses of those journeying to the Capitol.

Against the steps of the building's East Front, a gang of labourers had erected a temporary timber staging to accommodate invited guests and dignitaries who were now gathering to listen to Mister Lincoln's second inaugural speech. As the President took his place in front of the seated throng, there was a buzz in the air that told of a sense of hope and expectation. It would be a ceremony to witness and to cherish in the memory...something to tell one's grandchildren about...a new Presidency, a cause for optimism in these dark times. Old Uncle Abe was still at the helm to see the fighting brought to an end and to be hailed as a great victory for the Union. The death knell was already sounding for the Confederacy. It was only a matter of time.

Yet not all spectators who assembled around the Capitol's East Front on this chilly, early March day were in an optimistic and contented frame of mind. One was the celebrated actor, John Wilkes Booth. In the build-up to the ceremony he had taken his place at a choice vantage point – a lofty position above and to the left of the President's chair. He was immaculately attired in a tall silk hat and charcoal grey suit which only served to enhance his dark and debonair good looks. At his shoulder was his fiancée, one Lucy Hale, daughter of a Republican Senator and his passport this day to securing a place among the high and mighty. However, notwithstanding Miss Hale's presence, romance was far from the thespian's mind.

Other onlookers who could be numbered among the minority of malcontents were several of Booth's newly recruited cohorts. Standing in the milling crowd, yet close to the East Front staging and directly below the speaker's stand, were John Surratt and George Atzerodt; also, the druggist's clerk, Davy Herold and Lewis Powell, a strapping twenty-one year old who had served in the Confederate Army and ridden with Mosby's Rangers. As followers of Booth they all regarded Lincoln as the enemy. Yet, despite their contempt for the man who occupied the Executive Mansion, none shared their leader's depth of obsession – his haunting desire to wreak revenge upon the man for the suffering and destruction he had inflicted upon the Old South.

It was time for Abraham Lincoln to vacate his chair. Clutching his speech, he resisted placing it before him on the speaker's stand for fear that it might be snatched in the breeze.

"Fellow countrymen," he began. "At this second appearing to take the oath of the Presidential office, there is less occasion for an extended address than there was at the first..."

Thank God for that, thought Booth. *The man's words are sadly devoid of mellifluence and modulation. With a voice like that he would make a damned poor actor...as bad an actor as he had proved a President. After all, through his actions this tyrant, this nigger lover, had been responsible for slaughtering so much of the South's promising youth, creating a vast glut of young widows and grieving mothers. The bastard! His deeds must be avenged.*

"Ouch, John!" Lucy Hale emitted a short cry of discomfort. It was a trifling matter, so much so that she desisted from appearing at all inconvenienced. Instead she cast a coy and tender smile at her companion.

"Why," she continued, "your physical demeanour, dear heart, seemed to change for a moment. Your hand became taut and squeezed my own to the point of hurting me. I'm sure it was not intended…"

"Of course not, my dear," interjected Booth, embarrassed as he was by the inadvertence. "Nothing could be further from my thoughts…hurting you, I mean. If I did, I apologise profusely. No, it was just being here in my lover's presence and on such a special occasion. I allowed my thoughts to drift a while and I suppose…" He hesitated a moment. "Now…how might the poet put it?" pondered Booth, in a whisper meant solely for his lady love's ear. "What fond and wayward thoughts will slide into a lover's head!…Mister Wordsworth, the English poet, my dear. And you'll never guess his lyric's title."

"What would that be?"

"*Lucy*, my dear!"

"Really! How romantic! But how are you so familiar with the verse?"

"I have a liking for Wordsworth's poems and took a particular interest in that one on account of its title, dear Lucy."

"Oh…how charming of you. You must read it to me some time back at the National," remarked the Senator's daughter. There was a demureness in her manner which showed her to be quite flattered by what she regarded as the most touching and courteous behaviour on the part of her companion.

"For now, best listen to what Mister Lincoln has to say, Lucy," said the actor. "After all, your father may well choose to ask your opinion of his speech." Wilkes Booth settled back to listen to the remainder of the President's ramblings, making sure that, for the time being, he refrained from cupping Lucy's hand for fear of inadvertently squeezing it once more.

Lincoln droned on. To Booth his voice sounded dull and monotonous. In his head he repeated Wordsworth's words. *What fond and wayward thoughts will slide into a lover's head…* No fond thoughts drifted into the thinker's head as he listened to the speaker's words. *Such hollow pronouncements…*

"…With malice towards none," continued the President, "with charity for all, with firmness in the right…"

Bunkum. Too late for such sentiments you wreaker of suffering. Wilkes Booth took a sharp intake of breath. His nostrils flared. *You bastard…No, only wayward thoughts consume me where you're concerned. We must get you soon to Richmond. There you'll be held captive as a means of negotiating the release of thousands of poor Southern boys rotting in Yankee prison camps. Sooner rather than later. Damn your soul.*

★ ★ ★

Back in Port Tobacco, Rose Wheeler wondered when she would next see her common-law husband. He had cancelled his planned trip in early February to visit his cousin in upper Maryland on account of malaise and a lack of incentive – but not least because Surratt had sent a message saying that Booth was out of town. In consequence, he couldn't meet his new recruit until returning to the National Hotel later in the month. When that time came, George journeyed to Washington and, at John Surratt's behest, took a room in his mother's boardinghouse on H Street. He had returned home once during the last week in February to see Rose and Greta but it had merely been an overnight stay. George had met Booth the previous day and couldn't stop talking about the man. He seemed to be in awe of him and needed to get back to the city. Rose didn't quibble. Neither did she ask questions. After all, George had brought her a handful of cash. In accepting it, she assumed it came from Booth: either his own money or perhaps, indirectly, out of Confederate funds. Either way, it didn't matter. She was used to eking out what little housekeeping money came her way. Now there was a goodly amount of spondulix in her purse. It was certainly more than Rose was accustomed to and sufficient to ensure there would be food on the table for the foreseeable future.

In departing once more for the city, George said he would be booking into his usual hostelry, the Pennsylvania House. He would no longer be staying at Missus Surratt's boardinghouse. The accommodation he found cramped and musty. That was what he told Rose but, in truth, he had been barred from the property. Missus Surratt had soon taken a dislike to the furtive, dishevelled lodger who crept about the place and reeked of liquor. She remembered him from when, unexpectedly, he had called at the tavern in Surrattsville, one January evening the previous year. An unsavoury individual. That's what she thought of him then. It was an opinion which became the more entrenched after George had spent two nights under her roof. And it wasn't her imagination: a couple of the young lady boarders had sought an audience with her to complain that the man from Port Tobacco made their skin crawl and they were fearful of him. But it was when he broke house rules – when his landlady discovered two bottles of whisky secreted under his bed – that she chose to show George the door.

★ ★ ★

It was now the fifteenth of the month, the night of the ides of March.

"Come this way, gentlemen," said the proprietor's assistant in a pandering, coaxing voice as he led the way through a heavily draped restaurant bright with flaring gaslight.

A pall of cigar smoke hovered just below the ornately moulded ceiling. Waiters scurried to all quarters at the beck and call of a room of customers who all expected prompt attention when they dined at Gautier's. The new arrivals dutifully followed their companion without drawing attention to themselves. Meanwhile, at the dozen or so occupied tables, the diners' engrossment in despatching and enjoying their savouries and sweetmeats, in their constant chatter and indulgence in after-dinner liquor and cigars, was the complete antidote to the outside chill on Pennsylvania Avenue.

The proprietor's assistant laid his knuckles against the oak panelled door to one of several private rooms located behind the main dining area and kitchens.

"Come in," came the immediate response.

The lanky Lewis Powell opened the door to the pervasive fumes of whisky and brandy and an atmosphere thick with tobacco smoke. His comrade, the more diminutive John Surratt, followed in his wake, leaving the proprietor's man hovering in the corridor, as if expecting further instructions from within.

"Why, Lewis...John...welcome my good fellows." It was Wilkes Booth who spoke, his voice unusually raspish. "So what kept you? You've a lot of catching up to do, my friends," said the host with a chuckle.

"Is there anything we can bring you, Mister Booth, sir?" came a voice from the corridor, the assistant proprietor knowing, full well, that the actor's reply would be in the affirmative.

"A few more cigars, Edmund, if you please. Whiskies for our new arrivals...oh, and send your man back with another round of drinks for the rest of us...same again, Edmund."

"Very well, sir."

"Oh, and some more oysters. My friends will be peckish, I'm sure."

"In answer to your question, John, we had to escort the young women back to H Street," said Surratt, once the door had closed and he had the thespian's undivided attention.

"Of course," reasoned Booth. "They couldn't be expected to fend for themselves. Too many rogues and libertines abroad on the city's streets at night."

In providing his two friends with access to the Presidential box for that evening's performance at Ford's, Wilkes Booth recalled having given John Surratt two extra tickets and with these the recipient had chosen to treat two of the young boarders at his mother's establishment.

"So, how was the performance?" enquired Booth, as he savoured firing a slug of French brandy down his gullet, then cut and lit himself another Connecticut cigar. How was *Jane Shore*?"

Meanwhile the others in the room – Arnold and O'Laughlen, together with Davy Herold and George Atzerodt – seemed pre-occupied and already moderately inebriated as they chatted animatedly over their whiskies.

"Can't say it was to my liking," muttered Powell. "Too far removed from reality…all those dandified costumes and fancy language…"

"Well, I have to admit to enjoying it and so, I believe, did our two young companions," interjected Surratt. "Being lifted out of the eighteen sixties just occasionally…in this case back to medieval England…can be a pleasant diversion. It's good for the soul…but then, if, like Lewis, you've no particular liking for history, I can appreciate how such a play might cease to entertain and appear dull."

"Poor Lewis…but look here," exclaimed Booth as a negro waiter entered the room bearing drinks, cigars and oysters upon a large silver tray. "Remove your coats, take the weight off your feet and enjoy a little sustenance," he continued, signalling to the waiter – by way of facial expression and gestures – to decant the tray's contents on to a central loo table.

The attendant proceeded to comply with the actor's wishes, then filled the now barren tray with a multitude of empty glasses and dirty plates that littered all quarters of the room. Before he withdrew, Booth cast a few coins of appreciation upon the piled plates, causing the fellow to smile humbly and nod profusely in gratitude. It tickled the performer, in that moment of benefaction, that the negro's cotton coat was as pearly white as his woolly head was black as jet. But his amusement was not evident in his countenance. There was a stern look upon his face, as it reacted to a passing thought. *If Lincoln has his way the likes of that nigger will be treated as our equal. Metaphorically speaking, that contrast between black and white will be swept away forever and this Country will go to the devil. He must be stopped.*

Once Surratt and Powell had become seated and Booth's expression had mellowed, the host returned to the subject of the evening at Ford's.

"So what did you think of the box? Fit for a President?"

"A bit cramped I thought," said Powell. "What I mean is that I'm tall and so is Lincoln."

"So what you're saying is that the box is not fit for this President," responded Booth.

Lewis nodded.

"I'd put it another way. Hatred of this President may have jaundiced my mind but I'd say he's not fit for the box rather than the other way round. The fact is he's not fit for anything, that murdering bastard...save the gallows. Then the undertaker can find a suitable box for him. You're all fully aware of my intentions to abduct the fiend and cart him to Richmond. There he can be used as a bargaining pawn...as surety to secure the release of thousands of poor Southern soldiers rotting in Federal prison camps. Well, I've been giving the matter a lot of thought recently," said Booth, "and I think our best opportunity would be to seize Lincoln when he's occupying that damned theatre box."

"That sounds a pretty bold idea," remarked Powell.

"Bold and ambitious," agreed Surratt.

"Well, that's partly why I gave you those tickets for this evening's performance...so you could familiarise yourselves with the layout of the place and..."

"I didn't expect the theatre box to be so close to the stage," said Surratt before Booth had finished what he was saying. "I'm sure Lewis here, being the strong muscular fellow that he is, could easily prise Lincoln from his seat and drag him down on to the stage."

"I don't doubt it," confirmed Booth. "It would take a bit of careful contriving, mind you. Once subdued and bundled backstage, our catch would need to be hurried through the stage-door into Baptist Alley. I'm sure I could rely upon my old friend, Ned Spangler, to be ready with our horses. Then, once on to F Street we'd make a dash for the Navy Yard Bridge and in no time be in Maryland and on our way to Charles County." A gentle smile of satisfaction played upon the actor's face as he rotated his wrist and watched the remnants of his brandy swirl around its glass. Hitting upon the idea of gathering his team together over liquor and oysters seemed to be paying dividends. But his satisfaction was short-lived.

"It's absurd, John. God-damned reckless." The utterance came from the mouth of Sam Arnold.

"What is?" exclaimed Booth, somewhat taken aback by the forcefulness of the other's remark.

"Your plan to seize Lincoln during a theatre performance. It would be rash. I'm surprised that someone with your intelligence would even consider it."

Wilkes Booth looked thunderstruck. It enraged him to think that someone was prepared to question his wisdom and to thereby humiliate him in front of so many other players in his little clique of accomplices. He hit back. "How dare you denigrate my idea in such a dismissive fashion. I'm not opposed to constructive criticism, Sam, but I'll not listen to brickbats from someone who is living here in the city at my expense and has to date contributed nothing of any moment."

"Damn you, John. If you ask me you're all talk." The words that spilled from Arnold's mouth were slurred, testimony to the fact that he had drunk too much whisky. "Good God, man, it was last summer when you told me and Michael, here, of your plan to seize Lincoln and what have we achieved in over six months? Precisely nothing at all and now you talk of some crackpot scheme to capture the man in a crowded theatre."

"I'm inclined to agree with Sam," exclaimed Michael O'Laughlen. "It seems to me, as I've said before, that our best chance of laying our hands on the President is when he takes one of his carriage rides out to the Soldiers' Home. He's rarely well guarded and out in the country there tend to be few people about. In contrast, in a packed theatre there would be too many people to upset the apple-cart."

Across the room Wilkes Booth slammed down his empty glass and looked daggers. Inwardly he was seething. The others...Surratt, Powell, George Atzerodt and Davy Herold remained tight-lipped. They held the actor in too high a regard, in too much esteem, to challenge him and to rile him in this manner. Arnold and O'Laughlen, however, were childhood friends of Booth and, although they admired him for his achievements, they were not in awe of him in the same way as the remainder of their fellow conspirators.

"If you intend going ahead with this plan to capture Lincoln in Ford's then I don't wish to be part of it," continued Arnold in garbled fashion.

"You're a rat, Sam. As an old friend I never envisaged you being guilty of recreance. I like to think we're running a taut ship as far as our little coterie is concerned but, if that's the way you feel, I can dispense with you. And that also applies to you, Michael," snarled Booth, as he turned to face O'Laughlen.

"It might be a taut ship but if you tell me I'm a rat, just remember that rats leave sinking ships, so perhaps it makes sense that I go. After all, if you proceed with such a scheme, this ship of ours will surely sink, be it taut or otherwise."

Booth was incensed. He sprang to his feet, raising his right arm as he did so, as if bent upon striking Arnold. However, before he had time to fully execute his move, Lewis Powell intervened by grasping his arm.

"No, John," muttered the former soldier as he restrained the assailant. "It's not in your character and you'll regret it. We're all supposed to be friends and in this together."

"You're right, Lewis," said Booth. "I don't take kindly to being ridiculed. It made my blood boil. But to see the end of a tyrant is our common goal and we must remain united."

Lewis Powell relinquished the hold upon his leader's arm as Booth slumped back in his chair and composed himself.

"I think the drink has got the better of some of us tonight," he continued. "Sam for one is soused as a pickled fish and, yes, I'll readily admit I feel a shade tipsy." Wilkes Booth paused a moment, took a scarlet 'kerchief from his pocket and dabbed his glistening brow. Then, swallowing his pride, he lent forward and proffered a handshake in Arnold's direction. "I shouldn't have threatened you in that way Sam," said the actor, as the two shook hands. "The drink has got the better of us both. Kindly accept my apologies."

"I spoke out of turn, John. I likewise apologise," mumbled Arnold with a hiccup, his words now as indistinct as ever, his eyes glazed. "You're right, my friend...it's the drink...I'm three sheets in...in..."

"The wind," said George Atzerodt, making a rare foray into the conversation.

"The wind," repeated Sam. "Thank you, good ferryman...yes, the wind. I started early, you see...playing billiards with..." Arnold succumbed to a bout of hiccupping and clearly had difficulty in saying his piece.

"He was over in Deery's billiard hall all afternoon with an old chum," explained Michael O'Laughlen. "I gather he pocketed more corn whiskies than he pocketed balls."

"I think we should perhaps call it a night," opined Booth. "I staunchly hold to the belief that my plan has a good deal of merit but we can't discuss it rationally and objectively while liquor has got the better of us. It can wait for another time. Meanwhile, my bed beckons." Booth signalled to Atzerodt. "Go outside, George, and see if you can rustle up that darkey, or our friend Edmund, to bring us a last drink for friendship's sake." Then, turning to John Surratt, he changed tack, raising his voice to ensure he was overheard. "I'll leave you some tickets for Saturday's production at Ford's, should anyone wish to attend. It's a benefit performance of *The Apostate* for my old friend, John McCullough, and I'm playing the lead…Duke Pescara."

"You'll need to do something about that voice of yours before then," suggested Surratt. "It's sounding a trifle croaky."

"It's nothing more than an irritating little ailment that has afflicted me from time to time over the last year or so," insisted Booth. "I'll be in fine fettle come Saturday evening. If not, then a whisky and water or two in the Star Saloon will do the trick. A medicinal drop of liquor just before I take to the boards is good for oiling my vocal cords and getting me through a performance."

"I think not," chortled the druggist's assistant, Davy Herold. "After all, the liquor you've swilled down your throat this evening has done nothing for them. Take a tip from me…try a warm infusion of sage with honey and vinegar. That would serve you better."

The advice fell on deaf ears as Atzerodt returned to inform Booth that the negro waiter would be along in a trice with a further tray of drinks.

"Splendid, George! First rate," said the actor, as he drew forth and squinted at his pocket watch. "By Jove," he remarked, "I didn't realise the hour was so late. But I'll relish the walk to my hotel along Pennsylvania Avenue. The night air should help clear my head of smoke and liquor fumes…unless, of course, that wretched canal is throwing up such a stink as to first curdle my brain."

Moments later the last round of drinks arrived. Then, once the woolly-headed waiter had taken his leave – flush with yet another tip from what had proved a profitable night's work – the somewhat inebriated Wilkes Booth took all by surprise. With the aid of a chair and with some difficulty, he clambered up on to the central loo table. There he stood, a mite unsteadily, his left thumb tucked into his vest pocket, his right hand clutching a glass of French brandy. He took a deep intake of breath and puffed forth his chest as if about to start spouting some of his lines. But no…instead there followed a heartfelt plea to his accomplices. "Listen here, my friends. Despite feeling a shade intoxicated, I am in sufficient command of my senses to acknowledge the harm which may be occasioned through an excessive intake of the demon drink." Wilkes Booth paused a moment, seemingly in need of time to collect his thoughts. His normally piercing eyes seemed misty, his eyelids heavy, the product of both liquor and fatigue, but principally liquor. "However comforting drink may prove," he continued, "there is no disputing that it can play havoc with one's natural inhibitions. Look at Sam, there…the dear fellow insulted me earlier and I make no bones about it…I was deeply hurt. Yet that was not Sam speaking but his liquor. And then I, in turn, in the heat of the moment, saw red and nigh on landed a blow upon an old chum from my schooldays. And now, as I reflect upon tonight's events, I recall to my fuddled mind some words of the celebrated English essayist and poet, Charles Lamb. The gist of those words I want to share with you right now, my friends, before we go our separate ways, for I consider them most pertinent in our current circumstances. The words Lamb penned were maudlin ones of reminiscence over the loss of old familiar faces. As I remember, his verse told of the disappearance of childhood chums and school-friends, then of old bosom pals who had laughed and caroused together, downing liquor to a late hour. Childhood chums, just like me and Sam and Michael here. Drinking companions…as we all are…bound by a common interest."

Wilkes Booth paused to take another swig of brandy. "The point I am making, I suppose, is that nothing remains the same. All things pass, including old familiar faces. With time and for whatever reason, all depart, all are taken from us…and, if I live to see old bones, I don't wish to look back, a lonely old man, only to see your long departed, familiar faces in my mind's eye and think what we might have achieved together. I want that mental vision to be a reminder of what we accomplished on behalf of our beloved nation. So we must remain a united group and, by the way, Sam is right…I have been dilatory. Now we have to seize the moment and, by whatever means, lay our hands upon this tyrant of a President as a matter of urgency and…I would suggest…before Easter is upon us. I will keep my ear to the ground to apprise myself of his movements about the city. Now friends, let us gather up our hats and coats and be on our way before dawn is breaking. I'll be in touch as soon as I learn of any impending opportunity which might secure us our goal. In the meantime, I imagine I might encounter some of you in the Star Saloon on Saturday evening… assuming you choose to avail yourselves of the tickets I'm leaving with Johnny Surratt."

Booth fell silent for a moment to drain his glass and adjust his necktie. "Now, who's going to help me down from this damned table before I take a tumble?"

★ ★ ★

It was a mild, bright kind of morning – a factor which had certainly contributed to John Wilkes Booth having a marked spring in his step as he turned the corner out of Pennsylvania Avenue and headed north on Tenth Street. The actor felt good, having slept soundly in his room at the National. He had also breakfasted well before repairing to the hotel lobby. There he had nestled into a comfy, spoon-back armchair with the express purpose of digesting both his meal and whatever titbits of news caught his eye within the pages of the *Daily Morning Chronicle*. Then, in due course, when he had exhausted this latter interest, he embarked upon a mid-morning constitutional which had become a regular event when resident in the city: a brisk walk from his hotel to the theatre and back for the purpose of collecting his mail. Booth had an arrangement with his friends, the Ford brothers, that his letters be addressed to him at the theatre. And, on this particular morning, he imagined there could be a few missives awaiting his collection, especially as he had failed to put in an appearance the previous day. It was then that the actor had slept in late following his eventful night of carousing at Gautier's.

As Booth approached Ford's Theatre he recognised two individuals on the adjoining sidewalk. One was an old friend, Ned Spangler, a forty-year-old who worked on the premises as a handyman and sceneshifter. The actor had known him since his youth when Spangler had undertaken carpentry work at the Booth family home. The second was Harry, the youngest of the Ford brothers and the theatre's treasurer, who was casting a watchful eye upon proceedings as Ned set about pasting bills on to a couple of placards.

"Good morning Harry…Ned," exclaimed Booth, chirpily. "And what are you busying yourselves with?"

"Good morning to you, John," said Harry Ford.

"G'morning, Mister John," replied Spangler, a greeting perhaps informal enough to reflect a time-honoured acquaintance, yet laced with sufficient deference to evince the gulf in the two men's social standing.

"Ned's pasting a few more bills advertising *The Apostate*," added Harry. "Being a benefit performance it would be good to achieve a full house."

"Are you saying that ticket sales are lagging?" There was a hint of surprise in Wilkes Booth's question.

"No, with a day to go they're selling well enough. But we could do better," suggested Ford. "The Presidential box is still not taken. It would be good to sell its availability to a party."

"Oh, so *he's* not coming to see me!" scoffed Booth, flippantly.

"The President? Why," quipped Harry Ford, "he's supposed to be watching a Tom Taylor play this very afternoon up at the Campbell Military Hospital. He'll not want to witness another production so soon."

"The Campbell Hospital you say?" enquired Booth, his voice distinctly more flustered than hitherto.

"Why, yes…that's my understanding," remarked Ford. "I've heard they're putting on a performance of *Still Waters Run Deep* to raise funds for the benefit of wounded men undergoing convalescence. It's a cause close to Lincoln's heart, as you can imagine."

"Do you happen to know the time of the performance?"

"Of course I do, John," said Harry. "We at Ford's pride ourselves in knowing all that is to be known in the city when it comes to who is putting on what and when. Come through to my office where I'll have a note of their curtain-up. Oh, and by the way, you've a fair few letters waiting for you."

Wilkes Booth did not tarry long at Ford's. It quickly occurred to him that if Lincoln was travelling out to the Military Hospital that afternoon then this offered a promising opportunity to waylay the scoundrel. Furthermore, coming so soon after the contretemps at Gautier's, the staging of a serious attempt to capture the President would demonstrate Booth's real commitment to carry through his much vaunted intention. In the circumstances, before the morning had run its course, he had hurriedly made arrangements for telegrams to be despatched to those who had attended the gathering at Gautier's. They were all required to meet their leader at a rather dowdy eating house on the northern edge of the city where Seventh Street ran into the countryside, a short distance from the Soldiers' Home and the nearby Military Hospital.

By two o'clock in the afternoon, Wilkes Booth had been joined by his several accomplices. All had answered the call which, after the events at Gautier's, came as more of a relief to the actor than a surprise: after all he knew the likes of Arnold and O'Laughlen favoured the idea of snatching Lincoln from his carriage when visiting the Soldiers' Home. To have been urgently summoned, therefore, to attend some unexplained, furtive gathering in the vicinity of the home would have surely aroused the pair's interest and had them scurrying to the rendezvous.

Booth was in animated and restive mood. In a corner of the otherwise deserted restaurant, he acquainted his recruits with what he had learnt from Harry Ford. "Lincoln should already be ensconced in the hospital function room waiting for the play to commence," he declared in a lowered voice. In his excitable and distracted state he had allowed his coffee to get cold as all the while he fumbled with a teaspoon and somehow managed to drop his lighted cheroot into the lap of the hapless Atzerodt. "I'm sorry it's short notice but we can't let the chance go begging," said Booth. "I will shortly ride over to the hospital to establish when the tyrant is due to leave and, importantly, whether he is accompanied by guards. If he has a cavalry escort, then that's most unfortunate and there's nothing we can do. Otherwise we'll all ride after the Presidential carriage and bring it to a halt. Perhaps you, Lewis, can concentrate on overpowering the driver and throwing him off the box. Meanwhile, Sam and I will set about quietening Lincoln, for which purpose I have brought some rope and strips of muslin to tie and gag the bastard. While we restrain him you'll have the responsibility, George, for binding his hands and feet…I'm assuming as a boatman you're good with knots. While that's happening, Lewis, and when you have disposed of the driver, proceed to take the reins and make for the bridge over the river's Eastern Branch. It's no distance and we can soon be on our way south with a grand prize."

A few minutes later an excited Wilkes Booth had mounted his horse and was heading in the direction of the Campbell Hospital. His accomplices remained in the restaurant to await his return and further instructions.

"This makes a lot more sense than that ridiculous plan to snatch Lincoln in front of a theatre full of people," said O'Laughlen. "He must have taken heed of what you were saying the other evening, Sam."

"Well, by damn, it sure does look that way," opined Arnold with a smile of satisfaction. "How the hell did he expect to prise the man out of his seat without encountering people rushing to his aid? Lincoln never sits alone. He's usually in the company of his wife and a number of guests. And what of others in the auditorium? Are they all going to sit idly by as their President is manhandled and dragged backstage?"

"I think John said he'd arrange for the lights to be extinguished before seizing Lincoln," suggested Surratt. "And we'd quickly subdue him with chloroform."

"The lights extinguished?" scoffed Sam. "How the hell could we expect to see our prey without light, let alone bundle him backstage? It's a ludicrous stratagem."

A half hour or so elapsed following Booth's departure. The band of conspirators continued to occupy their secluded corner of the room and conversation switched to more constructive deliberation upon the now realistic and imminent prospect of waylaying the President on an open, country road. From an upper room above the restaurant, the tinkling of piano keys became evident while the proprietor put in a rare appearance and promptly responded to the signal for more refreshment.

When the restaurant owner re-emerged minutes later, he carried a steaming pot of freshly brewed coffee with a pungency to truly whet the sense of smell.

"It's my younger daughter," he exclaimed, proudly, as he placed the coffee pot upon the table while assuming his customers had been enjoying the rendition overhead. "An arrangement by Franz Liszt…an etude. She's practising for a charity concert appearance being given by a group of young people. It's to be staged before the President next month."

The fellow's comment did not exactly fall upon deaf ears. Yes, it failed to draw a response, largely on account of the distraction and expectation aroused by the whinnying of a horse as a rider pulled up outside. Yet the irony of the remark was not lost upon any of Booth's cohorts.

As the proprietor departed, a shade piqued at not having heard any praise bestowed upon his daughter's piano playing, there arose the sounds of the entrance door being opened and closed. Booth had returned. Entering the main body of the restaurant, his expression alone said it all. Indeed, such was the mood etched upon his countenance that, before he had resumed his place at the table and uttered a single word, an air of despondency had already engulfed his little cabal.

"Lincoln's not there, damn it, so we're wasting our time…we've been thwarted. He was intent on attending the play but called off the visit at the eleventh hour." Booth struggled to keep his voice down, such was his state of annoyance and disappointment. "Wretched bad luck I'd call it," he continued, dispiritedly. "Apparently the hospital received a note of apology from the White House a mere half hour before curtain-up. It seems Lincoln had a change of heart…something to do with preferring to be present at a ceremony involving a captured Confederate flag."

"Are you sure about this, John? Might it be a ruse and instead someone has got word of our plan to waylay him?" asked Surratt, his voice wavering with tension. Seated beside him, a jittery George Atzerodt nervously fingered his slouch hat as he morbidly dwelt upon his friend's suggestion.

"No…no chance of that," said Booth, in an attempt to reassure. "I guess the swine unknowingly made the right decision. But mark my words… our luck will change and his will run out. And what I find as galling as Lincoln's absence is the irony that his more pressing engagement is right now being conducted in front of the National and probably in view of my own room, goddam it!"

In the immediate wake of this disclosure there was a hint of sardonic exchange in the eye contact between Sam Arnold and Michael O'Laughlen. Yet overwhelmingly their meeting of eyes told of further mounting frustration and a fading appetite for what they saw as Booth's impotent scheming.

★ ★ ★

It was the eleventh of April. Wilkes Booth had spent the morning in bed in his room at the National. He was neither ill nor tired but depressed and hung over. Brandy had been a solace to him during the past week or so, ever since Richmond had fallen, while the subsequent news of Lee's surrender had been hard to take. The Confederacy was dead and the realisation hurt.

As he struggled out of bed, a shade before midday, Booth's dishevelled appearance was the very antithesis of his normally debonair, outward appearance that had made him the idol of the city's theatregoers. He smelt badly of stale liquor, having spent the previous evening and half the night in a tour of Washington's drinking establishments – from the well-heeled to the seedy, it mattered not. Drink had at least offered the opportunity to dull his mind and soften the otherwise harrowing knowledge that Richmond was now in Federal hands. He had become very drunk, falling into such a state of intoxication as to have now rendered him unable to recall how he had ever got himself back to the National. Perhaps Lewis had helped him – after all, he remembered being in Lewis's company in the early evening, when he had first embarked upon his night's indulgence…

After attending to his toilette, including a thorough rinsing of his mouth with a freshening solution of chloride of soda, Wilkes Booth descended to the hotel bar-room where he ordered a whisky with water and a plate of fried oysters. He cast a cursory eye over a pile of recent newspapers that were strewn across an occasional table beside his chair. An avid reader, for once he resisted burying himself in the latest news. His oysters were enough to digest. Dispatches upon the demise of Lee's Army of Northern

Virginia were trumpeted across the papers and Booth, of all people, had no stomach for such scuttlebutt.

He needed a walk and a dose of fresh air to help clear his head. In consequence, having partaken of his lunch, he set off along Pennsylvania Avenue. It struck him that many of the folk he passed upon the sidewalk had a greater nimbleness in their gait than was perhaps customary, matched by a cheerfulness in their deportment. There was, after all, plenty to celebrate among Washington's populace in the conclusion of four years of strife and bloodshed. Yet although the recent news lifted a burden from northern shoulders, it bore heavily upon those of Wilkes Booth. Sickened and anguished by the sense of celebration in the air, he came to a halt as he approached Grover's Theatre, the façade emblazoned with posters advertising its production of *Aladdin Or His Wonderful Lamp*. Nearby, a flight of steps led up two floors to his favourite billiard hall above and behind the theatre. Booth felt more than ready to part company with the jauntiness pervading the sidewalk.

John Deery was a trifle irked by the newcomer's behaviour. John Wilkes Booth, however, was an old friend and, as a frequent visitor to his billiard room, a valued customer. On this Tuesday afternoon, Booth appeared morose, quiet and introspective – a far cry from his normal affability. He took to a table alone and, steely-eyed, repeatedly sought to pocket balls with a fierceness of action not usually applied to a billiard cue. This didn't go unnoticed to the proprietor. Instead Deery viewed his friend's conduct with consternation, fearful that his erratic use of the cue might rip the green baize. Yet he refrained from admonishing Booth for fear of giving offence and ending up losing both his friendship and his custom.

In his mind's eye and inner thoughts, meanwhile, Booth began to imagine each ball he struck as the head of Lincoln, his cue a gun barrel or a musket with bayonet fixed. Yes, Richmond had fallen and Lee had surrendered and the purpose of seizing the President had evaporated. But the fiend who had wreaked havoc and suffering upon the South remained accessible in this very city. *There is a way*, thought Booth to himself as his cue ball smote another ivory sphere with a hearty thud which, in his mind, he likened to the sound of gunshot. He would return to what he had previously envisaged: confronting Lincoln during one of his theatre visits. Except now there would be no bundling him backstage, no chloroform. Instead it would be swifter and altogether more deadly. He pocketed another ball and again likened the sound to gunshot. *I have never killed a man...never committed a murderous deed. But I could readily shoot this tyrant who calls himself a President. Perhaps this is my calling, my raison d'etre...the deed that will immortalise me and avenge the South.* Booth was now consumed by such thoughts. He convinced himself that all was far from lost. Into his mind came lines from Shakespeare's *Richard 111,* words he had spoken many a time on stage after slaying the dastardly King Richard on England's Bosworth Field. *The day is ours, the bloody dog is dead... the words of the Earl of Richmond. And how had Derby replied? Courageous Richmond, well hast thou acquit thee. How curious,* considered Booth, *that my character was applauded for slaying the usurping king.* The actor's thoughts began to run away with him. *Does this not tell me something? Is it not prophetic? Am I not destined to slay this President, this usurper of seceded territory and to be applauded as my character Richmond was applauded...that brave and gracious Tudor Prince who strangely bore the name of the cherished capital of the South I am surely set to avenge.*

After taking his supper at the National, John Wilkes Booth set out for the Herndon House at the corner of Ninth and F Streets. It was here that Lewis Powell had a room and the actor was intrigued to learn how he had found his way back to the National during the early hours of the morning. He was also aware that Abraham Lincoln was later due to speak to a crowd which had been gathering upon the White House lawn since mid-afternoon and he would not be returning to the National until well after dark. It was always reassuring, in such circumstances, to have his muscular young friend, Powell, in attendance, should some street ruffian seek to pick a fight. Booth was interested to hear what Lincoln had to say, conjuring up an unseen smile of satisfaction as he ruminated upon the prospect of this being one of the tyrant's last speeches. As he progressed along Pennsylvania Avenue, in the direction of Ninth Street, he was altogether in a far less troubled and a more determined frame of mind than when he had dragged himself out of bed earlier in the day. Assimilation of the thoughts which had permeated his head during the recent spell at Deery's had somehow lifted the gloom and even infused him with a sense of tranquillity when it came to deliberating upon his future actions. He now knew for sure what he expected of himself and of his accomplices.

"The fact is, John, you were sorely drunk and I had to help you back to the National at three this morning," admitted Powell as the two men sauntered through F Street in the direction of Tenth. At Booth's bidding, they were intent on downing a few glasses of liquor at the Star Saloon, next to Ford's.

"Did you manage to get me to my room without being noticed?"

"Not exactly. The hotel clerk was in the lobby and I had to lay you down on a chaise longue to search your pockets for the key. Once that was done the clerk summoned the night porter to help me get you upstairs."

"Damn it!" hissed Booth. "Sorry, Lewis…don't misunderstand me, I'm grateful for what you did but it would have done nothing for my image and reputation." The actor was a trifle vexed by having let himself down. "The trouble is you can't rely upon such people being tactful. It should be the same clerk on duty this evening. I'll make a point of greasing his palm with a dollar or two and trust he and the porter will act discreetly."

After a couple of drinks in the Star Saloon, Booth and Powell retraced their steps back to F Street, then set their gait westwards in the direction of the Executive Mansion. When they arrived at the White House, it was to witness several hundred Lincoln devotees already assembled on the lawn. In contrast to the solemnity etched on the faces of Booth and Powell, the milling crowd was in blithe spirits and seemingly heady with expectation. From across the greensward the hubbub of good-humoured banter and laughter was a reflection of the unbridled joy and relief which had gripped the citizens of Washington in the wake of the recent news of Union victory. Someone close to Booth and Powell announced that the President would appear in fifteen minutes, this causing a ripple of spectators to press forward in the rather vain hope of gaining a better vantage point. In contrast, the actor and his companion held back, choosing to incline their frames against the bole of an old mulberry. They appeared thoughtful, almost languorous, as they lit and drew upon cigars and wondered what pearls of wisdom would shortly spill from the tyrant's tongue to stimulate the appetite of his largely adoring audience.

In due course the President made his appearance, exiting the building through a pair of full length casement windows that opened onto a short balcony. With the twilight hour fast approaching, recently kindled lamplight in the room behind him starkly backlit his tall, angular frame. The crowd went wild on seeing their leader, many of the spectators giving vent to their emotion by waving flags and banners and throwing their hats aloft. Meanwhile, a brass band struck up that most popular tune of the Confederacy, *Dixie*, a declared favourite of Abraham Lincoln. In the wake of the fall of the Southern capital the President had no qualms about requesting the playing of *Dixie*, after all it had been written before the war by a fellow from Ohio living in New York. To John Wilkes Booth, however, its breezy sound drifting across the White House lawn was a thorn in his flesh, delivered before Lincoln had even uttered a word.

The band fell silent, the cheering subsided, the President signalled to the crowd with a wave of his hand. Composing himself for a moment, he unfurled his speech. An aide came out of the shadows and proceeded to stand at his shoulder with a lighted candle, directing the flickering flame so as to assist the clarity of his script. By now there was hushed silence. Soon the President began speaking. The substance of what he had to say concerned his plans for accepting the Southern States back into the Union and, in particular, whether or not the fledgling state government of Louisiana was worthy of being welcomed in its newly constituted form. And then there was the issue of how to deal with the state's former slave population, given that the new constitution had resolved to abolish slavery.

"It is unsatisfactory to some that the elective franchise is not given to the coloured man," said Lincoln. Booth cringed. "I would myself prefer that it were now conferred on the very intelligent and on those who served our cause as soldiers."

Booth flinched, his eyes bulging in horror. The blood drained from his face. He hurled what remained of his cigar upon the grass and ground it into the dirt with his heel.

"Good God, Lewis, do you realise what the bastard is saying?" As his shock turned to rage the actor's colour quickly returned. "So much for the white supremacy we hold dear. He's going to give the fucking nigger the vote, especially the intelligent nigger! Jesus Christ, Lewis, I've never seen an intelligent coon."

"I guess we ought to be moving away from here," murmured Powell, in a strained and lowered voice. Booth had great difficulty controlling his emotions. Such was his fury that he was beginning to draw attention to himself. "For God's sake, John, you're starting to raise eyebrows. Button up will you and let's get out of here," implored Lewis, who soon resorted to using his strength to bundle the incandescent Booth across the lawn in the direction of Pennsylvania Avenue.

As the two companions emerged from the White House grounds and headed east, Booth continued to grumble while Lewis did his best to pacify his friend.

"I don't think you appreciate the seriousness of this matter, Lewis. I really don't. Damn it, man, it means nigger citizenship..." A couple of scavenging hogs squealed in a nearby alley. "You might as well give those yelping animals the elective franchise. After all, to my mind blacks have the acumen, habits and colour of pigs squirming in their own muck. And, as far as that good-for-nothing scoundrel, Lincoln, is concerned, I'll see him bleed like a pig. By God, I will put him through. Mark my words, Lewis, that will be the last speech he will ever make. Now I need a drink...a brandy and by that I mean a bottle of the stuff."

★ ★ ★

"Good morning, Walker." It was a grumbled greeting which seemed laden with insincerity, as if its deliverer almost resented the utterance. The coloured desk clerk immediately recognised the voice and clearly felt its owner's presence to be of sufficient import to abandon whatever engaged his attentions nearby. And so he promptly emerged from the dingy recess which lay to the side of the counter beyond public view. Clambering back upon his high stool, he hurriedly wiped his mouth upon his shirtsleeve, it becoming obvious to the character he faced across the desk as to the nature of his pre-occupation.

"Good morning to you, Mister Atzerodt. And what can I do for you, sir, on this blessed Good Friday?" If young Walker had formed an opinion of George Atzerodt, over the not insubstantial time he had known him, it was that he found him a rather churlish little man and a poor tipper. Yet, as a conscientious employee, James Walker was always polite and respectful in his dealings with such regular customers.

"Is it tasty?" enquired George, who had only recently descended into the hotel lobby. The young desk attendant seemed baffled by the other's question.

"Your breakfast, man," declared George, in order to better elucidate his meaning.

"Why, yes, Mister Atzerodt. Some flavoursome pieces of flapjack, freshly made by my dear mother and dipped in dark syrup."

"Mmm, sounds good," said George in a mildly more congenial tone as he hungrily set his heart upon a piece of Missus Walker's syrupy flapjack. "Would you care to consider parting with a goodly portion in exchange for five cents?

"Why, I guess I can forego a piece for such a consideration," said Walker.

"Good. Now, before you attend to that, I need to settle my bill. I'll be back, you understand. As you know, I always bounce back to this place when

I have occasion to be in the city although, just now, I can't say quite when I'll return. Certainly tonight I've no need for that bed in room fifty-one."

"Okay, Mister Atzerodt, I'll attend to your account straight away and leave a note for Silas, the day clerk, who I'm dearly hoping will be here shortly."

Outside the front of the building, meanwhile, the hotel proprietor was examining the boot scraper which stood at the top of his flight of entrance steps. To his annoyance it had become loosened. He concluded that he would need to engage the services of a stonemason to remedy the problem. It was unlikely that he could entrust the repair to James Walker: the young negro was better suited to indoor jobbing for which there was a constant and greater call when it came to running the hotel. He could also be relied upon to perform the occasional emergency stint behind the reception desk, a role necessitated during the past few hours after the night clerk had cried off sick. As the proprietor turned his attention to another problem, a cracked pane of glass in the lobby window, he was distracted by a familiar voice, its owner freshly emerged from his establishment.

"G'morning Greenawalt." George Atzerodt stood upon the top step. His spluttered greeting flew from a mouth champing upon some patently enjoyable titbit. He carried an old carpetbag which was outwardly as greasy as the lank tufts of hair that spilled erratically from beneath his black, felt hat.

"Good morning to you, Atzerodt. You're out and about early," suggested John Greenawalt in a tone designed to elicit some explanation. It failed, his words only being met with a grunt from his guest.

Greenawalt was unsure of what he made of George Atzerodt. A regular visitor to the establishment, the swarthy German was unsavoury in both his habits and appearance but then many of his customers who chose to hire a bed at the Pennsylvania House on C Street were of similar kidney. George was certainly an enigma in Greenawalt's estimation. His outward aspect, of being perpetually attired in drab broadcloth, baggy pants and his perennial slouch hat was a sure sign of poverty. Yet the fellow always had money enough for a few whiskies. Indeed, his clothes reeked of spirituous liquor and when Greenawalt had recently engaged a tipsy Atzerodt in conversation he had spoken of well-heeled friends who would one day ensure he had enough money to keep him going for a lifetime. And what of the smart, moustachioed companion, who, of late, had sometimes called and occupied George in conversation – be it either in the lobby of the Pennsylvania House or outside on the sidewalk? Why would a well dressed gentleman of fashionable and urbane appearance seek to fraternise with such scruffy low life as George Atzerodt? It was a paradox, a conundrum, which left Greenawalt enduringly perplexed.

"Were you out and about last night watching the celebrations, Greenawalt?" enquired George, as he descended the entrance steps.

"No...I retired early to bed. Did you see any of it?"

"Yes, I took a turn about the city and watched the parade. Many of the government buildings were brightly illuminated."

"Well, Jim Walker tells me that about three this morning there was the sound of high-spirited revelry out here on the sidewalk and he heard something being thrown against the lobby windows. When he ventured out here, it was to find that a drunken mob had just passed by and I had inherited this broken window pane. If such is the outcome of the departing crowd's exuberance then good riddance to the celebrations."

"I wholeheartedly agree," said George, inwardly wishing that there had been no cause for celebration in the first place. "Incidentally, I've told young Walker that I won't be requiring a bed tonight and I've settled my bill." And with that George took to the sidewalk and set his bearing westwards along C Street in the direction of Pennsylvania Avenue.

The spacious lobby at the Kirkwood Hotel was altogether more dignified than what passed as such in the Pennsylvania House. It was a little before eight o'clock, perhaps a quarter of an hour after George Atzerodt had set off from C Street, that he presented himself at the hotel's reception desk and rang the bell. A pleasant smell pervaded the room wherein randomly placed vases of spring flowers added freshness and colour to its ambience. A smart, uniformed young fellow promptly emerged from behind some heavy drapes which screened an adjacent office from the public area.

"How can I help you, sir?" said the clerk, immediately convinced from the caller's dishevelled appearance that he was some itinerant hawker of cheap goods. The thought that he might need to call upon the authority of the assistant manager to send the man packing was swiftly entering his mind.

"Atzerodt's the name. I've been booked in here for just the one night and I'll settle my account in advance, if you please," said George, proffering a crisp dollar bill given him for the purpose by Wilkes Booth.

The hotel clerk must have momentarily looked a little unsettled as he turned his attention to perusing the visitors' ledger. "Ah...yes, sir. Mister Atzerodt, indeed. Yes... room one hundred and twenty six has been reserved for you. It's on the second floor. Now, there's your key, sir and, here...don't forget your change. Should you require supper later then please let me know in advance and by four-thirty at the latest. It's served in the dining room from six o'clock…"

On reaching the first floor landing George hesitated a moment. He recalled standing here earlier in the week. It had been late in the afternoon and he had engaged in conversation an elderly, military gentleman who had revealed to him the door to the Vice President's room. Andrew Johnson had taken to residing at the Kirkwood since being appointed as Lincoln's deputy. The arrangement served as a temporary expedient, pending his securing a family home here in Washington. The old gentleman had also shown George the ground floor dining accommodation. At the time, around four-thirty, as the German peered into the room, Johnson had been the sole person at supper, his coloured servant in close attendance. It now occurred to George, as he commenced his ascent of the second flight of stairs, that it was probably customary for the Vice President to partake of his supper at that inordinately early hour to avoid having to mingle with the other guests.

By eight-thirty, having cursorily accustomed himself to the new surroundings, George was stretched out upon his bed with sleep threatening to embrace him. *What was Booth up to now?* he thought to himself. *Without explanation he sent me here, to the Kirkwood, a few days ago, ostensibly to acquaint myself with the building's layout and, more particularly, to establish where the Vice President laid his head. Did he have plans for Johnson? Since Richmond had fallen and the Confederacy had surrendered there was no longer any purpose in apprehending Lincoln and carting him south. The same applied to Andrew Johnson. Booth hated Johnson, a poor white Southerner and, in his view, a traitor to the South, who had wheedled his way into high rank in the new Federal government. But why would he now feature in Booth's plans when in truth the horse had already bolted and, for what it was worth, the stable door was also slammed shut?… horse… stable.* The words reminded George of Booth's instruction. *Don't forget to go to Keleher and Pywell's livery stables before Good Friday morning has run its course.* Booth had told him to pick up a horse he had already made arrangements for the ferryman to hire. *You'll need the animal for the night's retreat* he had said. *Stable it at Naylor's during the day since it's handy for the Kirkwood.*

George somehow shook off his lethargy. He had good cause to feel tired. He'd spent the previous evening watching the parade and the grand illuminations before engaging in some heavy drinking late into the night.

When, in the early hours, he eventually fell into his bed in room fifty one, it was to be kept awake by the snoring of two neighbouring bedfellows. Then he had to be up and about early, at the behest of Wilkes Booth, in order to register at the Kirkwood Hotel. It was, in consequence, no easy task for George to clamber back on his feet after lying prone upon a feather bed the likes of which – in terms of comfort – fell beyond the compass of past experience. However, once he had done so, he wandered across to the marble topped washstand where he took up the jug and poured himself some water. Although the need for such nicety evaded him, he was in dire need of a shave. Instead, he simply sluiced his face with water, dabbed it dry, then made a cursory attempt to comb his matted hair. Without dawdling, he grasped his crumbled felt hat, left the room and descended to the lobby where he enquired as to the whereabouts of the hotel bar. Here he settled into a comfortable chair, ordered some breakfast and engaged the barkeep in idle chatter for all of an hour or so. In due course, with his victuals despatched and chased down by a couple of whiskies, George rose to his feet, thrust on his hat and set out eastwards along Pennsylvania Avenue, his destination being the livery stables of Keleher and Pywell on Eighth Street.

When George Atzerodt arrived at the stables, a short while before midday, it was to find that a dark bay mare had already been saddled and bridled for him. He paid the stable boy the requisite hire fee of five dollars, then took a ride out beyond the northern city limits to accustom himself to the animal. She was a frisky, young horse but, by a quarter to one in the afternoon, George had ridden back into the city, comfortable enough in the saddle and confident that he had become sufficiently well acquainted with the mare's handling. As he headed westwards along the Avenue he rode past the Kirkwood Hotel, later turning south on Fourteenth Street in search of Thompson Naylor's stables – a block away, on E Street.

John Fletcher, the stable manager, was already acquainted with George who had previously visited his yard with David Herold. He thought him a peculiar, slovenly little man, but then what did appearances matter when a customer could pull a goodly bundle of greenbacks from his pocket and settle his day's livery on the nail? George sat awhile upon a bale of hay and chatted to the coloured stable boy before sauntering back to the Kirkwood. In so doing, he couldn't resist interrupting his walk by stopping at the Union Hotel's saloon to sink two or three corn whiskies. He felt quite contented as he sat at the bar counter and threw the amber liquid down his throat. As far as he was concerned, he had met his commitments, his day's work was done. He had registered at the Kirkwood Hotel and had hired and stabled a horse, just as Booth had instructed. By two o'clock George had completed his walk to the Kirkwood. Dog tired, he entered his room, closing and locking the door behind him. He threw off his hat and kicked off his boots. Within minutes he was asleep, back on that most cosy of feather bed mattresses.

It was close on six when George emerged from the land of Nod, revived but feeling distinctly peckish. He realised that it was too late to think about taking supper in the dining room. He would have needed to notify the desk clerk long 'ere now. Perhaps the barman could rustle up something for him later. As he rose to his feet he spotted a folded piece of paper, lying on the carpet, just inside the threshold. Somebody had pushed it beneath the door as he slept. He bent down to pick it up.

Upon the sheet of writing paper was scrawled a note from Booth. George immediately recognised the handwriting...*George, come to the Herndon House – Lewis Powell's room – at 7 o'clock sharp this evening. It is imperative you come. JWB.*

"Damn. What is he up to now?" mumbled George under his breath. It was too early to wander over to the Herndon House but he felt in desperate need of a walk to shake off the languor in which he was steeped after nearly four hours of slumber. And so he resolved to take a brisk walk back to Naylor's yard, then to ride the bay mare over to the Herndon House to see Booth. Once the actor had had his say he would ride the horse back to Naylor's, then retire to the Union once again where he could reckon on obtaining some supper and something to wash it down. That, in George's mind, seemed like a good plan.

When Atzerodt presented himself at the stables on E Street, John Fletcher was nowhere to be seen, having recently departed to wherever he was intent on taking his supper. This was a source of irritation to George because, in the foreman's absence, the stable boy was immersed in attending to the demands of another customer. In consequence, by the time that business had been satisfactorily concluded and the boy had brought forth bridle and saddle and readied the mare for the road, it was all of twenty minutes past seven.

George spurred the little mare northwards on Ninth Street. He felt distinctly apprehensive, after all he was late and fully expected to be reprimanded by Booth for his transgression. As he hitched up his mount outside the Herndon House and ascended the entrance steps, he felt a surge of anxiety to the very pit of his stomach. In truth, not only was he in awe of the thespian but he was fearful of him. Yet the intimidation he felt was somehow conjured more by Booth's reputation, clout and good looks than by any sense of physical superiority.

The tentative knock on the former soldier's door was promptly answered by Powell who glared at the little German cowering before him in the passage. There was no love lost between Atzerodt and Powell who viewed the diminutive ferryman as a sly, next-to-useless member of the team whose expertise was all but rendered redundant by recent events. From out of sight, beyond Powell's lumbering frame, came Booth's voice. Despite Lewis's intervening presence, Booth knew the identity of the visitor at the threshold having just watched him, from Powell's window, ride up to the front of the hotel. Yet the actor's words came as a surprise to George since they were delivered in a strained whisper, not in the harsh tone he had been expecting.

"Where the hell have you been, man? My message told you to get here by seven sharp. It's now half past and we're on a tight schedule. Come in and close the door behind you."

Booth's frown told of his anger but he was minded to refrain from shouting since he had no wish to draw other guests' attention to the meeting about to take place. As Lewis stepped aside to enable George to enter the room, it was to find Booth peering out of the window in the direction of the Patent Office.

"That goddam place is still decked with illuminations. I'll give the citizens cause to remove them before this day is out, along with the rest of this city's pretty lights." A movement, closer to hand, down below on Ninth Street, distracted Booth. "Ah… that's good. Here comes Davy." A few moments later there was a further knock on the door. It was David Herold.

"Now listen here," said Booth in his whispered tone. "Time is of the essence and our plans have taken a dramatic shift in nature since earlier today. In a nutshell, our stratagem has become not one of capture but one of murder."

Lewis Powell's eyes seemed to sparkle at the mention of the word. Killing had been his business. He had fought in the Confederate Army and relished butchering Yankee soldiers. For him, pride flowed from having put paid to more than his fair share of bluecoats at Gettysburg, prowess attributable to his dexterity with the bayonet. Above all, it was the utter shock on his victims' faces, as he ran them through and twisted the blade, that remained

266

an abiding and endearing memory. Davy Herold's expression, meanwhile, appeared surprisingly impassive. As for George, he had already started to relax, in realisation that Booth had quickly turned his attentions away from any further rebuke for his tardiness. Suddenly, however, with the mention of murder, the blood drained from his features and he wore a look of horror.

"Before I tell you more, my friends, let me acquaint you with what has happened today," continued Booth. "I went to Ford's this morning, as usual, to collect my mail. I was told that the President and Missus Lincoln, together with General Grant and his wife, are due to attend the theatre this very evening to watch a performance of *Our American Cousin*. It struck me immediately that here was the windfall for which, unknowingly, we have been waiting. And it means this, my friends…a great responsibility, on this Good Friday, has been thrust upon our shoulders and, if we all show the resolve to successfully carry through our appointed tasks, together we will change the course of history…"

"You talk of *we*, John, but what of Johnny Surratt, Arnold and O'Laughlen?" asked Davy Herold, querulously.

"Don't fret yourself, Davy. If we adhere to our tasks then the four of us can complete the job. Johnny Surratt has been away in Canada on Confederate business and by now should be in New York on an important assignment. As for the others, they've bailed out, disillusioned it seems since last month's aborted effort to capture Lincoln. O'Laughlen, I believe, is still in the city but he's got cold feet and all that seems to interest him is trying to tap me for a few bucks. The commitment's gone. As for Sam Arnold, it seems he went back home to Baltimore. I've since been told he's gone south and taken up a clerking job at Old Point Comfort."

"Good riddance to both of them," snarled Lewis Powell. "So what have you planned for the rest of us?"

"First and foremost I will deal with the big fish in the pond," said Booth, withdrawing from his pocket a shiny derringer pistol which he handled lovingly. "Tonight that scoundrel Lincoln will meet his Nemesis in the form of John Wilkes Booth and this little shooter. I won't be remembered for my acting ability, by God, but for the way I avenged the South. I'll sneak my way to the Presidential box and shoot the bastard through the head while he's watching the play. I've been back to the theatre this afternoon and made all necessary preparations. Also, I've hired a horse from Pumphrey's and already stabled her in Baptist's Alley in readiness for my getaway."

Lewis Powell pursed his lips, then smiled broadly. "Bold and daring stuff,

John…I like the idea. But should I not come along with you? If General Grant's there he's usually accompanied by several military men."

"Well, I'll admit that might have been a problem but, earlier this afternoon, I just happened to see the Grants ride by in an open carriage. They had plenty of baggage with them and seemed to be heading for the railroad station. So I don't expect them to be at Ford's after all. Anyway, Lewis, you're not to be deprived of excitement, my friend," continued Booth. "Your mission will also be murder. You'll ride over to Lafayette Square, to Seward's place. The Secretary of State is confined to bed at present after that serious carriage accident. Force your way in and murder the bastard abolitionist in his bed. Davy can go with you, to hold your horse while you're putting paid to Seward. Equally, since your familiarity with Washington is left wanting, he can ensure you reach the Seward mansion and then guide your escape through the city streets and away into Maryland."

Powell and Herold didn't quibble over the mission that awaited them. On the contrary, as far as Lewis was concerned, he had a frenzied look about him as if eager to embrace it.

"Now that leaves you, George," whispered Booth, as he turned his attention to the silent boatman who had retreated to the furthest corner of the room, sheer terror and apprehension already etched upon his countenance. "You, George, will murder that traitorous Southerner Andy Johnson. You know where he lives on the floor below you at the Kirkwood. When you failed to arrive here on time this evening, Davy Herold went round to your hotel to hurry you up and to bring you a knife and a revolver. That's how come you appeared to arrive here ahead of Davy."

"With George being out at the time and clearly on his way here, I left the package with the desk clerk," said Herold.

"So George, when you go back, retrieve that parcel. I suggest you use the knife when undertaking your assignment. Using the revolver will attract too much attention. Just go to Johnson's room and sink the blade into the scoundrel's vitals." Booth eyed the hapless German, fully expecting, from his cringing expression, that the acquiescence shown by the other two conspirators would not be forthcoming. He was right.

"I can't commit murder, John, for God's sake," mumbled George, his face distorted with fear. He felt unsteady on his feet and slumped into a chair.

"I told you, John, that this little German runt would prove our Achilles heel when it came to the test," said Lewis, his voice tinged with frustration. "Look at him cowering there, frightened out of his wits."

"I can't do it, John," pleaded George. He looked a pathetic wretch as he sat blubbering in his misery, twisting his felt hat with vigour sufficient to wring water from a wet cloth. "You never mentioned murder, John, for God's sake…you never mentioned murder. All you wanted of me was to ferry Lincoln over to Matthias Point. For God's sake, that's all you wanted."

"Pull yourself together, man," insisted Booth, sorely frustrated that to raise his voice and bawl at the lamentable boatman would be rash. "I thought I could depend on you when it came to the moment of truth."

"The fellow's shit-scared, John," murmured Powell. "He's no good to us. Let me break his fucking neck like I'd break a chicken's."

"Calm down, Lewis. I'm sure we'll be able to rely on George when he's had a little time to dwell on what's required of him" said the actor, knowing full well his words would prove but a futile attempt to indulge the German's feelings. "Now, listen here, all of you," he continued. "I will enter the Presidential box and shoot Lincoln at about a quarter past ten when the play is well advanced. I want you all to act simultaneously, Lewis attending to Seward, George putting paid to Johnson." Booth directed his gaze at Powell and Herold, deliberately avoiding eye contact with Atzerodt. "When you have completed your night's work ride east for the Navy Yard Bridge. We'll rendezvous later at Soper's Hill."

"Remember that those two carbines of yours, John, are in the possession of the tavernkeeper at Surrattsville," said Davy Herold who had been responsible for delivering them to the safe house a few weeks previously.

"And they're there for a purpose, Davy. We'll make a stop at the tavern later tonight. I can also tell you that, this very day, dear Missus Surratt should have delivered my field glass into her tenant's hands and told him to have the shooting irons ready for us tonight. I knew that Johnny's mother was bent upon taking a trip down to Surrattsville today…for business reasons… so I paid her a quick visit this afternoon. That fellow, Weichmann, a friend of Johnny's, was taking her by buggy, so I prevailed upon her to leave my parcel with Lloyd, the innkeeper, and to tell him to be ready with the carbines. So all is set. By tomorrow morning, if all goes to plan, we should be in dear old Virginny. Now, time is short and I must be away. Remember what is expected of you all."

Across the room, George squirmed uncomfortably, such was his mental anguish. "I can't go through with this," he whined. "I can't."

Booth's patience was wearing thin. "Don't think that if you walk away from this you'll be able to go slinking back to Port Tobacco and resume the life you left behind. You'll be implicated along with the rest of us, Atzerodt, I've made sure of that. And if I evade capture and the authorities have not laid hands on you first, then I'll seek you out and blow your wretched brains out."

Minutes later, as George rode away from the Herndon House, his thoughts were in torment. He tried to reason why he had got himself into such a mess. He set his course back in the direction of Naylor's stables although he dearly wanted to turn east on Pennsylvania Avenue, cross the river and make his way quietly back home to Port Tobacco. Inwardly, he chastised himself for ever allowing Surratt and Harbin to coax him into joining Booth's band of conspirators. *Surratt and Harbin no less…and where were they now for God's sake? Johnny Surratt was tucked away in New York while Harbin was probably at home on the Potomac's Virginia shore, no longer expecting to assist with the conveyance of a captured Lincoln on the way south to Richmond. Both men would be oblivious to the bloody and momentous events which Booth intended should unfold this night. Both would welcome the coming dawn without the stain of blood on their hands.*

The dejected German eventually rode into Naylor's, dismounted the mare and left her in the safe keeping of the coloured stable boy. As he did so, John Fletcher came ambling across the cobbled yard, shouldering a bale of hay.

"Ah, it's you, Mister Atzerodt. I half expected it to be your friend, Mister Herold. He's due back about now with Charley, the horse he hired from us earlier."

George said nothing in response, knowing there was precious chance of Davy Herold putting in an appearance. He had other matters on his mind and would need the animal later to make his escape into southern Maryland.

"Can you do me a favour, Fletcher?" said George. "Can you tell your boy not to remove my mare's bridle and saddle this side of ten o'clock, only I'm likely to be needing her again later? I'm assuming there will be no problem keeping the stables open until that hour?"

"No, that's no problem. I'll still be around."

As Naylor's foreman stood at the stable gates and watched his customer saunter away along E Street, it struck him that the little German had become quite dispirited since he last spoke to him. His round-shouldered posture had become more pronounced as if he were weighed down by a millstone about his neck.

An hour and a half elapsed. At around twenty minutes to ten George reappeared. He was quite full of liquor, having done the rounds of several drinking establishments west of the Kirkwood House. He hadn't eaten, his seven o'clock yearning for supper having abandoned him. The fear and misery that gripped him had stolen his appetite. Imbibing alcohol, he had hoped, might steel him sufficiently to carry through his assignment. It was unlikely, of course, but as he re-entered Naylor's yard it was a prospect he had yet to entirely banish from his mind. A modicum of Dutch courage was beginning to stalk his veins.

"Would you join me in a drink, Fletcher, my good fellow?" said the ferryman, his words heavy and indistinct.

Fletcher hesitated a moment. He wouldn't have chosen Atzerodt as a drinking companion, particularly in his already tipsy state, but in truth his own throat was dry and he yearned for a glass of liquor. His customer also seemed intent on paying, which was a bonus. In consequence, the foreman instructed his boy to finish clearing up and to have Mister Atzerodt's horse ready for him when they returned in about ten minutes.

At the nearby Union Hotel Fletcher made quick work of sinking a refreshing cool beer while George preferred another whisky.

"I'm getting increasingly concerned about your friend, Herold, Mister Atzerodt," said Fletcher as the two sat huddled against the bar counter. He's over-staying his spell with our horse, you know. He's about two hours adrift...I just hope he's returned by the time we get back."

"Oh, I doubt Davy will be long now," opined George. "He's a trustworthy fellow."

As the two men stepped back into the night air, a faint drizzle had begun to fall. From nearby Pennsylvania Avenue the sound of a passing brass band, accompanied by the cheers and high jinks of pursuing spectators, testified to the sense of celebration which continued to grip the city.

"You know, Fletcher, if what I think will happen tonight does indeed happen, then you will be rewarded," mumbled George.

Fletcher wasn't sure he had heard his companion's words correctly, since they were slurred and the noise of the band and its followers was still in evidence. If he had, then they made little sense. He put the observation out of his mind, knowing Atzerodt to be well tight. When they reached the stables, John Fletcher seemed visibly irked since there was still no sign of Davy Herold and the hired horse.

"If you see your friend on the way back to your hotel, tell him to hurry up since I'm wanting to close up for the night. As for you, Mister Atzerodt, are you feeling OK to be up in the saddle? You seem a little edgy," said Fletcher, trying to be tactful. In fact, he had hit the nail on the head, for George's mental state was perhaps a greater burden than his evening's intake of liquor. "After all, she seems a skittish little mare, that horse of yours," continued Fletcher. "I doubt I'd want to ride her through the city at night."

"Ah, but she's good upon a retreat," mumbled George, as, grasping the pommel and with some unsteadiness, he lifted himself up into the saddle seat. To the yard foreman it was another riddle, which, again, he attributed to the German's inebriation. For a moment George hesitated as he settled into the seat and took time to pat the mare's withers. Then he sighed loudly, as if weighed down by many troubles, before suddenly urging the animal forward across the stable yard.

"Goodnight, Fletcher," he shouted as he set off eastwards towards Pennsylvania Avenue.

It was around five minutes after ten by the time George found his way back to the Kirkwood Hotel and retrieved the package which Davy Herold had left with the desk clerk. He immediately went to his room and unwrapped the weapons – a new revolver, some cartridges and a large bowie knife. Given the imbuement of his addled mind with false courage, George had still not entirely dismissed going through with his assigned task, even though, in truth, he knew himself incapable of such a deed. Booth had advocated the use of the knife, which, being sheathed, he promptly tucked into his belt, leaving the revolver squirreled away beneath his mattress. Then he departed his room and descended the two flights of stairs leading to the lobby. He dallied a split-second on the first landing, glancing at the door to Johnson's room. He felt his heart pounding in his chest. Once downstairs he headed for the hotel bar which was devoid of other guests. He ordered a whisky. For once he refrained from downing it in a single gulp but chose to savour it. His eyes rolled in their sockets. He had difficulty focussing upon the gas flame which hissed and flickered above the far end of the bar. His eyes drifted towards the ceiling. Somewhere up there Andrew Johnson was probably preparing for bed. He finished his drink and fingered the hilt of the bowie knife. His heart was in his mouth as he contemplated beckoning to the barkeep for another drink. Something stopped him. Out in the entrance lobby a single chime from the longcase clock marked the quarter hour. A quarter past ten. If true to his word, Booth would be stealthily approaching the President's box and reaching for his derringer pistol. The bloodthirsty Powell would be forcing his way into the home of William H. Seward. George shuddered. It was now or never. He rose to his feet, not quite knowing where they would lead him. He drifted into the lobby where he sat upon a tub chair and spent a couple of minutes scrutinising the flight of stairs with its polished rosewood banister that could aid his ascent to the Vice President's room. Was that where his destiny lay or was it to take a different turn? He thought again of Wilkes Booth and Powell. This was his moment of reckoning. He sprung to his feet. He could delay no longer.

Seconds later George emerged from the Kirkwood Hotel. He felt hot…he loosened his necktie and breathed in draughts of cool evening air, dampened by the soft drizzle that fell upon the city. He staggered down the entrance steps, unhitched and mounted the bay mare and was soon setting her at a trot eastwards along Pennsylvania Avenue. His Dutch courage had finally deserted him. He had defied Booth and, if nothing else, momentarily felt a sense of freedom, as if unshackled from the actor's stifling sway. Approaching Tenth Street, George became aware of some raised voices as several people began spilling out on to the Avenue. Above the clatter of the mare's hooves, he thought he heard two agitated passers-by talk of a shooting. He feared the worst: Booth had remained true to his word. He pulled up and rode into the end of Tenth. In the distance a significant crowd was milling outside the entrances to the theatre and the Star Saloon, extending in an umbrella-topped phalanx across the entire street. A low hubbub of noise emanated from this gathering, punctuated by the occasional shouted instruction, the odd convulsive gasp or sob. Standing high upon the stoop of the small flight of steps to a house directly opposite Ford's, a man in his shirtsleeves seemed to be beckoning to a new arrival to negotiate a way in his direction through the crowd below.

George sat back in the saddle seat for a few moments, spellbound by what he saw. In his imagination he fancied he smelled blood. In truth, the pervading odour was that ubiquitous mix of street mud and horse excrement, aggravated beyond measure by the more offensive and unwholesome reek off the Old City Canal. As George came to his senses, to the extent his inebriated state would permit, his overwhelming desire was to melt away into the night. He turned the bay mare about. Once he was back on Pennsylvania Avenue he resumed his journey eastwards, this time at a canter. Panic as much as fear now permeated his every sinew.

Minutes later George Atzerodt reached the Pennsylvania House, the seedy establishment he had vacated much earlier on this fateful day. He went to the bar and ordered a whisky but no sooner had he slugged it down his throat than he felt the urge to be on the move again. Leaving the hotel, he rode west, having made the decision, by whatever logic, to return the hired mare to the stables of Keleher and Pywell. It was approaching eleven thirty. After relinquishing the animal, he ambled northwards, chose to turn west on F Street and, for some inexplicable reason, began to drift back towards Ford's theatre. However, before he had ventured as far as the Herndon House, the scene of Booth's last meeting, George was startled by a group of Union Cavalry that came thundering by, in the process showering him with clods of mud. The incident somehow killed the morbidity which appeared to be drawing him back towards the scene of the crime, for, in its wake, he panicked, turned about and fled. Simultaneously, he had qualms about carrying the bowie knife that had been intended for his own murderous use and so he tugged it free from his belt and cast it into the gutter. In due course, panic-stricken, breathless and weary from his day's drinking, George once again found himself on Pennsylvania Avenue. Here he hailed a horse drawn streetcar bound from Georgetown to the Navy Yard and proceeded to clamber aboard. As he entered the conveyance he recognised an old acquaintance, one Washington Briscoe, and took the seat beside him. Initially Briscoe was pleased to have George's company, on the basis that having someone to chat with could help lighten the journey. He told him he was on his way to the Navy Yard – to his place of employment as a store manager.

"Have you heard this awful news about the President?" said Briscoe. "Seems an assassin got into his theatre box and shot him."

"I had heard," mumbled George. "Is he dead?" There was a distinctly edgy tone to his voice.

"I don't know but they're saying it looked bad. I just wonder…"

"Have you a nook in your store where I could lay my head?" continued George. It was an abrupt interruption verging on rudeness and prompted as much by the German's desire to change the topic of conversation as by his need for a place to sleep.

"I couldn't do that, Atzerodt. It would be against the rules and I could lose my job."

Washington Briscoe was a man of fairly temperate habits. He classed George merely as a past acquaintance, not a friend. He knew him to be a slave to liquor and could detect, by sight, sound and smell, that the man sitting alongside him was more than just liberally imbibed. Had George been of more equable and trustworthy temperament he might have made an exception and acceded to his request, since there was a little truckle bed in one of the outhouses behind the store. He could have nestled down there without any questions being asked but, as George reiterated his appeal for a place to lay his head, Briscoe stuck to his guns.

"No," he insisted. "It cannot be done, Atzerodt." There was no way Washington Briscoe wanted to encourage the disreputable little German and certainly no way he was going to permit him to infiltrate his place of work.

At the end of the line the two men said their farewells without any overt expression of animosity. George, after all, was used to being rebuffed, something his servile, cowardly nature was quite capable of coming to terms with. As he remained on the otherwise empty streetcar, while the driver finished treating his two horses to a drink and a bag of hay, George looked out towards the Navy Yard and the Anacostia River. Somewhere in the distance a clock chimed the midnight hour. *I wonder whether Booth was apprehended or whether he has already made his getaway across that bridge and found his way to Soper's Hill?* he thought to himself. It was a contemplation he continued to harbour as the streetcar pulled away, passed the Navy Yard's main gate and began rattling along on its return journey to Georgetown.

★ ★ ★

The time was around five thirty on Easter Saturday morning. Save for the wet streetcar rails which shimmered in the half light, Pennsylvania Avenue presented a dank, muddied expanse. George Atzerodt pulled his coat collar about his neck and ears and settled his chin closer to his chest as he pressed on towards the open ground that surrounded the White House. He had been surreptitious in his recent departure from the Pennsylvania House after spending the last few hours in a shared room, acquiring what little sleep he could. The other guests had been restless, one holding forth until late in the night about the tragic events at Ford's. George had tried to close his ears to the fellow's remarks but one thing he gathered was that Abraham Lincoln was not dead. The assassin's bullet had delivered a mortal wound but the President clung to life, lying on a bloodied bed in a boarding house across the street from the theatre. It was only a matter of time before he slipped away.

George was now bereft of money. Gone for good was Booth's generous allowance. It was the reason he had tried to persuade Washington Briscoe to put him up for the night. It was also why he chose to sneak away from the Pennsylvania House without paying his bill. However, he reckoned it was about time he was due a night's free lodging in Greenawalt's squalid establishment. He had stayed there on many occasions and because of his early start and the paltry amount of shut eye he had managed to accrue – courtesy of a garrulous room mate – he felt there was no better time than the present. Now, as he crossed the end of Tenth Street, George couldn't resist glancing to his right. The morning was unusually gloomy because of the grey skies which released a steady rain. In the distance, however, opposite Ford's, he could just detect an amorphous, huddled mass of individuals. No sound or movement emanated from this crowd. Gone was the commotion, the raw shock which had gripped last night's departing theatregoers. To George the scene suggested that Lincoln had yet to breathe his last. Outside the boarding house within which the victim's life was slipping away, a muted crowd stood vigil beneath a forest of black gamps, waiting for news of the inevitable.

The scene was sufficient to encourage Atzerodt to increase his pace, lengthen his stride and to bury his chin deeper into his enveloping grey coat. As he passed and left the Executive Mansion in his wake, he pondered on why he had ever got himself into this awful predicament. With the war now over, the demand for carriage painting would doubtless begin to pick up back in Charles County. He thought of Rose and Greta and when he might see them again. He suspected it could be some time, having resolved, while he sat on the streetcar the previous night, that it would be unwise to attempt a return to Port Tobacco. If Booth and the others had succeeded in their getaway and the authorities had become alerted to their chosen route, then southern Maryland could soon be awash with soldiers. He was safer to make his escape elsewhere and one place above all quickly came to mind. George had decided to slip away in the opposite direction: to Montgomery County and specifically to his old boyhood home – the farmstead his father and his Uncle Johann Richter had built in Germantown. In February he had cancelled the trip to see his cousin Hartman Richter who now ran the old farm. Hartman would doubtless be pleased to see him and he could immerse himself in work around the secluded farm and try to forget his woes. It was spring and there would be plenty to occupy him on the land.

At around eight o'clock the slovenly ferryman trudged into Georgetown, a district on the north western fringe of the city. Here he reckoned on purchasing a ticket to ride on the Rockville stage which was later due to stop at Cunningham's Tavern on the High Street. Yet, before George could contemplate buying his ticket, he had two pressing matters to address. Of these the more troubling was his lack of money. His second need was for sustenance, having eaten nothing since breakfasting at the Kirkwood almost twenty four hours previously. Now, after his lengthy trek out of the city, George was famished and hunger pains gnawed in his stomach. But the wily German had a plan, as well as time to execute it, before the stage was ready to depart for Rockville. First and foremost, he was acquainted with a fellow by the name of Caldwell who managed a grocery store, operating under the name of Matthew's and Company, on the High Street. He knew Caldwell from his Germantown days when the family had regular grocery orders placed with and sent out from Matthew's. In more recent times George would also call at the store when returning from visits to his cousin. On such occasions he would purchase liquorice – for which he had a liking – and stock up on his favourite tea. The thought that Caldwell might do him a favour was in his mind as he entered the grocery. It was ten minutes past eight. George found the prevailing smell – seemingly a fusion of ground coffee, tea, cheese and molasses – vaguely enticing. From behind the counter, John Caldwell was prompt in greeting his first customer of the day.

"Well, if it's not Georgie Atzerodt. Good to see you my good fellow. Have you been staying over at the Richter place?"

"No, I'm on my way there. I was due to visit Hartman a few weeks ago but then couldn't make it. Anyway, I was passing and thought you might be interested in purchasing this watch from me," said George, as he proceeded to withdraw a silver pocket watch from his vest. "It's a good timepiece...a German fuppe...a fob watch...made in Nuremburg in the thirties. It used to belong to my father."

"No thanks, George. It wouldn't interest me I'm afraid. I already possess a good pocket watch."

George looked downhearted. "The fact is, John, I've no money, not even two cents to rub together. Would you consider giving a loan to an old acquaintance?"

"Well, my dear fellow, the blunt fact is that I've no spare greenbacks to offer you."

"What if I left this in your keeping as security?" said George, imploringly, as he unfastened a revolver from his belt and placed it on the counter.

Caldwell lifted the weapon and examined it closely.

"It's a point three six cap and ball Navy revolver...from the Colt Armoury.

I purchased it six years ago and would be sorry to lose it. But I'm desperate for cash and prepared to leave it as security for a ten bucks loan. I will send you the money or bring it to you next week."

Caldwell seemed impressed with the revolver. Without further ado he opened his till and handed George two five dollar bills.

Minutes later George was knocking at the door of a modest, clapboarded home in West Street, which lay just off High Street, a few blocks from Matthew's grocery. Its neat front yard, studded with house leeks and bedecked with clumps of spring flowers – now a shade past their prime – was a manifestation of the sense of order and fastidiousness that characterised its occupant.

If I'm to cure my hunger without spending a cent, then this is the place to do it thought George, as he waited for the door to open. When it did, it was to reveal a bright-eyed little woman dressed in a handsome, blue bombazine dress, a tulle cap nestling upon her brindled head of hair.

"Why, pray, if I'm not mistaken it's Andrew Atwood. Goodness gracious, Andrew, this is a surprise. Come in, my dear, come in. It must be two years or more since you last came by." The harshness of the little woman's guttural accent seemed almost implausible, failing, as it did, to sit comfortably alongside her rather dainty and prim appearance. She was a petite woman with a complexion as fine as a parian doll, like Dresden porcelain. "You've called at the right time for I've just made a fresh pot of tea. Come in out of that damp weather and sit yourself down," insisted the little woman as she turned about and led her visitor back down the passage. "Here," she said, with a wave of the hand, beckoning George into the front parlour, "go in there and make yourself comfortable. I'll be with you in a trice with a hot cup of tea. Hang up your wet clothes here in the hallway."

George had known Lucinda Metz since he was a child living in the old family home out in Germantown. She and her husband had settled in the village some five years before the Atzerodts arrived, having emigrated from the fatherland as newly weds. Lucinda still knew George as Andrew Atwood, as did other friends and acquaintances in that remote community. His middle name was indeed, Andreas, or Andrew. Why Atwood?...well, perhaps his German background was a cause of some sensitivity to George as he was growing up, causing him to anglicise his surname. Clearly, in later years, once he had moved away from the family home, this ticklishness had become less of an issue for him. As for Lucinda, now in her mid forties, she and her four daughters had moved away from Germantown after she was widowed. She was not enamoured with the country, preferring to be closer to civilisation. For one thing, it offered better prospects for her daughters and, indeed, so it had proved. The two eldest were now happily married and living nearby. The third, a children's nurse with a family living on the Foggy Bottom side of Rock Creek, had recently announced her forthcoming betrothal. That left the youngest girl, now fifteen, who was still living at home and who, according to her mother, had become a most adept seamstress for her tender years.

Shortly Lucinda reappeared with a tray of tea and some buttered rye bread which she placed upon a small, walnut tripod table that stood close to George's elbow.

"Thank you kindly, Frau Metz. I'm famished so that bread is most welcome."

"Famished, Andrew? Why, when did you last eat?"

"Early yesterday," said George with a grimace designed to appeal to the widow's sense of compassion.

"Then a couple of slices of rye bread is insufficient," said Lucinda, adamantly. "It's not long since I had my breakfast and the skillet has barely lost its heat. Let me quickly go and prepare you something more substantial to send you on your way."

George refrained from uttering any words of discouragement, leaving his hostess to disappear once again into the bowels of her little cottage. Ten minutes elapsed whereupon the little woman emerged with a breakfast to sorely whet the ferryman's appetite. George's eyes bulged as an expression of surprise and relish, while Frau Metz – with a little prompting of her guest to remove the occupying tea tray – committed to the little tripod table a plate of grilled bratwurst sausage with sauerkraut, mustard and a good-sized chunk of buttered bread.

"That'll stick your ribs together, Andrew," said Lucinda, as George, without standing on any ceremony – excepting to offer a brief murmur of appreciation – launched into rapidly despatching the widow's generous offering.

"I'm assuming that you're on your way to Germantown, Andrew?"

"Yes, a long, overdue visit to the old homestead."

"Well, do give my sincere regards to your cousin, Hartman. He was in Georgetown last fall and called in to see me. I thought he was beginning to age."

"I suppose we all are, Frau Metz."

"You're right of course. I'm nowhere near as nimble as I was five years ago. And how are things in Port Tobacco? What of your good lady and your little daughter? Are they in good health?" Whilst Lucinda did not approve of her guest having taken a common law wife and siring a child with her, she would certainly not have made known her disapproval. Furthermore, she made it a rule never to be so outwardly judgmental as to permit her beliefs to hinder the outcome of her inquisitiveness. That would be counter-productive.

"Yes, they're fine, thank you," confirmed George, "but the war has killed my carriage painting business."

"Well, it's as well this wretched conflict's come to an end. Perhaps things will now take a turn for the better."

"I'm sure they will," added George, not knowing just when or, indeed, whether he would once again be able to turn his hand to his business. After all, Booth had declared that, if he walked away from his assignment to kill Johnson, he could not expect to go slinking back home to resume his old life. And while George hoped it was bravado, Booth said he had made sure to implicate him in his plot. At least the widow, for all her loquacity, did not hark on about the events at Ford's. Seemingly she remained oblivious to what had been exacted upon the President the night before. That at least was a blessing, since Frau Metz seemed as thirsty for anything vaguely newsworthy as a dry sponge is for water.

Once George had cleared his plate and spent a further hour or so chatting and drinking tea with his old friend, a glance at his pocket watch told him he needed to be on his way. As he bade farewell his thanks seemed quite effusive, gauged by his usual niggardly standards. The Widow Metz, through her own kindness and generosity, had made sure he was now far better fortified to continue his journey. It had been a hungry, shuffling Atzerodt who had earlier wandered into Georgetown. Now there was almost a hint of sprightliness in the gait of the grey coated figure that turned the corner out of West Street and made his way to the stage stop. While the conveyance was not due to arrive from Washington for fifty minutes, George was cognisant of this when deciding it was time to part company with Frau Metz. He now had money in his pocket and food in his stomach. It was time to throw back a few whiskies in Cunningham's bar.

The stage's principal role was to carry the mail between Washington and Rockville, for which purpose it held a Government contract. There was no great call for passenger conveyance beyond Georgetown but, if someone wished to make the journey, and there was space to be had, the operator was only too happy to take the traveller's money and be of assistance. George was one such potential customer this Easter Saturday morning. He'd had enough of walking for the day and, with cash to hand, was more than content to part with a dollar for a ticket to carry him the twenty miles to Rockville.

Having proceeded to sink a couple of whiskies at the bar counter, George wandered off across Cunningham's taproom clutching a third glass of liquor. He tucked the ticket stub, handed him by the landlord, into his vest pocket and settled down in an easy chair by the chimney fire to await the stage's arrival. In no time the inevitable happened. The cheery warmth from the grate, sleep deprivation and the tiring effect of George's early perambulation, were influences enough. Added to these were the widow's breakfast and a few whiskies. All conspired to soporific effect. It was left to the tavern-keeper, being aware of the sleeper's intention to travel, to raise him from noisy slumber with a raucous yell in his ear.

"The stage is here, Mister!," bawled Cunningham. "Stir yourself or you'll be walking to Rockville."

George struggled to his feet, bleary-eyed and, in that split second, blind to his whereabouts. The deep chime of the bar-room clock began striking twelve. It seemed a gross intrusion into his still awakening sense of perception, as, without comment, he drowsily made his way to the tavern door. The stage had just pulled up and the driver, a portly fellow by the name of Webster, was showing great agility in clambering down from the box. Alighting upon the sidewalk, he secured his team of chestnut bays to the tethering rail, then promptly turned his attention to assisting his departing passengers. Four had taken the ride out of Washington and all four parted company with the stage at Cunningham's Tavern. It left George as the sole traveller to journey on to Rockville.

The poker-faced little German, newly emerged on to the High Street, proceeded to brandish his ticket stub under Webster's nose. At the time the stout coachman was ferreting around in the rear boot, in search of the sole mailbag destined for Georgetown. .

"You can ride inside, Mister, or you can accompany me aloft," remarked the driver. "The choice is yours."

George peered overhead. The heavy grey skies that had spilled an intermittent rain and drizzle for the last two days were beginning to break, allowing soft shafts of sunlight to filter through. Since the weather was improving and a greater warmth beginning to burgeon, George resolved to travel on the box. It was also an opportunity to converse with the driver, which might help the journey on its way. In consequence, he proceeded to climb aloft.

"Well, Mister, let's get under way," boomed Webster as, in due course and after some close inspection of the hitching and running gear, he joined his passenger on the box. Then, applying deft control to the reins, the coachman released the brake. With a brief shout and a crack of his whip came the strained sound of taut leather and the ring of shifting metal as the stage lurched forward. It was underway once more amid the rhythmic clatter of hooves.

"Have you heard the dreadful news?" queried Webster, before they had journeyed too far.

"Yes," murmured George as he braced himself for the expected. "Someone shot the President."

"Yes...but had you heard he was dead?"

George's muscles tightened. He knew the wound was mortal and it was only a matter of time. Yet, for all that, it came as a shock...the stark realisation that Booth had succeeded in his bloody quest and now he, George Atzerodt, was an accomplice to murder.

"The news appeared to be on everyone's lips when we left the city earlier. Seems the poor man breathed his last shortly after seven o'clock this morning. It's said they know the identity of the assassin...apparently some well known actor."

George did not respond to the stage driver's remark other than in curt and dismissive fashion. "Yes, a wretched business," he said, "but tell me, you're not the usual coachman on this run are you? It's always been an older gent who's taken the reins when I've travelled it before."

"You're darn right, Mister. It's usually old Francis Kerns, my employer, who drives the afternoon stage into Washington, then brings it back out to Rockville the next morning. Yesterday, however, he had business in Rockville and asked me to do the run. It happens from time to time. I don't mind. I enjoy a change of scenery." So dramatic and consequential had been the events at Ford's, that the stage driver could be excused for trying to return to the subject. Indeed, he might well have found it strange that, on more than one occasion, his passenger appeared interested in reverting to more mundane matters.

After about twenty minutes the Rockville stage ran into the settlement of

Tennallytown which marked the boundary between the District of Columbia and the state of Maryland. Here congestion on the road ahead forced stage driver Webster to pull up behind a long line of stationary wagons.

"If I'm not mistaken this queue runs up as far as the Military Road… to what the locals call the Forts," declared the driver. "I'll wager you it's something to do with Lincoln's murder."

A few minutes later his suspicion was confirmed as a message was passed back from the head of the queue.

"Prepare to wait awhile," shouted a drayman to the two men perched high on the box immediately behind his cart. "It's the Army. They're searching each vehicle with orders not to permit the onward passage of any suspicious looking characters."

George flinched. *This is serious*, he thought to himself. *I can't hide…I can't flee. The stage driver would alert the bluecoats and give them a good description of me. Perhaps my one hope is to take a leaf out of Booth's book…I'll act. I'll go up to the picket post and try to act supremely confident, as if I've nothing to hide. I'll dupe those fucking bluecoats into letting me through.*

"I'm going to walk to the head of the queue and see just how long we're likely to be delayed," said George without further ado. Webster nodded in agreement. It seemed a good idea.

As he walked towards the picket post, George counted nearly thirty vehicles backed up ahead of the Rockville stage. Nearing his destination, he increased his pace and strode purposefully up to the group of Union soldiers who were busying themselves searching the two leading wagons and interrogating their drivers.

"Good afternoon, sergeant," declared George cheerily and with a broad smile on his face.

The non-commissioned officer, taken somewhat by surprise, turned on his heels and, for a moment, scrutinised the newcomer without response.

"I'm with the stage travelling to Rockville and thought I'd just enquire, on behalf of the driver, how long it is likely to take before we can expect to be waved through?" Inwardly George was pleased with himself. He felt that he sounded confident.

"Where are you Mister?" enquired the sergeant, prompting George to point in the direction of the stationary stagecoach.

"Back there, sergeant, where a farm track joins the road. The track is demarcated by that line of trees," said George.

Screwing up his eyes, the bluecoat tried to follow the line of the civilian's forefinger. "Look, Mister, this is an important business. I don't know whether you're aware but the President, no less, has been murdered and we're under orders to inspect all vehicles leaving the District of Columbia and to detain any suspicious characters. The road is busy and it's taking time. If your stage is back there near that tree line then I reckon it'll be three quarters of an hour or more."

At this moment the sergeant was distracted by a shout from his corporal. The junior non-comm had finished questioning the drivers of the two leading wagons while the four privates in attendance had completed a meticulous search of the vehicles.

"All is in order, Sergeant Chubb. Nothing suspicious," bellowed the corporal.

"Then you can wave them through and call up the next two," replied Chubb.

"This promises to be a long day for you, sergeant…and a thirsty one," suggested George.

"Well, we've water and coffee but I could dearly sink a glass of John Barleycorn. At least our regimental sutler has his tent pitched nearby and we can shoot up there and purchase the occasional titbit."

"Does he sell liquor, sergeant?"

"Good God, no. It's against Army Regulations. If he sold liquor to us he'd lose his right to supply goods to the troops," said Chubb ruefully. "But I can tell you this. The fellow's got his own barrel of cider in his tent. I'm not sure whether he had to secure exemption from his obligations to retain personal liquor but he certainly won't sell it to us since he knows the consequences. Yet I'm thinking he might be persuaded to sell it to a civilian if he can see a profit in it. So what I'm saying is, if you're looking to wet your throat, while you bide your time, you might care to try our sutler."

"So where can I find him, sergeant?"

"A hundred yards in that direction…along the Military Road. You can't miss his tent."

Ten minutes later George returned to the picket post, having paid a successful visit to the sutler's store. To his credit he had offered a sum sufficient to persuade the sutler to readily part with a goodly portion of his own cider. Now Sergeant Chubb, of the 13th Michigan Light Artillery, could only watch in amazement as the stranger gingerly carried before him six glasses of hard cider, balanced precariously on the lid of a former hardtack box.

"Something to wet your own throats, sergeant," exclaimed George in a palpably triumphant voice.

"Well I never! Bless you, Mister," exclaimed an incredulous Chubb, as he promptly ushered the beneficent stranger out of sight of the queuing travellers. Conveniently a log hut had been erected by the Army at the junction of the main highway and the Military Road. This offered ready cover should any of the men wish to relieve themselves behind it. Now its presence would extend to hiding the illicit despatch of raw cider.

"They're for you and your men, sergeant," assured George.

"Have you not got one for yourself?"

"I downed mine at the sutler's tent. I couldn't fit seven on the box lid."

"Then please take another, since one of the men abstains from alcohol."

"No, no, sergeant…have yourself a second glass. You're very welcome to it."

"Well that's most generous of you, Mister," declared Chubb, who, without further deliberation, beckoned the corporal to join him. "Corporal, this gentleman has kindly provided us all with a most palatable beverage to ease our toils. Ask no questions. Go behind the hut and sink your quota. Then instruct each of the others…save for the abstainer…to report to me in turn and they can do likewise. Now, how are matters progressing?"

"I think we're almost ready to let two more through, sergeant," said the corporal.

"Very well. Try to hurry things along but be vigilant."

While Sergeant Chubb was talking to his corporal, George had drifted away to chat with the owner of a wagon now nearing the head of the queue.

"That's a nice bit of scroll work on your cart," remarked George, noticing that the word 'Gaithersburg' was incorporated in the design.

"Thank you," replied the driver. "It cost me enough to have painted."

"Are you travelling there now?"

"I am indeed and will be pleased to get home. I'm a farmer and set off yesterday with a load of butter and eggs for the Washington markets. Pity about this hold up."

George knew the whereabouts of Gaithersburg. It was a village the other side of Rockville and a good deal closer to his destination than the stagecoach stop.

"Would you care to have some company on your ride home?" enquired George, realising that to travel with the farmer meant an earlier clearance through the picket post and a dropping-off point which was closer to Germantown.

"Why, yes," said the farmer. "Having someone to talk to will stop me nodding off. So where are you bound?"

"Germantown."

"Well, I can take you most of the way. Incidentally, my name's William Gaither."

"Thank you, sir. George Atzerodt's the name and I'm mighty pleased to make your acquaintance. By the way, do you like cider?"

"Why, I've a thirst alright and would dearly love some apple cider. Do you have any?" asked the farmer with a quizzical look, since he could see that George was bereft of any possessions.

"No, but I can soon get some." And with that George dashed away in the direction of the sutler's store, only to return minutes later clutching two more glasses of cider.

"Here's a brace to quench your thirst, Mister Gaither, in appreciation of your kindness in allowing me to ride along with you."

"I'm hugely grateful, sir, but this will make me nod off. You'll have to keep talking," suggested the farmer with a chuckle.

With that, George climbed up alongside Gaither. In a short while Chubb's men waved the preceding two vehicles on their way and signalled Gaither to move forward. Their inspection of his cart was fleeting since it was empty. Similarly, the farmer's interrogation was brief and interspersed with lively banter between the farmer's passenger and the soldiers, themselves a shade light-headed and ebullient thanks to their unexpected gift of cider. By the time Gaither and his new companion were being told to move on, George had all but forgotten his concern about being detained by the soldiers, such was the relationship he had forged with them.

"Give those receptacles back to the sutler my good fellows," were his parting words as he retrieved the two empty cider glasses from beneath the farmer's feet and handed them to one of the privates. Then he settled back in his seat and for once felt good about himself. He had excelled. He had duped the soldiers and, at least for the moment, could relax somewhat.

William Gaither and his passenger passed a carefree few hours chatting amiably as they journeyed through the benign and gently undulating farmland of Montgomery County. Ultimately, as dusk gathered, the farmer's wagon approached a fork in the road some three miles north west of Rockville and on the approaches to Gaithersburg. Gaither pulled on the reins and slowed the wagon to a halt.

"This, I'm afraid, is where we part company, Atzerodt," said the farmer, almost apologetically. "It's been grand to have your company and I wish you an enjoyable time with your cousin. Now, I'm assuming you know the way to Germantown. The road forks here to Derwood but you'll need to carry straight on. After about two miles take the fork to Barnsville which will lead you through to the Germantown crossroads. It's about eight miles."

"Well, thank you, Gaither. I too have enjoyed our companionship but… yes…I know my way and I reckon I'm ready to stretch my legs."

"It's only a pity my journey stops here but the farm lies up that track," said Gaither, pointing to the start of a rutted dirt lane which joined the main highway immediately opposite the road to Derwood. And with that the two men parted with a friendly handshake and went their separate ways.

In truth, as George watched the farmer's wagon disappear up the dusty, furrowed track, his resolve was to satisfy the more immediate need for a drink than to stretch his legs in the direction of Germantown. Fortuitously and from past knowledge, George was aware that, located hereabouts, was the property of blacksmith John Mulligan – an affable Irishman – whose forge doubled as a tavern. He knew Mulligan was as adept at dispensing whisky as he was at being a man of iron and the fellow kept a good stock of liquor. And so, five minutes later, the traveller had settled into the comfort of Mulligan's bar, where, for an hour or so, he chatted with his burly host and spent some more of his now dwindling funds on despatching the blacksmith's whisky.

Darkness had fallen as George bade farewell to John Mulligan and set off towards his destination. The day was ending for him the way it had begun – with a long walk, except now he was at liberty to feel more relaxed. He was well clear of the city, night had fallen and he was in countryside familiar to him. After trudging on for about two miles he took the left fork to Barnsville. The silence was profound, broken only by the fleeting sounds of wild creatures. George's mood began to lift as he ruminated upon his circumstances and began to persuade himself that they were not as dire as he had first imagined. Yes, he had conspired with Booth and the others but his intentions had gone no further than to abet the seizure of Lincoln and, in his role as a ferryman, to help deliver him safely to Richmond. Murder had never been on his agenda. When he was asked by Booth to kill Andrew Johnson he had defied him and, by so doing, reasoned he had rescued the

Vice President from that fate. For this he should be applauded. After all, had Booth instructed Powell to kill the Vice President then the likelihood was that he would now be committed to his coffin. These thoughts lifted his spirits as he continued on his way but the day's exertions were also taking their toll. Fatigue began to tell as George caught sight of candlelight flickering in a window some fifty yards ahead. As he drew nearer, the tracery of newly budding branches would intermittently become silhouetted against this welcoming light for he was now approaching the Great Seneca Creek where a wealth of woodland trees huddled around the banks of the fast flowing stream. An owl hooted. Moments later another lighted window came into view as the intervening branches melted away, leaving the sturdy, brooding bulk of the old Clopper Mill rising up beyond the creek.

I wonder whether Robert Kinder would let me stay the night, thought George to himself, for he knew the miller quite well. He crossed the road bridge and descended a flight of steps which led the visitor to the mill's entrance door that stood in the dark shadows of its looming water wheel. His initial rap drew no response. He tried again, this time with greater success. With a weighty creak of its hinges, the door opened to reveal the miller, Robert Kinder, clutching a candle holder. George didn't immediately recognise him. Lit from below, by the candlelight, his visage seemed eerily distorted. He had also shaved off the moustache which invariably appeared prematurely grey on account of being heavily flecked with flour dust. Kinder, in turn, encountered an even greater problem as he peered out into a darkness as black as pitch, sunken as the doorway was below the Barnsville road and the soaring water wheel. He had to thrust the candleholder in George's direction so as to cast light upon his visitor's features before there was any sense of recognition. George was first to speak.

"Hello, Robert. It's Geo…it's Andrew Atwood."

"Well, well, Andrew. What brings you here after dark?"

"I'm on my way to visit my cousin but fear I'm not up to making it all the way on foot tonight," explained George. "I was wondering whether you might be happy to let me stay?"

"Funnily enough, I was only chatting with Hartman Richter yesterday. We bumped into each other on the Darnestown road. But, yes, Andrew, you're more than welcome. I can't offer you a bed but I can give you a blanket and you can settle yourself down in front of the mill fire. You'll be as warm as toast."

"That would suit me fine," said George.

288

"Then come on in my friend," declared the miller, with a welcoming smile.

George slept soundly before the miller's hearth and woke to a bright spring morning. He breakfasted, tarried a while in conversation with his host, then leisurely took his leave around ten thirty. The lofty mill, of stone and mellow brick, no longer appeared sinister as, in the vivid morning light, George climbed its steps to the Barnsville road and, with a parting wave to the miller, set his gait in the direction of Germantown. About a mile into his walk he spotted a carriage – what appeared to be an old barouche – approaching from the opposite direction. As the vehicle drew nearer, the German recognised a fellow countryman astride the driver's seat. He was a gentleman in his fifties by the name of Hezekiah Metz who had first been introduced to George by cousin Hartman some two years previously. A successful and well known farmer in the locality, Metz slowed to a stop as he approached the long track which cut across the fields and led to his well-appointed home. Yet he refrained from turning into the lane, for the recognition was mutual and he resolved to wait for the walker to draw close.

"Well, it's Andrew Atwood, if I'm not mistaken," exclaimed Metz.

"Good morning to you, Mister Metz," replied George who immediately recognised the two Leaman brothers sitting behind the driver. He had known Somerset since they enjoyed a contemporary childhood, in Germantown, back in the late forties. He would come and play with George and Hartman on the family farm. As for Somerset's sibling, James, he was less known to George, having – as in the case of Metz – only made his acquaintance comparatively recently.

Sitting opposite the Leamans was a young lady whose identity George had correctly surmised before the farmer spoke again.

"Let me introduce you to my darling daughter, Elizabeth," said Metz. There was a hint of pride in his voice as he beckoned towards the young woman, smartly attired and bonneted in her Easter Sunday best. "The epitome of her dear, late mother in both temperament and good looks," averred the farmer with conviction. "Meet Mister Atwood, my dear...a cousin of Mister Hartman Richter." His words prompted an exchange of pleasantries. "And tell me Andrew," continued Metz, "are you acquainted with the Leaman brothers?"

"He sure is," declared Somerset with a hearty chuckle. "We used to fish and play together."

"So are you staying with Hartman?" enquired the farmer.

"I shall be," said George, "although he's not expecting me. I'm now on my way there, having journeyed from Washington."

"If you're not expected then you can't reckon on Hartman having a meal to put before you. Would you care to join us for dinner?"

"I'd be delighted to," proclaimed George, his features delivering a broad smile.

"Well," continued the farmer, "we're on our way home from church and Somerset and James here already have a long-standing arrangement to join us for midday dinner. With Lent behind us, my housekeeper, Martha...a former house slave and a cherished soul beneath my roof...has promised to serve up a meal fit for trenchermen and she's a damn fine cook. We're expecting an additional guest to join us later, a close friend of mine and another member of the local farming fraternity...Nathan Page...but there's still room enough for you at our table, Andrew. That's for sure."

Unseen by George, Elizabeth Metz appeared to wince at the thought of this rather dishevelled, grubby stranger being seated at their dinner table. Yet it was not in her making to be so churlish as to cause a scene and to embarrassingly rebuke her father in present company. When introduced to him a moment before, Elizabeth had felt uneasy at the way the stranger looked at her, for there was lustfulness in his furtive eyes. However, the damage was done. She immediately retained her composure and smiled blandly at the newly invited guest. As for her father, his hospitality towards Andrew Atwood was undoubtedly prompted by his visit to church this Easter morning. The sight of the approaching, ill-kempt figure of the man he knew as Andrew Atwood aroused in him a pang of conscience. He was beset with the need to show kindness, infused with a sense of renewed spirituality and a desire to exemplify the moral values of his faith.

"You'd best climb aboard, Andrew, and we'll head up to the house," said Hezekiah Metz.

"No, wait a minute, sir," implored Somerset Leaman. He had noticed the way Elizabeth looked a mite uncomfortable when introduced to Atzerodt and how she had momentarily reacted in the wake of hearing her father invite him to dinner. His reaction was instinctive. Elizabeth would be eternally grateful for his intervention. She wouldn't want the scruffy newcomer sharing the seat with her.

"To be honest, I could do with a walk, sir," added Somerset. "I'll join Andrew in a stroll up to the house. It'll strengthen my appetite for that fine meal which awaits us."

"As you please, Somerset…assuming Andrew is happy to accompany you. After all, he may be tired."

"No, I stayed over with Bob Kinder last night," said George. "I've only walked a mile from the Clopper Mill."

Elizabeth breathed a sigh of relief as Somerset Leaman alighted from the carriage. Then, without further deliberation, Hezekiah Metz galvanised his two horses into action, leaving the two walkers to promptly fall in behind. Ahead of them, the well sprung carriage creakingly lurched on its way between high banks, verdantly endowed with the new season's growth, while – above and beyond the half hood – the farmer's bobbing head remained clearly visible.

Soon the ageing barouche had disappeared from view. It was Somerset who was first to speak.

"So you've come here from Washington, Andrew. Tell me…are you the man who killed Lincoln?"

George's frame tightened visibly. He was shocked to the core. A few seconds elapsed before he could utter a word. Yet, by then he had noticed the broad smile on his companion's face: he was speaking in jest.

"Yes," spluttered Atzerodt, as his tattered nerves struggled to recover their composure. A moment later he raised a meek smile. "Of course I did."

"Well, Andrew, coming hotfoot from Washington, I suppose you're as well informed as any. What's the truth of it, my friend? Is it so?"

"Is what so?"

"That Abe Lincoln has been killed."

"Yes, it is so. He died yesterday morning according to the driver of the Rockville stage."

"And what of Seward? Is it true his throat was cut?"

"Again, yes…according to the coachman. He told me Seward's throat was cut but that he had not been killed. Two of his sons had received stab wounds."

"It certainly is a wretched business," said Somerset, in an almost disbelieving tone. "Someone at church this morning said he'd heard a rumour about General Grant also having been the victim of an assassin's bullet."

"I'm not so sure that is so or not," suggested George after some hesitation. "If he had been then I guess I would have heard of it."

It took ten minutes for George and his old friend, Somerset Leaman, to reach Metz's home since it lay well back from the Barnsville road. When they arrived, Martha, the black housekeeper, ushered them through to the backyard, where, seated together on an extensive greensward, James Leaman and his host were already in earnest conversation and enjoying a refreshing drink.

"Come and join us in a glass of my homemade cider," exclaimed the affable farmer. "Dinner will be served in about half an hour."

No sooner had George become seated than he got fidgety. The predominant topic of conversation seemed to focus on the price of locally grown produce and the extent to which the ending of the war might influence some change. It was not a subject to entice George's interest, unlike the sweet prospect that took his attention in the middle distance, lingering in the vegetable garden. George rose to his feet, finished his glass of cider and, with a murmur of sorts designed to excuse himself – a murmur so quiet and perfunctory that it fell on deaf ears – he ambled off across Metz's well manicured lawn.

Miss Elizabeth Metz numbered sewing and kitchen gardening as her principal hobbies and unlike most young women of her age – which George Atzerodt assessed to be around twenty or so – was not averse to getting her hands dirty. After returning from church she had decided to inspect her vegetable plot, where, a month previously, she had lifted and divided an old rhubarb crown, only to replant the several pieces of split rootstock in a new and lovingly prepared piece of ground. Now, as she crouched uneasily on her haunches, her interest was twofold. Firstly, she was anxious to avoid dirtying her dress and petticoats before dinner: that would irritate her father beyond measure. Secondly, yet importantly, she was anxious to cast a critical eye upon her new crowns to establish whether they were showing expected signs of growth. She had not reckoned, however, upon the intrusion of the shabby and lascivious Andrew Atwood. He had eyed her with lecherous intent. Of that she was convinced and he made her skin creep.

"Rhubarb, eh," murmured George as he approached Elizabeth from behind.

The poor girl's heart sank and missed a beat.

"It should be doing well following this past week's rain and the boost of today's spring warmth. Do you enjoy gardening, Miss Metz?"

"I do enjoy my kitchen garden, Mister Atwood. It's where I can retreat from the world and become engrossed in my pastime, away from people who hold no interest for me," said Elizabeth rather pointedly.

It is no exaggeration to say that George found the farmer's daughter a most attractive young woman. Nearly two months had elapsed since last he had been with Rose down in Port Tobacco and he was beginning to feel a hankering for female company. Now, today, that yearning had been given fresh impetus in encountering the peerless Elizabeth with her fine proportion and stunning good looks. As he stood there beside her, he found her presence beguiling.

"You know, I have a good deal of experience raising fruit and vegetables," declared George. "My cousin and I used to spend a lot of time together, helping out on the farm and, of course, I'm knowledgeable about cultivating this local soil. I'll be staying with Hartman for a while, so I'd be delighted to come round from time to time, Miss Elizabeth, to give you the benefit of my skill." As George spoke he couldn't resist touching the girl's upper arm from which experience she immediately recoiled.

"How dare you be so bold, Mister Atwood," she exclaimed emphatically, yet in a hushed tone to prevent her voice carrying across the lawn to the ears of her father and his guests. "I beg you to keep your distance," she proclaimed with quiet insistence, "and don't call me Miss Elizabeth...it's Miss Metz."

Aptly chastened, George was not drawn to apologise and outwardly showed little sign of embarrassment, such was his stolid nature. Instead, he turned away and drifted back towards his host's gathering, only to find that, in his absence, its ranks had swollen.

"Andrew." It was Metz's voice. "Let me introduce you to Mister Nathan Page. Nathan...this is Andrew Atwood. Nathan farms land just down the road, in the direction of the crossroads. We've been neighbours for more years than I care to remember."

George shook Page's proffered hand. It was a handshake that Metz's neighbour found limp and indecisive, as if Atwood was indifferent to the introduction.

"Andrew used to live locally but now resides down in Charles County," added Metz. "He's on his way to stay with his cousin, Hartman Richter."

"Ah...yes. I'm familiar with the Richter place," said Page, a neat, dandy little man in his late forties. "It's a good spread, not far from my own but on the other side of the Darnestown road."

At this juncture Martha appeared on the back porch to beckon her employer and his guests indoors. Dinner was ready to be served.

At the dining table George took his place between the Leaman brothers while Elizabeth sat opposite, between her father and Mister Page. George felt sure that the object of his infatuation would have remained silent upon the events which transpired in the vegetable garden but that, behind the scenes, there had been some collusion afoot – perhaps involving the housekeeper – to ensure they were seated apart.

The ensuing conversation soon came round to the subject that was doubtless on most people's lips this Easter Sunday.

"Having travelled from Washington, Andrew tells me that Lincoln died early yesterday from his wound," said Somerset Leaman. "He was told by the driver of the Rockville stage which left the city in the wake of the President's death. Seward was also badly injured by his assailant."

George nodded in affirmation. He seemed nervous and agitated. At one point he dropped some beads of soup upon the tablecloth and proceeded, apologetically, to dab the spillage with his napkin. Across the table the affable, forbearing host placed no import upon his guest's agitation, while his daughter put it down to her recent rejection of his unwelcome advances. The German's uneasy behaviour did not, however, go unnoticed to the perceptive Nathan Page.

As the meal progressed, the conversation shifted to speculation upon the effects of the President's assassination on the incumbent administration and conjecture over Andrew Johnson's ability to step into the breach. It was left to James Leaman to return to the bloody events of Good Friday.

"A gentleman that Somerset and I were talking to outside church seemed to think General Grant had been caught up in Friday's outrage."

"I mentioned this to Andrew as we walked up the lane," said his brother.

"And what is your understanding, Andrew?" enquired James.

George shrugged his shoulders, before replying, having hardly uttered a word for some considerable time. "No, I don't suppose he was killed. If he was he would have been killed probably by a man who got on the same car that Grant boarded. But then, if the man that was to follow him had followed him it was likely to be so."

To his table companions, George's response appeared garbled and convoluted. To Nathan Page it implied something more. *Had Grant boarded a railroad car on Good Friday?* he thought to himself and *How come this Atwood was privy to Grant's movements?* Page's suspicions were aroused. He'd be prepared to wager that this nervous visitor knew more than he was prepared to admit.

With the meal concluded, the dinner guests repaired once more to the backyard, for the early afternoon was a sparkling one with a warmth surpassing anything the month of April had so far delivered. It was now turned two o'clock and George was anxious to resume his journey. He set about bidding his farewells and thanking Hezekiah Metz for his generous hospitality. Fortunately, he was spared having to confront Elizabeth who had considered it prudent to remain indoors and retire to her room. George's parting valediction was with James Leaman.

"Well, it's been good to see you again, Andrew, and I'm especially pleased that you and my brother have renewed your acquaintance. I know you are old friends. He used to speak fondly of your times together, fishing with you and Hartman in the Little Seneca Creek."

"Those were the days," reflected George. "Halcyon, trouble-free days and now what trouble I see."

"Why, what is there to trouble you, Andrew?"

"More than I will ever get shot of." George's words seemed laden with despondency.

George Atzerodt retraced his steps to the Barnsville road where he turned left and continued his westward journey. In due course, he shuffled into Germantown where he dallied a while, for the mid-afternoon sun now radiated warmth more reminiscent of summer days. The tiny settlement that huddled about the old crossroads had changed little since his childhood. After resting for ten minutes, stretched out on the grass, George commenced the last stage of the pilgrimage to his boyhood home, as he took to the Darnestown road and headed south. After about a mile, he came upon the familiar dirt track that led up through the cornfields to a sylvan copse which stood upon a shelf of higher ground. There, among the trees – still sparse with foliage – he could see the two-storey, clapboarded farmhouse, which, twenty years before, had been lovingly raised up by the toiling hands of his father, Heinrich and his uncle, Johann Richter. He was back home.

Eleven

Upper Maryland
April 1865

It was Easter Monday morning with little to trouble Corporal Reynolds other than an increasingly rasping and irritating cough. This he viewed as the legacy of a recent cold which had afflicted him in the wake of several nights' exposure to unseasonable chill while on picket duty along the railroad. Being just a cold, the original ailment had presented him with no good cause to respond to morning sick-call, since he thought the surgeon would scoff at him for wasting his time. The residual cough, however, was perhaps a trifle more disconcerting, not least because of what had happened to his father. That was always in the back of his mind, so much so, that, as he looked down upon Relay House station, he thought he might now pay a visit to the surgeon. Here in camp it was quiet enough. It was not as if the sawbones was under anywhere near the kind of pressure he would have encountered at the front. So, having already missed Monday sick-call, he would respond to it tomorrow morning. He could hopefully seek reassurance from the surgeon or, if nothing else, obtain an elixir to ease the problem.

William stood upon a raised timber platform, a walkway comprising an integral part of the works, inside the abatis, which capped the fort's natural outer cliff face. This offered an uninterrupted view of the railroad station and, more obliquely, the southern flank of the white, timber-clad Relay House. It had been part of the defensive works thrown up by the Engineer Corps when, after completing Baltimore's Federal Hill fortifications four years previously, they had come here with a commitment to safeguard the viaduct over the Patapsco.

Beyond the railroad tracks, a lone private was facing a long and humiliating day as he marched up and down the station platform attired in a wooden overcoat. The poor fellow had been convicted of robbing a hen roost in nearby St. Denis. Now he was taking his punishment, the top and bottom of a barrel having been knocked out, leaving the casing to be placed over his body. Upon the man's head, that emerged from the top of the barrel, his forage cap was stuffed with orange, hen's feathers, while, to front and back, he had to suffer the humiliation of signs proclaiming that he was a 'Chicken Thief.' Otherwise the extensive platform was largely deserted save for two soldiers – part of a guard detail – with responsibility to keep an eye on the miscreant and to make sure he did not deviate from the execution of his punishment.

Alone with his thoughts, William spent but a few minutes casting a reflective eye upon the scene. From a purely selfish standpoint it had been a smart move to part company with Molleys Town where he would have still been struggling to make ends meet. Now, less than two months after stowing a grand sum of money in the Government Bank, the war was over and, with the Two Hundred and Thirteenth being a green regiment, he had been spared any further perilous encounters on the front line. The time here at Fort Dix had been easy enough, save for the tedium of policing the railroad and the monotony of drill routines with which he was all too familiar. What the future held was anyone's guess. The President had been brutally murdered but that was not a matter to impact on soldiering life at Fort Dix, or so William imagined. There had been no suggestion since the surrender of General Lee that the regiment might expect to be disbanded any time soon. It would doubtless be mustered out of service in the fullness of time, although, until then, there was surely little purpose in continuing to prepare for field duty. Indeed, while no waning of vigilance had been sanctioned along the railroad, for fear of reprisals from southern sympathisers, the intensity of drilling had become markedly reduced.

The shrill whistle of an approaching Baltimore bound train, as it ran across the Thomas Viaduct, closely followed by the sounding of fatigue call, awakened William to his senses and to the fact that he was due to supervise a work detail. As he retraced his steps towards the assembly point by the garrison flag-staff, he was suddenly confronted by First Sergeant Robert High.

"Ah, there you are, Corporal Reynolds. The Captain has just requested that you report to him immediately."

"Very well, Sergeant," replied William briskly. "But what should I do about the fatigue detail I'm about to oversee?" he added, haltingly.

"Don't you worry about that, Corporal," insisted the Sergeant. "I'll make sure other arrangements are made. In the meanwhile, make haste to Captain Snyder's quarters. Apparently it's a matter of some importance."

"Yes, Sergeant," said William, obediently.

"Come in," shouted the Captain in response to the tentative knock on his door. William entered, removed his forage cap and, closing the door behind him, promptly stood to attention.

"Sergeant High said you wanted to see me, sir."

"Yes, Corporal, I did. Come in and sit yourself down." Theodore Snyder glanced briefly in William's direction, then returned to scrutinising the unfurled map which lay before him on his tooled-leather desk top. His words were in no sense haughty towards his junior, non-commissioned officer; on the contrary, they struck a soft and welcoming tone.

William obeyed Snyder's invitation and seated himself opposite his commanding officer. After two minutes silence the Captain sighed, looked up and shifted his spectacles above his eyes, such that they adopted an easy angle of repose upon his forehead. "So what did you think of last evening's memorial service, Corporal Reynolds?"

"I thought it very moving, sir. I thought the gentleman's words were heartfelt and delivered with fervour."

The gentleman to whom William referred was a warm-hearted Presbyterian minister from Elkridge. The clergyman had expressed a wish to conduct a service in memory of the country's beloved President, so cruelly cut down on Good Friday. It was specifically intended for the officers and non-comms of Company H and was held in a reception room down at the Relay House.

"There's only one thing I'd mention, sir," continued William. "Interestingly, in his eulogy, the minister drew upon a verse in Revelations... 'he that killeth with the sword must be killed with the sword.' I think a few of my fellow corporals felt it was directed at the role of the soldier. I sought to persuade them otherwise."

"Well, our dear late President, in waging this just war on slavery, did not consider his actions to be at variance with a strongly held faith. You were right to convince your comrades that the pastor's words were not directed at our brave soldiers, simply because they shoulder arms. No... his words were directed full square at the assassin and his accomplices.

Interestingly, Reynolds, he told me he is a close friend of the pastor from the Presbyterian church in Washington where the Lincolns worshipped. And he was proud to recount news which had just reached him…that his good friend had been present at the President's death bed and had prayed while he breathed his last."

"Now," continued the Captain, with greater emphasis in his enunciation as he prepared to change tack, "the nub of why I have summoned you here this morning is not to do with the service but very much to do with the assassin and his accomplices."

"Yes sir." William looked attentive, albeit quite taken aback by the Captain's final sentence.

"The fact is, as one of the military garrisons in the state of Maryland, we've been instructed by the War Department to keep an eye out for any suspicious looking characters in the wake of Mister Lincoln's assassination. I am also in receipt of a copy of a communication sent on Saturday evening to the Chief of Police in Baltimore." At this point Captain Snyder rose to his feet, drew down his spectacles and grasped a piece of paper which lay beside his map. "I'll read you what it says…it's from Charles Dana, Mister Stanton's Assistant Secretary at the War Department and it specifically refers to a character by the name of Atzerodt in the following terms. *The assailant of Mister Seward has been known here by the name of G A Atzerodt. He is twenty six to twenty eight years old, five feet eight inches tall, light complexion, brown from exposure, brown hair, long and rather curly moustache and goatee, dark from being dyed, rather round-shouldered and stooping. He wore dark pants, vest and coat with a long grey overcoat and a low slouched hat, much worn.* There is also mention and a given description of John Wilkes Booth, the assassin of the President. However, my understanding is that Booth is known to have made his escape into southern Maryland where Charles County is being scoured by cavalry." The Captain let the sheet of paper fall back on to his desk and removed his spectacles.

"That's very interesting sir, yet, with respect, why are you allowing me to be privy to such information?" said William in an uncertain voice.

"The thing is, Corporal, I don't think we can leave this entirely to the police. We continue to be very careful when it comes to searching trains passing through Relay House station and that must continue. If anything we must increase our vigilance. But I feel that in addition we need to show a little resourcefulness and for that reason I have decided to send forth a search party. Now, the letter sent to the Police Chief concludes with the following remark. *Atzerodt is believed to have left this city this morning at six thirty in the Baltimore train.* Well, if he did travel to Baltimore on Easter Saturday morning then he's either moved on, perhaps to Philadelphia or New York, or he's gone to ground in the city in which case, yes, let the police do their work. But what if, like Booth, Atzerodt fled the city into open country? Seemingly no one answering this man's description is believed to have gone south like the assassin. So where do you reckon a fugitive would attempt to sequester himself if you rule out going north or south?"

"Well, you're left with east or west sir," replied William, rather nervously, since it seemed an all too obvious answer to a question hardly worth posing.

"Precisely Reynolds...obviously, you may say. Yet, if you look east, it's not too far until you run up against the Chesapeake Bay. Go west, however, in the direction of Winchester, or north west, towards Frederick, then the world's your oyster. And that's my hunch...that this would-be assassin may have done just that. It's a long shot, Reynolds, but I'm thinking that Howard and Montgomery Counties should be searched for Atzerodt. And that is where you come in."

"Me, sir?"

"The very same, Corporal."

"I mentioned a search party and I'd like you to lead it, Corporal Reynolds. So why me, you may ask. Well, as you know, this Regiment's a green one and, as far as Company H is concerned, you are my most experienced Corporal who has endured arduous service in the Gulf. As for the men who accompany you they could remain here and follow the usual daily routines but where does that get them? With the war as good as over they're not going to see field service and the Regiment will be mustered out in due course. They might as well be chasing assassins as being here polishing their accoutrements and learning how to put one foot in front of another."

"Yes, sir," said William. "And when do we leave, Captain?"

"You'll leave Fort Dix this afternoon with a party of twelve men. The identity of those men is currently being decided by Sergeant Coleman who is to randomly draw names from a hat. Now, get to your feet and take a look at this map. I would suggest you head off in the direction of Clarksville, then across towards Rockville or Gaithersburg and beyond, as far as the Chesapeake and Ohio Canal. That will ensure you cover a wide sweep to the north and north-west of Washington. The important thing is that you remain alert and vigilant throughout. Keep your ear to the ground and make it the business of you and your men to question as many local people as possible. Try to establish whether locals have noticed anything out of the ordinary, anything vaguely untoward, since Good Friday and... most importantly...whether any suspicious looking strangers have been seen answering the description of this man, Atzerodt."

★ ★ ★

George had retired to bed in the early hours of Easter Monday morning. He felt safe here in the old farmhouse, in the bosom of his German relatives who had expressed delight in his unannounced arrival. On Sunday evening, as George and the family reminisced about times past, old Uncle Johann and his wife Annie, now in their mid-sixties, had been the first to wilt, retiring to their bed at the stroke of ten o'clock. It had become a ritual in recent years, explained Hartman, for his parents to make for the land of nod as soon as the hall clock struck ten and little would deflect them from that habit. By ten-thirty, Hartman's wife, Mary – having tired herself with an afternoon of weeding in the backyard – had fallen asleep in the comfort of her chair. Excusing himself, Hartman had risen to his feet and made for the scullery where he found and lit a candle, placing it firmly in the sconce of a little brass chamberstick. With this he had returned to the parlour to coax his slumbering wife into a vague state of consciousness before assisting her in her ascent of the stairs.

A further three hours elapsed before the two cousins had retired. They had drunk whisky and chatted at length, recalling their childhood days on the farm. They had even laughed together. George couldn't recollect when he last had reason to express himself in that way or, at least, when his mood had been at all conducive to laughter. Finally, Hartman had felt inclined to persuade his cousin to go to bed.

"You'd better get your head down, George, if you're to notch up a decent bit of sleep, only from tomorrow you'll have to share your room for a few days."

"Share it, Hartman! Dear God, with whom may I ask?" The visitor was accustomed to sharing a room at seedy hotels, notably at the Pennsylvania House, but was a trifle miffed at the thought of having to do so in the old family home.

"With the Nichols brothers. They're a couple of local youths who you'll get along with fine," said Hartman, reassuringly. "They work for me on a casual basis. I first had cause to use them back in January, when they assisted me with the winter ploughing. More recently, they were here helping me hoe and spread muck and then, just before Easter, they planted potatoes in the top field. They're good workers and keen to earn a dollar or two. This week we must start planting the new corn seedlings in the lower field. Perhaps you'd care to help us George to earn your keep," chortled Hartman, as he placed a chummy, enveloping arm across his cousin's shoulders. It was not entirely a tongue-in-cheek remark for Hartman Richter felt he should reap some reward for his hospitality. He also knew, only too well, that, left to his own devices, George would be inclined to sit around and do nothing.

The Nichols boys arrived at six o'clock on Monday morning and – under Hartman's watchful eye – were soon busily engaged planting the lower field. By ten o'clock the warmth radiating from the rising sun – a warmth enhanced by the angle of the lower field as it fell away towards the Darnestown road – had prompted Hartman and the youths to cover their heads. Knowing the planting to be back breaking work, George opted to carry the occasional tray of seedlings from the shady sanctuary of the front porch to the scene of planting; also to repeatedly gather and carry water from the well which lay beyond the site of the former tobacco shed. He would then follow in the tracks of the two youths and diligently apply liquid nourishment to each and every little plant. By the time the day's work was done, Hartman Richter was able to look back on what had been accomplished with a good deal of satisfaction. As for George, he felt less troubled than when he had arrived the previous day. Filling his day with work on the farm had been a distraction that served him well. It was only a remark by cousin Hartman at supper which brought him up with a jolt.

"Funny thing, George," said Hartman, "but they're saying the actor, Wilkes Booth, killed old Abe Lincoln. Now, if I'm not mistaken, he was the young fellow we saw on stage in Baltimore in some Shakespearian play… it must have been about ten years ago. He forgot his lines and received a lot of heckling from the gallery. Do you remember?"

"Why, yes," replied his cousin. "I vaguely remember." George's relaxed demeanour had melted away, his face now drawn and ashen. A few seconds later came a further utterance designed to deflect Hartman from pursuing the topic.

"At what time in the morning do you wish to resume planting? If it's that early I'll probably need to ask these young 'uns to give me a shake."

With that, George bid his cousin goodnight. Reaching his room, the sight of the slumbering Nichols boys, dead to the world and sprawled across the double bed, filled him with dismay. He would need to bundle the youngsters together, towards the far wall, thus releasing the nearer half of the bed for his own use. Before doing so he pulled back the scant curtain and peered out into the night. The darkness was complete, the panes glistening with running water. Since George and Hartman had ventured on to the front porch before supper, to smoke and down a whisky, a steady rain had begun to make its presence felt across upper Maryland.

★ ★ ★

Stealthily, the hum of the telegraph wires that hugged the railroad line had become discernible to the alert ear. Gone for a while was the relentless hubbub of tumbling water as it gurgled over broken rock and boulders. Instead, unfettered from such impudent obstructions, the Patapsco had deepened, slackened its pace and fallen quiet, drawing breath before the turmoil came again. The well-trodden path which coursed between river and railroad was familiar to all since it linked a series of picket posts located at regular intervals to the west of Relay. Twilight had come early this Easter Monday as the party of infantrymen reckoned they had trudged five miles since passing beneath the stoop of the Relay House.

The day's early promise of a repeat of Sunday's warm and clement conditions had failed to materialise. Gone was dawn's high cirrus, its azure palette having succumbed to the bullying advance of rain clouds off the Chesapeake Bay. Gloweringly dark, they had spilled a brief shower before the soldiers had ventured beyond the high knoll upon which sat Fort Dix. Some respite had followed, only for the rain to set in with greater intent. From the tangle of overhead branches, through the newly breaking greenery of maple, beech and white oak, percolated the constant drip of rainwater. Underfoot, meanwhile, the churning and sometimes squelching trudge of thirteen pairs of army brogans seemed to heighten the pungency that rose from a woodland path muddied by dank earth, spring rain and last fall's spent foliage.

It had been a hurried departure from Fort Dix which had left William Reynolds' party devoid of overcoats or for that matter, any dog tents. Yet at least, when the rain set in, they could call upon their oil cloth ponchos which they had collectively donned at the last picket post. Now, as they pushed on in the direction of Ellicott City, William had in mind that the Engineer Corps had erected a trestle or pontoon bridge across the Patapsco, just beyond the next picket post. In his limited knowledge it was a crossing that offered something of a shortcut, avoiding the need to venture too far north westwards as dictated by both river and railroad. Instead it would set him and his party on a course across rolling farmland and hopefully in the direction of the turnpike which would carry them south westwards towards the settlement of Clarksville. That, in Corporal Reynolds' considered opinion, would represent a good start in his search party's seemingly over-optimistic quest to track down Booth's German accomplice. The following day enquiries could begin in earnest. They would question anyone they encountered on the turnpike and randomly search as many farm buildings as possible. Wayside homes would be visited to establish whether local folk had recently encountered any suspicious looking strangers or persons behaving oddly.

"The bloody heavens must be shedding tears for the President," remarked a young Scotsman by the name of George Boyd. .

It was a remark that broke a spell of silence during which all thirteen men had been alone with their thoughts. Apart from the chink and rub of accoutrements, only the pitter patter of steady rain had continued unabated as it percolated through the woodland canopy.

"Seems a goddam ridiculous and futile enterprise, searching for this feller if you ask me…like looking for a needle in a haystack," opined Jacob Martin, a fresh-faced youth from Mechanicsburg. "And as for this bloody rain…"

"Shut up, Martin, you big wart," interjected Ed Thompson with a yell. He was a burly lad with a cheerful disposition who was inclined not to brook excessive bellyaching from those he felt had little cause for complaint. "Look upon it as a welcome break from routine. At least it gets us away from Fort Dix and the tedium of drills and picket duty. As for the rain, you've no reason to grouse. You've got yourself a tarred sennit hat, after all, unlike the rest of us. My poncho's not preventing the rain passing behind the collar of my tunic."

"Mine neither," remarked a ginger-haired lad from Lebanon by the name of Bob Craig. "I've a veritable stream to rival the Patapsco coursing down my back."

"I'd rather do drills or picket duty on a stomach with cookhouse victuals and the promise of a dry bunk to look forward to," bemoaned Martin with a rueful expression. Private Thompson resisted reacting once again, sensing it to be counter-productive and only likely to fuel yet more peevish utterances from the mouth of his irritable comrade.

"I reckon it's the Captain looking for some advancement," chirped Henry Reed, a rawboned farmhand from Princeton, New Jersey.

William Reynolds couldn't help overhearing his subordinate's comment, what with Reed being close to his shoulder. "In fairness to Captain Snyder," he asserted, "the War Department has ordered all army garrisons locally to keep a weather eye open for any suspicious looking characters in the wake of the President's murder. In other words, anyone who might have been an accomplice in the conspiracy to kill Mister Lincoln."

"And that includes this fellow, Azrot, Corporal?" enquired Reed.

"Atzerodt…yes, a German character, by all accounts."

"And is there intelligence to lead us to believe we might be on this fellow's tail?"

"Not exactly, Private. There is a suggestion that Atzerodt travelled by train to Baltimore early on Saturday morning. Other than that we are acting entirely on the Captain's hunch that this fellow has bolted in a north westerly direction from Washington."

"A hunch, eh? Well, perhaps young Martin is right…that it's a bit of a futile business if we're acting on a hunch," said Henry Reed with a tinge of despondency in his voice.

"Quite so, Private," said William, "but just remember that we're in the Army and we're merely acting under orders. It's not for us to reason why but to simply do as we're tol…" Before William Reynolds could quite finish his sentence he was bedevilled by a fit of coughing.

"Looks as though this damn weather might have given you a cold already Corporal," suggested Private Reed.

"No…not a cold, Reed, just a wretched cough that's been troubling me of late." Only then did it cross William's mind that his intended sick call on the morrow would, for the time being at least, need to go by the board.

Several minutes elapsed during which the men once again fell silent. For a while the sound of trudging feet, sucking on muddy ground, threatened to upstage that of the teeming rain as it filtered through the woodland canopy. Then the rhythmic gurgle of a small tributary came to the fore, tumbling eagerly through a culvert beneath the railroad, as if anxious to adopt the more serene pace of the river it was about to enter.

"Who goes there!?" The customary interrogation was far from unexpected. Over the last few weeks every member of Corporal Reynolds' search party had been called upon to take their turn at picket duty along the road. All had become familiar with this dank woodland path that linked the picket posts, including the section now encountered, a stretch that ran through a stand of piney woods until it reached the westernmost post to be serviced by the soldiers from Fort Dix. Furthermore, Reynolds' phalanx of infantrymen had been challenged several times already by lone pickets walking their beats between the string of posts. Yet no challenge had matched the shrillness with which the alert sentinel now bellowed his enquiry. It immediately jolted the majority of the approaching foot soldiers out of the solacing pre-occupation of their inner thoughts.

"Friends…Corporal Reynolds from Fort Dix with a party of twelve infantry soldiers," announced William in reply to the interrogation.

"Then advance, Corporal, with the countersign," shouted the sentinel.

William proceeded to move forward. Beneath the sylvan canopy twilight was spent. Darkness now prevailed. Beyond the man standing picket, a lone moth caught William's attention. Seemingly undeterred by the rain, it flickered busily in the glow of a kerosene lantern that illuminated the entrance to the post's log hut. Its persistence held the corporal's interest until he had advanced as far as the point of the young picket's bayonet. There was mutual recognition between the two men, yet the duty private – an Irish fellow by the name of Tom McCormack – regarded William with steely eye. For a sentinel there was no such thing as overtly expressed recognition. Protocol demanded that he knew nobody but expected everybody to whisper the countersign if they were to be permitted to proceed on their way.

"I'm not privy to the day's countersign, Private, but I have a pass for myself and twelve good men from your very own Company. Here…" said William, proffering the warrant that was endorsed by the lavish signature of Captain Snyder. A fellow picket and another familiar face – his weapon at secure arms – now appeared at his colleague's shoulder, his purpose being to relieve the first sentinel in barring William's way. Meanwhile Private McCormack withdrew to join the flickering moth beneath the lamplight, there to scrutinise Captain Snyder's warrant. It was, in truth, something of a charade but it would be remiss of him, before a non-comm, not to adhere to the rules of conduct of a standing picket.

Thus were concluded the formalities at the last picket post. Minutes later, Reynolds' party had crossed the sappers' bridge to the Howard County side of the river and were making their way south westwards by way of field boundaries and the guiding light of an old tin candle lantern. And all the while the rain teemed in torrents.

"In about half an hour we'll think about making camp," declared William in a strident voice intended to carry down the line.

"Pity we can't find a nice cosy barn to get out of this weather. Perhaps we'll come across one of those tobacco sheds piled high with sweet hay in which to rest our heads," suggested a rather gentle fellow by the name of Joe Todd. Young Toddy hailed from Philadelphia where he had worked in a private academy and by all accounts had had some involvement in bookbinding. It was a career he'd been content to pursue until his father reminded him there numbered several prominent minutemen among his Connecticut forebears and that he should proudly do his bit by shouldering arms for the Union. Yet the poor fellow's wheyfaced appearance and genteel manner were reasons he was often picked upon and regarded as a fish out of water in the ranks – a burden which, to his credit, he handled well.

"That's wishful thinking if ever there was," remarked Ed Thompson. "You don't see too many of them old baccy sheds in this neck of the woods…not as many as before the war at any rate. The farmers have taken to planting corn instead of tobacco. That's those little green seedlings, Todd, which you keep trampling underfoot."

"I think you can all forget about your home comforts tonight men, let alone those lumpy mattresses in the Fort Dix barrack room," shouted William with a chuckle. "In the hurry to depart they've sent us out bereft of dog tents but then they'd have been next to useless in this weather. We'll use our rubber blankets as makeshift tents. They'll serve us better than a bit of cotton drill. And we'll get a good camp fire going, boil up plenty of coffee and see what we can make of our rations. That said, we may have difficulty in rustling up some dry kindling."

"That's not a problem, Corporal," chirped the freckle-faced Scot, George Boyd. "I started to gather up some dry twigs in the woods as soon as it started raining and I've kept the bundle wrapped up in a piece of oilcloth."

"Top rail, Private Boyd," said William, reassuringly. "Now that shows initiative befitting a soldier on a mission such as this."

"Do we have any lucifers, Corporal?" enquired Eugene Patterson, a boy from Lancaster, Pennsylvania. Both in temperament and appearance, Patterson constantly reminded William of his old friend John Downer back in distant Portsea. The similarities were striking.

"I do so happen to have a tin of friction matches I recently purchased from the sutler," said William.

"Bloody camp fire. What I'd give to dry myself and warm my hands on the barrack room stove." Once again, it was the griping voice of Jacob Martin.

"For Christ's sake, Private Martin, no more of your bellyaching. The damn war's drawing to a close and you've got good Federal greenbacks in the bank...unless, of course, you've chosen to squander your bounty money already," yelled William, in a tone which showed him to be irked by the attitude of the young moaner from Mechanicsburg. "Believe me, a drop of spring rain is no cause for complaint. It's child's play when put in perspective. I'd like to see how you might have coped down in the Gulf, Martin...seeing how you'd have dealt with the hardship of tramping mile upon mile in oppressive heat...marching at route step in footwear that has rendered your feet raw, your socks matted with congealed blood the colour of the wayside blackberry juice that binds to your chin stubble... your throat and nostrils thick with dust thrown up by the multitude on the dirt road ahead. And all this, Martin, with the prospect of a battle to fight. Believe me," continued William, a mix of anger and exasperation hanging in his voice, "for a man trudging that hard road the temperate conditions of a wet spring evening in the heart of Maryland would be a joy to savour. So pull yourself together, man and count your blessings."

It was a summary chastisement, a scolding that silenced not only the cosseted and curmudgeonly Private Martin but all who followed in Corporal Reynolds' wake. For ten minutes the absence of conversation was as palpable to the senses as William's words had been sobering. In its place the noises of men on the move came to prevail above the unwavering soft sound of drenching rain: the squelching of army brogans wading through mud and mire, the rhythmic rub, rattle and jangle of accoutrements. To William the vocal reticence was satisfying. He had made his point. It was left to him in due course to break the quietude.

"Here we appear to be in the lee of a copse and upon relatively elevated ground. We'll make camp here...it seems as good a spot as any," he declared, holding high the candle lantern to help familiarise himself with the immediate surroundings. "Private Boyd, now's the time to bring forth that kindling you've gathered and I need two volunteers...let's see, now... Privates Clothier and Gordon, step forward."

Frank Gordon, a former tin plate worker from Chester County, Pennsylvania, was, to his credit, prompt to answer William's call.

"Take this lamp from me Private and see what you can find in that

thicket to help us build a decent campfire. Tom Clothier can assist you…
by the way, where is he?"

"He can't be of any help to me, Corporal," replied Gordon, a tinge
of glibness in his voice. "He's already gone ahead but not to gather
firewood."

"There's no such thing as can't…and what do you mean, he's already
gone ahead?"

"He's been feeling sick since we crossed the river, Corporal."

"River sickness…a bit like seasickness I suppose," quipped the lanky
Albert Bray, a former longshoreman with a sharp sense of humour.

"Spare us the levity, Bray, and go and help Private Gordon to find
something to burn," ordered William peremptorily. .

"Tom has yet to spew up but it seems the Virginia Quick Step has now
taken hold of him," explained Frank Gordon. "He's already taken himself
into that thicket to empty his bowels."

★ ★ ★

It was around six o'clock on the morning of Tuesday, the eighteenth of
April. George Atzerodt woke in a cold sweat. He'd been dreaming about
Booth and the others and it had been a far from pleasant experience. Initially
he found himself alone in a room with that ogre, Lewis Powell…or so he
thought. Time and events had become distorted. They were back in the
Herndon House, the scene of the last meeting. Then Davy Herold appeared
but he remained silent, sitting impassively on Powell's bed. Powell paced
up and down, his eyes throbbing, pleasure etched on his face. His hands
dripped with blood…his victim's blood…Seward's blood. Distressingly the
drips were unrelenting. Now Booth was in the room. He too wore a smile,
one of self-satisfaction. He sat in a corner, the customary glass of brandy
in his right hand, the shiny derringer pistol with which he had intended
killing Lincoln clasped in his left. Smoke spiralled from the little pistol's
barrel and strangely it kept spiralling, just like the blood kept dripping
from Powell's hands. Booth and Powell seemed to talk animatedly, yet to
George no sound emanated from their mouths. The actor suddenly gulped
back his cognac. He started to laugh, as did Powell…again, no sound. Then
Booth turned his eyes upon poor George…wrathful, hateful-looking eyes
that sent the recipient scrambling away and tripping over the hearth rug.
Spread-eagled and cowering on the floor, the little German glanced up to
find Powell standing over him. He felt the sensation of warm blood dripping

on his face and in his eyes. He screamed. Then Booth spoke again but now the terrified carriage painter could hear his bellowed words.

"We've all done our duty you insipid little wretch but what have you achieved? Nothing, save scurrying away like a sewer rat and all to no avail. I told you, Atzerodt, that I've already made sure you're implicated, no fear of that. Don't think you're safe lurking out there in Montgomery County." George's heart missed a beat. How did he know where he was? There was a hideous smirk across Booth's face. "Kick him, Lewis," shouted Booth, whereupon the strapping, former Mosby Ranger planted a boot into George's loins. The little German yelled in agony as he writhed around on the increasingly blood-drenched carpet. "Kick the bastard again, Lewis," screamed Booth, mockingly. The bloodthirsty Powell needed no further invitation to administer kicks into the ribs of the hapless Atzerodt. He proceeded to deliver a volley of painful blows. The imagined pain was excruciating but suddenly it was no longer envisaged in the labyrinth of his mind but real…real but remarkably less agonising.

George was awake and recoiling from the discomfort of being trampled upon by one of the Nichols boys as the youth hastily clambered out of bed to empty his bladder. The German was on the brink of cursing but thought better of it, for the youth had unknowingly brought an end to a grim and distressing nightmare. George remained in bed as he recovered his composure and freed his mind from the events that had tortured it. He banished thoughts of rising and getting himself dressed, despite the comparatively late hour. Cousin Hartman was in the habit of being up with the lark at five o'clock but George saw little purpose in promptitude this Tuesday morning. He could hear the incessant sound of raindrops against the window panes. Such inclement weather would need to relent if there was to be any prospect of making further inroads into Hartman's spring planting. George could afford to be lazy.

★ ★ ★

Tuesday's was a rude awakening under the grey skies of Howard County. William thought he heard a cock crow and, in all likelihood, he did, but as he came to his senses it was to recognise that it was the sound of retching that came to the fore…that and the constant thrumming of falling rain upon his tent. Monday evening's incessant downpour had continued throughout the night with little respite. Tom Clothier, once he had emerged from the thicket, continued to remain in a sorry state and had required assistance in pitching his tent. He had forgone his supper and spent a troubled night, courtesy of repeated bouts of the flux. Yet it was not poor Clothier who William heard vomiting but the young Scotsman, Boyd, and a lad by the name of Samuel Evans who hailed from west Philadelphia. Both had felt queer and become feverish and diaphoretic during the night. Poor Boyd had even dispensed with his rubber blanket shelter and allowed the heavens to soak him through in a vain attempt to lower his temperature. By daybreak Clothier remained prostrated and devoid of energy, such had been the severity of the ailment, while Evans and Boyd had reached the stage where they too were scurrying for the privacy of the adjacent thorn thicket.

After a breakfast of sowbelly, beans and Baltimore hardtack, washed down with liberal amounts of sweet coffee, William had to make a decision regarding what to do about his three invalids. The severity of their ailment rendered them unable to put one foot in front of another, let alone to be ready to undertake the rigours of the first full day of their assignment. In William's mind the matter was clear: Clothier, Boyd and Evans would have to be left behind. They could rest up until their sickness had passed and they felt well enough to retrace their steps back to Fort Dix.

"What do we tell the guys standing picket along the railroad, Corporal?" enquired Clothier. "We'll have no pass from Captain Snyder or knowledge of the countersign."

"Don't fret on that account, Private," replied William, reassuringly. "I'll write you out a pass myself and give a full account of the unfortunate events that have befallen you."

Leaving the unfortunates to find their feet, the now depleted search party – muddied but breakfasted and refreshed – picked their way across a quarter of a mile of sodden pasture beyond which nestled a tiny settlement. Reaching the hamlet and coming upon a dry piece of ground beneath the overhang of a wayside barn, William called for a brief halt to enable all to divest themselves of their mud-caked brogans. Several minutes later, footwear picked clean by bayonets and handfuls of wet grass, the men were better placed to take to the Clarksville pike and begin their day's work in earnest. It was a task they performed with diligence as they accosted and questioned passing travellers and randomly interrogated the occupants of roadside homes regarding anything untoward they might have noticed. Yet nothing of any import was reported that might point to a transitory sighting of the man Atzerodt. On occasion William would demand a search of farm buildings that might offer seclusion to a fugitive, yet, unsurprisingly, nothing out of the ordinary was happened upon – nothing, that is, save for the energetic antics of a copulating young couple in a hayloft east of Clarksville. Then, by mid afternoon, as Reynolds' search party crossed the Patuxent into Montgomery County, the wretched ailment that had already depleted the group began, yet again, to show its hand. Young Joe Todd, pallid-faced at the best of times, complained to William that he was feeling out of sorts and within the hour had to be excused his search and interrogation duties. Thereafter, as the group approached the market town of Brookeville and with the afternoon now well advanced, the poor fellow had great difficulty keeping up with his comrades. And while Toddy tried to cope with innards that were becoming ever more boisterous in their protestations, yet another man fell victim to the affliction. This was a flaxen-haired Irishman, a softly spoken chap, barely out of his teens, by the name of Oliver Burke. Strangely, the flux afflicted the unfortunate Hibernian with far greater rapidity than it threatened to embarrass Joe Todd. In no time poor Burke was forced to scurry away to empty his bowels in the dubious privacy of a roadside ditch. In contrast the wretched Todd still laboured under griping intestinal pain that for him was the drawn out precursor to an explosive defecation.

It was becoming all too evident to William Reynolds that this forbidding ailment now threatened to bring Captain Snyder's enterprise to its knees. But then there arose a stroke of good fortune. Following in the soldiers' wake came the sound of cantering hooves. In the distance could be seen an advancing buggy, a sprightly, dapple-grey horse between the shafts. A minute or two later, as he neared the group of infantryman, the driver pulled on the reins and brought his animal to a halt.

"Is everything in order with you folks?" queried the buggy's smartly attired occupant. His question was posed in tandem with a look as effective as any spoken enquiry upon the purpose of such a soldiering presence on the outskirts of Brookeville. Indeed, it prompted William to refrain from any direct answer to the gentleman's question in favour of offering an explanation as to his party's origin and objective.

"Good afternoon, sir. We're from the Two Hundred and Thirteenth Regiment, Pennsylvania Volunteers, currently garrisoned at Fort Dix near Relay Junction. We're making enquiries as to anything untoward that may have been observed in the locality…"

"Untoward?…in Brookeville?" There was surprise etched in the buggy driver's words, indeed, even a hint of indignation.

"We've been ordered to scour the countryside for one of the conspirators involved in the killing of the President," explained William. "It's thought he might have tried to escape in this general direction."

"Well, it sure seems a pity that you've had to venture forth in such inclement conditions," observed the gentleman. "I take it your quest has yet to be labelled a success?...and I see you've a more immediate problem," he added – a clear reference to the unfortunate, bare-arsed Irishman, still cowering with his predicament in the nearby drainage ditch.

"You're right, sir. We're plagued with some intestinal ailment that's already caused me to lose three of my party and right now I've two others succumbing to the illness. By coincidence William's words were underlined by the sound of Joe Todd beginning to retch.

"You'll be aware that there is a good deal of secessionist sympathy in these parts, Corporal, what with Maryland having been traditionally a slave-owning state," said the gentleman, "and although the war is all but done, feelings can run deep. With that in mind you may struggle to find much compassion towards your plight. But I can see you are in need of a little help and it is perhaps fortuitous for you to have encountered me on your travels. Let me introduce myself. My name is Hughes...Josiah Hughes... and I'm the bursar at a preparatory school but half a mile from here. Now, the afternoon is well advanced and I can see that this wretched weather, let alone the ailment, has taken its toll upon your strength. If you are ready to curtail your duties for the day, I'd like to invite you to accompany me into town. I can at least offer you a roof over your heads this coming night...in the grounds of the Brookeville Academy. It's nothing special, you understand..."

"A dry spot to rest our heads would be greatly appreciated, Mister Hughes," declared William. "By the way, my name is Reynolds and your kindness is much appreciated. You've come upon us today as our Good Samaritan."

"Something of an exaggeration I would suggest, Corporal," chuckled Hughes. "For one thing, I doubt it ever rains like this on the road to Jericho. That said, and for the reason stated a moment ago, I suspect you're more likely to encounter the uncaring Levite in these parts than someone willing to come to your aid."

At this juncture the bursar clambered out of his conveyance, released the brake and, grasping his horse's collar, began to walk animal and vehicle on the final stage of his journey into Brookeville. Meanwhile, William called for his men's attention and, once poor Todd and Burke had recovered their composure, ordered them all to follow in the buggy's wake. William then moved forward to accompany Mister Hughes.

"Well the weather seems to have eased, thank God," declared the bursar before they had ventured but a few steps. "I'm on my way back from Catonsville where I had to attend an important meeting. By the time I'd crossed the Patapsco River the rain was so heavy I wished I'd stayed put. Trouble is, I needed to get back today in readiness for a meeting with the Principal tomorrow morning."

"Will he mind you offering us this kind hospitality?"

"Sorry, Corporal, what do you mea...?"

"The Principal, sir...will he mind?"

"Good Lord, no. He's a committed Union man."

"And you, sir?"

"The war has touched a multitude of families. I sometimes feel a sense of guilt in never having enlisted," remarked the bursar, reflectively. "It doesn't help knowing that my younger brother did volunteer and ended up losing an arm while fighting for the Union at Chancellorsville. In truth, being able to help the likes of you boys, however meagre my assistance, helps assuage such regret...just a little, you understand."

William nodded. "We're most appreciative, sir."

"Well, you and your men will at least spend a night under cover. You can't venture into the school proper, you understand, what with the sickness in your midst, but we've a disused building in the grounds awaiting demolition. In actual fact it's a former dormitory, since replaced by more commodious facilities. You'll find plenty of cobwebs but the place is dry and there are probably enough bedsteads to accommodate you all. I'll make sure some bedding is brought over from the school laundry and will organise a kerosene lamp or two and a few candles for good measure. Also, if any of you have damp uniforms then I'm sure we can arrange to have them dried by the laundry-room stove."

"That's most generous and thoughtful of you, Mister Hughes," said William.

"It's the least I can do, Corporal. And if it helps you in your mission to track down this killer, then it'll gladden my heart that somehow I made a small contribution."

Shortly, William and the bursar, followed by what had now become a rather disorderly group of infantrymen – with the unfortunate Burke and Todd struggling to keep up – arrived in front of the Academy, a well-proportioned stone building of Maryland granite. Making his way to the side of the establishment, Mister Hughes led the way down a short entrance drive which, beyond a well framed, sylvan approach, terminated in a secluded stable-yard. Here he tethered his horse and buggy to a hitching rail and beckoned to the school's stableman to do the rest. He then ushered his followers across the yard towards a gated access into the school grounds.

"Bring your men this way, Corporal Reynolds," said the bursar, as he unlocked and held open a heavy oak door that looked entirely at home, recessed as it was in an equally formidable stone wall. "Come on through and I'll introduce you to your night's billet. And, while you get yourselves organised, I'll go and see the school cook and see what we can get you in the way of a hot meal…something a bit more nourishing than army rations. Oh, and by the way, Corporal," said Hughes, after a moment's hesitation, "you might have problems with your men getting sick but…and I don't want to sound alarmist…that cough of yours sounds none too grand."

★ ★ ★

"Good morning, Mister Griffiths," declared the new arrival as he hesitated a moment upon the threshold of the dry goods store which doubled as the local post office.

"Well, good morning to you, Mister Page," replied the postmaster while surreptitiously eyeing the wall clock to satisfy himself it was still ante meridiem. "It's good to see you," he continued, observing the caller over the top of his spidery pince-nez. "Come on in, won't you?…out of that dreadful weather."

Nathan Page finished shaking the rain off his felt hat and his coat tails before he did as Griffiths requested.

"It's almost midday, yet you're only the third customer I've had all morning. That's unusual for a Wednesday, but then I suppose not many would choose to venture out on a day like this. And to think you must have ridden over from Germantown in such inclement weather, Mister Page," said Griffiths with an admiring glance.

"Well, Postmaster, I've been wanting to get some newspapers despatched…since before Easter," remarked Page, as he simultaneously withdrew two packages from the dry sanctity of his overcoat's inside pocket. "I sat in all day yesterday hoping that the rain would abate but to no avail.

315

When it was still pouring down this morning I resolved that it should no longer inconvenience me. I would ride out in it and show some fortitude."

"That's the spirit, by Jove," said a smiling Griffiths as he took his place behind the post office counter. "Pass me your packages then, my good fellow. Are you in need of any additional stamps, Mister Page?"

"Yes, please…half a dozen five-cent and a dozen of two-cent denomination, if you will," declared Page, drawing forth a crisp dollar bill.

Moments later Nathan Page gathered up his change and carefully tucked the spare stamps into his vest pocket. As he folded together the two-cent Black Jacks he couldn't help but dwell upon the forlorn features of the silver-haired seventh President.

"You know, Griffiths, it seems sad to me that such a great man as Honest Abe has gone to his Maker without seeing himself depicted upon a U.S. postage stamp," declared Page. "The British do it better in my reckoning, showing their beloved and incumbent Queen on their stamps. Yet here we are, in eighteen sixty-five, still having old Jackass's physog eyeing us sternly from our letter wrappings!"

"I suppose it's just the way we do things, Mister Page. But I'd wager you that Abe Lincoln will have his day soon enough."

"Tell me, Mister Griffiths, before I take my leave…am I right in thinking that Mister James Purdom still lives nearby? I did visit him here in Darnestown before the war…when I leased him some of my land for a while…but I can't recall the precise location of his property."

"Mister Purdom?…why yes. His farmhouse is but a stone's throw from here. Come," said the postmaster, ushering his customer towards the window beside his property's rear entrance door. "Do you see that group of houses on the left side of this lane, flanking my store? Well, Purdom's place is entered directly opposite that last property. In other words, it's hidden away behind those trees bordering the end of my backyard."

"Well, I'm much obliged for that, Mister Griffiths," said Page. "I require a word with him while I'm here in Darnestown but, before I go, I'm in need of a new razor and some underwear, both of which I'm hoping to find amongst your stock."

In his earlier dealings with James Purdom, Nathan Page had recalled the man as being a rather secretive fellow who kept himself to himself. It had, therefore, come as no surprise to him to learn – a year or so previously – that the Darnestown farmer was an undercover army informant. It was an understanding that arose when supping a beer with a distant cousin who, in turn, had evidently gleaned the information from the indiscreet whisperings of an inebriated, former neighbour of Purdom's. Yet Nathan Page was not privy to whether or not this alleged role of the farmer was common knowledge in the Darnestown community. In consequence, he made no mention of his purpose in calling upon Purdom as he bade farewell to Postmaster Griffiths.

In truth, what had unfolded at Hezekiah Metz's Easter Sunday gathering had intrigued and puzzled Nathan Page. The unsavoury, dishevelled dinner guest, Andrew Atwood, had behaved and responded oddly when the topic of Lincoln's assassination had cropped up. It was behaviour which had stirred suspicion in Page's thoughts and for the past three days he had felt uneasy, as if he needed to share those suspicions. Remembering what he had been told about James Purdom, he had resolved to call upon the Darnestown resident sooner rather than later. He was not aware, of course, how long Atwood was intent on staying with his cousin but, if this man was somehow involved in the dastardly events recently played out in Washington, then it behove Page to ensure that his presence locally was made known to the authorities. If he told Purdom, then he felt his duty would be done as a responsible member of the community. Purdom would presumably act accordingly. And so, with that realisation in mind, Page had sat indoors the previous day feeling somewhat irked by the unyielding weather. Perhaps Wednesday would be more conducive to saddling and bridling his blue roan gelding, *Spirit*, and taking a leisurely ride over to Darnestown, ostensibly to visit the local post office but primarily to call upon James Purdom. As it happened, come Wednesday, the weather had proved no more obliging, the rain continuing to fall, sometimes in torrents. Page, however, felt he should delay no longer and such resolve had caused him to arrive sopping wet at Griffiths' door, a shade before noon.

Minutes after departing the Darnestown post office, Nathan Page dismounted his horse and led it by the snaffle rein up the gritty drive to Purdom's place, an impressive, sturdy-looking home of Seneca sandstone and clapboard. The recent mild weather had swollen the buds of dogwood and redbud trees that spilled beyond the confines of a clump of woodland on the far side of the house. As he approached the property, Nathan Page felt cheated that, had it been a fortnight later, he would have been treated to a profusion of blossom. It occurred to him that his approach must have been spotted for, hardly had he released his grip on the knocker, than the studded, timber door swung open to reveal the presence of a bright-eyed young girl. Almost simultaneously the voice of a more mature woman rang out from an indeterminate place within the darker confines of the house.

"Who is it my dear?"

"Mister Nathan Page," announced the visitor before the girl had made an utterance. "To see, if at all possible, Mister James Purdom."

The girl appeared to tender a perfunctory form of curtsey before retreating towards the gloomier confines of the front entrance passage. She was replaced, in a trice, by a rather lank, sinewy, middle-aged gentleman.

"Why, Page, my good fellow, it's been a long time since we last met," remarked Purdom in a mildly effusive manner. "What brings you to my door on a day like this?" It was not Purdom's tall and mildly gaunt appearance or, indeed, his somewhat gushing, opening gambit that conjured memories of their last meeting. No, it was the rather distinctive convergent squint in his left eye that had been Page's abiding recollection of the army detective.

"Well, in answer to your question Mister Purdom, I have the impression that you are a good Union man and that…how shall I put it?…throughout the war you have constantly been in the habit of keeping your ear to the ground."

"Hmm. Quite so, Mister Page," said Purdom after a moment's hesitation. "Well, you'd better come in out of this weather if you think we need to talk. Tether your horse to the rail over yonder."

Nathan Page did what was asked of him before the Darnestown farmer ushered his Germantown counterpart into the entrance hall and thence into his cosy front parlour "Settle yourself down in that chair, my good fellow, but first let me relieve you of your coat. Do you also wish me to unburden you of that parcel?" asked Purdom.

"It's OK…just some purchases from your local store," murmured Page. "It can go in here," he added, slipping it into one of the capacious pockets of the overcoat he was in course of handing to his host.

"How about a glass of brandy, Mister Page?"

"That would be most welcome, thank you…just the thing to warm the cockles of my heart."

The host proceeded to decant two glasses of French brandy. As he did so no words were exchanged. The only sounds were the heavy tick of the parlour clock and the enticing gurgle of liquor into cut glass goblets. Purdom then crossed the room and handed a brandy to his unexpected guest before manoeuvring his lengthy frame into a walnut wing armchair. Once settled he removed his spectacles and rubbed his eyes. "Now my friend, I won't embarrass you by asking how you came to learn of my covert activities. It doesn't matter now, of course…the war is done and with it so is my need to remain ever vigilant. How did you put it?…ah, yes, keeping my ear to the ground. Now I'm left with only the farm to run, which, as a fellow husbandman, you will know well enough, is quite sufficient to keep a man occupied. Anyway, I'm intrigued to learn why my past activities appear to have drawn you here today and especially in such wretched weather. Kindly elucidate, my friend, and sate my curiosity."

"Are you acquainted, Mister Purdom, with Hezekiah Metz?"

James Purdom looked quizzically at Nathan Page. "The name's familiar. If I'm not mistaken he farms land along the Barnesville road…not far from your own…"

"Precisely. A friend and neighbour of mine. Well, I was among a number of dinner guests at his midday meal on Easter Sunday. One of the others was a fellow who Hezekiah had encountered on his return from church that very morning. He was tramping towards Germantown. What prompted Metz to invite the fellow to dinner baffles me. Admittedly, it seems he was known to my friend, having been a Germantown resident in past times, but the fellow was a scruffy, unsavoury type who could have done with a good bath and a change of clothes. Well, the strange thing is that he had travelled from Washington and was noticeably agitated, especially when the conversation turned to the subject of Mister Lincoln's murder. What little he said on the matter was puzzling and, to my mind, unintelligible. Talking to the others, after this man had taken his leave, I gained the impression that they, likewise, had found his behaviour strange. But I suspect it was only me who put two and two together. To put it bluntly, Purdom, I think this character was somehow caught up in the tragic events that befell the President and Secretary of State Seward. I'm not saying he's capable of killing, for he struck me as too timid a creature for that, but I'm sure he's had some connection with the plot."

"Good God, man, I wish you had come to see me on Monday," declared Purdom, a noticeable sense of exasperation in his words. "After all, three days have passed. What was the fellow's name and did he say anything about where he was heading?"

"I don't think we have any worry on that score. His name is Andrew Atwood and when I encountered him at Metz's place he was not far short of his destination. He said he was on his way to his cousin's farm…a man by the name of Richter who farms land…"

"Hartman Richter...I know the fellow by sight," said Purdom, his words no longer mildly laced with irritation. "Richter farms land this side of Germantown....rising ground to the west of the Germantown road. How long was this Andrew Atwood intent on staying with Richter?"

"He didn't say exactly but he told Metz's daughter that he'd be there for a while, helping his cousin out. But I'd wager that if my assessment is correct then he'll be planning to lie low at his cousin's place for some considerable time."

"I'm sure you're right, but there is no time to dally. My understanding is that the army is scouring southern Maryland in search of Lincoln's killer, the actor Wilkes Booth, but there are others on the loose. That said, a number of Booth's accomplices were successfully apprehended on Easter Monday. You are right to have shared your information with me, my friend, and I, in turn, will make sure the authorities are aware of Atwood's whereabouts. Allow yourself not to worry further. I will attend to what's necessary."

An hour or so later James Purdom had donned a mackintosh riding coat, harnessed one of his driving horses and hitched the animal to his buckboard wagon. In the wake of Nathan Page having departed, he had quickly resolved to embark upon the journey of twenty miles to Monocacy Junction in order to pass the information to the garrison there. His intended destination lay just short of the city of Frederick, where the Baltimore and Ohio railroad crossed the Monocacy River. It had been the scene of a Confederate victory the previous summer and like Relay, was a strategically important location where Union soldiers were stationed to guard the road. In carrying out his undercover activities, James Purdom had occasionally had dealings with several of the garrison's officers and non-comms and, importantly, he knew there were horse soldiers billeted there...troopers who, if ordered to do so, could ride hard to Germantown for the purpose of interrogating and arresting this suspicious character, Andrew Atwood.

On the western fringe of Darnestown, Purdom bore right, where the road forked, to set his course in the direction of Germantown. Having crossed the Great Seneca Creek and being a mile or so south of the village, he realised he was in the vicinity of the Richter farm. A moment later and just ahead, a slew of freshly deposited mud, carried off the cornfields by the heavy rain, clearly denoted the end of the dirt track which led up to the farmhouse. As he drove past, Purdom glanced left, up towards the clapboarded building on its raised plateau. The rain had eased for a moment and, through a gap in the intervening copse, he thought he caught sight of a couple of figures busying themselves stacking wood. They looked like adolescents. Purdom concluded that neither was Andrew Atwood.

Half an hour later and several miles beyond Germantown, the undercover detective's buckboard splashed its way into the sloughy main street of the farming town of Clarksburg. Given the weather conditions, he felt he had made satisfactory progress towards his destination, having by now completed half the distance. He also deemed it time for his horse to have a good drink and was aware that a stone trough for such purpose was to be found outside the local blacksmith's shop that lay just ahead on the right. As he neared the forge he noticed a lone horseman, attired in the uniform of a Union Army trooper, bring his steed to a halt, dismount and lead his animal to the drinking trough. It seemed both travellers were of like mind.

"Enough wet stuff here to water the horse population of Montgomery County," joked the trooper, as he, in turn, became aware of the stranger with the buckboard unhitching his chestnut gelding nearby.

"That's hardly surprising I suppose," remarked Purdom, "given that the heavens have provided constant replenishment over the past forty-eight hours."

"Well, mister, I've not seen rain like it since I was in New Orleans and a storm blew in from the Gulf. I was passing through Hyattstown a short while ago and the constant, heavy rain had turned the Great Road there into such a mud bath that my poor stallion was struggling up to his fetlocks in mire."

"The Great Road can be a muddy route at the best of times," observed Purdom. "Tell me, soldier, where are you garrisoned?"

"Near Frederick, mister. A place called Monocacy, near where our boys got whipped by Jubal Early last summer."

"Wallace's men may have been beaten but the battle certainly dealt the Confederates a blow in their ambitions to seize Washington. That fight probably saved the capital from falling into enemy hands," opined the farmer. "So are you returning to Monocacy today?"

"Why, yes sir, I sure am. I've only made the journey out of necessity and on a pass to allow me to retrieve my overcoat. I surely wouldn't have chosen to ride the twelve miles here today…not in these wretched conditions. Trouble is I left my coat here yesterday…in the tavern you've just driven by, back there beyond the general store. I just hope the landlord has it in his safe keeping."

"And what is your regiment, my good fellow?"

"The First Delaware Cavalry."

"Then you'll be acquainted with George Lindsley?"

"Why yes, he's one of the sergeants in our company…Company D."

"And you'll be seeing him later?" asked Purdom, a hint of hopeful expectation in his voice.

"I sure will, mister. As a matter of fact we rode out together down the pike…I left him but half an hour ago in Hyattstown. He had some army business to attend to there."

"Well I'm mighty pleased to hear this, soldier. You see, I'm heading for the Monocacy military post right now and, if none of your officers are about to give me an audience, I'll ask for Sergeant Lindsley."

"So you're acquainted with Sergeant Lindsley?"

"Well, put it this way…I've had cause to speak with him in the past on some delicate matters. I found him most approachable and a man with integrity. Given the circumstances I think you may be in a position to do me a favour, Mister…?"

"O'Daniel, sir," said the trooper, in response to the other's meaningful pause. "Private Frank O'Daniel."

"Let me explain," said Purdom, "and where better than in the comfort of that drinking establishment you're heading for? By the way, my name's James Purdom. I'm a landowner and farmer from Darnestown, about ten miles due south of here, below Germantown."

A few minutes later, with horses watered and secured to the tavern's hitching rail, the two men sat together by the cosy taproom fire. Purdom's gangly legs were stretched out in front of him, glorying in the drying warmth that radiated from the grate's glowing embers. For his part the cavalryman was not irritated by the farmer's monopoly of the fire's comfort. On the contrary, he was momentarily overjoyed by having just retrieved his missing overcoat and grateful to Purdom for the whisky he had bought him.

"Take a look at this, Frank," said the elder man as he pulled a folded sheet of paper from an inside pocket. "If nothing else it should allay any thoughts there might be in your mind that what I am about to tell you is bunkum. On the contrary, it is to be believed and treated seriously."

O'Daniel took and unfolded the document. It was a short statement, signed by Secretary of War, Edwin Stanton, which announced that James Purdom was an authorised detective in the service of his Department. In particular, it instructed all officers and soldiers in the service of the United States to afford him assistance and protection.

The undercover detective then proceeded to recount what Nathan Page had told him earlier in the day while Private O'Daniel listened attentively. "If you can convey what I have told you to Sergeant Lindsley then that, Frank, will save me journeying further. I cannot stress the importance of this information too strongly and I dearly hope your superiors will send a posse to the Richter farm with a view to apprehending Atwood. They'll probably need a guide to locate the farm, in which case tell them to call on me. They know where I live. I'll gladly show them the way, whatever the time of day or night."

Ten minutes later Private O'Daniel was back in the saddle, having given a promise to Purdom that he would assiduously attend to what was asked of him. With a departing wave of his hand to the Darnestown farmer – newly perched back on the seat of his buckboard wagon – the cavalryman set in his spurs and made off at a gallop towards Monocacy.

★ ★ ★

At Brookeville, some fifteen miles to the eastward as the crow flies, the day could not have begun better for Reynolds' depleted search party. Breakfast was brought to the soldiers' sleeping quarters at fifteen minutes shy of six o'clock in the arms of the school cook, a jovial negress called Alice. Adorned in a blowsy old tarletane gown, the dear soul cackled and laughed at her own mutterings, all the while setting her fleshy, glabrous jowls at a tremble. At first her breeziness left the still drowsy men from Relay a trifle nonplussed as she sallied forth in two separate forays from her kitchen, each time clutching a tray laden with lashings of hot rashers, eggs, grits and coffee. As she returned to the old dormitory, bearing the second tray, she also carried a clean linen table-cloth, pinned betwixt elbow and waist. Meanwhile, the now expectant breakfasters, promptly stirred from their lethargy by sight and smell, had eagerly raised a makeshift table from trestles and planking that lay stacked against one wall of the building. Upon this Alice spread her cloth with a flourish. Then, still cackling to herself, the cook retired temporarily, only to reappear with china cups and plates and silver-plated cutlery which she distributed upon the breakfast table along with her dishes of steaming victuals and coffee.

"She serves a damned good breakfast does that nigger woman," observed Albert Bray. "I'd sure like to be a pupil at this school if that's the kind of fare she dishes up."

"Less of the nigger," snapped William, irked by the former

longshoreman's dismissive tone. "It's derogatory. She seems a sweet woman and we've spent the last few years fighting to free the likes of her cousins from Southern bondage."

All the men, with the exception of Burke, Todd and Bob Craig had made swift work of downing their breakfasts. The young Irishman and the wan-faced boy from Philadelphia had spent restless nights interspersed with occasional dashes into the dank and inky academy grounds to rid themselves of troublesome, inner turbulence. They both showed no interest in their meal as they continued to languish in their beds. As for Craig, he had drunk coffee but merely picked at his meal as he complained of feeling off-colour.

At ten minutes after six a rap at the door signalled the arrival of Mister Hughes. As Ed Thompson promptly opened the door, it was to find the school treasurer clutching a large canvas bag containing an assortment of sky blue pants and tunics.

"Good morning, gentlemen," declared the charitable bursar. "I trust you've spent a comparatively restful night. I've just come hot-foot from the laundry-room where your clothes have been transformed. Bone dry they are, so you have the prospect of spending a more comfortable day on patrol. It's only unfortunate that it is still raining with little sign of it abating."

"Well, thank you for your kindness, Mister Hughes," declared William. "We'll be on our way shortly and get from under your feet."

"So where will you be heading?"

"Well, I've been looking at my map and guess we'll be pushing on towards Gaithersburg, then making for a place called Seneca which I see lies close to the Chesapeake and Ohio Canal. That done, we will have scoured an arc between Fort Dix and the Potomac River."

"Well, Corporal, I wish you well. You'll know when you've reached Seneca. It's a busy place for quarrying and cutting redstone which is shipped out by way of the canal. Incidentally, your arrival yesterday evening generated quite a bit of excitement among the boys who remain here…those who didn't return home to their families for the Eastertide vacation. I'm sure they'll be looking forward to telling their fellow pupils that the place was swarming with Union soldiers in their absence," chuckled Hughes.

"Hardly swarming, sir," came William's somewhat forlorn retort. "I started out on Monday with twelve fit men. Now I have but seven although another is showing signs of going down with the ailment. That leaves me only six men and…"

Ironically it was an untimely remark. The sound of retching filled the room. Then William felt one of the men brush against his shoulder as the fellow launched himself helter-skelter towards the open door. The bursar, meanwhile, seeing the approaching soldier, deftly stepped aside to permit him to go on his way unhindered. Moments later the sound of the man expelling Alice's breakfast into nearby shrubbery rent the air.

Astonishingly it dawned on William that he only had five fit men. He had automatically assumed that the fleeing figure had been that of Bob Craig, since the red-headed boy from Lebanon had felt unwell over the last hour or so. As for Burke and Todd, they were now over the worst of it when it came to diarrhoea and vomiting. But, no. The wretched figure who was soon to waveringly make his way back into the old dormitory was none other than Jacob Martin.

"I fear I spoke too soon," said William, lamentably.

"I see it's a real problem for you, Corporal, in terms of your mission, but rest assured these men can remain here until they are fit to return to barracks," said Mister Hughes, reassuringly. "I will ensure that cook attends to their victualling needs…"

"Can't we all stay?" quipped Ed Thompson at the thought of his ailing comrades being plied with Alice's cooking. It was a remark which William chose to ignore, troubled as he was that his party was now below half strength and with the real prospect of losing yet further men. At this moment the blessed Alice appeared beyond the open door.

"I'z jest thought dat mebbe you'z sodjers might 'preciate some of ol' Alice's griddle cakes an flapjacks. Fresh cooked dey are, dat's fo' sartin," chuckled the cook, her dimpled face radiant with delight. "An I'z a l'il sack of Indian meal to take wid ye to make yerselves a porridge."

"Well, that's most thoughtful of you, Alice," remarked a beaming Mister Hughes. "Most thoughtful."

"Yes, thank you ma'am," exclaimed William. "And thank you for that fine breakfast."

"Why those cakes will be a grand supplement to our remaining rations," said Bray, chirpily, "especially as the damp weather has got into my haversack and speckled my iron crackers with mould."

"Fresh flapjacks will be a damn sight more palatable than what we've got, that's for sure," exclaimed Henry Reed with enthusiasm.

"Well, here's trusting they help sustain you in your search for this so-called conspirator," declared the bursar. "Doubtless, if you succeed in your mission, we'll read about it soon enough in the Washington press and Alice here will surely feel she can take some credit for having sent you away with full stomachs."

"Zactly, Maister Hughes, zactly," insisted the jovial cook. "Arter all, I figger it's sump'n to crow 'bout an Alice is al'ays good at crowin'."

Half an hour later William and his much depleted search party had bid farewell to their kindly hosts, leaving Burke and Todd and the newly afflicted Craig and Martin to recuperate in the comparative comfort of the Academy's former dormitory. The mood that prevailed among the six survivors was quite sombre as they pressed on beneath the turbid skies of Montgomery County, skies which continued to send down volleys of cold rain. This sour state of mind was largely provoked by the gathering opinion – albeit that this fell short of unanimity – that Snyder's plan to hunt down this fellow by the name of Atzerodt was a futile one. William, for his part, did not share that view or, at least, if he did, he kept his own counsel. As leader of the group it did not behove him to express dissidence over the Captain's stratagem. To his mind it was not important that the mission might be ill-conceived. The fact was he and his men were fulfilling their orders and that was an end to it. Of far greater concern to William Reynolds was the fact that he was only left with five able-bodied men. He could not afford for any others to fall foul of the ailment. Inwardly, he said a prayer. Outwardly, he did his best to appear upbeat, anxious to inspirit his men and lessen their frustration.

As Wednesday ran its course, William felt satisfied that he had achieved as much as he might have wished for in the circumstances. The questioning of passing travellers and the occupiers of wayside homesteads proceeded in the same manner that it had on Tuesday, although the scouring of farm buildings had to be set aside. By what in soldier parlance was time for dinner call – midday – the party came upon the fringe of the village of Gaithersburg where William called a halt to partake of rations and brew coffee. It was a stop where, to great satisfaction, all indulged in dipping and despatching Alice's griddle cakes and flapjacks.

"An uneventful morning, men, but we have done well to venture this far," said William with a sense of satisfaction ringing in his voice.

"Uneventful, Corporal, that's just it…that's the nub of it," pondered Frank Gordon.

"I thought we might have been on to something a mile out of Brookeville," declared Eugene Patterson, "when that old feller said he'd seen a suspicious character furtively making off with a brace of chickens under his arm."

"So did I for a moment," reflected William. "But then in no way did he answer the description Captain Snyder had given me of Atzerodt."

Leaving Gaithersburg during the early afternoon, William chose to take the Barnesville road, the very same route George Atzerodt had trodden after dark on Easter Saturday. Yet the search party did not venture as far as the Clopper Mill. Had it done so, interrogation of the miller might have thrown up some valuable information about a certain Andrew Atwood who had spent the night stretched out before Robert Kinder's hearth that previous Saturday. Instead, halfway between Gaithersburg and the mill, the soldiers turned off the Barnesville road towards Seneca, some eight miles distant in a south-westerly direction. It was about a mile further on that Reed and Patterson began to complain of blistered feet. While this was an inconvenience to William, in that it served to curtail progress, it was at least only that – a mere hindrance. After all, the day was well advanced with no apparent sign of any additional men falling victim to the dreaded sickness. All it meant was that, come candle lighting – with a peppering of flickering glows ahead telling of an approaching settlement – the now small group of Union soldiers was still a few miles short of Seneca village. Yet it was a delay that was to prove fortuitous – lucky in that circumstances contrived to conjure up another roofed shelter in which the men could lay their weary heads but also providential in the wider scheme of things.

From beyond a curve in the road ahead the noise of hammering was clearly audible. What also now occurred to Reynolds and his men was that the rain had actually stopped. Not only that but, silhouetting the cresting tops of nearby trees, a soft, orange light from low in the western sky eerily lit the belly of an overlying wrack of dark cloud. It seemed to point to a better day in prospect on the morrow.

"Good God...soldiers if I'm not mistaken." The infantrymen had by now rounded the approaching bend. The voice, shrill and startled, came from within a wooded clearing open to the road and hedged-in behind by lofty stands of mature white oak. The men from Relay drew to a halt as the owner of the voice – discernible in a twilight set fleetingly into recession by the retreating rain clouds – was spotted descending a ladder he had propped against a rickety-looking barn.

"So what brings you boys in blue to a sleepy place like Darnestown?"

asked the labouring man, hammer in hand, as he finished climbing down from his lofty perch. His bronzed, lustrous pate suggested a healthy, outdoor life while the sparse strands of argentine-coloured hair that fell untidily across it told of advancing years.

William proceeded to explain what had brought him and his men to the locality and how his party had suffered misfortune at the hands of some wretched ailment. "Our quarry happens to be a German fellow by the name of Atzerodt who fled Washington after the President was killed and who was allegedly in cahoots with the assassin."

"Well, I ain't noticed anything untoward in and about the village these last few days. It's been mighty quiet, what with all this bad weather. No...I guess the only quarry you'll likely to find hereabouts is a damn big sandstone pit over at Seneca." The old fellow paused a moment to chuckle at his own witticism. "Anyway, you boys look done in. If you want to spend the night in my barn you're welcome to do so. It sprung a few leaks during this damn awful weather and I've been up there with hammer and nails and hopefully cured the worst of it. There's a bit of clutter inside but over in the far corner there's a good pile of hay and straw that's stayed nice and dry. You're welcome to bed down on that."

"Well, that's kind of you, sir," declared William. "We'll take you up on that offer if you don't mind." They were words which drew expressions of relief across the faces of William's weary charges, not least those of Reed and Patterson who proceeded to divest themselves of their brogans, anxious to assuage their blistered heels.

"Cut out the sir, Corporal. I'm just a woodsman like my father before me. Timber's my business...that and all manner of jobbing work on the land. Bit of a jack of all trades, I suppose. The name's Jake, by the way...Jake Dempsey."

"William Reynolds...Two Hundred and Thirteenth Pennsylvania Volunteers."

"Pleased to make your acquaintance Corporal...and the rest of you boys. That's my home...across the road," said Jake, beckoning with his hammer. "My wife's just lighted a lamp...see, there...through the trees. That's a sure sign my supper's ready. Now, if you need any water just come across to the house but be sure to call before nine. I go to my bed at nine, you see. Oh, and you'll need a lantern..."

"No, we come equipped with a tin candle lantern which has served us well in our travels. But is it alright to light a fire out here in the open?" enquired William. "So we can cook some supper and brew some coffee?"

"Why, of course. There's plenty of good kindling inside the barn and you can help yourselves to logs from beneath the outside overhang. They should be dry enough to burn well," said the woodsman, as he turned his attention to a mewing black cat which had suddenly appeared from nowhere to squat on one of his boots. "My cat knows it's time for his supper too. He's a damn good mouser, by the way, so I'll wager you'll not encounter any vermin in the barn to disturb your slumbers. Incidentally, did you say that fellow you're after is German?"

"That's right…or, at least, from German immigrant stock."

"Well, perhaps tomorrow you'd do well to take the road west out of the village, then the north fork sign-posted Germantown. The settlement located around the crossroads there, on the Barnesville road, is so named after its connection with German immigrants. It might just so happen that someone knows of the fellow. Just a suggestion, for what it's worth."

"Well, we might just do that, Mister Dempsey," said William. "Thank you for the information. Oh, and, if we can accept your kind offer of water, we'll come over to your home shortly to replenish our canteens."

An hour or two later the six remaining infantrymen sat upon upturned fruit boxes before a cheery camp-fire. The earlier dispirited mood of the majority had dissipated. With a supper of stewed pork and beans already committed to their stomachs, the men whiled away the evening by jawing about their lot and about their former civilian lives. When it came to William, he avoided any mention of his life afloat but regaled his men with captivating yarns of his past soldiering in the Deep South. The prevailing mood was now of a more reflective nature and William remained quietly optimistic that he might just have seen the last of the wretched ailment that had devastated his party. After all, no others had fallen victim since breakfast. The men seemed at peace with themselves, sitting out of doors on a mild spring evening and under a starry sky while clutching their cups of coffee. A not unpleasant freshness pervaded the air after the several days of rain, a cool scent laced with the smell of decay, of dank earth and old trodden foliage and woodland mast, heightened in its intensity by the wet conditions underfoot.

A kettle of hot coffee sat among the bounteous embers. William lent forward, grasped the long handled dipper and took his turn to ladle more coffee into his tin cup. "I think we'll press on to Seneca village in the morning," he remarked. "Then we'll turn about and take a look at Germantown before setting a different course back to Fort Dix. If the place was settled by German immigrants there may be something in what Dempsey says."

★ ★ ★

"So where did you come upon this information, Captain?"

"Well, Major, I was told of it earlier this evening...by Sergeant Lindsley of my Company."

"So how did Lindsley learn of it?"

"From one of our troopers, sir...Private O'Daniel. He was down in Clarksburg this afternoon and happened to encounter one of the Army's undercover detectives...a man by the name of Purdom. Seems Purdom was on his way here from his home in Darnestown. He took O'Daniel into his confidence in learning he was billeted here. It saved him completing the journey..."

"I can understand that, Captain Townsend, what with the weather being so wretched. So what do you make of it? Should we despatch a posse to arrest this man Atwood?"

"To be quite candid, Major, I'm ambivalent when it comes to answering that question."

"You have doubts about taking the matter further? You surprise me."

"Yes. You see, I've had dealings before with Mister Purdom...on two separate occasions. They have led me to have misgivings over his reliability."

"Hmm...well, if nothing else, it strikes me the man is to be admired for his loyalty and commitment in resolving to travel here in the first place. The roads must have been atrocious."

"It's also twenty miles or more to Germantown. Not easy at night and, as you say, Major, the roads are in a parlous state."

"Germantown?"

"It's where Atwood is said to be staying...at his cousin's farm."

"And has Purdom had contact with this character?"

"No...but he was visited this morning by an acquaintance who, on Easter Sunday and, by a quirk of fate, found himself among guests dining at the same table as Atwood who had just arrived from Washington. Well, he described the stranger as a rather nervous, dishevelled character with a distinctly guttural, German sounding accent. Apparently he reacted oddly when the conversation turned to the President's assassination."

Major Enos Artman looked pensive. "Leave the matter for me to ponder over, Captain. I'll give it some thought and get back to you within the half hour. To be honest, my inclination is that we should follow this up, however much you question Purdom's dependability. Incidentally, are you aware of the location of the farm where this Atwood can be found?"

"No, Major, but we know where Purdom resides and he told O'Daniel that he's happy to act as a guide to any scouting party we send out…and at any time of the day or night."

"Well, as I intimated, before, Captain, this man Purdom strikes me as a diligent and committed Union man."

It was twenty minutes later and around nine-thirty in the evening that Solomon Townsend was stirred from a burgeoning sleepiness by his superior's hearty thump upon the door to his quarters.

"Did you say this fellow had a German sounding voice?" asked the Major before he had hardly crossed the threshold.

"That's what Purdom was told by all accounts. Oh, and I've just recalled that he mentioned to O'Daniel that the cousin with whom Atwood is staying is definitely of German stock. I think he said his name is Richter."

"Well, well," exclaimed the Major, a sense of concentration and inquisitiveness pervading his features. "This is all beginning to fall into place. Let me explain, Captain. Just after you left my quarters, I remembered that earlier this week I had received a message via the military telegraph from Captain Snyder. The Captain commands Company H, my regiment's detachment at Fort Dix…near the Relay House. It was to tell me he was sending forth a search party into the countryside, north west of the capital, to look for one of the assassins. It seems he had a hunch that one of Booth's conspirators had melted away in that direction and his mission had the blessing of Brigadier-General Tyler who is in overall command at Relay. Now, while that is not significant in itself, I've just cast another eye over Snyder's message and guess what? He refers to this conspirator as a man with the German sounding name of Atzerodt. So what have we in this intriguing mix? Richter…Germantown…Atwood? No, Captain…I'm inclined to think that this Atwood with the guttural voice and the fleeing Atzerodt could be one and the same. I'm therefore ordering you, Captain Townsend, to send out a scouting party immediately with instructions to call on Mister Purdom so that he might take your troopers to Richter's farm. There they shall arrest Atwood…or whatever he calls himself…and bring him back here to Monocacy. Tell them also to apprehend the cousin if there is any suggestion that they are in cahoots and Richter is privy to the other's skulduggery."

A short while later, at around a quarter past ten o'clock, a posse of six troopers – under the command of Sergeant Zachariah Gemmill of the First Delaware Cavalry – rode out of the Monocacy Military Post bound for Germantown, Montgomery County.

★ ★ ★

William Reynolds couldn't sleep. It was two o'clock in the morning. By his reckoning it was Thursday, the twentieth of April. Weary of tossing and turning, he cast off his blanket, rose to his feet and donned shirt, pants and belt in makeshift fashion. The others slept on, two of them noisily. William pushed open one of the barn doors. Outside a low mist hugged the damp ground. Despite having doused last evening's fire, a flickering glow was still discernible among the ashes. William picked up some straw and kindling wood, grasped the mess kettle and fumbled in his haversack for the drawstring bags which contained his coffee and sugar. As he crouched in front of the ashes and coaxed forth some flame into a bundle of straw, the intensity of the rural quietude was palpable. Just occasionally a night sound would intervene. In the distance an owl hooted. Then a short, sharp commotion back behind the barn…perhaps a red fox hunting down a cottontail rabbit. Now the kindling began to spit and inflame as William encased it with charred remnants from the old fire. From the barn, a snorer's inhalation was fleetingly apparent. Yet William's attention was now drawn to something less tangible than the discernible sounds pervading the night air. A gentle tremble, a quiver, a faint sensation in the ground beneath his feet seemed to be gathering momentum…a night rider…perhaps several… at a distant canter on the dirt road.

Having already nestled the kettle into the now rejuvenated campfire, William rose to his feet and picked his way out of the clearing, drawn by curiosity rather than apprehension. Being in its third quarter, the moon's light was meagre. Yet it was sufficient to shimmer the surface of lying water upon the receding road as it coursed its way eastwards, drawing William's strained eye to a point some seventy yards distant. Here the lane – for it was little more – became lost to the line of sight as it turned away behind stands of oak where they ran out to mark the edge of woodsman Dempsey's clearing. Meanwhile, the sound of the cantering hooves drew nearer. As William waited by the side of the dirt road, he took advantage of the cover provided by a lone tree. His right hand hovered close to the holster attached to his belt. He and his party had been equipped with revolvers when they departed Fort Dix, spared the encumbrance of unwieldy muskets.

Half a minute later the night riders appeared on the road. A coherent, yet dark and ill-defined body of men and horses. As they drew closer, William stepped out.

Trooper Longacre was first to see him. "Sergeant Gemmill!" he shouted in surprise. But it was the utterance of the lone infantryman that reached the Sergeant's ears a split second before that of his subordinate.

"Who goes there?" bellowed William, his frame stiffening, his hand already clasping the butt of his revolver.

"Whoa!" yelled the sergeant as he briskly reined in his steed, causing his party of troopers to do likewise amid a jangle of metal and the rub of leather.

"Good God, man, are you some sort of picket out here in the back of beyond? Kindly identify yourself, sir," bawled the cavalryman.

"Corporal Reynolds, Two Hundred and Thirteenth Pennsylvania Volunteers. And you, Sergeant?...who are you?"

"Zach Gemmill, Corporal. Cavalry Sergeant...First Delaware."

"And what brings you here, Sergeant, at the dead of night?"

"I might ask the very same of you, Corporal," spluttered Gemmill. It was a response which prompted William to disclose the purpose of his and his much depleted party's presence in the depth of the Maryland countryside.

"Extraordinary, Corporal Reynolds. How quite extraordinary," muttered the horse soldier. "It seems we have a common purpose. Perhaps you and your men would join us in our quest to apprehend this man, Atwood, or whatever he chooses to call himself. It seems the scoundrel has gone to ground at his cousin's farm near a place called Germantown which I reckon is none too far from here...that's if I'm right in presuming this to be Darnestown."

"That's correct, Sergeant," said William, his heart having leapt at hearing of Atzerodt's whereabouts. He felt elated by the sudden realisation that the mission might yet meet with success and inwardly dwelt on how perceptive had been the woodsman in pointing the way to Germantown. "We'll be delighted to assist you, Sergeant, in taking Atzerodt into custody."

One of the doors to Dempsey's barn creaked on its hinges as Thompson and Reed, woken by the sound of the troopers' whinnying horses, emerged into the night air, struggling into their pants as they did so.

"Well, it looks as though you and your boys are in need of a little time and refreshment before you'll be fit to bolster our little posse. Which leads me to enquire," said the Sergeant, eyeing William's kettle nestling in the distant embers, "whether you could rustle us up a cup of hot coffee. Only our bellies are in need of a warm drink, what with being in the saddle too long. We should have been here long 'ere now but somehow took a wrong turning and found ourselves on the other side of Gaithersburg."

William was swift to oblige, detailing Henry Reed to attend to the troopers' beverage and Ed Thompson to return to the barn to rouse their still slumbering comrades.

"Our plan, Corporal, is to first locate the Darnestown post office," said Gemmill, as, minutes later, he crouched before the heat of a now lively fire and sipped at his coffee. William listened attentively as the flames' reflective glow illumined and played upon the Sergeant's swarthy features and his bristly, greying moustache. "There's a house at the back of it which belongs to a Mister Purdom," continued Gemmill. "Apparently Purdom's an army informant who's offered to guide us to Atwood's hiding place. I'd suggest that while we seek out our friend, you and your men get yourselves organised and be ready to join us on our return. Hopefully that'll be within the hour but I guess it depends upon us first encountering the goddam post office and how deep a sleeper is our man Purdom."

Twelve

Upper Maryland
20th April 1865

Downstairs the hall clock struck four. It registered only with Hartman whose resting state, being well above the nadir of lowered consciousness, enabled him to draw comfort in the knowledge he could slumber on for another hour or so. Along the corridor, George and the Nichols brothers continued to sleep heavily. In the room opposite, the vibrating sound played upon old Johann Richter's soft palate offered a sole challenge to that of the striking timepiece.

Outside, below the lower field that fell away to the Darnestown road, Sergeant Gemmill's troopers eased their charges to a halt. In front of them, James Purdom beckoned the Sergeant to move forward, whereupon, from the seat of a heavy two-horse wagon, he pointed the way up the hill to the farmhouse nestling beyond the trees. Behind the army informant, within the confines of the wagon bed, sat William Reynolds and his foot soldiers.

"We'll part company here, Sergeant, only, as a local man, I wouldn't wish to be seen by Richter and known to have brought you soldiers to his home," declared Purdom, as he clambered down from the seating slat. "It's a fine morning and dawn's breaking so I'll enjoy a saunter back home. As I've said, you keep the wagon. You'll need it to convey these infantry boys along with Atwood back to Headquarters."

"That's mighty helpful of you, Mister Purdom, sir…mighty helpful."

"Think nothing of it. As horse soldiers I know you'll take proper care of my animals. Just be sure to get them and my cart safely back to me within a day or two."

Ten minutes later, with one of the troopers left on the road to guard

Purdom's property, William and his men began a gradual ascent of the dirt track which led to the farmhouse. Any resentment among them that had stemmed from their early, rude awakening had been quickly dispelled. The hardship of recent days was about to bear fruit, added to which the men had just despatched a flavoursome refection in the form of a well-salted hot porridge prepared from Alice's cornmeal. They felt, in consequence, well braced to face the day. Close on the heels of Reynolds' foot soldiers came Gemmill's horsemen. Behind them, dawn's first light cast a soft lustre above the far horizon. At some distance, the sound of a crowing cock broke the eerie silence while ahead a small flock of birds, suddenly startled by the advancing bluecoats, spiralled their way out of the newly planted cornfield.

Before the soldiers had reached the line of trees that crested the incline, Sergeant Gemmill rode forward so as to confer with William.

"I suggest, Corporal, that once beyond the trees, you place your men in such fashion as to encircle the house," whispered Gemmill. As he spoke he bent forward, low in the saddle. "We can't be too careful...just in case the scoundrel makes a run for it."

William nodded in agreement.

Moments later, the Sergeant and his men dismounted and led their animals to the edge of the spinney that capped the rising ground. "Private Ross...you stay here with the horses," ordered Gemmill, tersely. He then beckoned his remaining men to follow him. Once beyond the trees the Richter home rose starkly, ghost-like, its shabby white clapboard and shingles in need of fresh paint, the peeling timbers of its ornate, irregular-shaped side porch showing the onset of decay. Otherwise it struck William as a handsome edifice, an ornament that warranted a better prospect.

"I'll take two of my men with me to the front door, Corporal Reynolds. You proceed to deploy your men accordingly," said the Sergeant. "Young and Longacre come with me. Williams and Baker...go and circuit the building and stand close guard at any other doorways into the house. If you find none, come back and remain out here on the side porch."

It was fifteen minutes after four and the snare was set. Sergeant Gemmill, with two of his men at his shoulder, laid his fist heavily upon the main entrance door which issued on to the stylish side porch. He repeated the action several times before an approaching footfall could be heard upon creaking stairs.

"Who is it?" called a meek voice from within.

"Federal soldiers," boomed Gemmill. "Kindly open up."

Moments later came the sound of a bolt being drawn, then the door was eased partly open. Clutching his Colt army revolver, for fear of encountering resistance, the Sergeant thrust a boot against the lower frame. His action promptly rendered ineffective what tepid resistance remained. The door swung quickly about its hinges, in the process revealing a narrow faced, bearded individual who stood forlornly in his nightshirt beyond the threshold.

"Are you Richter?" said Gemmill, firmly.

"I am," muttered the other, nervously.

"Are you harbouring a man by the name of Atwood, only we've good reason to believe he's here?"

Hartman Richter hesitated. His silence irritated Gemmill.

"Well, man?" demanded the Sergeant, impatient to hear from the ruffled farmer.

"No." It was a faint-hearted utterance.

"Your lying, damn you," declared the visitor in a raised tone. By now, Richter's wife, Mary, on hearing Gemmill's voice, had descended the stairs and stood at her husband's shoulder.

"No, he's not here," said Hartman, sheepishly. "He was here…but he left yesterday. Said he was going to Frederick."

"Frederick, eh?" Sergeant Gemmill took a deep breath, the product of exasperation. "Well, Mister Richter, I'm not so sure I believe you and I'm going to search the house." The Sergeant promptly crossed the threshold and ushered forward the two troopers who hovered behind him on the porch.

This proved too much for Mary Richter, realising that her husband was about to be unmasked as a liar.

"There are three men in an upstairs room, Sergeant," she bleated in a shrill voice, hoping to partly redeem the situation. "The room directly above us is occupied by my husband's mother and father. Kindly don't disturb them. Instead, turn right at the top of the stairs and go to the far end of the landing. You'll find Hartman's cousin there together with two farmhands. George is known locally as Andrew Atwood."

"Thank you, Missus Richter, only there's nothing to be gained by being uncooperative," said Gemmill, as he simultaneously cast a penetrating eye in her husband's direction. "Not unless you want to incriminate yourself." It was a pointed remark which left Hartman cringing with awkwardness and embarrassment. "Perhaps you would be so kind as to fetch me a light."

Mary Richter hurried away in the direction of the scullery, returning moments later with a lighted lamp. Grasping this in his left hand, Gemmill ascended the staircase without further ado, promptly followed by Troopers Young and Longacre. Trooper Williams, meanwhile, having left Baker to guard a doorway immediately beneath the fugitive's bedroom window, had returned to the side porch. He now stepped into the entrance hall to keep a watchful eye on the shame-faced Hartman Richter.

The three soldiers who climbed the stairs clutched their drawn revolvers. Pushing open the bedroom door at the far end of the landing, they were confronted by the sight of the Nichols brothers cowering against the wall on the far side of the bed. Amid the lamplight both youths appeared wide-eyed and terrified. Closer to the bluecoats and sprawled across the outer half of the bed, an older man seemingly slept on. Yet Gemmill was not to be fooled. He sensed that he feigned sleep. The fellow looked unsavoury and the room smelt of stale sweat. Even in the poor light Gemmill noticed that the undergarments, in which he had taken to his bed, were in dire need of laundering for they were as grey as a Rebel's tunic. He was left in little doubt that this was the dishevelled creature who had arrived in the neighbourhood on Easter Sunday and immediately aroused local suspicion.

The Sergeant placed the cold barrel of his revolver against the man's temple. He was quick to respond. In the lamp's glow the whites of his eyes contrasted markedly with his dark, swarthy features. He glanced furtively about him and flinched at the touch of Gemmill's colt.

"What's your name?" growled the Sergeant as he applied added pressure to the weapon, the barrel of which remained thrust against George's head.

"Atwood." George's reply was indistinct. Perhaps it was "Atzerodt" he uttered but Gemmill had difficulty in understanding the German's response, not least because of his guttural pronunciation. Yet he was in scant doubt that this was the man he had been sent forth to hunt down.

"Get yourself out of bed and dressed," ordered the Sergeant. "You're coming with me." George proceeded to obey the order, only to be promptly bundled out of the room and down the stairs into the front entrance hall. Here his cousin Hartman stood sheepishly alongside Trooper Williams. Mary Richter, meanwhile, had disappeared, allegedly to reassure and calm her elderly in-laws, rudely wakened from their slumber. The other person present was William Reynolds, who, hitherto, had been attending to the strategic placing of his men about the farmhouse.

"This, Corporal Reynolds," declared Sergeant Gemmill, as he finished jostling George down the stairs, "appears to be the scoundrel you've been looking for these past few days." The Sergeant proceeded to leave George in the custody of his three troopers while beckoning William to join him out on the side porch.

"I'm damn sure this fellow is our man but Mister Purdom says there are a couple of brothers called Leaman who live close by and who could verify this. He's given me directions to their place. Apparently they were at the Easter Sunday dinner where this Atwood…Atzerodt…whatever he's known as, gave rise to suspicion. I intend to take the prisoner there so they might identify him before we return to Monocacy. Incidentally, there are two young farmhands sharing Atwood's room. I'm sure they're harmless enough but I mean to arrest Richter since he tried to deceive me…said Atwood wasn't there, then claimed he'd gone to Frederick yesterday. I think we need to interrogate him as well. By the way, I've brought no goddam irons with me to shackle Atw…"

"That's no problem," interjected William. "I've some handcuffs in my knapsack which I left in the farm wagon. I'll accompany you back down the farm track so as to retrieve them. You can then manacle Atzerodt's hands before you seek a further opinion on the prisoner's identity. As far as Richter's concerned we'll find some rope to bind his hands. Leave that with me, Sergeant."

An hour later, with all the horses newly watered from the farm's well, the soldiers were ready to depart. Two of Gemmill's troopers were detailed to remain at the farmhouse to act as a guard while another, Williams, took the farm wagon reins, leaving his own steed to be led by rope and halter. William Reynolds and his infantrymen returned to the confines of the wagon bed where they were joined by the hapless George Atzerodt – his identity freshly confirmed by his old friend, Somerset Leaman – and by a disgruntled and protesting Hartman Richter. After his initial timidity, Richter had now found his voice. Perhaps, understandably, he was unable to fathom why he was being taken into custody.

★ ★ ★

It was twenty minutes short of midday. Saddle weary and in need of sleep and sustenance, Sergeant Gemmill's men crossed the Monocacy River by way of the Georgetown turnpike and rode into camp near Frederick Junction railroad station. As they did so, a Wheeling bound train rumbled and rattled its way across the railroad bridge, its shrill whistle startling Purdom's mares, unaccustomed as they were to the manners of the iron horse.

"Well, Sergeant," shouted Private Baker, "I guess we've managed this well as it's almost time for dinner and I'm sure ready to fill my bread basket."

"You can forget your own victualling, for the moment, Private," insisted Gemmill before turning to address his several troopers. "First and foremost," he continued, "you'll need to gather up some nosebags and seek out the stable sergeant. Then tether the animals to the picket rope and give them a good feed and watering. You can eat once that's done. Then you'll need to give the horses a decent grooming. Oh…and be sure to take good care of Mister Purdom's animals."

Once the party had drawn to a halt, Trooper Williams jumped down from the driver's seat and strode to the rear of the wagon where he lowered the tailgate. William and his men proceeded to vacate the conveyance in the company of the manacled Atzerodt and Richter.

"Corporal, take the prisoners and sit beneath the spread of that shade tree," said Gemmill, as he gestured towards an umbrageous old mulberry. "And Private Bender, if you're still tending to your horse come dinner call, leave it with our hungry Trooper Baker to finish off and be sure to take Corporal Reynolds and his men to the cookhouse."

At this moment the Sergeant caught sight of the commanding officer, summoning him from a distance. "Private Young, kindly take my animal and have him fed and watered," declared Gemmill. "I'm off to report to the Major."

Enos Artman was standing at the entrance to the log hut – a requisitioned B & O building – which served as his quarters here at the Monocacy military post. He greeted Gemmill with a broad smile and a hearty slap on the back. "Step inside Sergeant. I've just been attending to some paperwork. Got up to stretch my legs and noticed through the window that you'd arrived back…and with a good deal more bodies than you set out with, if my eyes aren't deceiving me. I'm hoping you're going to inform me that one of them is Atzerodt. Now, sit yourself down and tell me what has transpired."

Sergeant Gemmill proceeded to recount the events which had unfolded since he and his scouting posse had ridden out of camp the previous evening. The Major sat opposite him and listened attentively, emitting just the occasional grunt of acknowledgment or appreciation until the Sergeant had finished his narrative. Then he rose to his feet.

"So has Atzerodt admitted any involvement with Booth? It was thought he was the assailant of Mister Seward but it is now understood he was intent on murdering the Vice-President."

"Well, sir, he strikes me as being too timid to kill a fly, let alone a Vice-President. And, in answer to your question, he has said precious little, short of asking me if he might bring some shirt collars and a plug of tobacco along with him. Astonishingly he has not even asked why he's been arrested. He's a sullen sort and quiet as a mouse, unlike his cousin. Richter became quite belligerent for a time when I decided to arrest him."

"So do you think he's in cahoots with Atzerodt?"

"Frankly, sir, I don't know. I think he was incensed and bewildered by our appearance on his doorstep. Yes, he tried to deceive us regarding his cousin's whereabouts but I doubt there was malicious intent. But I acted on the side of caution by taking him into custody."

"You did well, Sergeant. Get the prisoners some water and victuals and I'll interrogate them separately later today. Now, tell me a little more about these foot soldiers you've acquired…Corporal Reynolds and his men."

"Well, actually, sir, I believe they're from your own Regiment. Reynolds said that he and his men belonged to a Pennsylvania outfit…I can't remember which…and they were garrisoned at Relay."

"Just as I thought," said Artman, reflectively. "The search party sent out on Monday by Captain Snyder. Yes, they'll be from the 213th…from Company H."

"So you'll know them, sir?"

"Not exactly, Sergeant. You've got to appreciate that my Regiment was newly raised in February and full of green boys. Within days, detachments were sent to Annapolis and to strategic locations along the railroad, including Relay and Frederick City. I held the rank of Captain commanding Company I until early last month when I was promoted Major and, for my sins, was despatched here to take command of this post. So you see, Sergeant, I am not acquainted with these fellows from Relay. Now, I must take my dinner and I recommend you do likewise. We'll talk later in the afternoon, once I've had the opportunity to question the prisoners. Oh… and well done once again, Gemmill…you've done a grand job."

★ ★ ★

At four o'clock in the afternoon Sergeant Zachariah Gemmill once more found himself in the company of the post's commanding officer.

"Now, Sergeant," began the Major, "I've spoken at length with Atzerodt and Richter. Hard work, it was, questioning Atzerodt and although I failed to coax an admission of guilt from him, I gleaned sufficient to convince me

341

that, yes, we have our man. And, of course, we know for sure, courtesy of this Mister Leman tha…"

"Leaman, sir…Mister Leaman," interjected the Sergeant.

"Quite so…Mister Leaman…that he is the individual who gave cause for suspicion on Easter Sunday. Now…as for his cousin, the man Richter, I too share doubts as to whether he might be implicated in this business. To be honest, he was quite forthcoming and rather convincing in the responses he gave to my questioning…quite the antithesis, in fact, of his relative who seems a peculiar and disreputable kind of fellow. Indeed, if he belonged to the animal world I'm convinced he'd be the type to crawl under a stone. As for Richter, well we can't be entirely sure of his innocence so I suggest we play safe and let Washington decide."

At this point it struck the Major that Sergeant Gemmill appeared a touch distracted. "Anything troubling you, Sergeant?" he enquired. "A few hours ago you came in here looking as though you'd found that pot of gold at the end of a rainbow…and, by Jove, you had of a fashion. Yet now you're wearing the kind of furrowed brow in which you could surely plant potatoes."

Gemmill shifted awkwardly. "Yes, sir," came the retort. But I don't want to talk out of turn about a superior, Major."

"Out with it, man. What's troubling you?"

"It's Captain Townsend, sir."

"And what's Townsend been doing to upset you?"

"Well, sir, he wanted to talk to me about a reward."

"A reward? For the capture of Atzerodt?"

"Yes, sir."

"It's something I was about to mention to you, Sergeant. The news has come through only today from the War Department. It's not something for you to worry about…on the contrary, you and your men have played a central role in the scoundrel's apprehension and will surely qualify for a share of the money if I have my way."

"Yes, sir…thank you…but the Captain was asking me an hour ago to think about signing an agreement to divide the reward money between him, myself and Mister Purdom."

"What?!" scoffed the Major. "Good God!" A mix of scorn and irritation hung in his words as he strode across to the front window. For a moment, alone with his thoughts, he looked vacantly into the distance. Beyond the station buildings, at Frederick Junction, he watched smoke rise lazily from the balloon-type stack of a stationary locomotive as it took on water.

The cunning bastard. Artman had taken an immediate dislike to the Cavalry Captain after arriving at Monocacy the previous month. *Not only was the Captain opposed to sending a posse to apprehend Atzerodt but now he had the impudence to connive to get his greedy hands on a portion of the reward. The swine was using his officer's status to exert unreasonable pressure upon a subordinate in his own company. Damn the fellow. His action was reprehensible. He'd played no active role in events. It had been me who decided to send out that posse. Had matters been left to the Captain, Atzerodt would still have been in hiding at his cousin's farm. No, damn it, I'll do whatever's necessary to thwart the rascal's ploy!*

"Frankly, I don't know what to do, sir," continued Gemmill, as the Major turned away from the window, "what with the Captain holding the rank that he does and…"

"Don't do it under any circumstances," insisted Artman. "That's my advice. You mustn't feel intimidated." Artman looked pensive before proceeding. "Look, my dear fellow, I'll be straight with you. It doesn't behove me to be critical of a fellow officer's behaviour in front of one of his own men and a subordinate at that but here I'll make an exception. Your Captain Townsend is surely thick-witted if he thinks he can wheedle his way into persuading the authorities that he should lay his hands upon any of the reward money. The fact is, he was not in favour of sending forth a scouting party and he only instructed you to ride out after I ordered him to do so. You, on the other hand, along with your troopers, would be fully justified in receiving a share and so would the loyal and diligent Mister Purdom. After all, he acted so promptly in furnishing us with the information regarding Atzerodt's whereabouts. So what I will do, Sergeant, is write to Colonel Ingraham, the Provost Marshal at the War Department, and make a strong case that you and your scouting party…and Mister Purdom…should be appropriately rewarded. In the meantime, I will make a point of speaking to Captain Townsend. I intend to leave him in no doubt that all contact with the War Department, regarding the reward money and pertaining to the attestation and verification of claims, will be channelled exclusively through me. I'll not mention our conversation, Gemmill. That's between us and these four walls. Hopefully you'll hear no more of his trying to take unfair advantage of you."

The Sergeant had listened heedfully to the commanding officer. He seemed greatly relieved to hear his advice and intended course of action;

also quietly blithe at the emerging prospect that he and his men be the recipients of a portion of this newly announced reward. Yet, after delivering a heartfelt expression of gratitude and, being a fair minded fellow, his thoughts immediately changed tack. "What of Corporal Reynolds and his men, Major? Should they not be eligible for some of the reward? They spent several days and nights scouring a huge tract of Maryland for Booth's accomplice. And then, to cap it all, sir, they ably and willingly assisted me in apprehending the felon and conveying him here."

Major Artman once again appeared ruminative, momentarily alone with his thoughts. "You, know, Sergeant, that's a commendable sentiment and, if I'm to be honest with you, I'm sure you have a point. However..." There was another pregnant pause before the Major continued. "I like to think of myself as a just man, Gemmill, but perhaps what I have to say rather undermines that notion. The fact is, I'm confronted here by a sort of conundrum which leads me...for the second time, goddam it, and in as many minutes, to speak out of turn. Forgive me, Sergeant but, as I've already said and...putting it bluntly...I'm not familiar with those men, notwithstanding they are fellows from my own Regiment. I'm also proud of the fact that we at the Monocacy military post have done well to apprehend a man who is implicated in a heinous crime. Naturally, it is my wish that we should take credit for our actions and I certainly have no desire to see acclaim heaped upon Captain Snyder at Fort Dix. The Captain seems to have acted on a whim that Atzerodt had fled into rural Maryland and events have shown him to be correct. I suppose he and his men should be commended, although it strikes me that his mission was doomed to failure...rather like looking for a needle in a bottle of hay. And to think those green foot soldiers were oblivious to Atzerodt being right under their noses when you encountered them."

"Yes, sir," reasoned Gemmill, "but with respect and, in fairness to Reynolds, the poor fellow started out with twelve men, the majority of whom he lost to illness. And they had to endure atrocious weather. Also I think Corporal Reynolds would be riled to hear himself referred to as green. After all, he was telling Private Williams that he had served with General Banks' forces at Port Hudson and on the Red River..."

"Well, if that's the case, Sergeant, I speak out of turn and do the Corporal an injustice. Yet I somehow doubt if Snyder's party would have tracked down Atzerodt of their own accord. I'd wager they would have returned to Relay without their man. And there is another issue to consider here, my good fellow, and I readily admit that it's a mercenary one. It might just deter you from worrying too much about Corporal Reynolds and company."

The Major wandered yet again to the window, drawn perhaps by the sound of an approaching westbound train crossing the Monocacy River. "The reward money for Atzerodt's arrest I understand to be substantial so I suggest we do nothing to hasten the dilution of its apportionment prior to the day decisions are made about its recipients. What worries me, Sergeant Gemmill, is that if Reynolds and his men start clamouring for a share they may well have quite a strong case. I acknowledge they will doubtless become aware that a reward is on offer, especially if Captain Snyder is in the know, but I suggest it is not for us to plead their case. Leave that in the lap of the Gods."

The Major's words left no doubt in Zachariah Gemmill's mind that he would do well to drop his advocacy of Reynolds' case. The Sergeant had never had a great deal of time for the infantry but he had found Reynolds to be a likeable man. He had also proved a cooperative fellow when he needed his support at the Richter farmhouse. It occurred to Zach Gemmill that perhaps it wasn't simply a matter of Artman being protective towards his scouting party. *No, there must be an ulterior motive: the Major was thinking of his own pocket, let alone his reputation. But, then, good luck to him*, thought Gemmill. *Unlike the undeserving Townsend, he had at least insisted that a party of troopers should go after Atzerodt.*

"So what now becomes of the conspirator and his cousin, Major?" asked the Sergeant, as he prudently chose to pursue a separate issue.

"He'll be taken to Relay this evening, along with Richter and in the company of the men from Fort Dix. An eastbound train is due to leave the Junction at six-thirty. However, I've had second thoughts about leaving the prisoners in the charge of Corporal Reynolds. You see, when they're taken off the train at Relay station I don't want them carted up the hill to Fort Dix and into the clutches of Captain Snyder. No, I want them taken straight into the Relay House where Brigadier-General Tyler has his quarters. The General has overall command at Relay and I want him left in no doubt that we at Monocacy have apprehended these men and delivered them into his safe keeping. So, it may come as no surprise to you, Sergeant, that I want you to accompany Reynolds and his men and the prisoners back to Relay. I've already sent the Brigadier-General a telegraphed message informing him that Atzerodt and Richter have been arrested and will be delivered to him tonight. He's acknowledged my dispatch and intends to arrange for the prisoners' early conveyance to Washington by military train."

"Very good, sir," said Gemmill. Although touched by the degree of trust the Major appeared to place in him, he felt despondent that he couldn't look forward to getting his head down sooner rather than later. After all, it had been a sleepless and hectic night.

★ ★ ★

The six-thirty eastbound train had been delayed by a problem on the line just east of Harpers Ferry. It was a problem exacerbated at Frederick Junction where arrangements were made to couple an additional car to the rear of the train, ostensibly – so passengers were told – for the discrete use of the military.

It was ten minutes after seven when the fireman opened the cylinder cocks. Soon the locomotive began to move forward amid a cacophony of hissing steam and the repetitive throb of billowing emissions from its stack. The familiar commotion prompted Major Artman to venture, not for the first time this day, to the window that looked out towards Frederick Junction station. In the last car, Sergeant Gemmill, together with William Reynolds and his men and their handcuffed charges, had settled down for the journey to Relay. William found himself taking a long, hard look at the shifty Atzerodt who sat opposite him, shackled to the sergeant. The prisoner's eyes constantly avoided any direct contact with those of his custodians. Instead they appeared to focus upon the floor several paces along the car. Fleetingly, William's train of thought took him back to Camp Belger. Sergeant O'Malley was putting the new recruits through a spell of drill and addressing a lad by the name of Simpson. *What are you meant to be looking at?... At you, sergeant...At my feet, Simpson. These things at the end of my legs, man, because they're fifteen paces in front of you. Fix your eyes on the ground fifteen paces ahead. The furtive German would have been good at focussing on a drill sergeant's feet,* thought William. *The furtive German...* the words and notably the adjective that came into the young man's mind suddenly redirected his inner reflection. Now he was back in the gypsy encampment on Southsea Common, listening to Ned's old Gran. *He's someone you will encounter on the way...a furtive man if ever there was...yes, I'm sure you'll find he's a German.*

Only now had the old crone's words come back to William. Here in his presence was Gran's mysterious foreigner who was constantly looking over his shoulder. He had doubted her pronouncements regarding the soldiering blue tunic and the furtive man but time had shown her to be a formidable clairvoyant. As William sat in that final car marvelling upon his conclusions, Major Artman watched until the train – with its prized cargo – had disappeared from view across the river bridge and was wending its way beside Bush Creek. A gentle smile of satisfaction spread across his features.

Thirteen

CHRISTIAN STREET, PHILADELPHIA
NOVEMBER 1865 - JANUARY 1866

"Willie, do you hear? Time you got out of bed. It's eight-thirty and the Reverend Appleton is due to call at ten."

Mina had been busying herself sweeping the little bedroom hearth and raising a shine upon the black-leaded fender. She knelt upon a scrap of old oilcloth which afforded her knees some efficient protection from the splintery floor timbers. As she spoke, she finished drawing together and heaping the unburned coals across the grate's waning embers. It was only November but winter's chill was already in evidence. Her sick husband needed to be kept comfortable yet she was bent upon practising economy with the stock of fuel that had been laid in the coal hole at summer prices.

"We can't let the minister see us in such a mess, Willie. If you get up and have a wash, I'll make the bed and get you some breakfast."

In the absence of a reply, Mina returned the poker to its resting place in the hearth, raised herself to her feet and turned to face her ailing husband. To her surprise he had lapsed into slumber during the ten minutes or so she had toiled before the hearth. It presented a dilemma. Under other circumstances it was what she would have hoped for, since poor Willie had had a night of hard coughing. What little sleep he'd grasped had been fitful and short-lived. She had earnestly wished to tidy the room and spruce up her husband's appearance before Appleton came to call but he was desperately in need of some peaceful slumber. Just now that sleep seemed untroubled enough. His breathing was shallow and rasping but he was in no sense agitated or prone to cough. She would leave him be, persuading herself that the good clergyman would be disappointed to learn that she had opted for the alternative, simply for the sake of semblance, normality and his own benefit. After all, circumstances were far from normal here in Christian Street and the Reverend Appleton was only too aware of that.

Mina sat herself down upon the bed and watched her husband. The sight of his gaunt, pallid features tugged at her heartstrings and placed tears in her eyes. Feelings of deep sadness and dejection had permeated her mind and maintained a perpetual presence ever since Doctor Jackson had diagnosed Willie's illness. Beyond that distressing day a month had elapsed. Only the initial feeling of shock had subsided but, as for melancholia, it remained a potent force. It was a constant, hovering below the surface, filling her last pillow thoughts at night, looming large during unsleeping moments in the small hours, dominating dawn's awakening reflections. Yet, to Mina's credit and despite her tender years, she had portrayed remarkable stoicism over recent days by putting a brave face on matters. Perhaps, in part, it was something to do with becoming resigned to the grave predicament facing William. Somehow she had begun to demonstrate an ability to rise above and suppress the despair and disconsolation which flowed in the immediate wake of being told of his plight and prognosis – the anguish which had torn her apart and rendered her inconsolable and spiralling downwards into a grasping web of self-pity. Of course, there were those unforeseen occasions when, taken off-guard, a trigger could cause lugubrious thoughts to surface in a trice; and with those thoughts tears would quickly well and tumble. Yet Mina's change of perspective was less to do with reconciling herself to William's predicament and more to do with her little heart-to-hearts with the affable and kindly Reverend Appleton. He would coax her aside during visits to William's bedside, taking care to be out of the patient's earshot. She was at ease with the clergyman to whom she would talk candidly; and all the while he would encourage her to put her trust in the Lord.

Mina dabbed her eyes, then placed her head upon the pillow next to William. It was but a short while ago that she would have lain there beside her husband and cried herself into fits. Yet such were the comforting and persuasive words of Mister Appleton and the power of prayer that she had surely been spiritually blessed with some meaningful consolation, a crutch to help sustain her in her torment. She recalled a particular piece of advice from the genial clergyman. Although at odds with human nature, in the face of such wretchedness, he had implored her to try to let go what bitterness and resentment she felt over William's plight. "Man's time is short," he had said "and we shall all encounter death. In William's case, the Lord has seen fit to call him in the prime of life, implying that in His mind his life's work is already done. Put your trust in God and ask Him through your prayers to hasten unto thee. You'll be acquainted with Saint John's Gospel, Mina, my dear…well, might I suggest you turn to it anew. John tells of Christ comforting his disciples with the promise of heaven, telling them not to let their hearts be troubled and assuring them that he will not leave them comfortless but come to them. If you believe in Him, He will surely bring solace to your troubled heart." Then, on his very last visit, earlier in the week, the dear man had disclosed to Mina that, throughout services at the Mediator, a candle always burns brightly for Willie. In addition, he told her that the congregation regularly says prayers…prayers calling upon the Lord, in His goodness, to mollify the heaviness and distress that William's illness has cast upon her young shoulders.

As she lay alongside her husband, Mina reflected upon these disclosures and the earlier advice the Minister had proffered. She had been touched to hear of the succour afforded to her and Willie by the churchgoers at 19th and Lombard Streets. It had been a great comfort to both of them, as had the greater commitment on her part – through daily prayer – to turn to her faith. Twenty minutes passed. Thoughts waned as sleep also threatened to engulf Mina. Yet, on the very brink of slumber and being attuned to the often capricious nature of William's state of rest, she was herself drawn back from that threshold by indistinct mutterings from her bedfellow. Raising her head from the pillow and glancing to her right, Mina observed that Willie's brow was beaded with sweat. His eyes remained closed but he was gripped by a mild tremor. His lips shaped words yet his attempted utterances were all but mute. Then his agitation appeared to subside and he became more restful. Yet it was to prove a deceptive serenity. Within a short time, William resumed his murmurings, although, with the waning of his discomposure, what sound he emitted became more distinct.

"Nurse…nurse…water please…water." Moments later Willie let out a sigh of exasperation, then opened his eyes.

"You were dreaming again, Willie," declared Mina. "Sounds as though you were back in the hospital."

"You're wearing that same jasper green dress with the rosebuds you wore that Saturday morning in Naylor's…the day we first met."

"It's scruffy now, Willie dear. I've started to wear it when doing my dirtier chores."

"Yes, my love…you're right, I think I was back in the hospital. Back in the Jarvis General."

"You seemed to be calling for a drink. Anyway, Willie," continued Mina, now anxious to harness what time remained before their visitor was due, "you've just had a beneficial half hour's sleep. Better than nothing. It's just turned nine and remember that Mister Appleton is calling in less than an hour. He has had to change his routine by visiting you this morning because of other commitments later in the day."

"You'll show him up, will you? Save me getting washed and dressed and struggling down to the parlour. Only it's been another bad night and I'm feeling quite beset with lethargy."

"If you wish, Willie, but I'll first bring you up a jug of hot water so you can at least sluice your face. I'll also fetch you a bowl of porridge…and I'll look you out a clean nightshirt. We can't have the minister seeing you in a garment spattered with phlegm and spittle. While you attend to your toilet I'll tidy your bed."

It was a few minutes after ten when Mina responded to a single thud of the door knocker upon its plate. As expected, the Reverend Samuel Appleton stood upon the short flight of entrance steps. He promptly removed his customary felt hat, in mannerly greeting, as Mina ushered him into the dark entrance hall where he unburdened himself of his Raglan cape and scarf and committed the garments to one of a number of wall hooks.

"So how are you this chilly morning, my dear and how is the patient?" enquired the faithful rector.

"Bearing up, thank you, sir," said Mina, her words lacking conviction. "The last few nights have been difficult for Willie…a lot of coughing and little sleep. And when slumber does come calling it tends to be fitful and he's apt to dream or have nightmares."

"So is he down here in the parlour?"

"No, Reverend, he's waiting for you in his room. I fear he fell asleep a little more than an hour ago and, being in need of it, I let him be. He didn't slumber for long but again his dormant mind seemed to be at work, if that's not a contradiction. He began to mouth words and was soon awake again," said Mina, as she beckoned the clergyman to ascend the stairs.

"How are you today my dear boy?" queried Appleton, airily, as he was ushered by Mina into the couple's bedroom. He tried, as always, to sound upbeat in William's presence, despite, between frequent visits, invariably noticing some incremental deterioration in his young friend's appearance.

Mina, having followed her visitor into the room, turned away and added a few knobs of coal to the fire, before making her exit.

"Not so grand, sir. The past couple of nights have been a torment. I'm often awake and it gets me thinking too much."

"I'm told that a little laudanum in a drink is efficacious when it comes to inducing sleep but you'd do well not to listen to me, William. Speak to Doctor Jackson."

At this point William was beset with a coughing fit which was to last for the greater part of a minute. As the poor fellow struggled to stem his abrupt expulsions, the clergyman grasped a glass of water from the rickety occasional table drawn up to the bed and stood ready to press the receptacle to the other's lips. William, meanwhile – being well propped up with bolster and pillows, in preparation for the minister's visit – took hold of one of several scraps of clean white muslin that Mina had expressly left upon the counterpane. This he held to his mouth until his hacking subsided, only to then withdraw it swiftly and surreptitiously beneath the confines of his bed linen. His purpose was to prevent his visitor witnessing the gory secretions drawn up from his lungs. Then, after accepting the proffer of water, William lay back upon his pillows, exhausted by his exertions. As he did so, the Reverend Appleton cast a pitiful eye upon his ailing friend, inwardly reflecting on how so wan, gaunt and hollow-eyed he was becoming as the illness took greater hold.

"I am so sorry, sir," declared William, rather diffidently and once he had regained some composure.

"Do not concern yourself on my account, dear fellow, unless you'd prefer me to go, in which case I completely understand."

"No, no, sir. I'm inclined to a lot of coughing, as you know, but I'll be alright in a moment and I do so appreciate your visits. It's very kind of you and a great comfort to me…and, indeed, to Mina."

"Mina tells me you've been prone to dream recently," remarked the clergyman after an interval and sensing his host was sufficiently at ease to resume their dialogue.

"That's right," said William. "Indeed, only this morning I fell into a short sleep and was told by Mina I was saying things that implied I was reliving my time in hospital."

"So was that the field hospital you told me about…on the occasion you received your leg wound?"

"No, it was more recently…back in June."

"I was not aware you had been admitted to hospital only a short while ago. So where was this William?"

In the city of Baltimore…the Jarvis US General Hospital."

"What were the circumstances that led to your admission?"

"Well, it's a long story, sir, but…"

"Oh, no, my boy," implored Appleton, "don't launch yourself into some lengthy account just to sate my curiosity. I don't want to start you coughing again."

"That's not a problem. It doesn't follow that talking causes me to cough. It can be tiring after a while but I refuse to be a slave to my ailment. Anyway, I'll try to be relatively succinct," assured William.

"It began in late April. My Company had been quartered at Fort Dix, near the Relay House, in Maryland, since early in March. We were standing picket along the railroad and preparing for field service. Then, at Easter, I was sent on a special mission. Shortly after my return to Fort Dix, on April the twentieth, a part of my Company was ordered to report to Camp Parole in Annapolis…"

"Camp Parole. Wasn't that a holding camp for paroled Union prisoners waiting to be sent home or returned to their regiments?"

"Yes, a sprawling, overcrowded place on the edge of the city. The Union parolees would arrive by steamer from Southern prisons as part of an exchange arrangement with the Rebels. By this time peace had been concluded and we'd been informed there was a party of liberated Rebels on the loose and causing trouble in Annapolis. Word was that they were bent on burning the place down. Anyway, we were sent for to quell the disturbance since the soldiers on guard duty at Camp Parole were relatively meagre in number and couldn't be spared. We managed to arrest a number of the guilty parties and took them back to camp but sadly they exacted their revenge in the most dramatic and devastating way. For whatever reason, they were not detained under lock and key but were free to wander within the confines of an enclosed yard. Yet what no one realised was they could reach a barrel that stood outside and in which fresh meat was steeped in salt to keep it. They must have slipped a dose of poison into the brine before the meat was cooked and then given to us for breakfast."

The Reverend Appleton's expression suggested he was engrossed in what William had to say but was quick to discourage his young friend from continuing when he paused to ask for a further sip of water.

"Are you sure this is not too much for you, William? If it's tiring then pray stop right now…you can tell me more of this incredible story when I call later in the week."

"No, sir, it's not a problem. Now, where was I?…ah, yes…within fifteen minutes of eating the meat I understand that eighty-five men were laid out and, of these, thirteen were dead. I was one of the unfortunates. I was insensible for a long time. I also experienced the most violent vomiting and coughing which probably implied that the poison had been administered quite heavily. Yet equally, and in all probability, the intense nature of the vomiting was my salvation, in that it managed to rid my system of sufficient of whatever baneful substance had been dispensed into the brine."

"Quite possibly, but given the strength of your faith, I warrant the Good Lord may have had something to do with it," remarked the rector. It was a telling comment, accompanied by the hint of a wry smile. "So what happened to you then?"

"Thirty-five of the men, including myself, were admitted to hospital. At first we went into the camp hospital. However, although the war had ended and the exchange of prisoners had drawn to a close, the Camp Parole facility was still overcrowded and, as a consequence, conditions were poor. You've got to realise that, in the recent past, prisoners had been ferried up the Chesapeake in their thousands, many suffering debility and disease from their time in Confederate prison camps. In consequence, the camp hospital struggled to cope, even when I was there back in May. Within a short period of time I was transferred, along with others from my Company, to the Jarvis Hospital, on the western fringe of Baltimore."

"I've heard of it, William. Wasn't it a big house requisitioned by the Government to accommodate the wounded?"

"Yes, but patients were housed in individual wards, newly erected throughout its grounds. Mine enjoyed a fine prospect which looked out across some pleasant, undulating countryside."

"How long were you there?"

"A few weeks. They told me I was very lucky to have survived. I had become very hoarse and quite lost my voice but, then, I'd been troubled for some time by bad and persistent coughing. I did complain to the physician but he assured me it was bronchitis and treated me for such. But it was not a happy time there. The black contract nurse assigned to my care was wonderful, a cheerful and jocular soul but, to be honest, I preferred being in the field hospital back in Louisiana, coping with my leg wound. While in the Jarvis I could hardly move, such was the agony caused by the strain of all that vomiting back at Parole. And, being prone to cough, the action of doing so was little short of purgatory upon my tortured vitals and ribcage. Then, shortly after my admission, I found it difficult to sleep, which was unlike me. The main reason was the presence, in my ward, of a young trooper whose leg had been mangled at Five Forks. Seems the sawbones should have amputated on the field but there was hope that the limb might be saved. Well, things later turned nasty and they brought him into the Jarvis to remove his foot. The couple of days and nights after he'd been under the surgeon's saw and catlin had the poor boy beset with dreadful pain and calling out for his mother. But it was not long before that good healer, time, and the morphine injections bestowed a greater serenity throughout the ward. Sleep came easier, which was as well, for I found it a joyous relief from the particularly vile odours that pervaded the place. Very few of the men on the ward were capable of rising from their beds to attend to the calls of bladder and bowels and so the nurses and attendants would be constantly scurrying around clutching chamber pots. And despite, for fear of reprimand, rigorously covering the content of those pots with muslin drenched in lavender water, the practice simply failed to nullify the stench. Sometimes it would prompt me to retch, again a most unwelcome reaction in view of my terribly sore ribs."

"Couldn't the sashes be thrown open to let fresh air do its work?" queried the still attentive listener.

"It was attempted but to little avail, sir. The days and nights back in June were balmy and unruffled by anything beyond the softest of zephyrs."

"So when were you released from the hospital, William?"

"It was late in the month and by then I had recovered from the poisoning. The ward master presented himself early one evening, just before the supper bell rang, to announce that those men considered capable of rejoining their regiments would be discharged the following day. He also announced that those who, by reason of disability, were not considered sufficiently fit to return to their regiments but were, nevertheless, thought to be capable of going home, would be discharged from both the hospital and the military. Well, it transpired that I was considered to dwell within that latter category. I had been examined two days prior by the Assistant Surgeon who had apparently concluded that I was no longer considered capable of performing my duties as a soldier because of incipient phthisis…"

"Consumption of the lungs," interjected the minister.

"Yes, but that was not explained to me at the time and another physician in the hospital had told me not to worry…that it was only bronchitis. There was also my old leg wound which was viewed as another obstacle to remaining a soldier and, I have to admit, it can occasionally reopen and be troublesome. In fact, it was one of the reasons I decided to give up working in the mines. Anyway, the following day…I think it was a Monday and the twenty-sixth of June…I parted company with the Army. I wasn't sure where to go but I was already vaguely acquainted with Philadelphia and Baltimore, having entered upon my enlistments in those cities. Well, I tossed a coin and it came down tails which meant that Philadelphia won. Later that week I checked into Naylor's Hotel in Dock Creek and, within a week, I had landed myself a job as a ledger clerk. Strange to say it was also where I met Mina…at Naylor's. She and her mother still work there on Saturdays, helping the landlord's wife with washing and ironing."

"Well, well," remarked the visitor, "what with everything else you've told me about, it seems you've had a great deal to contend with during the course of your young life…so much adversity."

Yes, I have had an eventful life, thought William to himself, *but I have not been entirely candid with you. I fear that I have not told you of all that went before.* He had, in fact, been reticent about telling the minister of how he came to be in the Country. Shame had been at the root of it, being loath to tell a man of the cloth that he had been a deserter from Her Majesty's Navy. Yet the Reverend Appleton, being an astute and intelligent man, had long since put two and two together and, for want of not wishing to exact embarrassment upon William, had always prudently refrained from enquiring upon the young man's salad days.

"Now, my friend, let us dwell a while on Scripture. I thought today we might reflect upon the lessons to be gleaned from Jesus' moral teachings in his Sermon on the Mount…in essence, what he has to say about our devotion to God and our compassion for others. But first let us embark upon our customary recital of your favourite psalm," declared the clergyman, as he laid a hand upon William's *Book of Common Prayer* that was ever-present at his bedside. In passing, as he thumbed through its pages to find The Psalter, the visitor chose to enquire upon the whereabouts of William's mother-in-law. "I haven't seen Missus Thompson when I've called on you of late," he declared. "I trust all is well with her?"

"I have to say that I have been critical of my mother-in-law in the past," admitted William, opting to reply to the minister's question in a somewhat oblique manner, "but I thought for good reason…on account of her indolence and slatternly ways. I know you may think ill of me for that, knowing what the Bible says about sitting in judgement of others, but I have learned to become more accepting, more amenable towards her since we all came to live here in Christian Street. I have seen a different side to my mother-in-law. Since she became acquainted with my situation and, knowing Mina had to finish at the laundry and me being unable to work, I have seen her adopt a more determined effort when it comes to breadwinning and keeping the wolf from our door. But yes, she is well and most days is busying herself down in the scullery with the considerable amount of washing and ironing she now takes in. That's probably why you've not set eyes on her recently. Occasionally, and to her credit, she finds time to come up here and chat with me for an hour or so upon all manner of things. But, you know, I often sense that the sympathy she might hold for me in my plight is somewhat hollow." William hesitated a moment to reflect on his comment. "No," he continued, "perhaps that's the wrong choice of words…perhaps that's unfair of me. I'm sure Widow Thompson is sincere in her sympathy and she's genuinely most concerned, that her younger daughter herself faces the prospect of being widowed. It's just I sometimes detect that what kind words she has to offer are delivered with an underlying inference that I've only myself to blame for my illness… as if I should have taken greater care of myself. Well, I have always tried to live a good life, although it has sometimes proved a harsh one because of my career. And, for all I know, ending up with consumption may have been hereditary from my father. He died of the disease twelve years ago."

"Taking greater care of yourself is far from easy when you lead the arduous life of a soldier at war," observed the listener. "Missus Thompson is clearly something of a Job's comforter to you, my boy…and unfairly so. But as you surmise, it is perhaps a reaction coloured by an anxiety derived from the sadness and disappointment she feels about her daughter's uncertain future. Put it down to human nature, William. As to whether your illness is one that can be transmitted from one generation to the next, I know not. Yet, being unfortunate enough to contract it, however that may happen, is hardly something for which you should be held responsible. Perhaps when you feel strong enough in yourself and when you consider the time is right, you ought to have a frank discussion with your mother-in-law. And if I can assist you in that regard, don't hesitate to ask me. I will gladly talk to Missus Thompson for you."

A week or so elapsed during which time William experienced some modest improvement in the quality of his nights' rest. This he and Mina attributed to the efficacy of a new syrupy elixir – taken at bedtime – which had been recommended by the good Doctor Jackson. It appeared to be beneficial in terms of both reducing William's tendency to cough and in helping to promote wholesome sleep.

It was now mid-November. The morning of Friday the seventeenth dawned bright and clear, yet mild enough to be spared of a frost. As William opened his eyes upon the new day, the brightness which infused the room immediately told him that the forenoon was well advanced. The bedroom curtains had been drawn back and he could detect something of a breeze. Across the street, he watched a mere handful of dying leaves hold stubbornly to their progenitor as they flittered in the stiff draught. He likened them to unwilling fledglings, frightened to depart the nest and wondered, in his despair, whether he would live to see that same tree in leaf once more. Such melancholic thoughts typically featured in his waking moments; it was then, with impact, that reality and all it meant to William flooded into and gripped his consciousness. In the grate the early fire had fallen to ash. The little gilt-brass carriage clock upon the mantelshelf showed the hour to be twenty minutes shy of ten.

A few minutes passed and there came a knock on the door.

"Hello…Mina?" called William. His tone was hesitant, suggesting he harboured doubts over the identity of the caller. After all, he would not normally expect Mina to knock. The door opened to reveal Widow Thompson clutching a cup of tea, her bare forearms flushed from their recent immersion in hot soapy water.

"Good morning, William."

"Good morning, mother-in-law. Where's Mina?"

"Mina's gone out. She's taken Josie with her. She didn't want to wake you."

"Taken Josie? Is she not working today?"

"No…for some reason the millinery shop is not open today."

"And where have they gone?"

"I thought they said they were minded to go up town to look in some dry goods stores. They said something about walking as far as Broad, then getting the horse-car to Chestnut or Market Street."

"I would have thought Mina might have mentioned last night that she was planning to go up town today," insisted William, a hint of resentment in his voice.

The remark was ignored by Ann Thompson as she committed the cup of tea to the occasional table beside the bed. "Mina asked me not to wake you before nine-thirty and then to bring you a drink. Now, I've yet to stop for my own breakfast and was thinking of preparing some hot oatmeal. Would you like a bowl? I've also Josie's sourdough bread if you'd care for some?"

"I'd certainly like a bowl of oatmeal please…but nothing more."

"Would you like me to bring you some hot water first?"

"After my breakfast would be soon enough, Missus Thompson…thank you. I'll then wash and dress and sit up here until Mina returns. I'm feeling somewhat brighter than I have for some time now and propose to devote what's left of the morning writing a letter to my mother."

"Have you yet to hear from her?" enquired the widow.

"Yes, it was several weeks ago when I last wrote, telling of my situation since leaving Baltimore. Worryingly, that was the third letter I've sent since the end of June and I still await tidings from home. I'm dearly hoping a fourth missive might conjure a response."

"There must be a reasonable explanation, William," said Ann Thompson in a reassuring tone.

"I fear there is an explanation, mother-in-law, but would question whether it might be seen as reasonable. I have a strong suspicion my Uncle James continues to exert a peremptory and disquieting influence over my mother. You see, my past behaviour, when a youth, does not sit comfortably with the high-minded way he conducts his own life. I am afraid that, in his opinion, my actions have gone beyond the pale and I know he regards me with contempt. I wrote to him back in March, while at Fort Dix, and asked his forgiveness but I have never received a reply."

"Is that the gentleman who runs the alehouse?"

William sensed that because of her own suspected misgivings about his past behaviour – albeit far less trenchant and founded on selfishness as opposed to ethics and good character – Widow Thompson was happy to deflect the substance of the conversation to something more pedestrian.

"Oh, no…that's dear Uncle Charley. A nicer fellow you could not hope to meet."

"Ah, yes, Mina has told me about your favourite uncle. Now, without further ado, I'll go and fetch you some breakfast, then bring you a jug of hot water."

By half past ten William had breakfasted, washed and dressed. He had refrained from asking Ann Thompson to bring him pen, paper and ink, all of which were squirreled away in a tin box he had committed to a corner cupboard in the parlour. He felt sure she would have difficulty in retrieving them and knew from her tetchy demeanour – after carrying up his hot water – that she was anxious to get back to her laundering in the scullery. Instead, William gingerly took to the stairs, grasping the rail as if his life depended on it. In truth, it probably did, for if he were to have lost his footing on the frayed carpet and be sent tumbling into the hallway below, it could have signalled the end of the poor fellow. However, having successfully negotiated the descent and retrieved his tin box, the task he then faced was to prove a daunting one. The effort required in dragging himself back up the stairs – his right hand preoccupied in clutching his stationery – took an inordinate amount of time. And, as he gripped the stair-rail with his left hand, William was shocked to see how pale and sunken was his flesh which lay between bone and tendon and how prominent were his veins. His straining fist looked aged. By the time he had attained the first floor landing he felt exhausted and was gasping for breath, as if he could not have managed one more step. There and then he contemplated slumping down upon the landing and resting awhile yet, in truth, he knew that he would not be able to pull himself up. Furthermore, with Widow Thompson preoccupied with her laundering, he realised full well that any call for assistance would be unlikely to carry to the scullery. In consequence he avoided so doing. Instead, once he had caught his breath, he pushed open his bedroom door and walked unsteadily across the room. Relieving himself of pen, paper and ink, by placing them upon the little occasional table which served as his writing desk, William proceeded to collapse on the bed, beset with yet another coughing fit. In time his discomposure subsided and he fell into a light sleep only to be roused, in due course, by the distant chime of Dreer's clock. It was midday and by the time William had come to his senses he could hear the sound of familiar voices below, followed shortly by Mina's tread upon the creaking stretchers.

"How has your morning been, Willie?" enquired Mina, as she entered the room, her cheeks suffused with a healthy glow after the walk from Broad Street.

"A disappointment if I'm honest. I had intended to begin writing a letter to my mother but I fear that fetching my stationery from the parlour rather finished me off. I was forced to rest instead."

"But didn't mother come up to wake you?"

"Yes, with a cup of tea, shortly after half past nine. I was already awake. She then brought me some breakfast and water for the basin."

"And you didn't ask her to get your stationery?"

"I doubt she could have found it. In any event, she was busy in the scullery."

"Nonsense. She wouldn't have minded," said Mina, emphatically. "It's that pride of yours Willie."

"Anyway, Mina, my love, why didn't you tell me last evening that you were planning to go up town with Josie? And what did you want in those Market Street stores that is not available locally?"

"I have a confession to make, Willie. I've not been shopping. That was a fib but don't blame Mother for it. It was my doing. I told her to tell you that. But I have, in truth, been up town with Josie."

"So what drew you both there?"

"Well, you know I've been feeling nauseous at times just recently and more tired than usual?"

"Yes, my love…a reaction, I'm sure, to the situation we find ourselves in."

"That's what I thought but Mother suspected otherwise and this past week I've had a couple of dizzy spells. There have been other things as well," said Mina, rather coyly. She paused and took a deep breath, her cheeks now uncommonly flushed. "Mother said she'd bet her bottom dollar on me carrying a child." These particular words were delivered with a greater velocity than hitherto, as if Mina felt ill at ease over their utterance and anxious to dispatch them and move on. "Well, Josie has a friend who lives on Arch Street. She's a woman of mature years with a wealth of experience in midwifery who received her training at the city's Nursing Society. With my sister not working today she arranged for us to visit her friend so that I could talk to her privately about my symptoms."

"And so what came of your meeting?"

"She said I'm certainly with child…to be born, God willing, in the spring." As she imparted the news, tears welled in Mina's eyes. She looked at William inquiringly, not knowing how he might react. She found his expression difficult to read. The prospect of fatherhood would normally be something to thrill the heart but Mina's fear was that the disclosure might compound her husband's despair, knowing almost certainly that he would not live to see his child's birth.

William was slow to react to this momentous information. Then his eyes likewise filled with tears. Mina initially feared the worst – that it was destined to add to his misery. Yet, moments later, he conjured a smile, the likes of which she had not witnessed since they had first stepped out together, back in those heady days of July. "What wonderful news, Mina… what wonderful news."

It was what Mina had hoped to hear. William's lacrimation comprised tears of joy. That realisation caused her to sob uncontrollably. As she did so she drew herself close to her husband and hugged him in a vice-like grip. Then, as she loosened her hold on his wasted frame, he gently wiped away her tears with his hand and smoothed her brow.

"In the spring you say?"

"Josie's friend thought it should be early April," confirmed Mina.

Neither said what they were both thinking: that William's prognosis meant he was unlikely to survive beyond Christmas and that any chance of his lasting until April was indeed a bleak prospect.

"I hope it's a boy, Willie. If it is I'll call him William," declared Mina, prompting her husband to spill another few tears.

"A boy or girl, my dear, it matters not…so long as its birth is unhindered and it is blessed with good health. And now I have even greater reason to write to my mother, to tell her the news. Surely that would inspire her to reply. I was only telling your mother earlier that I have now written three times since June and have received nothing in return."

"Well, it was not so long ago that you last wrote and two mail steamship crossings take time," claimed Mina, reassuringly. "On the other hand, I also have a suspicion that that letter never left these shores. Do you remember, Willie, you were feeling somewhat better at the time and, with the weather being clement, you decided to take a walk to the Post Office?"

"I do, but it proved too much. I quickly tired but fortuitously came across that dear little girl who lives over the back, in Montrose Street. When she saw how weary I was she kindly offered to go to the Office for me."

"So you gave her the letter with the money for postage."

"I did, my dear."

"Well, I suspect the temptation was too great."

"You may be right, Mina. I was perhaps too trusting," admitted William, reflectively. "I will write home this afternoon and, to the extent that I can remember, will try to repeat the content of my last letter. If you're right about the little girl keeping the postage money then my mother will still be unaware of our marriage and will know nothing of my illness. At least I will be able to tell her that, with God's mercy, there will come another little Reynolds into the world."

"And I will take your letter to the Office myself," insisted Mina.

★ ★ ★

Mina stood at the parlour window and peered out on to the street. It was candle lighting time but she was in no hurry to illuminate the room. Her mood was pensive, introspectively detached. Across Christian Street, on the corner of Twenty-Second, a vendor of hot chestnuts appeared to be conducting a brisk trade among passers-by. He took a moment to stoke and shuffle his embers, then stooped to gather some more chestnuts from the sack at his feet. Cutting their leathery skins, he tossed them into the perforated metal tray that served as his toasting pan. As he took a minute to warm his hands above his tiny furnace, two young ragamuffins appeared from nowhere to proffer their meagre coinage in exchange for a bag of the vendor's wares. Mina wondered if they had illicitly come by their small change and whether, since the day's dawning, the fleshy, white kernels would be the first nourishment to pass their lips.

Watching those infants scurrying away, clutching their hot chestnuts and almost colliding with another customer in the process, it seemed to Mina that little had changed. She recalled previous Christmases, upwards of ten years past, when she and her sister, Josie, would be treated by their father – now, sadly, deceased – to a bag of roasted chestnuts. They'd love to accompany him from their home on Willow Street, across the railroad, southwards to Callowhill Street. It was there that an elderly chestnut vendor with a long white beard would regularly set up his pitch and roast his wares well into the night. His lively trade was, in part, down to the good reputation he forged in his ability to roast the sweet nuts to perfection. Yet, in no small measure, it was because the local children had it in their heads that the old man with the beard was a close assistant to Saint Nick. Some even said he was Santa Claus himself, a conjectured eminence he sought to perpetuate by never putting in an appearance on Christmas Eve.

As Mina had been used to a rather impecunious upbringing, the Christmas that beckoned promised little change from the austerity of Willow Street. With William's finances having suffered through his inability to work and, with increasing reliance upon Ann Thompson's and Josie's modest earnings, there was no room to aspire to anything approaching an abundant Christmas. Yet, had Mina's thoughts strayed beyond her own, personal experience, she might have been less inclined to the view that little had changed. On the contrary, for many folk, life had changed dramatically. The ravages of the war had spread misery throughout the homes of countless new widows and bereaved parents and siblings who now faced the first truly peaceful Christmas in five years, yet with an empty chair in their midst. Likewise, many a sturdy fellow had returned to his own fireside but at the cost of being a mere shadow of his former self. William was a case in point. Yes, there were some who had returned unscathed to be reunited with loved ones: men who no longer had to sleep under cotton drill beneath the stars or huddle for Yuletide warmth beside a camp fire. Perhaps they could revel in the familiarity and comfort of times past. Yet few folk remained entirely untouched, however indirectly, by the recent conflict.

"What are you doing there in the dark, Mina?" It was her mother, clutching a lighted candle which she placed next to the paraffin lamp, the sole occupant of an old, fruitwood games table that stood to one side of the hearth. She had entered the parlour fully expecting it to be empty but was surprised to see her daughter at the window, her form softly illuminated by the flickering glow of the fire.

"Alone with my thoughts, Mother," said Mina.

"Well, don't you fret and bottle up sad thoughts. It's not good for you. Last evening I finished reading a very good book. It was lent to me recently by one of my customers on the occasion I dropped round her ironing. *East Lynne* it's called...an intriguing story by Missus Wood. Its owner is in no hurry for its return so why don't you try it? A good story can pre-occupy your mind and lift you out of maudlin thoughts."

"I might try it, Mother, thank you...but I was not being mawkish. I was just watching the chestnut seller across the road. My thoughts drifted back to the bearded old vendor on Callowhill Street. Do you remember, father would take Josie and me there at Christmas time and treat us to a bag of his most exquisite roasted chestnuts?"

"I don't think the old man's been there for some years past. I think he went to the Friends Burial Ground soon after the war broke out. Sadly, all things do pass, my dear...like the early dew, the wind-driven chaff and the smoke from the chimney." She paused for a moment. "Now listen to me," she continued, apologetically, "now it's me being melancholic! Well, enough of this…I'm here because I forgot to trim the wick earlier." Ann Thompson carefully removed the table lamp's shade and chimney. Turning the screw, she raised the wick and removed the blackened top with trimming scissors plucked from their customary resting place on the mantelshelf. Then, as her mother lighted the lamp, Mina drew the curtains.

"I know you're trying to be kind, Mother…reminding me that all things… ourselves included…do pass, like chaff in the wind, as if Willie's condition is nothing out of the ordinary and that we might soon follow him out of this world. But it isn't easy to bear, believe me. It grieves me deeply. He is but a young man. Why can't he last as long as the old man on Callowhill Street?"

"Only the Lord Almighty can answer that question. Perhaps it is because he has already achieved so much in his short life that the Lord has decided the time is right. He has his faith to sustain him through this difficult time and, from what we're told, the Reverend Appleton's congregation is regularly offering up prayers for William. Always remember, Mina, that Blessed are those who die in the Lord. That should be a great comfort to you. Now…it's Christmas Eve and Josie says she will cook supper as soon as she returns from work. I've already prepared the vegetables, so there's nothing for you to do right now. So I suggest you go upstairs and spend some time with William. How is he today, by the way?"

"I fear he continues to slide down the slippery slope, Mother. I can see that he has deteriorated markedly in the last ten days."

"Yes, I know, his features have become so sunken. One can't help notice it."

"When he called yesterday, Doctor Jackson said he thought Willie didn't have long and that I should prepare myself for the inevitable. He thought he could even slip away before we enter the New Year."

"Has he visited today?"

"Doctor Jackson?…no, but I suspect he will look in before the day is done. He's a remarkable man, Mother. He's barely missed calling every day since giving Willie his diagnosis and won't brook any payment for his services. It's a measure of his admiration for an Englishman who has sacrificed himself fighting for the Union."

Some two hours later, with the household's supper already partaken and the pots and dishes washed and stashed away, Josie proudly conjured some spare lengths of coloured ribbon from her coat pocket.

"My employer, Missus Higden, said I was welcome to these scraps from our workroom if I could find a use for them. I thought they might just brighten our mantelshelves over Christmas so I gratefully accepted."

"I'll help you pin them up shortly," said Mina, "but first I'm making some tea for William. Would you care for a cup?"

"No thank you but Mother may."

"Where is she?"

"In the scullery. She has the last of her ironing to finish. She didn't want to be bothered with it tomorrow."

It was around eight in the evening and, out on the street, a crowd of wassailers were in the throes of drifting their way westwards towards the Schuylkill River. In so doing, they had resolved to stop somewhere in the middle of each street block, there to huddle about a hurricane lamp and deliver a few festive hymns from a selected repertoire. And, as they progressed, a few of their number would take a turn knocking upon front doors, armed with collection boxes with which to solicit monetary donations. Having just crossed Twenty-First Street, the group now clustered about a point on Christian Street's southern sidewalk, a short distance from the Reynolds' front door. Here they began to give voice to their first hymn. Meanwhile, approaching at a gentle trot from an easterly direction, came a two-seater runabout with the younger of two men at the reins.

The driver of the conveyance brought the vehicle to a halt, a short distance from the assembled carol singers, to allow the elder gentleman to alight.

"Thank you, son," said the departing passenger, his jovial utterance raised in competition with the nearby rendition of *Hark the Herald Angels Sing*. "If you'll be good enough to come and meet me a little before nine that would be grand." And with that he grasped an old travelling bag from beneath his vacated seat and turned away. Skirting the little group of singers, he was soon treading a familiar, brief flight of entrance steps, only to encounter an approaching collector while waiting for a reply to his knock on the door.

"For whom are you collecting alms?" enquired the gentleman.

"We're gathering money for poor and broken soldiers, sir," was the response.

"Then pass by, my good man, instead of joining me on these steps. Sadly, the poor fellow who lives here is not long for this world and is more deserving than most when it comes to being broken and needy. Indeed, for having served the Union so well, he warrants becoming a recipient rather than a provider of your funds." The gentleman opened his coat and fished in his vest pocket. Then, withdrawing his hand, he brandished a dollar bill and dropped it into the carol singer's box. "In the circumstances my good fellow, consider this to be his donation."

"Well, thank you kindly, sir...for your generosity," declared the other man as he doffed his slouch hat and made off. "Merry Christmas to you and your kin."

A moment later the door to number 2136 Christian Street was opened by Josie Thompson. She had remained in the parlour to sort through her ribbons and was therefore the most conveniently placed member of the household to answer the visitor's knock.

"Good evening, Miss Thompson," stated the caller. "Is Missus Reynolds at home?"

"Good evening to you, Doctor Jackson," came the reply. It was uttered with hesitancy as Josie sought to assimilate, in her mind, the fanciful delivery of the physician's greeting to the accompaniment of vocal music. "Yes, she is...in the kitchen making a pot of tea. Please step inside, sir, while I go and fetch her."

Doctor Jackson removed his stove pipe hat and entered upon the dingy, candle-lit hallway as Josie closed the front door behind him. It was with a hint of reticence that she did so, preferring to have dallied a moment on the threshold. She would have enjoyed listening to what remained of the choristers' presentation of *It Came Upon the Midnight Clear*.

A minute or two passed. Then, at her sister's bidding, Mina emerged into the entrance hall.

"Ah, Mina, my dear," exclaimed the visitor. "I'm so sorry I've left it late to call but today has been a difficult one. It might be Sunday and Christmas Eve but I've had a number of indisposed patients to visit and, much to my good lady's chagrin, have had to forego Sunday worship at the Mediator. I do so hate the winter with its many ailments but even on the day of rest I can't forsake my sickly patients. Perhaps some would consider me a poor Christian but at least tomorrow is Christmas Day and I can redeem myself. Now, how's William been?"

"Very poorly, Doctor. Earlier he was sweating profusely and at times seemed very short of breath. And his phlegm is increasingly speckled with blood. It also alarms me that his face has become so pallid and drawn, especially over the past week."

"I fear, my dear, that these are typical symptoms of incipient phthisis in its advanced state. I know it must be very difficult for you...bearing up to the strain of caring for a loved one in such a plight. It is to your credit, Mina, that you are coping so much better now," said the physician, warm-heartedly and with a compassionate smile."

"Mother and Josie have proved very supportive since learning of William's illness and I have a lot for which to thank the Reverend Appleton. His counselling has been a great sustainer, as have my own prayers."

"That's a blessing, my dear. Now...it's Christmas Eve," continued Doctor Jackson, not wishing to prolong deliberations upon William's sad predicament. Opening the catch that secured his travelling bag, he proceeded to extract some greenery from within. "This afternoon my wife took a knife to a holly tree in our backyard and I have brought you some of the sprigs to brighten your home. I doubt you would have seen a holly adorned with so many berries. Some say it heralds a cold winter. Whether that's true or not, the tree has certainly excelled this year. Oh, and I've also a few sprays of mistletoe that you are welcome to...brought to us by a house guest who arrived only yesterday from New Jersey."

"Won't your guest be offended, sir, if you've given away his mistletoe?"

"No, no," insisted Jackson. "We have more than enough, Mina...rest assured."

"Well, thank you Doctor Jackson. We'll place some about the hearth to make the parlour look cheerful. The rest I'll use to decorate the mantelshelf in our bedroom so that Willie can see it. Getting up now and coming downstairs is sadly becoming too much for him."

"Why...yes, my dear...but I am afraid that is to be expected."

"I've just made a pot of tea, Doctor, if you'd care for a cup."

"A warming cup of tea would be most welcome...thank you."

"Then if you'd care to go up and see William I'll be along shortly with tea for you both." And with that Mina disappeared in the direction of the kitchen.

"I've brought you some reading matter, William," began the kindly physician as he proceeded to occupy the rail back chair beside his young friend's bed. "It's something I've meant to bring you before now but I seem to be increasingly forgetful these days. I fear the war may have curdled my brain," he blithely declared. Then, turning to his travelling bag once again, he withdrew a bundle of old journals. They were secured with a ribbon which he untied and then placed the papers upon William's counterpane. "By the way, how are you finding living with your in-laws these days? I venture to ask because Mina's sister opened the door to me. I hadn't seen her for quite a time…I suppose on account of my normally visiting you when she is at her work. But I have to say the young lady struck me as being most personable…"

"I know I used to complain bitterly about Widow Thompson and Josie," admitted William. "When I first made their acquaintance, they both struck me as indolent, Josie being a chip of the old block and irritable with it. However, both have changed for the better since moving here to Christian Street. My sister-in-law still has her moments but she most certainly underwent a metamorphosis for the good once she secured her job at the milliner's. Now she is far more affable. And there is no disputing that both women have proved helpful and understanding towards Mina since learning of my illness and her gravidity."

"Well, that is certainly good to hear," declared the visitor with a smile.

"Thank you, Doctor Jackson, for these newspapers," said William, as he sifted through the pile of *Harpers Weekly* journals. "I will get a good deal of enjoyment reading them."

"To be honest, I think you're lucky to have them at all. My wife nearly threw the lot out, knowing that I'd finished with them."

William happened to thumb through the uppermost journal – that dated July 22nd 1865 – only for his attention to be drawn to some illustrations across a two page spread. They depicted the execution of four conspirators found guilty of involvement in the plot to kill President Lincoln. "Good grief," murmured William pointing to a head and shoulders portrait of a fellow in a slouch hat. "There's that poor wretch, Atzerodt, alongside pictures of Powell and Herold. Seems they can't even get his name right. It's not J.W. but G.A. Atzerodt. And these other rather graphic drawings show the poor devil on the scaffold with Herold, Powell and Missus Surratt."

William looked genuinely taken aback, prompting Doctor Jackson to cast an eye across the pages which had so distracted his patient.

"What so interests you about that man Atzerodt, William? A German scoundrel who got his just desserts if you ask me."

"I knew about the conspirators being found guilty and being hanged but didn't expect to see illustrations of their execution in print."

"I believe they're based upon photographs taken by Mister Alexander Gardner in the yard of the old Arsenal Penitentiary."

"Well, in answer to your question, sir, our paths crossed in April this year when I was still in the Army."

"You crossed paths with Atzerodt? And how pray did that come about, my dear fellow?"

"I felt sure I'd told you, Doctor."

"No, it's news to me…"

At this point William interrupted the conversation to clear his throat of phlegm. As he was doing so, the door opened and in breezed Mina with a tray of tea.

"A most timely entrance, my dear," exclaimed Jackson. "Thank you so much. I suspect William is in need of a warm drink and it will give him the opportunity for some respite from talking. In fact, as his physician, I think he would do well to have his drink and then lay back and rest. I will call again on Wednesday morning, the twenty-seventh, probably around ten-thirty," said the physician, as he thumbed through a small pocket book which listed his forthcoming engagements. "I have two house visits that morning, a few blocks from here. Once they're out of the way, I will have time to spare before my midday meal…then I see I'm chairing an afternoon meeting on the subject of anaesthesia and lessons to be learnt from the war. That's at the Jefferson Medical College. So, yes…sometime around ten-thirty, William…and, if you're feeling up to it, you can tell me about your encounter with that conspirator. I'm intrigued to hear more. Now, I don't know about you, but I'm beginning to flag after a busy day and, in my opinion, there's nothing to rival an efficacious cup of tea to revive the spirits. I'm not proposing to call by tomorrow, with it being Christmas Day or, indeed, on the twenty-sixth, since, as I mentioned, we're entertaining some house guests. However, should you need me, Mina, you know where I live and do not hesitate to come round. By the way, my dear, I haven't asked you how you are feeling…"

★ ★ ★

Christmas Day. As regards matters of routine, it was a day which started much like any other, as far as Mina Reynolds was concerned. She was out of bed at six-thirty attending to her household chores. Having swept up and carried out the ashes to the backyard, emptied the chamber pot, and trimmed and filled the lamp in the parlour, she took time to prepare some breakfast for herself and William. Upstairs, meanwhile, William woke to that split second of normality in which it takes the awakening mind to absorb the stark reality of one's dire predicament. Once again, he had spent a fitful night throughout which spells of coughing were interspersed with bouts of shallow and troubled slumber. Ahead, on the mantelshelf, Doctor Jackson's sprigs of berried holly and mistletoe reminded him – as if he needed reminding – that this was Christmas Day. It would be his last Christmas. That knowledge, that certainty, caused his wasted frame to tremble as he fought back tears. His thoughts drifted back to Christmases past, at home in Forton and Portsea. For a moment, his musing found him wandering along a packed Queen Street on Christmas Eve, drinking in the atmosphere, the bustle and blithe sense of excitement, the soft light cast by flickering candles beneath oiled paper, the wafting smell of frying onions and beefsteak and molten tallow. He looked up at an array of plump game and poultry suspended on metal hooks above a butcher's shop, only for the bedroom door to creak as it was pushed open, enough to draw William out of his state of abstraction. Now his gaze was focussed on a nondescript piece of grimy ceiling – nondescript but for the convergence of two separate cracks in the discoloured plaster. He lowered his eyes. Mina confronted him with a tray bearing tea and a plate of ham and eggs.

"How are you this morning, my love?" enquired Mina. "You seemed very agitated in your sleep last night." She purposely refrained from uttering anything resembling the kind of salutation normally traded on Christmas Day. After all, it was entirely inappropriate in the circumstances. Understandably, William was of like mind, knowing how unfitting it would be to wish his beloved anything approaching a joyful Christmas. They had agreed that, notwithstanding its religious significance, the day would be treated much the same as any other. They would not exchange presents, since William was now bedridden and unable to go searching for gifts. As far as he was concerned, there was nothing he wished for, save the restoration of good health; and, since that was not within the purview of earthly beings, he had told Mina that the best Christmas gift she could give him would be to keep praying for him and not to waver in her love for him. The one notable concession to it being Christmas Day was that William had asked Mina to arrange the purchase of a goose for the midday meal.

"Yes, I didn't have a good night at all," remarked William.

Mina was convinced that her husband's shortness of breath had become more conspicuous during the last few days; similarly, his voice had weakened perceptibly. However, these were judgements she kept to herself. "I've brought us a little breakfast, Willie," she declared, as she proceeded to raise her husband from his recumbent state and propped him up with pillows and cushions until he had adopted a sitting position. It occurred to her, as

371

she did so, how emaciated he had become, what with the illness having greatly diminished his appetite.

William proceeded to sip at his tea and pick at his plate of ham and eggs. Mina had cut the meat into small, manageable pieces but in no time, having consumed but a meagre portion of this fare, he seemed devoid of inclination to permit any further food to pass his lips. "I'm sorry, my dear, it's very good but I've no relish for it just now."

"That's perhaps not a bad thing," said Mina airily, "only it may just mean you'll be able to manage a few slices of goose later on."

William nodded and smiled weakly. "There is something that's playing on my mind a little," he confided in Mina. "I'm worried about what will become of you and our child once I'm gone. I think we need to spend a few moments talking to your mother, my love. Perhaps today…yes, today, if at all possible. Let it be sooner rather than later."

"Mother and Josie have just left to attend the early service at the Mediator and they're intent on preparing and cooking the midday meal on their return. I'll ask Mother to come up once that's under control or, if not, sometime this afternoon when we all have more time on our hands. For now, I'm going to set and light the fires up here and in the parlour."

Around eleven-thirty, as William idly perused some of the *Harpers Weekly* journals donated by Doctor Jackson, he was aware of more than a single footfall treading the creaking, lower flight of stairs. He was not mistaken. Mina entered the room, closely followed by her mother.

"Mother has answered your call, Willie. She preferred to do so now rather than after dinner."

"Quite so, Mina," declared Ann Thompson, "only I'm thinking that, once the dishes are cleared away and the pots washed up, I'll be ready to put my feet up before the parlour fire. If you can't have a rest and a quiet nap on Christmas Day, when the day's chores are done, then I don't know when you can."

"Thank you, mother-in-law. I appreciate your acceding to my request but I've become increasingly anxious of late as to what the future holds for Mina, when Almighty God sees fit to call me. I think it fair to say that my thoughts have become increasingly more focussed on that issue since learning that Mina is carrying our child. Firstly, there is the matter of accommodation. As far as the rent is concerned, O'Farrell the landlord is paid up until the end of February. I think there is sufficient money left in my account at the bank to cover another half year's lease here in Christian Street but, of course, what I had when I left the Army was savagely diminished by physicians' fees…until the blessed and compassionate Doctor Jackson came on the scene. Beyond that and, sooner, if you so wish, you may need to think about renting a more modest property than this to ensure a lesser drain upon finances. What I have done…as Mina is already aware…is to have filed a claim with the Clerk to the Orphans' Court for an invalid pension. I have also engaged an attorney to act for me in that regard. And, of course, when I am gone, Mina, you will have the right to apply for a widow's…"

"Oh, don't, Willie…please don't talk like that," sobbed Mina. "It's too distressing."

"I know my dear. It's lamentable for us both but I am afraid that's reality and we can't shirk facing up to it. I was about to say that you will have a right to a widow's pension. Again, there will be the need to appoint an attorney… Mister Poulson of Mathews Poulson would be a good man to represent you. But more importantly, today," continued William – simultaneously catching the eye of Ann Thompson – "is to ask you, dear mother-in-law, if you can find it in your heart to promise me that you will not forsake my dearest Mina and the child? I earnestly request you to afford them all the succour they require at the time of their greatest need…when, in the wake of my demise, there will be no husband and no father figure to discharge that responsibility."

"It goes without saying, William, that I will do what you ask and I am sure Josie will also play her part." Ann Thompson was irked by what she saw as an underlying suggestion by her son-in-law that she might fall short of being compassionate towards her own daughter and future grandchild. However, given William's serious predicament and it being Christmas Day, she thought better of giving vent to her irritation. Instead, she did well to suppress any overt display of annoyance. "Mina is my own flesh and blood and will not want for help and assistance while I am around to provide it," she continued.

"Thank you, Missus Thompson. That is a great comfort to me and brightens my Christmas Day." Inwardly, William reflected upon the past indolence of his mother-in-law and Josie. Of course, only time would tell – when William had gone to his grave and when Mina had given birth to their child – whether Ann and Josie would continue to adhere to their reformed ways. After all, old habits are inclined to die hard. Nonetheless, William was cheered by his mother-in-law's expressed commitment and trusted it was made with conviction and sincerity.

"I'd best now get back to the kitchen," declared Ann Thompson, "only Christmas dinner does not cook itself. I left Josie to finish preparing the vegetables and, fortunately, I found time to clean, pick and singe the goose before going to church...which reminds me, William...the Reverend Appleton asked me to wish you and Mina a peaceful and restful Christmas. Now, I've still to stuff the bird and to get it spitted. That done, we should have our Christmas dinner ready to eat in about an hour and a half."

★ ★ ★

Doctor Elisha Boyleston Jackson, sitting on the rail back chair beside William's bed, stretched out his legs and yawned. "What a sorry state I'm in William. It's as if I've already done a day's work and it's only eleven o'clock. I suspect my lethargy is down to over-indulgence these past couple of days, although I wonder whether the warmth of your room is something to do with it. That said, it's good to come in out of the cold."

"So where had we got to on Sunday?"

"Not very far, excepting that you told me you'd crossed paths with George Atzerodt."

"Well it's quite a long story, Doctor."

"Then only tell me if you feel up to it, my boy. If it proves too much for you then there is always next time."

William proceeded to recount the events which surrounded the mission entrusted to him by Captain Snyder. The physician listened attentively, save to occasionally interrupt the narrator, since he was concerned he should not overtax himself. He was also insistent that his patient should partake of intermittent sips of water. In consequence, perhaps half an hour elapsed – interspersed with abundant short pauses – during which William described all that transpired between leaving Fort Dix on Easter Monday and delivering the shackled prisoner and his cousin to the Relay House a few days later.

Once William had concluded his story, Doctor Jackson appeared to hold back from any immediate response, feeling the need to take stock of what he had heard. "That, William, is a remarkable story," he eventually declared. "If I didn't know you as well as I do I would have reacted to such a yarn with incredulity, my boy. But tell me, what happened to Atzerodt and Richter once you and the remnants of your party left them with Sergeant Gemmill at the Relay House?"

"I believe the Sergeant delivered them to Brigadier General Tyler and that the following day they were taken by train to Washington."

"Yes, their destination was the Navy Yard where Atzerodt was held onboard the *Saugus*. The cousin, Richter, was later released but Atzerodt was transferred to the Arsenal's Old Penitentiary. He was subsequently tried with fellow conspirators before the military commission, found guilty and sentenced to hang...hence the images in that edition of *Harpers Weekly*. But tell me, William, what did Captain Snyder have to say about your involvement in the apprehension of this man? He must have been pleased...to think his intuition proved correct...that this scoundrel had, indeed, gone to ground in rural Maryland."

"Actually, Doctor, I don't know what he thought of our comparative success. You see, on our return to Fort Dix, the Captain was away in Baltimore, on army business. By the time he returned, I was at Camp Parole, helping to deal with problems caused by liberated rebels in Annapolis. I believe I've told you about the poisoning incident, my admission to hospital and my discharge from the Army."

Jackson nodded. He had quizzed William about his medical history when the Englishman had first agreed to become his patient. "You seem to under-estimate your involvement in the arrest, my good fellow, when you talk of comparative success," he remarked.

"I say comparative because, in the final analysis, we only assisted in Atzerodt's arrest. We didn't track him down. If the troopers hadn't turned up that morning, my plan was to move on..."

"Stop a moment, William," insisted the physician. "You're becoming increasingly out of breath and, before long, I suspect you'll have one of those coughing fits. Just rest for five minutes and I'll do the talking. You know, you do yourself and your fellow soldiers an injustice, my boy, by underestimating your contribution. Yes, you happened to be in the right place at the right time, but you had endured a most trying manhunt in such arduous conditions...conditions which would have seen lesser men give up. Also, it strikes me you showed admirable leadership and strength of character which led you to play an active role in this scoundrel's apprehension. And what if the posse of cavalry had not shown up? From what you've told me, you were intent on visiting Germantown later that day, given the mention of German immigrants by the woodsman. You may well have run the wretch to earth of your own accord."

William's change of expression, though subtle, was sufficient to imply that he was not prepared to take issue with the good doctor's observations.

"Your efforts, William, deserve recognition and it seems to me that circumstances have conspired against you…fate that is, along with…I suspect…the deft hand of others." Doctor Jackson's countenance had changed. His furrowed brow was a reflection of some concern. "What worries me is that some substantial rewards were on offer to those who could show they had participated in the apprehension of the conspirators. That would surely include you. Furthermore, I can remember having seen a newspaper advertisement…perhaps during the past month or six weeks… which amounted to a copy of a General Order issued by the War Department. If my memory serves me correctly, it required that persons considering themselves eligible for those rewards should file their claims and their proof to such claims with the Adjutant General. The validity of claims was to be subject of adjudication by a special committee and, of course, a time limit was stipulated within which they could be submitted. The trouble is, William, I had no cause to take note of where I saw the notice or, indeed, when the period to submit claims was said to expire. It may have done so already."

"It matters not, sir," said William, with indifference. "If I am honest, I have to say that I do not consider I should be rewarded for what amounted to merely doing my job. I am a firm believer that you should always diligently do your duty in whatever calling you pursue."

"Goddamn it, William, you certainly are incorrigible. At least when you demurred over accepting my services, I at least had the persuasive ability of Sam Appleton to coax you down the path of acquiescence. A good slice of Government money would serve Mina and the child well, my dear fellow…"

"Yes, Doctor, I understand what you're saying, but I am opposed to ill-gotten charity."

"Ill-gotten?!" exclaimed the physician. "Good Lord, my boy, it would be your entitlement. You surely are a proud man, William."

"I have my dear mother to blame for that, Doctor."

"And how might that be?"

"I suppose it all goes back to one Good Friday, some ten or twelve years ago."

"Here, before you launch into a further tale, you'd best take another drink," insisted the visitor, as he picked up the nearby glass of water and drew it to William's lips. "Now, before you continue talking are you sure you feel up to it?"

William nodded. "What happened was that, in a moment of disappointment, I gave vent to frustration by kicking against a brick wall and, in so doing, I damaged my right boot. Shortly afterwards and while on my way home, I encountered our village clergyman…Old Parson Veck we called him…who happened to notice that the sole of my boot was hanging off. Unfortunately, he wrongly surmised that my mother couldn't afford to buy me a new pair and, in consequence, he graciously gave me a shilling out of his own pocket. He directed me to take the shilling to a forthcoming second-hand clothing sale and there to purchase a sturdy pair of boots."

"A kind gentleman, indeed," remarked Jackson. "And you were happy to accept the parson's shilling?"

"I was, but I was yet to learn my mother's lesson. Another drink, please, Doctor," said William. "Thank you," he gasped, as Jackson pressed the glass to his lips. "I'll take a short pause as well."

"Please do. You're not to overtax yourself, remember."

In due course, William chose to take up the story once more. "On hearing about the clergyman's gift and of its purpose, my mother was incensed, claiming she had never had cause to accept charity. She angrily declared that she would need to fall into the most dire state of destitution before agreeing to such and, even then, she'd find it difficult. Charity, she said, was for the poor and needy and it was an affront if the parson viewed her as being poverty-stricken. In fairness to my mother, she was, of course, unaware that my boot was damaged because I had only defaced it but a short time earlier."

"Did you tell her?"

"I fear I lied. I think I told her that I had tripped over a flagstone. Anyway, mother confiscated my shilling before returning it to me on Easter Day with the instruction to place it in the offertory and to tell the parson that I had done so. Then, the following week, she marched me off to the village cordwainer and purchased me a new pair of boots."

"So your mother was a very proud person," observed the physician.

"She was. 'Stand on your own two feet' she would say. According to my grandmother, she was too proud for her own good but the fact is, I admired her stance and took a lesson from her that day. I suppose my mother's pride has always burned within me."

"Well, I guess that explains a lot, William, but I can't help feeling a shade sorry for the parson. He clearly had good intentions and was concerned for your well-being. Sadly, the little episode was based on a misunderstanding."

"Parson Veck was a good person, sir…the best of mankind. See here, Doctor," said William, as he stretched out and grasped his *Book of Common Prayer*, then extracted a morsel of material from within. "A small remnant of a palm cross given me all those years ago by Old Parson Veck. I've carried it with me ever since, through a great many adventures. Precious it is, even though little of the token now survives."

"And what is this…another keepsake?" said the visitor, pointing to a little fabric drawstring pouch that had rested by the prayer book.

"Yes…another gift bestowed on me along the way." William picked up the little moth-eaten bag, untied the string and allowed the contents to fall into the palm of his hand. "A collection of whalebone buttons…a parting gift from a good friend. He wanted me, in time, to have them sewn upon a fine silk waistcoat…what you call a vest…when I could afford to purchase one. It never happened, of course, but I will leave them with Mina, so she might use them to adorn an item of clothing for our son or daughter."

"I have to say, William, my friend, that given what you've just told me, there's little point in pressing you further upon the matter of the reward money. It's academic, anyway, I suspect, because the time for registering claims has probably expired."

"Well, Doctor, perhaps now you have a better understanding of why I adhere to such conviction when it comes to matters of charity…and I doubt I'd feel any differently were I not the broken reed in life's watery landscape that I've turned out to be."

"What you have said has been fascinating and you've been close to bringing tears to my eyes," admitted the visitor. "Now…I want you to rest this afternoon, as I suspect you have probably exerted too great a strain on yourself, talking so much. It was perhaps remiss of me, as your physician, to have permitted you to do so. Anyway, I must be on my way because this afternoon I have to be at the Jefferson Medical College and time moves on," said Doctor Jackson, his eyes fixed on the mantelshelf clock. "I'll see you tomorrow, William. Oh, and remember to keep taking that new elixir at bedtime."

"Yes, Doctor, I take it religiously since I find it beneficial. By the way, please ask Mina on your way out if she can come up. It's been a few days since I last shaved and I'd be grateful for her assistance."

"Certainly, my boy."

"Good day, Doctor Jackson and thank you."

"Until tomorrow, then, my friend," said the departing physician…"oh, and just one thing. What did you make of Atzerodt?"

"A queer fish, Doctor…a scruffy, sullen and furtive little man. It was difficult to prise a word out of him on the road to Monocacy or on the journey back to Relay. He looked so disconsolate I began to feel sorry for him. And I doubt he was capable of killing a rabbit, let alone a human being."

★ ★ ★

Friday 5th January 1866. Beneath the roof of No. 2136 Christian Street, Philadelphia, William Reynolds finally succumbed to incipient phthisis – consumption of the lungs – at the tender age of twenty-three. It was a bleak, bitterly cold beginning to the New Year, a day which heralded the start of a weekend associated with the coldest temperatures ever known in the city: temperatures that caused the city's Schuylkill and Delaware Rivers to freeze over.

★ ★ ★

So Willy has gone, my beauty, my eldest born, my flower ;
But how can I weep for Willy, he has but gone for an hour,
Gone for a minute, my son, from this room to the next ;
I, too, shall go in a minute. What time have I to be vext?

Alfred Lord Tennyson
'The Grandmother' (1859)

POSTSCRIPT

With the novel being based on fact, this postscript sets out a number of profiles to summarise what became – to the extent that I am aware – of many of those real-life characters who inhabit the story. What information I have springs largely from my own researches over the years. However, as regards the profiles pertaining to characters who – to a lesser or greater extent – had some involvement with the Lincoln assassination or its aftermath, I have found the following publications to be particularly helpful to draw upon: *The Lincoln Assassination Encyclopaedia* by Edward Steers Jr (Harper Perennial, New York, 2010) and *The Lincoln Assassination Underground: A Selection of Graves of People Associated with the Assassination of Abraham Lincoln* by John Muranelli and Edward Steers Jr.

★ ★ ★

William Reynolds Following his death, on 5th January 1866 at the age of twenty-three, his body was interred in Macpelah Cemetery located at Washington Avenue and 11th Street, Philadelphia. It is understood that, in 1895, the remains from the burial ground were transferred to Mount Moriah Cemetery at 62nd and Kingsessing Streets.

Mincora (Mina) Reynolds On 29th January 1866 Mina chose to send the following touching letter to her mother-in-law, Charlotte Reynolds:-

Dear Mother,

If as such I may be permitted to address you. 'Ere this no doubt you have received word that Willie has passed from this world to a better home above. Mr. Appleton kindly promised to write to you and let you know all the particulars of his death, he is the clergyman who visited him so faithfully and kindly administered to his wants, both temporal and spiritual. Sad no doubt, very sad must you feel to know that your only one has gone forever from this earth away, but let us not sorrow as those without hope for does not the Bible tell us Blessed are the dead who die in the Lord. I have often thought that I would like to see you and believe me, "Mother" and "Home Sweet Home" were not forgotten by Willie though he was far away from both. You think he did not answer your letters, he wrote twice; he took one with him as he went to take a walk, being at the time somewhat better, gave it to a little girl whom he met with the money for postage, perhaps the temptation was too great for her, I do not know. The other I took to the Office myself. We received your letter with the money you so kindly sent and believe me we were very much obliged and thankful for the same. The papers you sent I received with much pleasure and have read with a great deal of interest. I would be very glad indeed to receive an answer to this letter if you think it worthy of a reply and although we may never meet on Earth I trust we may all three meet where parting is unknown. Your truly sorrowing daughter,

Mina Reynolds

Interestingly, and contrary to the suggestion that Charlotte Reynolds did not reply to her son's missives, it is clear, from the above, that she did send him letters. Moreover, it seems Charlotte had reason to think that William failed to reply to her correspondence.

On 16th April 1866 Mina gave birth to a boy. She named him William after his father and had him baptised by the Reverend Appleton. Two and a half years later, in October 1868, having contracted consumption from her late husband, Mina passed away at the tender age of 17 years and 7 months. She was interred in the burial ground at Union and 6th Streets, Philadelphia. It is understood that, in 1971, the bodies from the cemetery were removed to the Philadelphia Memorial Park at Frazer, Chester County, Pennsylvania.

Charlotte Reynolds William's mother continued to live at 31 King Street, Portsea until the early 1870s and probably until the death of her mother, Margaret Black, in 1873. Then Charlotte moved house – to 'Baroda Villa', Victoria Road, in neighbouring and more fashionable Southsea. In July 1874 her social standing experienced something of a transformation when she married a widower, John Gieve, at the tiny and remote Saxon church known as St Hubert's Chapel, Idsworth, near Rowlands Castle in Hampshire. The Gieves came from a family of Hugenot refugees who had settled in Devon where they were engaged in the trade of cordwainery. By the 1850s, John Gieve's brother, James, had acquired an interest in a Portsmouth tailoring business that had earlier listed Lord Nelson among its customers. The firm continued to flourish, the name Gieve becoming synonymous with naval outfitting and well known throughout the Royal Navy. Today it survives as Gieves and Hawkes of Savile Row, London and elsewhere, with a worldwide reputation. At about the same time that John Gieve's brother took up tailoring, his sister, Elizabeth, left Devonshire and set up home in Davies Street, Mayfair, where she established herself as a much favoured dressmaker and milliner to Queen Victoria. One can only surmise, given the professional expertise of the London and Portsmouth branches of the Gieve family, that the congregation which ascended the earthen path to the little chapel in the field at Idsworth, would have been especially well attired.

Charlotte Reynolds had clearly married well and enhanced her social standing, residing with her second husband in a substantial house in Tyrwhitt Road, Brockley and later back in Southsea – at Outram Road – in an area known as Havelock Park. Charlotte passed away in May 1890, a year after her husband's death. She was 68. She and her husband are buried together in Southsea's Highland Road Cemetery.

Margaret Black Before he entered the Royal Navy at the age of 15, William Reynolds had grown up – from his earliest times in Malta – with his grandmother, Margaret Black, ever present in the family home. Understandably, therefore, he was very close to his Grandma, a relationship doubtless assisted by the fact that he was an only child. William's affection for his grandmother was always evident in his letters home. Margaret continued to reside with her daughter Charlotte in King Street until her death in March 1873. She is buried in Highland Road Cemetery, Southsea, in the same grave as her son, William James Black.

William James Black To avoid reference to another 'William', he is referred to as William Reynolds' Uncle James in the story. He died at Queenstown, the port of Cork, in Ireland, in December 1871, while serving aboard H.M.Steam Troopship *Orontes*. He was 45 years of age and on the day of his death the *Orontes* sailed for Portsmouth where four days later – in the presence of a party of men from his ship – he was buried in Highland Road Cemetery, Southsea.

Charles Black A Portsea street directory of 1867 shows William Reynolds' Uncle Charley to be still the landlord of the *Sheer Hulk* tavern at 19 The Common Hard. He died of chronic bronchitis at 13 King Street – a short distance from the former family home in that same thoroughfare – in November 1883, at the age of 55. He is also interred at Highland Road Cemetery.

Henry Aubrey Veck The Reverend Veck – old Parson Veck – was born in Bishops Waltham, Hampshire, in 1785. After a curacy at Alverstoke, near Gosport, he became the first vicar of St John's, Forton, in 1841. He was a much respected clergyman in the Gosport area and, in October 1862, was honoured by congregation and friends with the presentation of a testimonial of esteem and respect. He died in June1866 and, with burials having ceased at St John's, his body was interred at nearby Elson.

Samuel Appleton The Reverend Appleton, who Mina Reynolds cited as having visited her husband so faithfully on his death bed and administered to his temporal and spiritual wants, had begun his rectorship at the Church of the Mediators, 19th and Lombard Streets, in 1860. He remained rector of the church for over forty years.

Elisha Boyleston Jackson Writing to his mother, in the autumn of 1865, William Reynolds stated :- *I do not know what I should have done only for an old doctor named Jackson who is very patriotic and took me under his charge gratuitously because of my serving the country and having no friends. He came to the house and examined me thoroughly and told me my case. He said, my boy, I am not going to lie to you or tell you that you are well when you are not. Your case, he said, is very distressing, one of your lungs is entirely gone. Write and tell your mother, he said, that you are labouring under rapid consumption. He then promised he would do all he could for me, he calls constant every day.*

Pension papers held in the National Archives, Washington DC and pertaining to William and Mina Reynolds, disclose that the Doctor Jackson to whom William was referring was Elisha Boyleston Jackson MD, who, on 15th November 1867, wrote :- *I hereby certify that I did attend professionally in his last illness, William Reynolds, dec'd., late of Comp. H, 213 Regt. Pa. Vols. and that he died at Philadelphia, Pa. on the 5th day of January 1866 of consumption of the lungs.*

Dr Jackson had been born in December 1826. He graduated in 1852 and, contrary to the storyline's suggestion that he was attached to the Army, he was actually an Assistant Surgeon in the United States Navy during the Civil War. He married his second wife, Emma Foulon, of Philadelphia, in 1864 and was certainly still resident in the city in the 1880s.

It is interesting that William Reynolds referred to Jackson as an 'old doctor' bearing in mind he would only have entered his fortieth year at the close of 1865. Perhaps this was simply a reflection of premature ageing and the lower life expectancy associated with mid-Victorian times. Also, at twenty-three, William was himself of relatively tender years.

George Andrew Atzerodt The day after being transferred to Relay, Atzerodt – together with his cousin Hartman Richter – was taken by military train to Washington where he was placed in chains aboard the ironclad *Montauk* and later on the *Saugus*. He was subsequently taken to a cell in the Old Federal Penitentiary at the Washington Arsenal (now Fort McNair). Atzerodt was tried before a military court and sentenced to death by hanging. He was executed in the late morning heat of 7th July 1865 along with Herold, Powell and Mrs Surratt on gallows erected in the penitentiary courtyard. He and his fellow conspirators were buried near the scaffold. When later disinterred, Atzerodt's remains were reburied in Glenwood Cemetery, Baltimore.

John Wilkes Booth After shooting Lincoln in the head at the Ford Theatre, Booth began his escape by jumping down on to the stage, in the process falling awkwardly and fracturing a small bone in his left leg. Leaving by the rear stage door, he mounted his horse and rode for the Navy Yard Bridge which he crossed at around 11.00pm. About half an hour later he met up with Davy Herold, at the agreed point of rendezvous known as Soper's Hill, before the two men rode on together to the tavern in Surrattsville, then managed by John M. Lloyd. Herold had panicked, on hearing screams, as he waited with Powell's horse outside Seward's home. He fled and, like Booth, minutes before him, rode for and made his escape across the Navy Yard Bridge. When the pair reached the Surratt Tavern they collected a carbine before proceeding on their way. At around 4.00am the fugitives presented themselves at the tobacco farm of Dr Mudd where the physician gave them hospitality and splinted Booth's broken leg. Subsequently, Mudd was to deny – to little avail – that he already knew Booth or was in any way implicated in the plot against Lincoln. Later that day – Easter Saturday – Booth and Herold left Mudd's home and secured the services of a free black to guide them through the Zekiah Swamp to 'Rich Hill', the home of the well-respected Confederate agent, Samuel Cox. Cox arranged for the two men to be hidden in a pine thicket and instructed Thomas A. Jones to take care of them and to facilitate their crossing of the Potomac. Since troop activity was quite busy, a crossing was not attempted until 20th April when, late in the evening, Jones made available a rowing boat and watched his charges start for the Virginia shore. However, Booth and Herold strayed off course and ended up in a creek further up river on the Maryland side. Here they lay hidden until the 22nd when a second attempt to cross the river met with success.

With the help of Confederate agents – including Thomas Harbin – and Rebel soldiers on the Virginia side, Booth and Herold eventually found sanctuary at the farmhouse of Richard Garrett and his family, four miles south of Port Royal. It was 24th April. However, a troop of soldiers from the 16th New York Cavalry was now in pursuit of the fugitives and finally tracked them down to the Garrett farm, arriving there in the early hours of 26th April. The troopers surrounded the tobacco barn in which Booth and Herold were hiding. Booth held his ground and wanted a shoot-out although Herold decided to surrender and was taken alive by the soldiers. Lieutenant Doherty, commanding the posse, decided to set the barn ablaze so as to flush out Booth. The fire spread quickly, illuminating a figure inside. A shot rang out and Booth slumped to the ground. He died after about an hour and just before dawn, stretched out on the farmhouse porch.

Booth's body was interred at the Washington Arsenal but was removed to the Booth family plot at the Greenmount Cemetery, Baltimore, in 1869.

David Herold After surrendering to the soldiers at the Garrett farm, Davy Herold was taken to Washington where he was held in the ironclad *Montauk*. In due course, at the conspiracy trial, he was tried and found guilty and sentenced to be hanged. He went to the scaffold with Atzerodt, Powell and Mary Surratt on 7th July 1865.

Lewis Powell On the evening of 14th April 1865, Powell arrived at Secretary of State Seward's home and gained entrance by posing as a messenger bearing medicine. At the time Seward was confined to his bedroom as he convalesced from a carriage accident. When Powell was denied access to Seward's bedroom, mayhem ensued. The politician's son, Frederick, sustained a fractured skull while Seward's male nurse and his eldest son, Augustus, were also drawn into the fray. During the fracas, Powell succeeded in stabbing the Secretary of State and causing him to fall from his bed. He then fled from the house, thinking he had mortally wounded Seward (who actually survived the knife attack) and, in the absence of Herold to guide him out of the city, went into hiding until Monday 17th April. On that night, hungry and weary, he made the mistake of visiting the Surratt boardinghouse at around midnight, at a time when Union detectives were present interviewing Mary Surratt. Both he and Mrs Surratt were arrested, Powell being placed aboard the *Saugus* on 18th April. At the conspiracy trial he was sentenced to hang and was executed with his fellow conspirators on 7th July.

Although initially buried in the prison yard at the Washington Arsenal, Powell's remains were later disinterred and reburied in Holmead Cemetery. Disinterred again, in 1884, when the use of that cemetery was discontinued, the recovered remains only amounted to a skull which ended up in the Smithsonian collection. Eventually this was reburied close to the grave of Powell's mother in Geneva, Florida.

Mary Surratt Following her arrest at the boardinghouse, Mary Surratt was placed in the Old Capitol Prison. Described by Andrew Johnson as the person who, as far as the assassination plot was concerned, *kept the nest that hatched the egg*, Mrs Surratt was found guilty at the military trial and sentenced to be hanged. She was executed with Atzerodt, Powell and Herold on 7th July 1865 – the first woman to be hanged by the Government – and is buried in Mount Olivet Cemetery, Washington D.C.

John Surratt On the day of the assassination, Surratt was in Elmira, New York. Hearing of Lincoln's death and of there being a substantial reward on his head, John Surratt fled to Canada, eventually travelling to England and then to the Vatican. There he became a papal guard but was recognised by an old school friend. He was arrested, then escaped, only to be arrested once again and returned to the USA. He was sent for civil trial but was not convicted and survived Government attempts to bring him back for judicial examination.

Surratt became a teacher in a Rockville academy and, while there, delivered a lecture at the local courthouse admitting to his role in the conspiracy to capture Lincoln, but not to kill him. Moving to Baltimore he was married and became an employee of the Old Bay Line shipping company. He died in 1916 and was buried in the city's New Cathedral Cemetery.

Samuel Arnold A member of Booth's conspiracy to capture Lincoln, he was charged with murder and, at the military trial, was found guilty and sentenced to life imprisonment. This was to be served at Fort Jefferson in the Dry Tortugas, Florida. In 1869 President Johnson issued a pardon to Arnold and he returned a free man to his native city of Baltimore where he lived until his death in 1906 at the age of seventy-two. He is buried in Green Mount Cemetery.

Michael O'Laughlen On 17th April, knowing the Baltimore police were on his tail, O'Laughlen turned himself in. He was convicted for his involvement with Booth and, like Arnold, was sentenced to life imprisonment in the Dry Tortugas. However, while at Fort Jefferson, O'Laughlen caught yellow fever and died there in 1867. He is buried in Green Mount Cemetery, Baltimore.

Ernest Hartman Richter Although taken into custody and imprisoned, Hartman Richter was eventually released when it was concluded he had not been embroiled in the conspiracy. He returned to his farm in the Maryland countryside and lived until 1920. His body lies in the grounds of the Neelsville Presbyterian Church, Neelsville, Maryland.

Johann Atzerodt After leaving his brother George and the dwindling carriage painting business in Port Tobacco, John Atzerodt became a detective working for the Maryland Provost Marshal, James L McPhail, in Baltimore. When he heard that his brother was being sought in connection with the assassination, John Atzerodt drew McPhail's attention to the fact that his sibling was known to visit the Richter farm. McPhail proceeded to send a posse to Germantown, only to find that George Atzerodt had been taken into custody a few hours previously.

Nathan Page Although imparting information to James Purdom which led to the arrest of George Atzerodt, Page was not a recipient of any of the reward money. He died in 1899 and was buried at the Riffleford Baptist Church in Darnestown.

James Purdom It was in the purview of a Government committee to consider and submit recommendations regarding the apportionment of the several reward monies offered for the apprehension of the conspirators. In considering how to distribute the $25,000 reward pertaining to the arrest of Atzerodt, the committee expressed the opinion that Purdom should be entitled to a liberal share amounting to $3,000. With Congress having the final say on apportionment, he received $2,878.78. On his death, James Purdom's body was interred in the grounds of the Darnestown Presbyterian Church.

Frank O'Daniel Although Private O'Daniel submitted a claim for a portion of the reward money, this did not succeed. His remains lie in the Arlington National Cemetery in Arlington, Virginia.

Zachariah Gemmill The committee recommendation regarding the entitlement of Sergeant Gemmill was that he should receive $5,000 of the reward money. He actually received $3,598.54. He lived until 1922 and is buried in the Emmanuel Episcopal Cemetery in New Castle, Delaware.

Gemmill's six troopers, namely, Christopher Ross, David Baker, Albert Bender, Samuel Williams, George Young and James Longacre also shared in the reward money. The committee recommended they should each receive $1,166.67. In actuality they each received $2,878.78.

Solomon Townsend Captain Townsend did not receive any portion of the reward money.

Enos Artman Major Artman kept to the undertaking he gave Sergeant Gemmill, that he would write to Colonel Ingraham, Provost Marshal, at the War Department, drawing attention to the fact that Captain Townsend had sought to persuade the Sergeant to sign up to the reward being distributed equally between him – namely, Townsend – Gemmill and Purdom. He said he felt it his duty to see that the men who had made the arrest were not taken advantage of by parties with more influence. Interestingly, the Major stated that he had instructed Sergeant Gemmill not to sign such an agreement as he did not consider that either himself or the Captain were entitled to any of the reward.

In contrast, the deliberating committee submitted that Major Artman was entitled to much greater consideration than his subordinates and recommended that he should receive $10,000. In fact he was awarded only $1,250.

Major Artman was mustered out with his Regiment in November 1865. He died in 1912 and is buried at West Laurel Hill, Philadelphia.

Ann Thompson Interestingly, as with Dr Jackson, William Reynolds perceived his mother-in-law as being old – 'an old widow woman' he called her in writing to his mother. Yet she was only in her mid-forties at the time. Ann Thompson became guardian to her daughter's infant child, William, on Mina's death in October 1868. She wrote regularly, throughout the 1870s, to William's paternal grandmother, Charlotte Reynolds (later Gieve), apprising her of her grandson's progress. As for the younger and orphaned *William Reynolds*, he was eligible, as an orphan from the city, to enter the Girard College, Philadelphia, which he did in May 1874. He left the college in September 1882. In September 1896, William Reynolds and his wife, Mrs M A Reynolds, were appointed to the positions of master and assistant matron at a reform school – the Ferris Industrial School for Boys at Marshallton, near Wilmington, Delaware. They left those positions in June 1899 and took up posts as officer and matron at a similar establishment at Glen Mills, Pennsylvania. In a letter dated 21st August 1900 their address was given as House of Refuge (Cottage No. 10), Glen Mills.

ACKNOWLEDGMENTS

I am bound to commence by expressing my gratitude to those custodians of William Reynolds' letters who went before me, albeit that none are here to accept my thanks. Not least, of course, there was my great-great aunt, Charlotte Gieve, formerly Reynolds, who, at the outset, chose to keep those several letters penned in 1865. That said, what mother would resolve to discard such poignant missives from her only son, notwithstanding that, in William's case, the way he had led his brief life might not have found favour in all quarters? The fact is I feel blessed to have had those letters placed in my safe keeping fifty years ago by which time they had already remained intact for a century. Without them my life would not have been enriched, as it has, by the fascination of wishing to learn more about the young man who produced them at the close of such a short, arduous and eventful existence.

Looking back over those fifty years of custodianship, I suppose there were two key events – which I have chance to thank – that strengthened my commitment to ensure that Reynolds' story was not left untold. One I have already mentioned in my *Introduction* in Volume One – that occasion, in 1983, when Colin Welland showed an interest in writing a cinema screenplay based on my researches at the time. Whilst Colin's intent was dashed by the necessary financial backing failing to materialise, the very fact that an Oscar-winning screenplay writer had shown faith in the storyline could not fail to stoke my enthusiasm. The second event came in 1993 when I met Charles Jacobs of the Montgomery County Historical Society in Rockville, Maryland. He had arranged for a friend, Doctor Edward Steers Jr., to take me and my family out to the site of the Richter farmhouse at Old Germantown, stopping at such places as the earlier location of Mulligan's bar, the old Clopper Mill ruins and the site of Hezekiah Metz's home where Atzerodt had partaken of Easter Sunday lunch and stirred suspicion. Ed Steers, a microbiologist by profession and former Deputy Director of the National

Institutes of Health, was an amateur historian with a keen and in-depth knowledge of Lincoln, the assassination conspiracy and its eclectic bunch of participants, not least the hapless Atzerodt. Since that meeting, twenty years ago, Ed has written extensively by drawing upon his expertise as a Lincoln aficionado, producing among other books the much acclaimed *Blood On The Moon: The Assassination Of Abraham Lincoln*. Ed Steers has also become a close personal friend to whom I am indebted for his willingness to read my emerging manuscript and for his constructive advice and criticism based on extensive knowledge of his area of interest. I am also grateful for the loan to me from his personal library of several histories of Civil War Union regiments which proved helpful references. In addition I wish to thank Ed for his agreeing to write the Foreword to this novel.

I am also grateful to Lizzie Craig, my younger son Philip's partner, for her ability to conquer my ageing computer's occasional, irritating idiosyncracies as a word processor. I also thank Lizzie for engaging the assistance of her former German teacher, Christoph Link, in translating passages of the Atzerodts' conversation – which appears in Volume One – from English into German. Thank you, Herr Link. Furthermore, while on the subject of language, I apologise to students of the old Scottish and Cornish tongues if, as I suspect, my sole reliance upon relevant language dictionaries has led to shortcomings in Volume Two.

Lastly, my appreciation is directed to a pivotal confederate (small c!) who became immersed in the process of compiling this story: my wife, Theresa. In part this is for the reason stated in my *Dedication* but also for her unwavering encouragement as I have plied her with the story on a page by page basis over the last seven years or so. In turn she has diligently proof-read each page and, where appropriate, offered much valued constructive criticism from a grammatical standpoint. Theresa was also influential in my decision to tell William Reynolds' story by paralleling it with that of George Atzerodt to the point that their lives converged in April 1865.

Addendum

I have not produced a *Bibliography* for the simple reason that the research work I undertook, which eventually enabled me to compile this story, has been extensive upon the subjects of the American Civil War and mid Victorian history. More significantly, it has been research work and reading extending back to the 1960s, since when scribbled notes I amassed for future reference came from copious sources. Indeed, the origins from which most of those notes derive I could not hope to recollect since that knowledge has become lost in the mists of time. However, I would choose to refer to two particular books which I kept close to hand when writing about Reynolds' army life.

One was a 1996 reprint of a regimental history published in 1866 titled *Record of the 114th Regiment N. Y. S. V. : Where It Went, What It Saw And What It Did* by Dr Harris H. Beecher. This proved an invaluable and indispensable aid for which I am again indebted to my good friend Ed Steers. Ed presented me with a copy of the reprint as a memento to mark the occasion, in 2007, of our first visit to his and Pat's lovely home in the mountains of West Virginia. Secondly, I would choose to refer to a most useful little book which I purchased in the shop attached to the National Museum of Civil War Medicine in Frederick, Maryland. Again, it is a reprint of a book first published in 1887 titled *Hardtack And Coffee* or *The Unwritten Story Of Army Life* by John D Billings, its value being in its portrayal of the ordinary soldier engaged in routine matters on a daily basis.

AJH

Lightning Source UK Ltd.
Milton Keynes UK
UKOW06f0315131015

260413UK00004B/73/P

9 780993 336911